THE *Malibu* DESTINY

BELLA CHRISTINA

Vinci Books

vinci-books.com

Published by Vinci Books Ltd in 2026

1

A CIP catalogue record for this book is available from the British Library.
Paperback ISBN: 9781036733919
The EU GPSR authorised representative is Logos Europe, 9 rue Nicolas Poussion, 17000 La Rochelle, France contact@logoseurope.eu

By Bella Christina

The Kensington Brothers

The Malibu Arrangement

The Malibu Destiny

The Malibu Secret

Bella Christina as Ainsley Keaton

Sconset Beach

The Beachfront Inn

The Beachfront Surprises

The Beachfront Reunion

The Beachfront Secrets

The Beachfront Girls

The Beachfront Sunsets

The Malibu Girls

The Beachfront Christmas

The Beachfront Retreat

The Beachfront Crush

The Beachfront Winery

Orchid Island

The Orchid Island B&B

The Orchid Island Restaurant

The Orchid Island Gallery

The Orchid Island Christmas

The Orchid Island Wedding

The Orchid Island Theater

Bella Christina as Annie Jocoby

Fearless

Fearless

Secrets & Lies

Trapped

Illusions

Beautiful Illusions

Deeper Illusions

End of Illusions

Ryan Gallagher

Exposure

Exposure

Focus

Close Up

Broken

Broken

Saving Scotty

Ever After

Always

Temptations

Dangerous Temptations

Twisted Temptations

Dark Temptations

Wicked Temptations

Bella Christina as Rachel Sinclair

Kansas City Legal Thrillers

Bad Faith

Justice Denied

Hidden Defendant

Injustice For All

L.A. Defense

The Associate

The Alibi

Reasonable Doubt

The Accused

The Hate Crime

Secrets and Lies

Until Proven Guilty

Southern California Legal Thrillers

Presumed Guilty

Justice Delayed

Insanity Defense

Wrongful Conviction

The Trial

Chapter One

ROMAN

I prowl through my exclusive oceanfront resort in Palos Verdes, each step of my custom Ferragamos echoing off Italian marble like a warning shot. Imperfections assault me from every angle—the Rothko that maintenance can't seem to level in the east wing feels like sandpaper against my nerves, some brat's sticky handprint desecrating my twenty-foot glass walls has my teeth grinding until my skull throbs, and Christ, those peonies—edges already curling brown barely a day after I ordered fresh ones. This isn't merely a resort; it's meant to be my bulwark against the world's endless tide of mediocrity, my testament to the standards everyone else has abandoned.

All the rooms and bungalows in this resort start at $1,000 a night and go up to $100,000 for the luxury packages connected to the top suites with hand-carved Balinese furniture and Italian marble soaking tubs that could fit a family of four. My guests expect Egyptian cotton sheets with thread counts higher than most people's credit scores and champagne that costs more than a month's rent in most cities. This is not some fucking Marriott where you can get away with wilted orchids drooping in dusty corners and mass-produced watercolors hanging at a three-degree tilt.

I storm across the marble lobby, my voice bouncing off the twenty-foot ceilings. "Marcus!" The concierge's shoulders hunch as if bracing for impact. Charlie should be here taking this heat, but the maintenance manager conveniently vanished the moment I spotted the disaster. "That Rothko is crooked enough to fall off the damn wall, and those peonies look like they died last week." I jab my finger toward the smudged window. "Find Charlie. I want him here with cleaning supplies in five minutes. Call Nicolle's for fresh arrangements—I don't care if you have to drive there yourself." My fingers snap toward the massive canvas that would require a construction crew to adjust. "And get that painting straightened. Everything fixed by the time I circle back. Understand?"

Marcus lowers his head. "Yes, sir." He's barely old enough to drink—some USC hospitality program kid with big dreams of running his own hotel someday. His shoulders slump under my criticism. Too bad. The real world won't coddle him like his professors do. If anything, I'm preparing him for the shitstorm that is hotel management. His eyes might be all wounded right now, but he'll thank me later when some entitled guest is screaming about thread counts at 3 AM.

I glance at my Patek Philippe and curse. Three minutes behind schedule for the marketing meeting. Unacceptable. I stride faster through the lobby, my jaw clenching at the sight of a crumpled brochure on an otherwise immaculate marble side table. Someone's getting written up. When I push through the conference room doors, eight faces snap to attention. Good. They're all here. They should be. Anyone walking in after me wouldn't just be late—they'd be unemployed. Not that I'm looking to fire anyone today, but rules are rules. The Verde Resort didn't become what it is by tolerating mediocrity.

Two hours later, the marketing meeting wraps up, but my day's marathon has barely hit mile one. My schedule knows no mercy—Dubai's on the line at dawn, Tokyo keeps me up past midnight. Between reviewing the Milan property blueprints, analyzing quarterly projections, and playing referee between our temperamental executive chef and some Saudi prince demanding white truffles in August, there's no pause button in the luxury hospitality game.

By noon, I've personally escorted the Crown Prince of Abu Dhabi and his twenty-person entourage to their presidential suite and prepped the staff for tomorrow's Danish royal arrival when my phone buzzes. Miranda, my luxury services director, has apparently green-lit a new "exclusive experience" without my approval—a tarot reader.

A what? I nearly choke on my espresso. A tarot fucking reader? I can already see it: some crystal-clutching charlatan in flowing scarves charging our billionaire guests two grand to light "cleansing candles" and babble about mercury retrograde.

Absolutely not. This five-star property isn't transforming into some incense-soaked retreat center on my watch. We cater to people who run countries and corporations, not consciousness workshops. Next thing you know, we'll have barefoot "spiritual guides" wandering the marble lobby, offering chakra alignments between spa treatments.

I sprint down to Miranda's office, skidding to a halt at the sight of her visitor. The woman perched on the edge of the chair can't be a day over thirty—all tumbling dark hair and honey-gold eyes that catch the light like expensive whiskey. But what is she wearing? Some Eileen Fisher knockoff draped over premium denim, paired with scuffed Pradas that have seen better days. I feel my lip curl. This is the Verde, for Christ's sake. We have sheiks dropping fifty grand on champagne towers and A-listers booking entire wings. Our helicopter pad has a waiting list. Our yachts don't even dock—they hover. And this woman thinks she can waltz in here dressed for a Target run and land a job?

She smiles at me and Miranda stands up. "Mr. Kensington, this is-"

I lock eyes with this woman and keep them there as I address my resort manager. "Ms. Baudelaire. A word." My glare at this woman could turn the Caribbean to ice as Miranda glides to my side and follows me out of her bungalow office.

Once outside, I hiss, "Who exactly is that woman?" I can't believe this. Miranda has been my right hand since I leveraged Grandfather's $40 million loan into what's now a $50 billion luxury empire. Through every punishing 18-hour day that built this place, she's been there. Yet here I am, contemplating her termination because she's interviewing... what? A fortune teller?

"Roman," she responds, her British accent precise as a surgeon's knife. Miranda embodies everything this resort stands for—aristocratic pedigree (her father's an Earl), Oxford polish, and a willowy six-foot frame crowned with that immaculate blonde bob. Her makeup never smudges, her diplomacy never wavers. She's the perfect concierge to the elite, solving their problems before they know they have them. "I anticipated you might resist adding tarot readings to our luxury experiences."

"Damn right I'm fighting this. What is she, some kind of fortune teller?" My fingers rake through my hair, pulling it tight against my scalp. "If she's so good at predicting the future, she should've seen security escorting her off the property. Which is happening in about five seconds."

Miranda folds her arms across her chest, her eyebrows arching in that way that silently calls me out for being a complete jerk. Which—fair enough.

"Finished with your tantrum?" she asks, voice clipped.

I exhale slowly. "The floor is yours."

"Right. So I was at the Kimpton Fitzroy last month—"

"That old Victorian palace where royalty stays when they're slumming it in London?" I interrupt, unable to help myself.

She ignores my commentary. "They've added tarot readings to their amenities. I tried it on a whim, and it was... illuminating. Turns out, it's becoming quite the trend. I've looked into it—luxury hotels worldwide are adding metaphysical services to their concierge offerings. The demand is significant."

I raise an eyebrow. "Tarot readings? At The Verde? Since when?"

"Since the data supported it," Miranda says, not missing a beat. She ticks off points on her manicured fingers. "Client surveys, focus groups, the works. Turns out our VIPs are desperate for someone to tell their fortune between spa treatments." She shrugs. "Ms. Sydney comes highly recommended. Has her own shop on Venice Beach. They say she's the real deal."

"I'll be the judge of that," I mutter. "And if she starts waving crystals around or communing with dead relatives, you're fired."

Miranda just smiles that knowing smile of hers. We both know my threats are empty. I've been "firing" her for years.

But good help—especially help that calls me on my crap—is harder to find than an honest psychic.

I slam the door behind me as I re-enter Miranda's office and drop into the chair across from Ms. Sydney. Her resumé crinkles in my grip. "So. Why Verde?"

She tilts her head. "I'm sorry, you are...?"

"Kensington," I snap.

"Ah. As in Roman Kensington, who owns this resort."

No shit, Sherlock. I resist the urge to slow-clap.

She straightens her spine. "Mr. Kensington, I sense you weren't expecting me and have doubts about what I bring to the table."

"Impressive deduction. What's next—you'll guess my zodiac sign?" The sarcasm drips from my voice before I can stop it. But Jon Bevin, the five-star chef at our flagship restaurant, just handed in his resignation for some Food Network gig, and my patience was thin to begin with. Though if I'm honest, my default setting isn't exactly sunshine and rainbows anyway.

She smiles knowingly. "Oh, I already know your zodiac sign. You're an Aries."

I lean back, arms crossed. "A what?"

"An Aries. Born late March to late April. Stubborn, ambitious, fiery, natural leader." She ticks each trait off on her fingers. "Basically, you."

I narrow my eyes. April 15 is my birthday—she nailed it. But there's my Wikipedia page, my *Forbes* profile, the *Wall Street Journal* piece last quarter. Any halfway competent person would've researched me before walking in here and would discover my birthday. This little parlor trick doesn't prove anything except she can use Google.

She mirrors my stance, arms crossed tight against her chest. "Look, Mr. Kensington," she says, voice steady despite the flush creeping up her neck. "I battled the 405 all the way from Venice Beach because your recruiter called about a tarot position for your VIPs. That's an hour of my life I won't get back. So if you don't mind, I'd like to finish what I started with Ms. Baudeliere." Her eyebrow arches like a challenge. "It's not my problem if you're out of the loop on your own company's hiring practices." Something dangerous flashes in her eyes, and I return it with a glare cold enough to make hell freeze over.

I lean forward, my jaw tight. "Let me make this crystal clear. Your employment at this resort is my decision, not Ms. Baudeliere's. I sign the checks around here. You want in? You go through me."

"Fine," she says, her eyes darting to Miranda like a lifeline. I catch the glance—she's hoping I'll walk away so she can work her mumbo-jumbo on my more susceptible employee. Fat chance.

I check my watch. The Blackstone meeting starts in fifteen minutes. Any sane CEO would delegate this tarot card situation and move on. But I'm not going to. If I leave now, Miranda might turn my five-star establishment into some New Age retreat center with incense and wind chimes. No thanks. This tarot reader either impresses me right now with something substantial, or security shows her the door.

"So," I say, leaning forward. "Why should I let you stay five more minutes on these resort grounds?"

Without a word, she reaches into her worn canvas bag and pulls out a deck of tarot cards. The cards make a soft shuffling sound as she divides them into two neat stacks on my desk. Her gaze meets mine directly—steady, unblinking.

"Mr. Kensington," she says, gesturing toward the twin piles. "Choose one."

I fold my arms across my chest, jaw tightening. The last

thing I need is some fortune-telling nonsense. But Miranda's insistence echoes in my head—something about high-profile clients requesting this service. I exhale slowly. Perhaps my skepticism is limiting me. If the ultra-wealthy are paying for this, there must be some value I'm missing. The only way to know is to let her demonstrate.

She fans the cards across the table, studies them with narrowed eyes. "This is a 17 card Celtic Cross. Much more involved than the typical 10 card spread." Her mouth twitches as she studies them. "I see a child with deep scars," she murmurs. "Alcoholic father who vanished early. Mother has died. You've navigated life feeling abandoned, and now even within your own family, you stand alone."

My gaze snaps to Miranda. That's it—Miranda's fired for real. If she fed this fraud my personal history, crossed that line to get her friend hired...And she must have. How else would this Lilith Sydney know about my father's drinking, his disappearing act, my mother's death when I was barely two? How else would she know my brothers have ostracized me because I refuse to welcome our father back with open arms?

But "child with deep scars"? I'm the fucking CEO of a $50 billion international resort. I'm thirty-three years old. Not a fucking "child with deep scars."

I lean forward. "What in those cards tell you all that?"

She nods. "The reversed King of Cups at the center shows someone trapped by trauma, unable to move forward, emotionally unstable, unreliable, making poor decisions. That's your father. The Devil crossing signifies an addiction or entanglement—clearly not yours but your father's."

"Okay," I say, narrowing my eyes. "Go on." In spite of myself, I'm becoming intrigued.

She nods and points to some more cards. "Your foundation card—the Five of Cups—speaks of loss and disappointment. The Tower in the past confirms a sudden upheaval: his abandonment."

I sit back in my seat and nod for her to continue.

She points to the future card: "Four of Wands—a joyful reunion waits. But your present mindset is the Five of Swords: resentment, unwilling to forgive."

My fingers drum the polished wood. Cool blue light from the window frames her profile. I glance at Miranda. "If I find you breached my privacy—fired. Understood?"

Miranda simply nods. "On my honor."

Lilith returns to the spread. "Eight of Cups—abandonment, walking away—surrounds the situation. Position nine: Six of Cups—longing for reunion but fearing repeated loss. Yet The Sun as the outcome promises lasting joy. So…"

"Sounds like you might have the happy reunion with your father after all," Miranda says, clearly amused.

I lean in closer. "That thing you mentioned—about me feeling isolated in my own family. How can you tell?"

"See this?" She taps the upside-down card. "Reversed Ten of Cups in your house position. It represents your current situation—family discord, tension, fighting. And considering this entire spread revolves around your father walking out and those unresolved wounds, I'd say you're in conflict with your family over your father suddenly showing up again."

"Hold on. How could you possibly know about him coming back?"

"That your father returned to your life?"

"Exactly."

"Simple," Lilith says. "All these abandonment cards appear in your past. But here—" she points, "the Six of

Cups, symbolizing reunion, sits in your present. And these cards here that suggest you and your father will eventually reconcile, they're all in future positions."

"What about my mother's death?" I ask. "How did you figure that out?"

Lilith tilts her head. "Queen of Cups beside the Three of Swords, both in past positions. Deep grief connected to a maternal figure—significant enough to appear prominently in your reading."

I drum my fingers against the custom mahogany desk that cost more than most people's cars. Miranda's eyes are fixed on Lilith, her expression almost reverent. If Miranda had leaked information about my family's darkest secrets, she wouldn't look this genuinely awestruck now. The abandonment by my father. My mother's passing. The ongoing cold war with my siblings since Dad suddenly decided to reappear in our lives and I told Dad to fuck off while the rest of those pussies rolled out the red carpet. The cracks in my foundation that I've spent years concealing. The deep psychic wound that this woman somehow sees.

How could Lilith possibly know? The Kensington name appears in headlines weekly—my four brothers running their corporate empires, Connor collecting his Oscars, Kalen's face on billboards for sold-out concerts—but certain topics remain untouchable. Any journalist who's ever profiled us knows: mention the family trauma, and your access vanishes permanently. Red line. So, none of the 100s of profiles on us have ever mentioned our family's history.

Yet somehow Lilith spoke directly to wounds I've never displayed publicly.

Maybe there's something to her abilities after all.

I exhale sharply. "You're hired." I snap my fingers at Miranda. "Contract. Now."

My Patek screams five minutes late. Fuck. The investors are waiting. I despise tardiness—it reeks of weakness— but something made me stay rooted to this damn tarot reading until the bitter end.

I sprint down the corridor, my Italian leather shoes hammering the marble. Doubt claws at my throat.

What the hell was I thinking? Bringing in someone who just gutted me with her eyes, who peeled back my skin without permission and read the entrails of my ambition?

Too late to turn back now.

The beast is already in the house.

Chapter Two

LILITH

I can't stop grinning as I drive home from Verde resort, my cheeks actually aching. The job is mine! God knows I need the money with how Mystic Tides has been performing lately. Summer brings the sunburned tourists flooding into my little psychic shop on Venice Beach, wallets open after a day riding waves or baking on towels. But winter? The boardwalk empties out, and so does my bank account. This Verde gig couldn't have come at a better time.

Just imagine—me, reading tarot for actual royalty and A-listers! That's who stays at Verde, after all. The elite. The one-percenters who'll pay triple what my regular clients shell out for a glimpse of their gilded futures.

The Verde will only see me twice a week, with all my tarot readings crammed into those days, but oh my God—the space they've given me there! Picture this: a private luxury beach cabana with cream-colored canvas walls that billow like sails in the ocean breeze, teak floors polished to a honey-gold sheen, and a ceiling fan spinning lazily above a white linen chaise lounge. Floor-to-ceiling windows facing the ocean, a mini fridge stocked with San Pellegrino, and an actual assistant who brings fresh fruit every hour.

The only problem? Roman Kensington, the owner of this resort. Every time he looked at me, his eyes narrowed like he's spotted a counterfeit bill. I could practically hear his thoughts: "Fraud. Con artist." And sure, I've seen the type—psychics who charge $1500 for "blessed" candles that supposedly break spiritual chains, or sell $1000 crystals with promises of instant wealth. The ones who whisper "You're cursed" just to charge thousands more to lift that imaginary hex.

But my shop? The price tags match what you'd find at any retail store. My readings cost forty bucks for half an hour—peanuts in this industry. When Mrs. Abernathy came in last week convinced she needed some kind of super-expensive "ultimate spiritual package," I sent her home with a $15 journal and told her to write down her dreams instead. I've built my business on helping people find clarity, not emptying their wallets. In a world where everyone seems to be chasing the next dollar, my little corner operates differently. If only Roman could see that.

I get to my shop, the little bell clinking as I walk in and see Jack, my roommate, my partner in crime (and in this shop) ringing up a sunburned blonde who looks like she needs aloe much more than she needs crystals, poor thing. Jack sees me and his eyes light up. "Lil! Spill the tea, girly. How did it go?"

"I'm in!" I grab a chunk of rose quartz from the display, rubbing my thumb over its smooth surface. Rose quartz is the stone of gratitude, and I always try to be grateful for all the abundance that comes my way, like this new gig. "Can you believe it? Me, reading cards at Verde! A-Listers, billionaires, royalty - those are the only people who could afford to stay at Verde, so those will be my clients there."

Jack finishes with the sunburned girl before turning to me. "Slow your roll, psychic woman. You're acting like the Harry and Meghan will be on your client list."

"Why not?" I toss my hair. "Meghan would totally get a reading."

"Girl, please." Jack rolls his eyes dramatically. "Next you'll be telling me you're besties with Oprah."

"You laugh, but Angie Banicki reads for Gwyneth Paltrow and Emma Roberts. Not to mention Usher. That could be me someday!" I frame an imaginary marquee with my hands. "Lilith Sydney: Tarot Reader to the Stars!"

Jack leans across the counter. "Forget celebrities. Tell me about those gorgeous men serving drinks poolside."

Typical Jack—I'm living my dream and he's thinking about eye candy. "Oh, I'm sure the cabana boys will be just as polished as everything else at that place. It's where the beautiful people play, after all."

Speaking of beautiful people...Roman Kensington is walking perfection. The resort is like a living *Vogue* magazine, but that makes sense when the owner himself belongs on *GQ*'s cover. He probably has a "gorgeous people only" hiring policy. Shame he seems to despise me...

Jack narrows his eyes at me. "Lil," he says, catching me mid-daydream. "I know that face. Which ridiculously hot resort person has you all flustered?"

I can't help but sigh. Roman's dark waves that he tries—and fails—to tame with expensive product. Those obsidian eyes that see right through you. The way his Tom Ford suit stretches across shoulders that could carry the weight of the world. Beneath that polished - and heartbreakingly beautiful - exterior lurks something untamed. I saw it in his eyes, and the cards confirmed it. Turbulence swirls beneath his surface, and God help me, that only makes him more attractive. I've always had this self-destructive thing for complicated men, and Roman is a beautiful, tangled knot of complications.

Not that it matters. He exists in a stratosphere I'll never reach. I can't seriously consider him—but that won't stop me from dreaming. Who could blame me?

"Why do you say that I'm daydreaming?"

"Oh, puleeze," Jack says, slapping his hand on the counter hard enough to make the crystals jump. "When you said 'beautiful people,' your eyes practically rolled back in your head. Now spill it before I die of suspense."

"It's nothing," I say, my cheeks burning as I imagine Roman's razor-sharp jawline, those piercing dark eyes that could melt steel. God, I'm pathetic—like some teenager fantasizing about a celebrity she'll never meet. "It's just—"

"It's just WHAT?" Jack leans in so close I can smell his cinnamon gum.

I take a deep breath. "Well, the owner of this place, Roman Kensington," I begin.

"Roman Kensington? The Roman Kensington? Holy mother of—"Jack clutches his chest and collapses against the booth. "That man is walking sex. I literally had to fan myself through that twelve-page *Vanity Fair* spread where he was wearing that charcoal Armani suit with no tie. Annie Leibovitz should've been arrested for what she did with that camera."

"I forgot about your *Vanity Fair* obsession," I mutter, suddenly desperate to see these photos.

"Well, right. He's been in that magazine twice. Once was a profile of him and his brothers, and once a profile of just him. And oh my God…" He grabs my wrist. "You're going to be working for an absolute adonis, Lilith. I would kill—KILL—to be in your second-hand Pradas now!"

Oh great - now I'm really intimidated. *Vanity Fair.* Twice. Once just him—all chiseled jawline and brooding stare, no doubt—and once with the whole Kensington dynasty. I flip through the mental images: Roman in Tom Ford, lounging on some mid-century furniture worth more than my car, while Annie Leibovitz adjusts the lighting. Of course the glossy magazine crowd can't get enough of guys like him. Rich, gorgeous, powerful—he's like catnip sprinkled with cocaine for that set. And his brothers...

"Why did *Vanity Fair* feature his brothers too?"

Jack's eyes widen as he slams his palm on the counter again. "Are you kidding me right now? You don't know about the fabulous Kensingtons? Jesus Christ, what planet have you been living on?"

My face burns. "Sorry, I—"

"Listen," Jack leans in, voice dropping to an urgent whisper. "Roman is just the tip of the iceberg. That family is like some genetic experiment gone perfectly right. Eight brothers—all of them walking gods with bank accounts that could bail out small countries. Connor's got three Oscars on his mantel and makes grown men weep with his performances. Kalen sells out Madison Square Garden in four minutes flat."

"Wait. Connor and Kalen Kensington are his brothers?" My stomach drops as the realization hits me like a freight train. "Holy shit."

"And that's not all." Jack's fingers grip my wrist. "Max runs Kensington Pictures with an iron fist. Ansel dominates the music industry. Silas has half the celebrities in Hollywood dripping in his jewels. Asher throws parties that make the Met Gala look like a backyard barbecue. And then there's Cameron—" Jack laughs bitterly, "—poor Cameron only saves lives as an ER doc at Cedars."

I feel dizzy. But then again, I saw in those tarot cards the truth about Roman and his family. In those cards, I saw the absolute tragedy that befell that family - the alcoholic father who left when they were young, the mother who died when they were even younger. The turbulent relationship Roman has with his brothers. Those beautiful, powerful men were forged in the same hellfire that created Roman—abandoned by their broken father, never really knowing their mother. The glittering Kensington empire was built on a foundation of absolute devastation. Talk about a beautiful house built on a foundation of sand…

I clear my throat, desperate to change the subject. "Well. Looks like I'll be gone two days a week at Verde. Think you can survive without me?"

Jack's eyes flash playfully. "Oh, I'll survive just fine," he says, voice dropping lower. "Picture it—me trapped here with the unwashed masses pawing through crystals while you're down there with the gods and goddesses of Verde." He leans in, close enough I can smell his cologne. "And Roman Kensington, who makes mere mortals weep with his perfection. Maybe light a black candle for me while I'm rotting away in your absence."

"I'll do that."

Then I exhale slowly. This position could be everything I've wanted.

If only Roman Kensington didn't look at me like I was something stuck to the bottom of his Italian leather shoe.

Chapter Three

ROMAN

Over a week later, I slam through the doors of Blackwood Boxing at 5 AM sharp, my knuckles already itching for contact. The downtown gym reeks of sweat, blood, and ambition—a cathedral of pain where Caspian Blackwood and I have shed more than just our family legacies.

His name might be emblazoned across the building in cold, unforgiving steel, but Casp's been taking punches for me since we were five-year-old brats at Westlake Prep. I can still see him with that stupid bowl cut, splitting his last peanut butter cracker with me after I'd gotten my ass handed to me by a third-grader. We battled through prep school together, then conquered Harvard's cutthroat halls, demolishing bottles of Macallan and our competition with equal ferocity, forging ourselves into weapons while lesser men slept.

I duck between the ropes and into the ring where Casp is already warming up, his taped knuckles flashing as he shadowboxes. "Hey," I say, adjusting my own hand wraps.

The familiar smell of sweat and disinfectant fills my nostrils —oddly comforting.

I'm training for an charity MMA match at the Rancho Palos Verdes Charity Gala this December, and Casp's gym —one of seven he owns across Southern California—has become my sanctuary. Something about the rhythmic thud of gloves against the heavy bag, the squeak of shoes on canvas, helps unravel that perpetual knot between my shoulder blades.

My brothers call it my "Sonny Corleone complex"—this hair-trigger temper that's always simmering just below the surface. After this, I'll head to the private Verde beach where Ansel and Max are waiting with our boards, the ocean being the only other place where that red haze truly lifts. "Let's go."

So, for the next hour, Casp and I lose ourselves in the rhythm of combat—my knuckles connecting with the dense leather of his training mitts, the sharp snap of his roundhouse kick barely missing my jaw, the grunt of his exhale as I take him down to the sweat-slick mat. We transition seamlessly from the clinch work of Muay Thai to the ground game of Jiu-Jitsu, muscles burning with each escape from an armbar.

By the end of it, my gray shirt has turned nearly black with sweat, salt stinging the small cut above my eye, every fiber in my shoulders and core screaming in protest—but the chaos in my mind has finally, mercifully, gone quiet.

I haven't been this fucking rattled since I met my father standing in my granddad’s goddamn living room after twenty-two years of radio silence. I’m still thinking of that tarot reading that gutted me like a fish. How the hell did she do that? Those cards sliced through every defense I've built, exposing raw nerves I thought I'd killed years ago. She laid out my relationship with my father, the darkness I keep chained inside me, my disappointment in myself—everything I've buried so deep I can barely acknowledge it. And she did it with such casual precision it felt like being hit by a fucking freight train.

But Christ, it's not just the reading making my hands shake. It's HER. That beautiful woman is a force of nature —barely 5'4" but she fills the room like a storm. That black hair falling around her face, skin like burnished bronze, and those eyes—those goddamn topaz eyes that don't just look at me but through me, like I'm made of fucking glass. And not a single tremor of fear when I glared at her. Not one. Goddamn, that's rare.

Even Miranda, who's been with me since day one, spent her first year flinching every time I raised my voice. Now she's family, the only person besides my brothers and Casp who calls me on my shit. But this woman—Lilith—she stood her ground from the first second, announcing to me that she would finish the interview-whether I liked it or not-with a confidence that made my pulse spike. I can't stop thinking about her. I can't stop wanting her. She's crawled under my skin in a way that terrifies me, and God help me, I want more.

Casp tosses me a towel, his eyes narrowing. "Jesus Christ, Roman. You nearly took my fucking head off in there. What the hell's going on with you?"

My knuckles are raw, blood seeping through the wraps. I don't even feel it. The rage that fueled me through three brutal rounds has burned down to embers, leaving something else smoldering in its place.

"I met someone," I say, wiping sweat from my face. "She's like nothing I've ever..." I slam my fist against the locker. "Goddamn it, she probably wants nothing to do with me."

Casp knows me better than anyone—knows how women have always clawed for a piece of me. They smell the damage, the power, the billions, and they come hunting. Vultures circling, thinking they'll be the one to save the “broken billionaire.” I've had stalkers, obsessed models, executives who wouldn't take no for an answer.

Even Casp's sister Serafina, also a hotel magnate—two years, a diamond ring, and I felt nothing. Nothing. I'd stare at her sleeping beside me and feel absolutely fucking hollow. I couldn't manufacture what wasn't there, so she cheated, which relieved me - gave me an excuse to walk away without looking like the bad guy to Casp.

They say when you settle, The One appears just to torture you. Maybe that's why I've burned every relationship to the ground. All these women, and I've never once felt anything real. Until Lilith. And it's tearing me up inside.

Casp glances at his watch. “You still meeting Ansel and Max for surfing?"

"Of course," I say. "Saturday surf is sacred to Max."

The thought of hitting the waves with my brothers loosens the knot in my chest. We're all expert surfers—Dad's doing. He insisted we start at four, same as he did with all eight Kensington boys. I remember my first time at Big Sur, ten-foot swells on what Dad called "a calm day."

Lance Williams—the five-time world champion—steadied my board while I trembled in my custom wetsuit. I bawled the entire six-hour drive home, soaking the leather seats of Dad's VW Bus. Strange to think about it now—how gentle he was that day, how he never once snapped at me despite my hysteria. Just kept one hand on the wheel, the other reaching back to squeeze my knee whenever the sobs got too violent.

I close my eyes. Before Dad left, he'd kneel down to my height when I'd break something in one of my rages. He'd place his hands on my shoulders, not to restrain but to steady. "Roman," he'd say, his voice low and even, "breathe with me." And I would. He saw the storm in me and never feared it.

Then one morning, his side of the bathroom counter was empty—aftershave, razor, toothbrush, all gone. Seven brothers looking to me, to each other, for answers none of us had. I shake my head. Twenty-two years later, and my jaw still clenches at the memory. No. Some absences can't be forgiven.

“Anyhow, gotta go,” I say. “Meeting Ansel and Max at the resort’s private beach to surf, like you said. Want to join?”

Casp handles himself on a board like he was born on one, though he doesn't always join us. Sometimes Max brings Gianni, or Ansel drags Finn along. Then there's Celeste, Max's wife. I wince every time I see her pink beginner board strapped to the roof of Max's Jeep. She's been at it less than a year, and it shows—paddling too early, missing perfect swells, face-planting into the whitewash. Max hovers around her like she's made of glass, holding her hand through the basics while we carve up the good breaks without him. I can't fault her—she seems decent enough—but Christ, the way my baby brother follows her around with those puppy dog eyes. Whatever. His life, his choices.

Caspian shakes his head. "Rain check. Swamped at work." He tosses me a towel. "Your offense was solid today, though. Next session we'll drill defense." He takes a swig from his water bottle, then points it at me. "You've got the fire, man—that temper works when you're throwing punches. But you're telegraphing your moves when you get emotional. Gotta keep that brain engaged while the heart's pumping." He taps his temple. "Balance, brother."

I nod, acknowledging his point. My MMA technique needs refinement—more strategy, less raw emotion. But I'm off my game today, thanks to Lilith's damn tarot reading. The cards shouldn't have rattled me, yet here I am, unsettled by how accurately she pegged me.

I'm already at my resort's private beach when Max shows up solo.

"Hey, Rome," he calls out. "Just us today. Ansel bailed, and Connor's stuck filming again. I swear we'll drag him out here someday."

I snort. "When pigs fly." Connor wouldn't be caught dead on a surfboard. Too busy collecting awards and magazine covers to get his perfect hair wet. Three-time "Most Beautiful" in *People*, *Time*'s 100 Most Influential—my brother's come a long way from the kid who couldn't look anyone in the eye after Dad split. I still remember Granddad dragging him to that middle school audition. Connor was so terrified he threw up backstage, then walked out and nailed the lead role. Now he's Hollywood royalty, though he still blushes and stares at his shoes during interviews. Some things never change.

"And Celeste?"

"Home with Violet," Max says. I smile. I'm surprised he didn't want to also stay home with his little girl, but I'm grateful for his company today.

Max and I paddle out past the break. Between waiting for decent swells, he brings up Mom's memorial service again. Thirty years in the ground, and suddenly we need a do-over because Dad finally decided to grace us with his presence. Cameron's organizing the whole thing—says it'll be "more meaningful" now that none of us are snot-nosed kids who barely understood what was happening the first time around. The Catherine Kensington remembrance ceremony, with the complete Kensington collection in attendance.

I've made my position clear to everyone: as long as Dad shows his face, mine won't be there.

"We'll all be there, even Ansel and Silas," referring to the two brothers, besides myself, who were most likely to be wary of Dad's return.

I cut him off. "Not giving into peer pressure." A swell rises beneath us like a gift from the sea gods. I ride it toward shore, Max carving the curl beside me. The timing couldn't be better—no more talk about Mom's memorial. Once beached, I paddle back out, arms burning against the push of the tide. Max follows. We bob like corks on the surface, scanning the horizon. That's surfing for you—ninety percent waiting, ten percent adrenaline. But those waiting moments? That's when my brothers and I really connect. When life's bullshit gets aired out between sets, nothing but endless blue surrounding us.

"Rome," Max says, pressing. "At least talk to Cam about the Memorial. He really needs your input."

Max buzzes around me like a fucking gnat sometimes. Love the kid to death—love all my brothers—but I've never had that bond he shares with Ansel, or what the twins have. The four of them pair off naturally: Asher with Silas (identical twins), Kalen with Connor (also identical twins). Then there's Cameron, who was busy playing dad while Granddad ran his Fortune 500 empire and Grandma ruled the society pages. That left me—Roman, the odd man out.

At school, I'd be throwing punches while Kalen and

Connor, both younger than me, would try to back me up but couldn't land a hit to save their lives. Look at them now —Connor just accepted a best actor Oscar while Kalen is selling out arenas and can play three instruments like a god - piano, guitar and, weirdly, a cello. Those two are talented as hell, but soft. And the older twins? Asher with his genius IQ and Silas running the family jewels division? They'd rather negotiate than fight.

So there I was, the only Kensington who could break a nose properly, standing alone in the middle of six brothers paired like Noah's fucking animals and one other brother on the outside like me. Thank Christ for Caspian. When everyone else paired off, he became the brother I chose—the only guy in my life who understood that sometimes problems need to be solved with fists instead of words.

I guess that's why I don't feel much heat about skipping this memorial service. No one brother and I ever formed a real alliance, so there's no one who can guilt-trip me effectively. Silas stood with me initially when Dad showed up, both of us giving the cold shoulder, but Asher got to him with that lawyer-brain of his. Classic Asher—all rational arguments and zero emotion. And Silas? He folded like wet cardboard.

Look, I care about all of them, don't mistake me. But we've never been a united front, any of us. So when they call to lecture me, their words just slide right off.

I spot the wave bearing down on us. "Max," I say, "kindly shut the fuck up." I pop to my feet, catching the swell as it carries me shoreward, Max right beside me. We call him Little Max as a joke—nothing little about my 6'4" (same height as me) baby brother. He commands his surfboard the same way he commands his movie studio: with precision and flair that draws everyone's eye. At sixteen, scouts were begging him to go pro, but Max always had Hollywood in his sights. The stubborn bastard knew exactly what he wanted and went after it. Hard not to respect that.

Just then, Nina Harrington, my royalty concierge, appears on the shoreline, her arm flailing in my direction. Damn it. Saturdays are supposed to be sacred—my one day off after grinding through six straight days of fourteen-hour shifts. Still, Max's voice has been grating on my last nerve, so I paddle toward her, grateful for the interruption. "Mr. Kensington," she says, breathless as I approach. "We have a situation with Baroness Janssens from Belgium. Her helicopter can't take off in this wind, but she's determined to make the San Francisco Opera tonight. What should we do?"

I grip the towel, wiping sweat from my face. "We're taking the Chinook," I snap. Not just any helicopter—our military-grade CH-47, built to slice through gale-force winds like they're nothing. "I'll handle this personally." For a woman who drops fifty grand a night, I'll fly the damn thing myself if I have to.

I jab a quick wave at Max before storming toward the resort. I need to change and get the baroness airborne. I pull on a t-shirt to go with my blue swim trunks, intending to grab a golf cart to take me to my suite in Building A.

But the moment I hit the marble lobby floor—Christ. There she is. That light blue sundress clings to curves that make my mouth go dry, the fabric a perfect contrast against her olive skin. She's gliding toward the beachfront gazebo like she owns the place, already commanding the space we set up last week. My fists clench involuntarily. The same primal hunger that hit me last week slams into me again—harder this time. I want to drag her into the nearest empty room and ravage her until neither of us can stand. The force of it makes me furious. With her. With myself. With the whole goddamn situation.

She looks at me, her amusement like a slap across my face. "Mr. Kensington," she says, one eyebrow arching dangerously high. "Mingling amongst the hoi polloi, I see, looking like you're one of us." Her eyes rake over me. "When I met you last week, I thought you were an Adonis carved from marble, but now I see that you have feet of clay like the rest of us mortals." She shakes her head and strides toward the door, the sunlight catching subtle auburn highlights in her hair.

I lunge after her. "Ms. Sydney!" My voice tears from my throat. She whips around, those topaz eyes burning into mine. "If you must know," I growl, "I was surfing, which is why I look like this." I rake my fingers through my salt-crusted hair, furious at myself. What the hell am I doing, standing in my own goddamn lobby half-naked in nothing but swim trunks and a shirt that clings to every muscle? I never let anyone see me as anything but immaculate in Tom Ford or Brioni. The humiliation scalds me from the inside out as Lilith Sydney's gaze lingers on me, seeing straight through to my core.

She dismisses my apology with a wave. "No need to worry. It's just amusing to see you wandering through your hotel lobby half-dressed as if you own the place—which, of course, you do." Her gaze drifts momentarily to my damp t-shirt before meeting my eyes again. "And that disheveled hair? Very Renaissance masterpiece meets California surf culture." She playfully fans herself. "Pardon me while I recover."

I roll my eyes despite being unable to look away from her face. Something about this woman throws me off balance—she shows no fear, no intimidation, and speaks to me with a familiarity that should get her fired for mocking my appearance.

Words fail me, so I retreat into the hotel, waiting impatiently for my golf cart to take me to my suite. Baroness Janssens has tickets to *Madame Butterfly* in San Francisco tonight—a critically acclaimed production of her favorite opera. She's counting on me, and I won't disappoint her. I'll personally ensure she boards our military-grade Chinook helicopter within the hour.

After the golf cart takes me to my suite, I storm into it, shower and dress in one of my immaculate Brioni suits, my hands still unsteady. Damn, that woman bothers me. There's only one way to fix this. Lilith Sydney has to be terminated—immediately. I don't care if she somehow nailed every detail in that reading. Lucky guess. Coincidence. Whatever. The fact remains: I can't have some tarot-flipping hippie getting under my skin like this. Nobody messes with my equilibrium. Nobody.

I check my watch. The moment the Baroness's jet leaves our airspace, I'm telling Miranda to handle it.

I get the Baroness up in the air and then I get to Miranda’s office. She doesn't even look up from her laptop when I slam her office door open. "I want that tarot reader gone."

"I just hired her, Roman. She's under contract." She finally meets my gaze, unflinching. "If you want her gone, handle it yourself."

No one else in my empire would dare speak to me that way. But Miranda's desk still has the coffee ring from when we stayed up all night eleven years ago, running numbers on napkins, wondering if my grandfather's loan would be enough to transform this crumbling property into something magnificent. I'd paid him back within twelve months with interest.

Now my resorts dot coastlines from the French Riviera to Sao Palo Brazil, Sardinia to Crete to Lake Como, Italy to Dubai to Beijing to Auckland, New Zealand. The flagship's guest list reads like a global Who's Who. But Miranda remembers the twenty-two-year-old kid terrified of becoming the family failure. She believed before anyone else did, which is why she's the only person whose "no" I accept.

“Fine,” I say. “Where is she now?”

“She's down at the beach cabana. Doing a tarot reading for Countess Vandermeer of the Netherlands. So, I suggest you wait—"

I cut her off with a wave of my hand. Wait? When I want this woman gone from my resort immediately? I storm toward the door. I won't barge in on royalty—I have some standards—but I'll be right outside that cabana platform when she finishes, ready to tell her to pack her crystals and disappear. Permanently.

I slip into the vestibule of the cabana, realizing Lilith is already deep into a reading. “Countess Vandermeer,” Lilith says in that steady, soothing tone, and I can hear the Countess’s soft sobs. Guilty as I feel for eavesdropping, I can’t tear myself away—I’m curious to see how Lilith handles nobility.

Part of me hopes she botches the tarot reading. It would reflect poorly on the resort, sure, but it would also hand me the perfect justification to terminate her contract.

The fact that I’m willing to sacrifice business optics just to be rid of her should tell me something.

Chapter Four

LILITH

My first client is a Countess! I text Jack the news, already picturing myself reading tarot for actual royalty. He sends back a thumbs-up emoji, then deflates me: "Countesses are peers, not royals." Whatever.

When she glides into my cabana, she's clutching a Birkin that probably costs six months of my shop rent. Mid-fifties, spine like a ballerina's, face that gives nothing away. Blonde. Beautiful. The kind of woman who's never carried her own groceries. But beneath that perfect exterior, I see it immediately—a sadness so deep it's practically leaking from her pores.

She clears her throat. "I added your service to my package," she says, her English flawless, not a hint of an accent detectable. I've always been impressed by people who can slip between languages like changing clothes, their pronunciation so perfect you'd never guess they weren't native speakers.

"Tell me about Bridget," I say, my fingers working the deck.

"My daughter refuses to marry Count Willem Van Haarlem." She sighs, smoothing her silk scarf. "He's worth billions, runs a shipping empire. Security for life." Her perfectly manicured nails drum once against the table. "But Bridget wants Hollywood instead. Insists on 'marrying for love.' We've argued for months about this. I'm at my wit's end—that's why I'm here. I need guidance."

Oh, boy. This spread won't tell her what she wants to hear. Of that, I'm sure. Yet, I go through the ritual - shuffle the cards, cut them, ask her to select one of the decks, and then spread them out in the Celtic Cross. And I immediately see just what I thought I would.

"Your daughter has pulled away from you, but reconciliation is possible," I say, turning over the Six of Cups. "She needs space to chart her own course—the Nine of Pentacles. She craves independence, wants to stand on her own financially. Still, her love for you is genuine as shown by the 10 of cups, which is a promise of joy, but only if you loosen your grip. The Page of Cups in the spread shows her great affection for you, too. But let her choose her own path rather than imposing yours. That is the advice of this spread - let her chart her course and you will be close with her for a lifetime."

"But Ms. Sydney," the Countess protests in her perfect English. "I have already arranged for her to marry Count Willem. I have already arranged for her to take over the Vandermeer Foundation. What am I to do, Ms. Sydney?"

"Countess Vandermeer," I reply, "let's explore both outcomes. I'll do two spreads—one for the path where you compel her into marriage and charity duties, and another for her living the life she truly wants, with a man she loves and a career she dreams of." She glances up. "Does that sound all right?"

The Countess sniffs and nods.

"All right," I say, riffling the deck. "A quick three-card spread: past, present, future, for the scenario where she lives by your rules." I spread out the cards. The spread tells me everything I need to know. "Nine of Swords, Ten of Swords, The Tower."

The Countess presses her lips together. "The Tower—what does that portend?"

"A sudden upheaval," I answer. "The Nine of Swords in the past shows her fear of disappointing you. The Ten of Swords in the present signals betrayal and devastation. The Tower in the future shows upheaval, crisis, destruction of old beliefs. But let me get some clarity on that Tower Card. I need to see what exactly will happen in the future if your daughter is compelled to marry Count Willem and take over your charity." I shuffle the cards again. "Eight of Cups—walking away. Reversed Queen of Swords—she views you as manipulative. The Tower appears again, followed by Three of Swords—heartbreak—and a reversed Ten of Cups—shattered dreams, disharmony, broken family."

At that, the Countess breaks into fresh tears. I hand her a Kleenex and I go over to her side of the table and put my arm around her. I read my protocol for handling the Countess before the reading, so I know that she's warm, considered a people's Countess, and does not mind hugging. Indeed, she seems to enjoy my embrace, putting her head on my shoulder while she cries.

I lower my voice. "Countess, these cards tell me your daughter adores you. The Page of Cups we saw earlier—that's her, devoted and eager for your approval. She might follow your wishes—marry the Count, run the charity—but see this Tower card? It predicts collapse. Either the marriage fails, or she abandons the charity work, possibly both."

The Countess exhales slowly. "And if I simply... let her choose her own path?"

"Let's see." I turn over three new cards. "The Nine of Swords appears again in her past—all those sleepless nights worrying about disappointing you. But look at these next cards: Ten of Cups in her present and The Sun illuminating her future." I tap the bright cards. "The message couldn't be clearer. Release her from expectations, and she finds immediate joy, lasting love. The Sun promises fulfillment—whether she succeeds as an actress or simply lives authentically. Her happiness blooms when she's free to chart her own course."

"Oh, but her father will not approve."

"You're certain Count Vandermeer opposes this? Let's consult the cards about him." I shuffle the worn deck before laying three cards in a neat row. "Interesting. Eight of Swords in his past position—he's felt trapped, unable to speak freely. The Star illuminates his present—see how the figure pours water back to earth? That's hope returning. And his future..." I tap the final card, where a crowned figure holds a golden chalice. "King of Cups. A man of deep feeling beneath a controlled exterior." I lean forward, my voice softening. "These cards suggest your husband secretly supports Bridget's Hollywood dreams. I suspect she's already confided in him, and he's simply been afraid to contradict you."

The Countess releases a weighty sigh and shakes her head. "The Van Haarlems have been our closest friends and allies for generations. How am I supposed to face Willem's father with news that my daughter refuses the match? Bridget and Willem shared cradles as infants. This union has been written in our family ledgers since before they could walk. I've pictured their wedding day in my mind a thousand times. Must I bury that vision now?"

I shuffle the tarot deck, feeling that familiar tightness in my chest. This moment—when the cards reveal a truth that contradicts a client's deepest wishes—never gets easier. The Universe speaks through these cards whether we like its message or not. People only seek my guidance when they sense something's wrong - the satisfied rarely request readings. Yet how do I tell this woman that pursuing her cherished dream will only bring sorrow to everyone involved? The love for her daughter shines in her eyes. I believe she wants Bridget's happiness above all. Now I must somehow help her see that letting go is the greatest gift she can offer her child.

I lean forward, meeting the Countess's gaze. "I understand how difficult this is," I tell her softly. "When we believe we know what's best for our children, watching them choose differently tears at the heart." My fingers trace the edge of the spread before us. "But these cards speak clearly. A marriage to Count Van Haarlem will bring your daughter only misery—and worse, it will drive her from you completely." I pause, letting the silence emphasize my next words. "Deep down, what matters most is her happiness and her love for you, isn't it? The old wisdom holds truth: loving means releasing. Your daughter will find joy, Countess, but only if allowed to chart her own course. The cards have revealed this path. I hope you'll consider it."

She inclines her head. "When I hired you, I made a promise to myself to follow your counsel, regardless of my personal feelings. You're correct, even if it's difficult for me to accept. Bridget's happiness is all that matters." A sigh escapes her as she looks away. "Though I had hoped her path to joy would involve Count Willem and our foundation."

I rest my hand briefly on her shoulder. She acknowledges the gesture with a slight nod before rising to her feet. "I'm grateful for your guidance, Ms. Sydney," she tells me, smoothing her skirt. "I'll proceed as you've suggested. May it lead to the outcome we all desire."

She leaves and I start to put my cards away when Roman storms into the cabana.

Oh, boy.

Chapter Five

ROMAN

After the reading with the Countess, I slam through the cabana door so hard it bounces back and nearly hits me. My blood is boiling. That conniving witch Lilith is getting fired—right now. The more I think about it, the more I'm certain that she was tipped off about my father. Had to have been. There's no other explanation. The tarot spread she laid out—that "bulls-eye" reading that convinced me to hire her—was nothing but a calculated con.

My jaw clenches so tight my teeth might crack. She played me, exploiting my complete ignorance about tarot. Those cards could've meant anything—anything!—and she twisted their meanings to match information she already had. My hands are shaking. I don't know who betrayed me, who told her my secrets, but someone did. She's a fraud. A goddamn fraud. I'm going to watch her pack up every last one of those cards and escort her off my property myself.

Ms. Sydney's eyes lock with mine. "Mr. Kensington. Back so soon?"

"I'm terminating your contract," I snap, my jaw

clenched so tight it aches. "You're nothing but a fraud peddling mystical bullshit to desperate people. I won't waste another cent on your little performance."

"Sit down, Mr. Kensington." Her voice remains maddeningly serene. My blood boils, yet something in her unwavering stare makes my pulse quicken. No tears. No begging. Not even a flinch. She doesn't move a single card from the table, as if my command means nothing.

"I don't want another spread," I slam my palm against the wall. "I just want you gone. Right now."

She ignores me completely, her fingers dancing across the deck with hypnotic precision. The cards slap against each other with a rhythm that feels deliberate, taunting. She throws some cards out and her eyes suddenly widen.

"Your brothers are suffocating you," she whispers, her voice cutting through me like ice. "They're using your mother's memory as a weapon. But that's not why you're fighting them, is it? You adored her despite barely knowing her. It's him you can't forgive—your father. And there's more..." Her finger traces a card, trembling slightly. "You blame your youngest brother for everything. The same one who's now hounding you about honoring your mother. That's why you're digging your heels in until they bleed."

Despite my rage, I sit down across from her. She's somehow sensing the truth about Max—the truth I've buried so deep I barely acknowledge it myself. How can I admit I blame an innocent child? How can she see that every time I look at Max, I see the pregnancy our mother refused to end, even after her cancer diagnosis. I see seven siblings left parentless. I see our father walking away, unable to live life without his wife, our mother. My hands clench under the table. It's not fair. It's not Max's fault. But the resentment has always been there, festering. And Lilith sees it? I rack my brain trying to figure out who could have told her, then realize: no one could have. This poison has lived only in my thoughts—never shared with my brothers, with Miranda, not even with Casp.

I shake my head, my anger draining away. "Who told you?" I ask her.

Lilith's fingers trace the edge of the Death card. "Nobody told me anything, Mr. Kensington." Her voice drops to match the hushed lighting of the reading room. "These cards speak for themselves." She meets my skeptical gaze, her shoulders tensing under my scrutiny. "Your eyes say it all—you think I Googled you before before my interview, so I can throw out some cards that turn out weirdly accurate, but are just confirming what I already learned." She places her palm flat on the table, steadying herself. A shiver runs through her body, rippling the silver bangles on her wrist. "Some readers do that, you know. Cheat people, take their money, prey on their naïveté and desire to believe." Her throat tightens. "Last month, a woman came to my shop after spending five thousand dollars on a 'curse removal.' Five thousand." Lilith's eyes shine with unshed tears. "She couldn't make rent that month." She shakes her head. "I couldn't live with myself if I did something like that. I'm not the charlatan who sells candles who allegedly removes spiritual chains from people. I don't even try to clear chakras, not that I don't believe in chakra cleansing but because I'm not skilled at doing it. And I would never give a false reading just to make a buck."

"Well, somebody must've told you about-"

Just then, she receives a text. She looks at her phone and puts her hand to her mouth. "Oh, my. So sorry, Mr. Kensington, but I need to go. There's an emergency at my shop. Excuse me."

At that, she hurriedly packs up her cards and crystals and leaves.

I pull up her shop on my phone, jot down the address, and find myself heading there before I've even decided to go. It's not like me to chase after someone—especially not some hippie tarot reader who probably thinks crystals cure cancer. But the way she suddenly looked so panicked after showing me nothing but a calm demeanor… I can't shake it.

Plus, something about her has hooked into me, and I won't rest until I understand why.

Chapter Six

LILITH

I white-knuckle the steering wheel, screaming into my phone, "I'm coming, Jack!" His text had been three numbers that froze my blood: "911. Pipe burst. EVERYTHING FLOODING." My heart hammers against my ribs as visions flash through my mind—my precious first-edition Crowley texts dissolving into pulp, hand-painted tarot cards bleeding their colors onto the floor. Thousands of dollars. My entire life's work. Destroyed. And today—of all the cursed days—when I was reading for European royalty - oh, excuse me, peer, not royalty, right Jack?- at the Verde Resort! I slam my foot on the gas, cutting off a Lexus.

I crash through the door to find Jack frantically hauling soggy boxes, his guy-liner streaking down his cheeks. I immediately join him.

I'm elbow-deep in salvage when a shadow falls across the doorway. Roman. Towering at the threshold of the shop like some dark harbinger. Of course he'd track me down to gloat over my misfortune.

Jack's eyes widen. "Oh.my.god. Roman Kensington?

Here?" He fans himself with shaking hands. His voice runs down to a whisper. "Oh, Lil, those *Vanity Fair* pictures don't do him no justice, honey. He's even more beautiful in person, as if that's possible."

I whirl toward Roman, my voice cracking. "Mr. Kensington, if you've come to dance on the grave of my business—"

He says nothing, just rolls up his sleeves to reveal corded forearms. "That oak bookshelf—we need to get it out soon before it warps beyond repair. Just don't expose it to direct sunlight. And these Persian rugs need immediate attention." His voice is a battlefield command. He stabs at his phone. "Caspian, flooding emergency at Mystic Tides. Bring tools." He turns those steel eyes on me. "That oak display—help me move it before the water reaches the leg joints."

Just like that, the billionaire has seized control of my catastrophe—and God help me, I'm surrendering completely.

Roman's voice slices through the chaos. "Where is the water shut-off valve?"

Jack and I exchange panicked looks. "Uh…" Jack stammers while I stand paralyzed, my heart hammering against my ribs.

"Goddammit," Roman growls, then vanishes out back. When he reappears, water drips from his forearms. "Found it. What do you have to patch a pipe before this place becomes Venice Beach's newest swimming pool?"

My hands shake violently as I fumble through a drawer. "Duct tape?" I hold it out like a pathetic offering to an angry god.

Roman snatches it, his jaw clenched so tight I swear I hear his teeth crack. "Fucking amateurs."

Water surges across my floor—a relentless tide

devouring everything in its path. Jack and I frantically throw books into boxes while the pipe screams like a wounded animal, then suddenly falls silent.

Roman storms back in, shirt ripped off and his undershirt clinging to his torso, soaked transparent and molded to every ridge of muscle. My mouth goes desert-dry. Jack actually gasps out loud, his eyes bulging as if he's witnessing the Second Coming.

I force myself to keep moving, hands flying over crystals and pendulums, heart racing with dual panic—over my drowning livelihood and the electricity crackling through the air whenever Roman barks another command, his voice deep and uncompromising as thunder.

Then Caspian bursts through the door—another Greek god in human form. His dirty blonde hair is windswept, topaz-green eyes blazing with purpose. My breath catches as Roman gets on one side of the bookshelf, his veins popping along his forearms. Together they hoist the massive oak bookshelf as if it's made of cardboard, muscles straining against expensive fabric. The raw power radiating between them makes my skin flush despite the emergency.

"Water off?" Caspian asks.

"No, I thought I'd let the whole damn place flood," Roman snarls, eyes flashing. "I MacGyvered that pipe with whatever garbage she had and tied my shirt around it. Got the putty?" Caspian nods once, sharply. "Hand it over. You three—" Roman's gaze locks onto mine, sending electricity down my spine "—keep vacuuming while I save what's left of this place."

Caspian, Jack and I attack the flood with Caspian-provided Shop Vacs, the machines roaring like beasts as we suck up gallons of water. I drag the sopping rug in, my muscles screaming, and vacuum it until my knuckles turn white on the handle. The rug weighs a ton as I heave it back outside, my shirt now plastered to my skin with sweat. My pulse hammers in my ears—part panic, part physical exertion—as I vacuum the floor again with desperate intensity. Caspian fires up an industrial blower that howls like a hurricane, blasting the rug with hot air while Roman, his forearms bulging, hauls in the massive oak counter that normally takes two delivery men to move. The four of us work frantically, racing against time, shelving books and merchandise until my fingers are raw and my back threatens to seize.

When we finally finish, I collapse against the counter, gulping air. I dispatch Jack for food, and he returns with steaming pizzas, cold beer, and salad, and the four of us collapse on the floor, backs against the wall. "You guys literally saved my life today," I tell Caspian and Roman, my voice still shaky. "I would've been completely destroyed without you."

Roman's smile transforms his face from intimidating to breathtaking. "We're not done yet," he says, wiping sweat from his brow. "Those ancient pipes need replacing before they burst again and flood this place to the ceiling. They're practically fossilized—probably installed when Washington was crossing the Delaware."

We devour the pizzas like we're starving, and every time I glance up, Roman's eyes are burning into me. He tilts his head back to drink, throat working as he swallows, and I can't tear my gaze from the way his fingers grip the bottle. His A-shirt clings to his torso, damp with sweat, revealing not just muscles but the sharp definition between them, the dark ink of a tattoo disappearing beneath the fabric. When his eyes lock onto mine—those lashes casting shadows on his cheeks—heat floods my core. Jack clears his throat.

Jack flutters his fingers in Caspian's direction. "Yoo-hoo, Mr. Muscles," he stage-whispers, voice rising into a theatrical lilt. "I'm absolutely parched for fresh air. Let's go outside and count stars or commune with night squirrels or whatever you straight boys do in the darkness."

Caspian's eyes dart between Roman and me. "God, yes," he mutters. "It's like a furnace in here."

The door barely clicks shut before Roman's phone hits the floor. He takes another pull from his Heineken, never breaking eye contact. "Diego's coming in in the next several days," he says, voice rougher than before. "He'll tear out those old pipes, put in the good stuff. Type K copper." His tongue touches his upper lip. "Thickest. Heaviest. Most durable."

I nod. "So, Mr. Kensington…"

He rolls his eyes, the movement sharp as a blade. "You've seen my tattoo. You can call me Roman. Or Rome."

I nod, heat flooding my cheeks. "Roman," I manage, my voice barely audible. "What brought you here tonight?"

He shrugs, muscles rippling beneath his shirt. "I acted like an asshole like usual. And you looked panicked when you left the resort, so I had to come out here and see what was up. Good thing I came, too, because, I'm sorry, I don't think I've seen two people less competent in a crisis than you and Jack."

His laugh hits me like thunder, and something electric shoots down my spine. First that devastating smile earlier, now this laugh that makes my knees weak. For a fleeting second, he seems almost human—but there's nothing mortal about the raw power radiating from him. He's Ares incarnate, the god of war himself, with that tattoo mapping violent constellations across his skin. Even when he's being kind, danger pulses from him like a heartbeat.

I swallow hard. "I'll pay you back. Every cent."

Roman's laugh cuts through the air. "Don't insult me. Not after tonight."

"Diego, then. I need to—"

"Diego works for me," Roman snaps, leaning forward. "End of discussion."

"But dragging him out here, an hour's drive away—"

"Nobody loves driving in LA traffic for a job, but that's why I pay him triple what anyone else would." He tears off a chunk of pizza with his teeth, washing it down with a long pull of beer, throat working as he swallows. "Look, I was an absolute bastard earlier. Threatening your job like that."

"You literally saved everything I've built," I say, my voice cracking. "We're more than even."

His eyes lock onto mine. "Insurance. Tell me you have it."

My chest tightens. "Only for acts of God. If those ocean swells hit ten feet and breach the sea wall? Covered. But this?" I gesture at the devastation around us. "I'm completely exposed."

Roman slams his beer down. "Unacceptable. My insurance guy will call you tomorrow."

I feel the blood drain from my face. "I can't afford—"

"I've got it," he cuts in, voice like steel. "You think I want you at my resort giving readings while you're terrified of losing everything? This isn't charity—it's business. And to me?" He snaps his fingers inches from my face. "Pocket. Change."

I sigh. Pocket change to him is everything to me. "Well, thank you," I say.

He shrugs, checking the Patek Philippe on his wrist.

"Time to hit the road." His gaze lifts to catch Caspian strolling through the entrance, mid-chuckle at something Jack said. Jack's eyes are practically heart-shaped cartoon cutouts as he drinks in every inch of Caspian's frame. Meanwhile, Caspian remains blissfully oblivious to the effect he's having.

"Gotta bounce," Caspian says.

"Right behind you," Roman says, then turns to me. "Diego will be coming in the next few days with those copper pipes—guaranteed leak-proof. And expect a call from Brett about the insurance." His eyes linger on mine a beat longer than necessary. "Take care, Lilith." He tilts his beer bottle toward Jack. "You too, though between the two of you, I'm not sure who needs more supervision. Talk about blind leading the blind." A smile plays at the corner of his mouth as he shakes his head, then follows Caspian out the door.

He leaves and Jack flutters his hand in front of his face. "Oh. My. God. Two Greek gods just blessed our humble establishment with their divine presence. Shame they're both straight." He wiggles his eyebrows suggestively. "But one of them clearly has the hots for you."

"Roman? Please," I roll my eyes. "He drove all this way to make amends for being an ass. He tried to fire me earlier, you know. I just pulled your famous 'selective hearing' technique." I smile, remembering our tiny UCLA-adjacent apartment where Jack would recount his work stories over cheap wine. His manager had fired him during the dinner rush, but Jack simply continued taking orders like nothing happened. The poor guy was so bewildered he never mentioned it again, and Jack ended up serving martinis there until graduation - three years after the "firing."

Jack rolls his eyes dramatically. "Honey, please. Mr.

Luxury Resort CEO drove an entire hour through LA traffic—an hour!—just to say sorry? When he could've fired off a text?" He leans in, voice dropping conspiratorially. "That man didn't come all that way for an apology. He came for you." He fans himself with one hand. "And did you see those muscles in that tank top? I swear, those abs were so defined I could've used them as a cheese grater. And believe me," he adds with a wink, "I would've volunteered for kitchen duty."

Heat scorches my cheeks. "Well," I manage to say, my voice catching. Roman Kensington noticing me? I might as well be a dust mote trying to catch a supernova. The man is carved from marble and midnight, for god's sake. "He saved my ass tonight. I'll give him that."

Jack fans himself dramatically. "Sweet mother of mercy, Lilith. Did you see him take charge like that? I'm still recovering." He clutches his chest. "The moment that pipe burst and he just—" Jack mimes ripping fabric, eyes rolling back. "And then watching him and Caspian muscle that bookcase through the doorway? Pure. Physical. Perfection." He clutches his chest. "It's like Apollo himself stepped out of my mythology books just to make you his mortal conquest." That's Jack, always believing that gods walk among us.

Thinking about Roman's shoulders, I'm starting to believe it.

I grab Jack's arm. "Let's go. I need sleep or I'll collapse right here."

"Okay, little Lilith," he says, eyes glinting. "Just keep pretending there's not a wildfire between you and Roman god." Then he laughs. "Roman god. Good lord. It was right there the whole time."

I force a laugh but my heart hammers against my ribs as we walk the block home. The night air does nothing to cool the heat crawling up my neck. In bed, I press my thighs together, desperate to extinguish thoughts of those dark eyes, that jaw, those hands that could crush or caress. My skin burns everywhere he looked at me today.

God, I'm drowning. Wanting the boss like this? I'm playing with dynamite.

Chapter Seven

LILITH

I survey the store and feel like crying. It's not a catastrophe—Roman and Caspian hauled in their muscles and Shop-Vacs, so the floor and rug are bone-dry. We even aired the place out to chase away any lingering mildew—truly the worst smell in the world.

"So," Jack says, sliding books back onto the shelf. In half an hour the store opens, and I've got four readings lined up. No countesses or celebrities—fine by me. The rich folks at the resort are polite, but they're not my crowd. "Roman god."

"What about him?"

Jack waggles his eyebrows dramatically. "Honey, the universe is practically shoving Mr. Tall-Dark-and-Obscenely-Wealthy into your cosmic orbit! I mean, those cheekbones? Divine intervention. I'd sacrifice a goat if I thought it would help, but PETA would come for me, and I just got these nails done."

I shake my head. "He's gorgeous and loaded, but…"

"But?"

"He might not be emotionally available." I cock my head. "Come on, Jack: thirty-three, gorgeous, filthy rich, and still single? There's a story there. And I steer clear of emotionally unavailable men."

I don't tell Jack about the tarot spread I did for Roman. It revealed an absent, alcoholic father who abandoned him and his brothers, leaving deep scars of betrayal and grief. I sense auras in people who emit them strongly—artists glow magenta, spiritual types shine indigo. Most folks barely register. Roman's aura was jet-black: blocked energy, loss, distrust. The cards showed early trauma and loss, an alcoholic dad. My readings are accurate—that's why I have a solid reputation among L.A. tarot readers—and Roman proved it when he hired me on the spot.

Jack snaps his fingers in a z-formation. "Lil, honey, if he's emotionally unavailable, he's practically gift-wrapped for you! You're like a walking therapy session with better accessories. Remember that aura reader with the unfortunate turban situation? Even she said your aura is greener than my thumb after I killed that cactus—and killing a cactus takes talent, darling."

I laugh. "You've got it backwards. Green thumb means you can make things grow, not kill them. You actually have a black thumb."

"Semantics," Jack says with a dismissive wave. "What matters is your green aura. The healing energy you radiate." He wiggles his eyebrows suggestively. "Just what our brooding billionaire needs, if you ask me."

"I'm a compassionate healer," I agree. I've never seen my own aura, but every psychic I've met insists it's green. So if anyone can help Roman heal, it's me. But that doesn't mean I want a romance.

One, he's way out of my league—a billionaire versus a

tarot reader renting a tiny shop, living with a friend because I can't afford my own place, driving a used Prius I can't replace with an electric car. Two, I'm not even sure he wants my help. I can only guide people who choose to heal. While I wish I could do crystal healing or chakra balancing or aura cleanses, I'm really just good at drawing out emotions and identifying blockages—the first step toward real healing.

Still, I assemble a small gift in case I see him again: an amethyst for calm, a black tourmaline to absorb negativity, lemon balm to lift and soothe, hawthorn and rose to ease emotional pain. I tuck them into a silk-lined wooden box. He probably won't take it, but I prepare it anyway.

I smile when I look at my little gift. But who am I kidding? I probably won't see the guy again.

Even though I dearly hope I do.

Chapter Eight

ROMAN

Fuck. I can't shake that woman. She's fucking everywhere—in my dreams, in my goddamn shower thoughts, like some kind of jasmine-scented ghost haunting every corner of my mind. And the worst part? I'm not even fighting it. Me—Roman Kensington—the man who eats Fortune 500 CEOs for breakfast, who crushes multi-million dollar deals before lunch, brought to my knees by some barefoot crystal-worshipping witch with tarot cards. Jesus Christ. I'm losing my fucking mind, and I don't even want it back.

I couldn't help but smirk watching her and Jack flail around like it was the end of the world. A burst pipe? Please. Try handling a celebrity overdose, a kitchen fire during peak dinner service, or that time a guest released three dozen live doves in the grand ballroom. After running resorts for over a decade, I've developed a certain immunity to chaos—but I won't deny enjoying the chance to play hero for her tonight.

But Lilith will have to wait. Cam's called a mandatory Kensington summit for tomorrow night, and when the eldest brother summons, we all answer—unless we're looking to get disowned. I tell myself I shouldn't give a damn what they think, but that's bullshit and I know it. Kalen's flying in from his Australian tour, Asher's putting some royal Dutch gala on hold, and Silas is pausing his hunt for Napoleon's jewels in France. The least I can do is drive my ass the hour from Palos Verdes to Brentwood without bitching about it.

So, the next day, I drive to Cam's relatively modest house. And I say modest by Kensington standards—the place is a fucking palace to most of Los Angeles. Terracotta roof tiles catch the morning sun as I pull into the circular driveway lined with fragrant orange trees. The Mediterranean villa sprawls across the hillside, its cream-colored stucco walls punctuated by arched windows framed in wrought iron. Through the floor-to-ceiling windows, I glimpse the infinity pool that seems to spill right into the Pacific.

Cameron bought the place for $3 million a few years ago, it's now worth double that. My bleeding-heart brother might dedicate his life to the underprivileged, but his kitchen tells another story—gleaming copper pots hanging above a six-burner Viking range, marble countertops imported from Carrara, and a wine fridge stocked exclusively with bottles that never dip below three figures. Every inch of the place bears Eli Jones's signature touch—the same designer whose work graces the centerfolds of *Architectural Digest* and whose waiting list is longer than the line at the DMV.

I arrive to find my brothers sprawled across the terrace, Mai Tais in hand. Cameron stands at the grill, poking at what smells like swordfish. He spots me and abandons his post, arms outstretched. I return his hug stiffly. No need to make him look bad in front of the others. Besides, Cam's the only one I can stomach for more than five minutes. Maybe because we both never quite fit—him carrying Dad's shadow, me without a built-in buddy while the two sets of twins had each other and Max clung to Ansel. So Cameron got my loyalty by process of elimination. Even if he does drink these ridiculous umbrella cocktails.

"Roman! You made it!" He shoves a Mai Tai into my hand before I can protest. The smell of pineapple and rum wafts up, cloying and sweet. I grimace. I've never been one for sugar. At every birthday growing up, while my brothers fought over who got the corner piece with extra frosting, I'd be quietly scraping my frosting onto Ansel's plate. Cameron knows damn well I'd rather chew glass than drink this syrupy cocktail. A neat Macallan is my drink. Always has been. He's doing this on purpose—trying to force me into the "vacation spirit" like everyone else here.

My brothers rise from their seats one after another, each pulling me into a bear hug. I haven't felt Silas's vise-grip or Asher's backslap since Max's wedding in England the December before last. Kalen's been just as scarce. At least Connor's been around, shooting his latest film in the area. Max barely leaves the Kensington Pictures building these days, preferring to stay local with his wife and baby girl, and Ansel's finally letting his talent scouts do the traveling while he stays local. Between those three and Cameron, I've had some semblance of family nearby.

I take a seat as Cameron shoves a plate of seven-layer dip in front of me. Of course he made the dip himself—probably spent hours chopping tomatoes and mashing avocados when he could've grabbed a 7-layer dip at Ralph's in five minutes. Classic Cameron. While my other brothers would've served duck confit or caviar-topped deviled eggs and truffle-infused whatever prepared by a personal chef, my oldest brother serves up something you'd find at a Super Bowl party. Mr. Relatable, living in his multi-million dollar Brentwood mansion. But, when I put some Tostitos into the dip, I have to give Cameron credit. He does make a mean seven-layer dip.

"You make this from scratch, Cam?" I ask as I cram the Tostito chip and the dip into my mouth.

"Every bit of it," he says, chest puffing slightly. "Mashed the beans, diced the avocados, chopped the tomatoes and onions by hand. Grated the cheese. Even the salsa's homemade."

"What, no homemade sour cream created from the cow you milked yourself?" Ansel quips. Cam responds with a playful shove.

"Just because you barbarians can't boil water doesn't make me Gordon Ramsay," Cameron says. "Though I did sign up for those Sur La Table workshops. Learning Korean BBQ techniques next week."

Connor wiggles his eyebrows. "Got someone special to cook for?"

"Not anymore," Cameron says, his smile fading as he looks down at his plate. The brothers go quiet. We all remember the memorial service—Alecia's photo holding the tiny baby Stephanie. Over two years since the drunk driver took them both while they were on a grocery run in the middle of the night - Cam had the flu and they had run out of NyQuil, so Alecia went to get the cold medicine, taking the baby with her. The drunk driver ran a stop light, plowing into them at 70 MPH. Now Cam still keeps her favorite coffee mug in his cabinet. Still wears his wedding ring.

Out of all of us Kensington brothers, he's the one who

deserved that family the most—the one who remembers birthdays and asks how your day was and actually listens to the answer. The one learning to make bulgogi for nobody in particular.

Cameron wipes away a tear, then straightens. "Let's talk about the Kensington Foundation fundraiser. It's happening this month, and with Ash organizing, you know it'll be spectacular. We've landed Chris McKenna as host—yes, the Oscar front-runner everyone's talking about." He ticks off on his fingers. "For once, all eight of us will actually be here. Kalen's between tour dates, Asher's in town for the *Vanity Fair* and LACMA events, and even Silas is here to stay for awhile as he works with the Natural History Museum on their Napoleonic diamond collection." He smiles. "When Ash and I realized we had a chance to get all the Kensington brothers in one place—well, that's rarer than a planet alignment. We had to seize the moment." He points at Asher. "Take it away, Ash."

Asher's hazel eyes dance as he leans forward. "We're calling it 'Masterpieces in Motion,'" he announces, fingers fluttering like paintbrushes in the air. "The Patrician's ballroom will become a living canvas." His voice drops conspiratorially. "Imagine—Degas ballerinas posed in blue tulle, frozen mid-pirouette. Renoir's boating party brought to life—straw hats, champagne coupes, that golden afternoon light. We'll have *Las Meninas* with every ruffle and royal glance recreated, and Hopper's *Nighthawks* with that eerie diner glow. All of those masterpieces recreated with actors, costumes, sets, lighting, the works."

He speaks faster now, practically vibrating. "Each tableau shifts every half hour. Connor's donated one of his portraits for the auction—they've been impossible to get since Vanity Fair spotlighted him. Plus all the usual extravagances—dawn balloon rides over vineyards, those exclusive spa packages, private dinners with chefs who have three-year waiting lists."

Leave it to Asher to break the mold. Why the hell hadn't we tapped him for our event planning before? Right—he was always jet-setting across the globe, orchestrating galas for Saudi princes, Hollywood A-listers, and tech billionaires who'd pay six figures just for his table arrangements. The man could transform a paper clip and some twine into something worthy of a museum.

I sigh, torn between anticipation and dread. It looks like the event might not be so stale after all—I admit it, part of me actually looks forward to seeing these tableaus come to life. And yet, the knot in my stomach reminds me there's just one question hanging over it all…

"Dad coming?" I ask, more sharply than I intend.

"Yes," Cameron says, hesitating as if he can sense my tension. "He's bringing Patricia Jenkins as his date—Max's mother-in-law."

My chest tightens. Relief and fury war inside me. "Then I'm not coming," I blurt, crossing my arms as though I can barricade my heart.

Silas leans forward, his expression soft but firm. "Rome, I know you're angry with him. I am too." He sweeps his arm around to include the rest of the brothers, most of whom are staring at me like they're trying to bore right through my skin. "I'm still angry, but I want to slowly let our father back into my life. The Kensington Gala feels perfect for that. You don't have to talk to him if you don't want to—no pressure. But maybe it's good to see him, even if it's from across the room."

I swallow, torn. Part of me resents the idea and part of me—God, I hate to admit it—wants that tentative reunion.

But my anger burns louder. Fuck them. I don't want to be around my father.

I always enjoyed the Kensington Charity Galas before—pleasant enough, full of LA and Hollywood elite, the food divine since no expense was ever spared. It bored me, yet I liked seeing the family together. Asher makes it sound refreshing, thrilling even. But if my father's there, I can't be. The thought of facing him ruins it. It doesn't matter that I "won't have to talk to him." That promise feels like bullshit. I'll show up and they'll guilt me into conversation. Not today, not tomorrow, not ever.

"Listen, you fucking pussies," I say, voice cracking with the mixture of bile and regret I didn't know I still stored. "Why aren't any of you giving him more of a hard time? He was gone from our lives for twenty-two fucking years. His absence burned each of us differently. I get that he was grieving Mom. I get that he started drinking because he couldn't bear losing her. But how do you explain never once trying to get help? Just packing up and leaving us in the lurch? Cam—of all people—you forgave him too easily. You were the oldest, you should've been allowed to be a fourteen-year-old kid, not picking up his slack—giving up football, running the family."

Cameron shakes his head, hurt flickering in his eyes. "You don't remember it right, Roman. I helped, okay, but I never quit football to take care of you all. I cooked, I cleaned—Rosa helped too. Grandparents did most of the parenting." He half-smiles. "Without that, I wouldn't be the amateur chef I am today."

I blink back familiar tears—anger and shame mingling—"Bullshit," I say. "You answered all our questions, even though you had no answers either. You became our counselor, our emotional rock. You couldn't show your own grief because you had to be strong for us."

"I chose that role," Cam insists quietly. "No one forced me. It felt right, and I didn't mind." He lays a hand on my arm. Warmth rushes in, along with guilt. "What's this really about, Rome?"

I avert my eyes. My throat tightens. "I just—he hasn't earned our forgiveness."

"Rome," Max says, his tone gentle but firm, "Dad deserves a chance. Give that to him."

Words slip out before I'm ready. "Oh, that's rich coming from you." My voice thins on the last words. "If it weren't for you, we'd—" I trail off, mind rattling. Dammit. What was I going to say? Something so cruel. Something I wish I could swallow back.

Max's eyes harden. "We'd what? Finish it, Roman. Say it."

My pulse pounds. I stare at the ground, wanting the earth to swallow me. The words, though unspoken, echo in my brain.

Max steps closer. "You were about to say I caused all this. That if I hadn't been born, Mom would've survived, Dad wouldn't have gone off the rails, and we'd all be different men without that wound we all carry. Wasn't that it?"

I can't meet his eyes. "Yeah. Maybe not in so many words—but yes."

Cameron's face goes slack. "Roman. You weren't going to say that, were you?"

I feel the weight of their stares. I choke on the truth. "I —" I break off, voice barely a whisper.

Connor, ever the reserved one, clears his throat. "That's out of line. It wasn't Max's fault. Mom chose to carry him instead of getting treatment. And you're basically saying our mother shouldn't have given birth to him—wish he'd never existed." His words sting, yet I know he's right. The conflict inside me twists tighter: guilt at blaming an innocent, relief that I didn't actually say it, shame for thinking it.

I glance at Ansel, Max's staunch defender, expecting him to pounce. But he just gives me that look—the one that says "I'm disappointed in you"—and turns away. "I'm out," he says, voice flat. "Need to get away from this bullshit before I regret staying." He points at Cam. "Cam, no more frou-frou drinks. Get the Macallan." He looks around. "Who's in?" Every hand except Cam's shoots up, including mine before I even realize it. "Okay, everybody, let's go raid Cameron's bar."

As the brothers drift back toward the house, I stand alone for a heartbeat, my body humming with conflicting impulses: the urge to follow them inside for the scotch, the urge to bolt and never show up at the gala. A tight ache blooms in my chest. I hate them for wanting reconciliation, hate them for forgiving Dad so easily so that I'm on an island alone. I hate myself for secretly craving reconciliation. With a shaky breath, I follow, half-resentful, half-relieved, uncertain which feeling is stronger.

"Roman," Kalen calls, reminding me he's the only brother I haven't heard from tonight. "Come on in. We're on to the good stuff."

I shake my head but can't help feeling touched they still want me around after the awful things I nearly said to Max. I never spoke them aloud, but thinking them was bad enough. And Max hasn't done anything wrong. But if he hadn't been born, Mom might still be alive, Dad might never have abandoned us, and we'd have grown into different men, without those wounds or the fear of abandonment.

But would that life have been better? Maybe we all became driven professionals because we had something to prove. If we'd been coddled in a "normal" family, perhaps we'd never have pushed ourselves so hard. Who knows what trade-offs we made? Take Connor: he's an A-list, Oscar-winning actor adored worldwide, but only because Grandpa shoved him on stage to conquer his shyness—which only deepened after Dad walked out. Without that trauma, would he ever have acted?

I shrug. I'm terrible at these *Sliding Doors* scenarios—tweak one detail, and the whole world changes, often not for the better. Still, I'm grateful Max exists. I hope he doesn't think I regret his birth, because I don't. Connor was right: wishing Mom hadn't died is the same as wishing I'd never had Max as a brother.

I step back inside to find them clustered around Cameron's bar, finally drinking something real. Kalen hands me a neat Scotch. This is the true Kensington order —Grandpa sticks to Old Fashions, Cameron prefers fruity cocktails, and the rest of us are Scotch men.

I'm about to do something that feels like swallowing broken glass - apologize to Max. The words sit heavy on my tongue, bitter as aspirin. But would an apology even do the trick? I said what I said, each syllable a bullet I can't call back.

Before I can force the words past my clenched jaw, my phone buzzes. Miranda from Verde, her text practically radiating panic through the screen. Some A-lister throwing a tantrum that's escalating by the minute.

Normally, I'd shrug it off. After 10 years in luxury resorts, I've witnessed every celebrity meltdown imaginable -

from cocaine-fueled rampages through $10,000-a-night suites to near-drownings in infinity pools at 3 AM. The rich and famous, living down to their reputations.

I should text Miranda back, tell her to handle it herself. Instead, my fingers are already typing that I'm on my way. Anything to escape the suffocating pressure of seven pairs of Kensington eyes boring into me, waiting for words I don't know how to give.

"Guys, I need to bounce. Sorry, something is blowing up at the resort."

My brothers look at me with skepticism in their eyes, but they nod in understanding. Work is work. And they don't know that the text I received was about something that probably could've been handled without my input. They don't know that the main reason why I'm wanting to leave is because, well, I want to leave. I don't want to be around their judgment anymore.

Still, as I make the long drive to the resort, I'm feeling a pang. And, even though I don't want to think about it, I do – what would Lilith say about my inability to forgive my father? And what would she say about my inability to forgive my own brother? She was the one who understood that I have harbored resentment for Max. Latent feelings that I had never been able to acknowledge before she drew it out. What would she say?

More importantly, why do I care what Lilith would say?

I get to the resort and immediately find Miranda. "What's going on?"

"Blake Walsh is here, and he's on a rampage. He demanded the presidential suite—which is already occupied —then tried to bribe the concierge with a handful of crumpled hundreds. When that didn't work, he threw a martini at a pool attendant for bringing him regular water instead of Fiji, called the female bartender a vulgar name when she cut him off, and is now threatening to urinate in the koi pond. Three guests are livestreaming it, and *TMZ* just called the front desk."

I roll my eyes. Blake Walsh might have five platinum records hanging on his wall, but the guy's ego is bigger than his discography. Even Ansel wouldn't touch him with his label, and my brother signs almost anyone with a pulse and decent pipes.

I find myself smirking despite the headache brewing. Hotel drama like this barely registers on my crisis meter—though watching guests hold up their phones to capture his meltdown means I'll be putting out social media fires until dawn. Whatever. The Verde Resort thrives on buzz, good or bad. Besides, Blake's tantrum gave me the perfect excuse to bail on another excruciating family dinner, so I can't complain too much.

"I'll handle Walsh personally," I tell her, already loosening my tie. "And I'll make damn sure those same phones capture every second of it. Might as well turn his PR nightmare into our marketing dream."

I slam the mic button on my walkie-talkie, hunting for the pool attendant who's been tailing Blake's every move. I almost feel sorry for the guy—rumors are that Walsh has bipolar disorder. Whatever's going on upstairs, the elevator's stuck, so I'll have to talk him down. If talking fails, my MMA background's there as Plan B.

"Marcus," I snap. "Where is he?"

"Heading for the koi pond—he's about to piss in it."

My heart pounds. Those koi aren't decorations—they're alive. I rush to the pond, grab Blake from behind, and lock my arm around his throat. He gasps and struggles as I hold him—tight enough to stop him, not hurt him. Guests circle us with phones raised, recording everything. I see their shocked faces and ease my grip slightly. I want them to understand I'm restraining him, not attacking him.

"Back off!" Blake rasps, alcohol burning his breath.

"I'm calling the cops," I growl, voice cold. "This is private property. You try to drag my resort through the mud online, you'll regret the day you were born. I have fixers who will obliterate your reputation—no blood, just ruin you so completely you vanish from every directory."

I release him. Blake whirls, tears glimmering in his Irish accent. "You're Roman Kensington. You own this place." His voice cracks. "My Sheila… she's gone. She left me." He trembles, grief raw.

Not a crisis after all, then - he's grieving, not vindictive. He won't unleash an online assault come dawn. So I make a snap decision—get him to bed, post a guard, let Miranda soothe him tomorrow.

"Alexander," I key up the walkie talkie, "meet me at the koi pond."

Moments later, Alexander Papadopoulos glides in—my in-house diplomat for celebrity meltdowns. I gesture sharply: "Get him upstairs. Station yourself at his door all night."

Alexander eases to Blake's side, words soft but firm. Blake nods, defeated, and they melt into the crowd. Phones drop. The onlookers break into spontaneous applause. I acknowledge them with a slight nod.

Just another night at the resort: a viral meltdown that'll light up TikTok, free publicity I can't buy. And bonus—I dodge a tense dinner with my brothers.

Win–win.

Chapter Nine

ROMAN

The next day, I slam through the gym doors twenty minutes before Caspian. My veins are electric with leftover adrenaline from Blake's bullshit and that disaster dinner. I tape my knuckles so tight my fingertips throb, then attack the speed bag like it owes me money.

The rhythm builds until the bag's a blur, my fists connecting with machine-gun precision. I switch to the mannequin, driving my knee into its gut so hard the whole apparatus rocks backward. Sweat stings my eyes. Every punch carries the weight of my brothers' judgment, every kick fueled by self-loathing over Max. Fuck. The kid's carried enough on his shoulders—the family implosion after his birth wasn't his goddamn fault. I land a hook that would've shattered a real jaw, disgusted with myself for adding to his burden.

Caspian arrives at the gym. "You ready?"

I nod and say nothing. I just put up my fists and Caspian smiles.

"Today we're working on your Muay Thai. Your teeps need work."

For the next 45 minutes, we drill until rivulets of sweat cascade down my forehead, stinging my eyes. My knees slam into his black leather pads with a thunderous crack that echoes through the gym. My roundhouses connect with his padded ribs, the impact reverberating up my shin bone. In the clinch, my forearms tremble against his iron grip, muscles burning as if dipped in acid. I throw elbow strikes with such precision they whistle through the air—strikes that would split a man's temple like ripe fruit if they connected.

Between combinations, Caspian's voice cuts through the haze of my exhaustion, barking "Again!" and I summon what's left of my strength to deliver another blistering flurry of sok, te, kao, and tad until my lungs feel like they're filled with broken glass.

"Okay, I think that's enough training for today." Caspian tosses me a towel. "But you're still letting your emotions drive you instead of your brain. Emotions are vital—you have to dig into your pain and use it—but you also need logic. So what's really going on?"

I shake my head. How do I explain this without sounding like an even bigger asshole? Then I remember: this is Caspian, my best friend since I was five. If I can't tell him, who can I tell?

"Remember that psychic I hired for the resort?"

"Yeah— the beautiful woman who's got you enchanted."

I nod. Not going to try to deny that she has me enchanted because why? It's the truth.

"She did a tarot reading the other day and brought up

something I've always denied: I've been blaming my brother Max for things he couldn't control."

I admit how I've harbored resentment toward Max, even though it makes no sense—if Mom hadn't died and Dad hadn't lost it, Max wouldn't exist. I hate that I've ever wished he weren't born.

Caspian nods thoughtfully. "Good that it came up. It's like a splinter under your skin, festering until you pull it out. You're digging it out now. As for overcoming anger toward your brother—and your father—that's a bigger challenge."

My chest tightens. Max is innocent; I love him. But Dad made a choice—he walked away when we were kids, left without explanation. I can't forgive that.

Caspian meets my gaze. "You've got scar tissue years in the making. Use your rage, your sorrow, to become the fighter you're meant to be. You can win this charity tournament. It's about pride and it'll be great PR for the resort. I believe in you. Now, let's get back to sparring."

We spend the next hour drilling—my knuckles splitting against the heavy bag, sweat dripping into my eyes as Caspian calls out combinations. My muscles burn through jiu-jitsu sequences, the satisfying thud of my body hitting the mat again and again. By the time we finish grappling, my rash-guard is soaked through and my lungs feel scorched. I finally tap out, shower off the day's demons, and head back to the resort with my gym bag slung over my aching shoulder.

On the drive home, I feel calmer than I have in ages. The workout cleared my head, and a thread of reason about my father emerges. I don't want to be alone anymore. Even though I've felt like an outsider in my own family, I know my brothers have my back—and I have theirs. I just hate feeling marooned.

And, damn it, I'm eager to get back—because Lilith will be there. I don't want to admit I'm excited to see her, but I can't stop it. Somehow, this hippie has gotten under my skin—and, surprisingly, I don't mind.

Chapter Ten

LILITH

I catch sight of him across the room and my heart skips. "Blake Walsh!" His name escapes my lips before I can stop it. Those summers when we were kids feel both like yesterday and a lifetime ago. Now his face beams down from billboards, his voice fills stadiums worldwide, and I've got every album he's ever released.

I've watched his journey from those early days—just a kid shuttling between worlds, spending summers with his dad in L.A. while his mother raised him the rest of the year in Dublin—to the global phenomenon he's become today. The boy who once carried a backpack through LAX three months each year now has his name on billboards in every major city.

I used to beg him for stories about his Irish village—tales of emerald hills rolling into the wild Atlantic, morning mist hanging over ancient stone walls. Our Venice beaches have their own beauty, but they're sun-scorched, drought-stricken. In my imagination, Ireland was everything Los

Angeles wasn't—verdant, rain-kissed, a place where the earth itself seems more alive.

He bursts into my cabana and wraps me in a bear hug that smells of expensive cologne and jet fuel. "My lass! When I heard you were here, I couldn't stay away. Always told you you'd make it big someday, didn't I? Look at you now—reading fortunes for the elite!"

I snort. Blake's idea of "making it big" is relative. This from the man whose face is plastered across Times Square billboards, who's sold 100 million records, whose last world tour grossed a billion dollars, whose trophy room needs its own zip code to house all his Grammys.

Meanwhile, my "empire" consists of a drafty shop on Venice Beach where I sell crystals to sunburned tourists, and now this—a part-time gig shuffling cards for bored socialites. The closest I've come to fame is standing three feet away from someone who's been on a *Variety* cover—him.

Blake plops into the chair across from me, his face flushed and sporting that trademark grin that never quite reaches his bloodshot eyes today. I've always adored his Irish charm, but something's definitely amiss.

"Come on then, deal those cards and read my future. And honestly, Lilith? You're missing a marketing opportunity with your name. Something flashy like 'Madame Moonbeam' would bring in the big spenders."

I snort while shuffling. "Please. Lilith was literally Adam's first wife who told the Almighty to shove it, then spent eternity seducing men and stealing babies. Not to mention being the lead succubus - you know, the demons who have sex with men in their sleep. I'd say that's sufficiently on-brand." I study him while cutting the deck.

"You're looking rough around the edges. Your aura's practically the color of wet cement."

Blake winces. "Had a wee disagreement with a bottle of Jameson last night. Apparently I threatened the koi pond's dignity in ways I won't repeat. The video's making rounds, but my publicist is handling damage control." He shrugs. "Ah, I've seen worse than this mess. You know it's been a proper night when your morning begins with a mental list of apologies. The resort staff received either premium flower arrangements or top-shelf whiskey, depending on gender and severity of my offenses."

I can only smile sympathetically. Show me someone who claims they've never made an absolute fool of themselves after too many drinks, and I'll show you a teetotaler or a liar. We've all been there—myself definitely included.

I shuffle the cards, their worn edges catching as I separate them into two stacks on the velvet cloth. My bangles clink against the table. Blake hesitates, then chooses the left deck. I lay out the Celtic cross, each card landing with a soft thump. The reversed Queen of Swords appears next to the Tower card. Someone broke his heart—badly.

I tap the card with my turquoise ring. "The cards don't lie, Blake. See this King of Wands here? That's you." I point to the next card. "And the Fool—that's your path. You'll be embarking on a new journey soon. With the Queen of Cups right here." I slide my finger to the center where a darker card lies. "But the Devil crosses you." I look up, meeting his bloodshot eyes. "Your liver could use a break from all that Jameson."

Blake's laugh is warm but hollow, his bloodshot eyes crinkling at the corners. "Christ, wish I would've seen you yesterday - I wouldn't have gotten into that bloody fight with Jameson, a fight I clearly lost, judging by this hangover.

Now tell me. You mentioned the Queen of Cups. What does that mean?"

I smile. "Ah, the Queen of Cups." I tap the card where a robed woman holds a chalice. "She represents compassion, and she's facing your future position." I glance up at Blake across my small table. "Something's coming for you soon."

Blake's cards show his journey: the reversed Queen of Swords retreating into shadow while the Queen of Cups rises, bringing her intuition and compassion into his future. The symmetry of these twin journeys from criticism to care makes me smile.

Blake's eyes light up. "New love. How exciting." His smile widens. "Speaking of which, are you free Saturday? The Kensington fundraiser is happening, and I thought—"

A shadow falls across the cabana entrance. Roman stands there, jaw tight. "Lilith. A word?"

My heart skips. First-name basis now. Progress. "Mr. Kensington," I chirp, voice unnaturally bright. "Have you had the pleasure of meeting—"

"We've met," Roman cuts in, his gaze boring into Blake with laser precision.

Blake straightens, recognition dawning. "Roman Kensington. Your brother's label passed on me. Said I was 'difficult.' Bet he's kicking himself now, huh?"

Roman's expression doesn't flicker. "Fascinating. You clearly don't remember our encounter last night. Lilith, I need to speak with you. Privately."

I lift my chin. "Whatever you need to say can be said in front of Blake. We've known each other since we were kids." I pause deliberately. "And apparently, we're attending your family's fundraiser together."

My pulse races as Roman's eyes darken. Am I deliberately provoking him? Absolutely. Why? Because admitting I'm falling for this impossible man feels too vulnerable. He's Mount Olympus, I'm merely mortal. Besides, Blake is safe —practically a brother. His cards showed the Queen of Cups awaiting him, and while I embody some of those qualities—empathy, intuition—the energy of that card doesn't feel like me. My Virgo earth-sign self aligns more with the Queen of Pentacles anyway.

Roman's eyes—dark as polished obsidian—flare the moment I mention that Blake and I will be attending the Kensington fundraiser together. He's leaning against the marble post, one hand tucked into his pocket, the other brushing a strand of hair from his forehead. "Lilith," he says, his voice low and precise, "this resort has a policy: staff aren't supposed to mingle socially with guests. It's right there in your handbook."

I tilt my head, surprised. I'm notorious for reading every word of any handbook handed to me—fine print included —and I never saw a clause like that. Besides, I'm not technically "staff." I'm an independent contractor. I keep my posture casual, letting my confidence show. "I read that book cover to cover," I tell him. "No such rule. And anyway, I'm not on payroll. I'm a contractor."

Blake—short in stature but sun-kissed and effortlessly charming—leans in from behind me, a smirk playing on his lips. "Come on, lad," he says, voice warm as summer air. "Employees forbidden to date guests? Sounds like a relic of Victorian propriety."

I nod in agreement, brushing back my hair. "Exactly. And you gave me the manual yourself. Not a word about it. Blake's right—it's about as modern as corsets and curtseys."

Roman's expression hardens. He crosses his arms, the sleeves of his crisp white shirt stretching across his biceps.

His gaze locks onto mine—and I feel that familiar spark, like I'm being scorched from within. Then, abruptly, he looks away, jaw clenched. "Fine," he says, voice quiet but resolute. "There's no such ban. But there will be."

Blake reaches out with a grin and clasps Roman's hand. "In that case, I'll see you at the Kensington function—seeing as you're a Kensington." He nods toward the polished letters of the resort's crest behind Roman. "And your brothers, Ansel and Kalen. I know Kalen too—our world tours keep crossing paths. We've been duking it out at the top of Spotify for years. Friendly rivalry, I call it."

Blake strides away, golden light spilling across his retreating silhouette. Roman remains, rooted by the desk, his gaze sliding back to me. The hush of the terrace about 100 feet from the cabana presses in around us: distant laughter, the clink of ice in glasses, the faint tinkle of a piano from the outdoor lounge.

"Can I help you with something else?" I ask, indicating the silver tray of hors d'oeuvres—smoked salmon rosettes, delicate cheese towers.

He inhales, slow and steady. "I don't want another spread. I want you to skip that fundraiser with him. I don't trust Blake—he stirred up more drama here last night than anyone should."

I arch an eyebrow, the corners of my mouth curving upward. "Mr. Kensington—"

"Call me Roman," he interrupts softly.

I meet his gaze evenly. "Roman," I say, voice gentle but firm, "he's already explained: too much drink, a fresh breakup. I know that combination can be explosive—heartache and whiskey make for dangerous decisions. You know you've had a bad night when you wake up apologizing to three strangers before breakfast. I've been there more than once. Who hasn't? So, really, the best thing you can do is mind your own business."

His jaw tightens. "I just think you should stay away from him, that's all." He swallows hard, his dark eyes never leaving mine.

Heat radiates from that stare—something wild and possessive that makes my pulse quicken. Or am I imagining what I want to see? Maybe he's worried I'll stick out like a sore thumb among the designer gowns and family crests. The quirky tarot reader from Venice Beach mingling with LA and Hollywood royalty. He'd have to introduce me, explain why he has someone like me on his payroll. God, that would be mortifying for him.

I lift my chin. "Last I checked, Roman, I'm an independent contractor for your resort. Part-time. That's where our relationship begins and ends. You don't get to dictate who I see socially." I smooth my skirt, steadying my voice. "I'm attending your family's fundraiser with Blake, and that's final."

And now his stare burns through me like wildfire, igniting every nerve ending from my flushed cheeks to my trembling fingertips. My body betrays me completely—heat surges between my thighs, my breath catches, and I have to grip the edge of the table to steady myself, even as my mind screams in protest.

Just then, another man appears in the doorway. He's older than Roman—mid-fifties—with deep lines around his eyes that somehow make him more attractive rather than less. Something about him radiates warmth and hard-won wisdom. I find myself leaning slightly forward, drawn to whatever story is written in those weathered features, even as I notice Roman's jaw tightening beside me.

"What do you want and what the hell are you doing

here?" Roman snarls at the man, voice dripping venom. The older man's expression shatters, and my chest physically aches for him. The raw love radiating from him towards Roman is almost blinding. Why would Roman—wait.

Oh god. This is THE father. The one who abandoned them all. The ghost who haunts Roman's nightmares. Now I see it - they share that same aristocratic bearing, that same electric presence that makes the air crackle. Old money isn't just worn; it's embedded in their DNA, commanding the space without a single word.

The man's voice cracks. "Roman, please. I'm here for Max—he's bringing surfing equipment for your guests. I thought maybe we could—"

Roman storms off without a word, leaving the man frozen in my doorway, his face crumpling like he'd just watched his entire world burn to ash. My chest tightens painfully. Roman didn't just hurt him—he demolished him, left him bleeding emotionally on my threshold. Before I can stop myself, I'm wrapping my arms around this stranger, this broken man who radiates such raw pain it physically hurts to witness.

He clings to me like I'm a life raft, and over his shoulder, I spot Roman. He hasn't gone far—just down to the shoreline, hands jammed deep in his pockets, shoulders hunched like he's fighting a hurricane. He keeps whipping his head around to look at us, his jaw clenched so tight I can almost hear his teeth grinding from here.

Suddenly another gorgeous man appears—unmistakably Roman's brother. He's like their father reincarnated younger—those same piercing blue-green eyes, that same chiseled jawline, identical dark waves of hair. But where the father's hair flows wild and untamed, the son's is slicked back with enough product to survive a typhoon. When this new man's face splits into a smile, it's blinding—deep dimples carving into his cheeks, lighting up the entire beach.

"Max!" The father's voice breaks with desperate joy as they collide in an embrace.

"Dad!" Max clutches him fiercely. "Roman around?"

The father points shakily toward the beach where Roman stands, not fifty feet away, watching them. The naked longing on Roman's face is devastating—like a starving man watching others feast. His eyes burn with such hunger for that same connection that I can barely breathe watching him. His hands have curled into white-knuckled fists at his sides, trembling with the force of everything he's holding back.

Oh God. Roman is hemorrhaging before my eyes. His aura pulses crimson and black, a psychic scream so loud my ears ring. The cards in my pocket burn against my thigh—I don't need to read them to see the Tower, the Three of Swords piercing his chest. His jaw clenches so hard I swear I hear enamel crack as he watches his father's arms encircle Max—the golden child whose birth shattered everything. The betrayal in Roman's eyes is primal, animal.

My lungs seize. The energy crackling between these three men is suffocating me, a vortex of twenty-two years of abandonment, rage, and desperate, shameful yearning. Roman's eyes never leave his father's hands on Max's back. Those same hands never held him through nightmares, never taught him to shave, never steadied him when he stumbled.

Max approaches Roman, hand outstretched. Roman's entire body jerks back—pure instinct—before he forces himself into his brother's embrace. The violence of that contradiction splits my heart. Flinch. Embrace. Reject.

Need. I press my nails into my palms until they leave half-moons. Every cell in my body screams to cross the sand, to press my hands against Roman's temples and draw out the poison. But I stand frozen, watching him bleed.

My eyes lock with the father's, who's planted himself in front of me like a man awaiting judgment. "I'm Michael," he says, his hand thrust forward, weathered lines etched into his palm. His gaze sweeps over my crystals, my cards, as he inhales the sandalwood incense that coils between us like a living thing.

"Lilith," I say, my voice stronger than I intended. "I read tarot cards here."

"I see that." His eyes narrow. "You actually divine truth from those things?"

"Every time," I say, holding his stare. "Want me to prove it?"

He glances over his shoulder at Roman, who's standing rigid as stone beside Max on the beach, his eyes burning holes through us both. "God, no," he says, voice cracking. "Not with him watching. Though you must be something special to survive working for my son." The words "my son" catch in his throat like broken glass.

I grip his shoulder, feeling bone beneath fabric. "Listen to me," I whisper fiercely. "Your sons—all of them—have your blood burning in their veins and they all love you. Even him. Especially him." I somehow know that what I'm saying is the truth.

His eyes flood instantly. "He'll never forgive me," he chokes out. "And Christ, I probably deserve every ounce of that hatred."

I dig my fingers deeper. "No. Hatred is poison, not justice. Everyone walks through fire for their reasons. I don't know yours, but I see what you are—a Phoenix risen from destruction. Own that power. It's yours now."

Michael's eyes flood with unshed tears as Max comes back and wraps his arm around his father's shoulder, squeezing tight. My heart swells watching them—this sweet, gentle man with the aura that blazes golden like summer sunrise finally receiving the love he deserves. I burn to know if the others embrace their father with the same fierce devotion Max shows. If they do, Michael's wounds will heal like wildfire.

"Just dropped my gear with Roman's surfing concierge," Max says, then pivots toward me, hand thrust forward. "I'm Max. And you are?"

"Lilith," I manage, my voice catching.

His smile flashes white. "Lilith. Nice to meet you." He turns back, clasping his father's shoulder. "Gotta run, Dad. Saturday at the Gala?"

Michael's eyes dart anxiously. "Will Roman be there?"

"Working on it," Max promises, then gives me one last electric smile before vanishing into the crowd.

Michael's gaze finds Roman standing at the water's edge. Even from here, I can see the tension in his shoulders, the way his fists clench at his sides. Something about his stillness against the moving water makes my chest tighten. I want to go to him, to stand beside him until whatever storm is raging inside him passes.

I've always been the one who could brighten a room, ease someone's burden with a joke or a touch. But Roman's pain feels different—deeper than anything my usual light could reach. Still, I wish I could try.

Later, after readings for the elite—a billionaire who crushed my hand in his grip; a tech mogul's wife dripping in diamonds that could fund my shop for decades; a Duchess with eyes like glaciers; and an A-list actress whose presence literally stole my breath—I stumble up the beach, sand burning between my toes.

Later, when I'm walking through the lobby to go to my car, Roman appears without warning, dark suit and darker expression. He leans over the front desk, each clipped word making the staff member's shoulders tense visibly. When he looks up and sees me, something flickers across his face—recognition, maybe interest—before he deliberately turns away, jaw tightening. My stomach drops. Of course. I'm just another tourist with a crush on the handsome hotel owner, the kind of distraction he's learned to dismiss before his coffee gets cold.

Yet my heart pounds wildly as I trek the endless miles back to Venice Beach. Blake Walsh is taking me to the Kensington Gala! The same Blake who once made me tongue-tied in middle school is suddenly back in my orbit. So even though Roman's rejection scorches like third-degree burns—Jack will be devastated to find out that Roman's not interested in me after all—I've got a lifeline to cling to in this drowning sea of emotion.

Chapter Eleven

LILITH

"Guess what?" I say to Jack, practically vibrating with excitement. My silver bangles jingle as I grab his arm.

I can't stop thinking about going to the Kensington Gala with Blake Walsh. Not that I have a thing for Blake - god no. We spent six summers - ages 9 to 15 - building sandcastles and chasing ice cream trucks together, skateboarding on the Venice Boardwalk, and boogie-boarding in the ocean. Building bonfires with him singing with his guitar - always wildly talented, even then, but little did I know that he'd become one of the biggest pop stars in the world.

Then his father remarried that horrible woman with the pinched face who treated Blake like an inconvenient houseplant. After that, he stayed in Ireland year-round, sending me postcards of rolling green hills that made my heart ache with missing him.

But there was never that spark between us. Zero chemistry. Just friendship.

No, I'm not excited because I'll be going with Blake,

exactly. I'm actually excited because Roman will be there - brooding Roman with his black aura so dense I can practically see it swirling around him like storm clouds. When I did his reading last week, the cards practically trembled with the weight of his blocked emotions. My fingers tingled when they brushed his, sensing layers of trauma wrapped around his spirit like thorny vines.

Meanwhile, Blake's aura glows the most beautiful shade of rose-pink I've ever seen - the hallmark of artistic souls, compassionate and open. But of course I'd be magnetically drawn to the complicated man whose energy feels like a thunderstorm about to break, the man carrying around a lifetime of trauma like a second skin.

"What, love?" Jack asks, looking up from his phone.

"I'm going to the Kensington Gala with Blake Walsh!"

"Get out!" Jack shoves me back so hard my crystal necklace swings wildly. "Shut your actual mouth!"

I giggle. "I really am. I told you I know him, right?"

"You did, but I thought you were full of it, sorry! But, oh my god, Lilith. Blake Walsh?" Jack clutches his heart dramatically before breaking into the chorus of "Butterfly Effect," complete with the little shoulder shimmy that made the music video go viral. "But I'll believe it when he picks you up in his chariot, love."

"Well, you'll believe it soon, then."

Jack's perfectly groomed eyebrows arch mischievously. "And will the Roman god himself be there, per chance?" His voice lilts on the word "god," drawing it out with dramatic flair.

I shrug, fidgeting with a strand of my wavy hair. "Don't know."

Jack's eyes roll so hard I'm surprised they don't get stuck

in the back of his head. "Sweetie-pie-sugar-dumpling, it's the KENSINGTON Gala. The man's last name is literally on the invitation in gold leaf. He'll be there, front and center, looking like sex on a stick."

He leans in, bathing me in a cloud of his signature scent —Bergamot Billionaire or whatever ridiculous name they've slapped on a $400 bottle of eau de show-off. "Every A-lister with a pulse and a publicist will be there, darling. It's basically the Super Bowl of schmoozing, but with better shoes." He flutters his fingers like butterflies having seizures. "I'm positively green with envy. Speaking of green—" he jabs a perfectly manicured finger at me, his nail polish matching his statement earrings, "—that credit card of yours needs CPR. Nieman Marcus. Tomorrow. We need to find you something that'll make Roman's eyeballs pop like champagne corks!"

"Nieman Marcus?" I wince, the fluorescent lights of the bookstore suddenly feeling too harsh. "Not unless I want to max out my credit card and live on ramen for months. Either that or buy the dress and return it the next day, like girls do after the high school prom." I twist my grandmother's silver ring nervously. "No, I think I'll make my dress."

My fingers snap with sudden inspiration, the sound echoing against the crystal display case. "That's it! Oh god, the gala's in three days, Jack. I can't afford designer, but these hands can work magic with a sewing machine." I gesture toward the ceiling, mind racing. I can already envision the fabric, cool and lustrous between my fingers. "I know exactly what I need—emerald green satin that'll catch the light when I move. Easy to sew, drapes beautifully. Not as expensive as silk. I can get enough for $80 at that little shop on the boardwalk."

Jack's laughter fills the incense-scented shop, warm and melodic. "My god, you're such a Cinderella, stitching away at your magical gown."

"Well," I counter, absently straightening a stack of tarot cards, "Cinderella made her dress before those stepsisters tore it to—" I shake my head, my long earrings swinging against my neck. "You know the story. But no, Jack, I'm not waiting for any prince. I just don't have a grand to drop on a dress I'll wear once. But I'll have to get started tonight when I get home. Making this gown will take hours of my time, plus I need to find the material."

And then the man from the reading yesterday comes through the door, the crystal bell tinkling like wind chimes in a summer breeze. Max. Roman's breathtakingly beautiful brother with his sun-kissed skin and piercing jade eyes that crinkle at the corners. He has a dimpled smile on his face, his long, tanned fingers stuck in the pockets of his designer jeans as he saunters casually in, exuding California cool.

"Hi, Lilith," he says, stretching his hand to me, a silver Rolex watch glinting on his wrist.

"Well, hello. Max, right? Roman's brother?" I tuck a strand of my wild dark hair behind my ear.

He nods, his thick chestnut hair catching the light from the stained-glass window. "I live in Malibu, not too far from here. I wanted to…"

I sigh, the scent of sandalwood incense swirling around us. He's here to check me out, obviously, but why? Perhaps he thinks that I'm a fraud, too, and wants to warn his brother about me? Then I shake my head, my silver moon pendant swinging against my collarbone.

No. I don't get a bad vibe from this man at all. I don't really have a read on his aura—it's faint, almost see-through, like morning fog. Nothing like Roman's. Roman's aura is thick and dark, hovering around him like a shadow that never leaves. Years of buried feelings have hardened there, building up until he's trapped inside himself.

But this is the brother who Roman blames for the family falling apart, even if Roman would never admit to this, even to himself.

He nods again, shifting his weight on the creaking wooden floorboards. "My wife, Celeste. She's really into the crystal thing. I know nothing about it, and I'm embarrassed to ask most uh, psychics."

I smile, feeling the warmth spread across my face as I lean against the amethyst-topped counter. "I'm not really a psychic. I read tarot cards and I can sometimes see auras. I'm very good at reading tarot, though. Do you want to know more about it?"

He steps into the softly lit shop, eyes drifting over shelves bristling with polished quartz and amethyst clusters. "Actually, I wanted to surprise Celeste with something," he says, voice low. "Maybe a crystal, and learn a bit about tarot." He shrugs, the denim of his jacket creaking. "She's learned to surf for me—her arms burn and I know she hates it, but she'd never admit that. I thought if I dug into what she believes—what she really loves—she might open up. She's so guarded about her mystical side; she's convinced I'll mock it. Maybe if I knew more, she'd feel safe talking to me."

I brush a lock of black hair behind my ear and smile. "Tarot can be eerily accurate. Want a reading?"

He shakes his head, the harsh overhead light catching the golden flecks in his green eyes. "No. It's not a reflection on you, it's just that I don't necessarily want to know things. But maybe I should. How does it work?"

I run my finger along the edge of my favorite deck—deep

blue with silver stars that catch the light. "I'm not psychic," I tell him. "I can't see the future or read your past. These cards are just how the Universe communicates. They help me understand what's happening with the person sitting across from me." I pause, noticing his jaw soften. "But I can sense whether someone's good or carrying old wounds." Something about him feels genuine. Whoever Celeste is, she's lucky.

"And the crystals?" He gestures toward the velvet-lined display case, his calloused fingertips hovering over the rainbow of stones. "How do they work?"

"Well, they're blessed. At least, the crystals I buy are blessed by shamans in a ceremony with sage and moonlight." I smile, breathing in the familiar scent of sandalwood incense that permeates my shop. "So, they have healing and protective properties. You want to buy a crystal for Celeste, then?"

His stern expression softens. "We just welcomed our first baby. Got anything special for little Violet?"

I float toward my crystal collection, the hem of my skirt dancing around my ankles, and lift a milky white stone that catches the light. "Selenite—purifies a baby's space, surrounds her with calm energy." I place it in his palm, then add a sleek black stone flecked with emerald. "Black tourmaline. Nature's shield against negativity."

He reaches for his wallet, sliding out a Black Mastercard that gleams like onyx.

"Please, they're gifts," I insist, pushing his hand away gently.

"Absolutely not." His tone brooks no argument. I surrender, processing his payment before wrapping the stones in tissue paper.

As I hand him the small package, he lingers. "About my

brother, Roman..." He pauses. "He'd have my head if he knew I stopped by."

My curiosity sparks. I wait, eyes locked on his.

"Roman's...complex. Old wounds run deep in our family." He shifts his weight. "But something tells me you might reach him in ways others can't. He needs that—needs..." He trails off, then straightens. "Don't let his rough edges chase you away, okay?"

I blink and smile. This is a strange conversation, considering Roman's showed no romantic interest in me. But perhaps Max sensed something the other day when he came to my tent looking for his father and Roman? "I don't understand?"

He sighs. "Just don't let him chase you away, that's all." Then he lifts the crystals up and smiles. "Celeste will love these. Violet will too, one day. Right now, she's just a tiny baby who won't appreciate these crystals."

Later on, just as I'm gathering my things to dash to Fabric Planet before closing—I've been dreaming of that emerald silk for my gala dress—the bell above the shop door chimes. A courier in pressed gray slacks hands me a black velvet box tied with a single crimson ribbon.

Inside, nestled against black satin, lies a Painite pendant: deep red with dark flecks catching the light. It hangs from a delicate platinum chain. My fingers tremble as I touch it—most jewelers will never see one in their lifetime. A crystal this perfect is worth a quarter million.

A cream-colored card rests beneath it, the handwriting bold and slashing: "This crystal is said to align all seven chakras simultaneously. Thought that might appeal to your mystical side. Hope to see it gracing your neck at the gala. Roman."

I blink. First Max comes by with his cryptic words and now this…

Is it possible for a beautiful and stormy billionaire to actually be interested in little ol' me?

I suddenly can't wait for the gala!

Chapter Twelve

ROMAN

Damn. That woman fucking unravels me. I had to grip the doorframe when I overheard her in her cabana—laughing, actually laughing—while making a date with Blake Walsh. WALSH. The same degenerate I dragged out by his designer collar last night, threatening to have him arrested. The same entitled prick who thought my hundred-year-old koi pond was his personal urinal. And she's batting those lashes at him?

My jaw clenches so hard I taste metal. I need Caspian's face to pound into a punching mitt right now, but he's up in San Francisco babysitting some gym opening. Goddammit. My blood is scorching through my veins like jet fuel. First my father showing his face, then Max showing up, and now Lilith—LILITH—giggling with Walsh? The drywall won't survive the night. My fist is already twitching for it.

I get to the resort and find…Serafina. Sera fucking fina. She's in the lobby, leaning against the front desk, one manicured finger tapping impatiently on the polished marble. Her white Valentino sundress hugs curves that belong on a yacht in Monaco, not my lobby at 2 PM on a Tuesday. Blonde hair cascades down her back like liquid gold, catching the sunlight streaming through the floor-to-ceiling windows. Six feet tall with a gorgeous natural rack, legs for fucking days and a face that would make Margot Robbie jealous. Every man in the vicinity keeps stealing glances while pretending not to. She's definitely an Amazon goddess come to life, complete with that ice-queen expression that says she knows exactly what she's worth. And I have zero fucking interest in her. Sorry Caspian. Know she's your sister but no.

And why is she here? She owns a string of hotels herself—glass towers in financial districts with marble lobbies, where the rooms are $1,000 and up. They don't compete with mine, though they're all five-stars. Her hotels cater to businessmen who need a desk and Wi-Fi, while my oceanfront resorts welcome those same men when they're ready for flip-flops and family time. Shouldn't she be somewhere else right now, in the middle of the fucking day?

"What are you doing here?" I ask her, my voice echoing slightly in the vaulted ceiling.

She shrugs, the diamond tennis bracelet on her wrist catching the light. "I have a reading with Lilith Sydney today. Heard she's the best around. Want to check it out for myself. Caspian told me about her." Then she turns back to Noah, my front desk concierge, whose eyes are popping out of his skull. "Talk to you later, Noah," she purrs. Then she looks at me. "And you too, Rome. We should catch up." And then she leaves, every man's head turning as she glides out the door towards Lilith's cabana.

Goddammit. If Sera starts any drama, I won't hesitate to have security escort her out. Let her cry to her 50 million

Instagram followers—I couldn't care less. My jaw clenches as I remember our disaster of a relationship.

But something's off. I don't trust her sudden appearance.

I head down to the beachfront cabana where Lilith conducts readings when the weather permits. As I approach, Sera's voice drifts through the open windows.

"So you've got your eye on Roman Kensington." Her tone drips with condescension. "Just so we're clear—he and I were engaged. I'm only telling you this because, well, a psychic should know these things, right? Though I'm surprised you're not working one of those late-night hotlines. The pay must be better than this... quaint setup. Roman would never take someone like you seriously anyway."

I curl my fingers into tight fists. Everything in me wants to barge in there and drag Sera out by her designer heels, but I hold back. Wait. Breathe. How the hell did she find out about Lilith? Oh, right. Casp let it slip. I should be pissed, but even my best friend screws up sometimes. I'll let this one slide.

"You've misunderstood," Lilith replies calmly. I hear cards sliding against each other. "I have zero romantic interest in Mr. Kensington. He's my employer, nothing more. I'm certain someone of your... caliber would have much better chances with him. You have nothing to worry about from me."

That's it. I'm ending this bullshit now. I storm into the doorway of the cabana, my jaw clenched so tight my teeth might shatter. "A reading, Sera? Bullshit." My voice cuts through the air like a blade. I shoot a glance at Lilith, who's staring at the floor as if her life depends on it.

My blood is boiling, pounding in my ears, but I can't pin

down which part of this clusterfuck is making me want to put my fist through a wall. Is it Serafina's transparent lies? Her goddamn audacity to think she can snap her fingers and I'll come running back? Hell would freeze over first. Or is it that Lilith's denial felt like a knife to my gut? The way she spoke to Sera sounded so convincing—too convincing. Like there wasn't a single spark between us. Like I've been drowning in feelings for a woman who feels absolutely nothing in return. I'm marooned on an island again, just like with my brothers. And goddamn it, I'm tired of feeling like I'm on a deserted island.

Sera's voice slithers through the room like a viper. "Roman," she says, her red lips curling into a smile that doesn't reach her eyes. "I was just explaining to your little card-reader that she's swimming in waters too deep for her. Your world devours hers. Different planets entirely. When people cross those lines, someone always ends up destroyed. But she already knows this, don't you, darling?"

Lilith sits frozen, her fingers motionless on her deck, all color drained from her face. Of course Serafina terrifies her—Sera's presence is a fucking hurricane in human form. Six feet of runway perfection with a bloodline so blue it makes royalty look common. Vanderbilts and Rockefellers in her family tree. The kind of woman who's never heard the word "no" and wouldn't recognize it if she did.

My chest constricts watching Lilith shrink under Sera's gaze, cornered like prey. But the knife twists deeper knowing Lilith just denied everything to Sera—denied us. Oh, what am I thinking, "us." There is no "us." That's the whole fucking problem. I swallow the words rising in my throat. I won't chase. I won't make myself pathetic trying to extract feelings Lilith doesn't have. She's made it crystal fucking clear: whatever I thought was between us exists only in my goddamn imagination.

I pin Serafina with a steely glare and jerk my head toward Lilith, who still won't meet my eyes. "Sera," I spit out, voice low and raw. "Let's go."

Serafina's lips curl into that victory grin—she's rattled Lilith to her core. As we back away, I spot a line of gleaming VIPs queued outside Lilith's cabana, guests clamoring for her tarot readings. It's absurd how these high-rollers—people who make more before breakfast than most people make in five years—flock to have their futures divined. Maybe I should put a tarot deck into every resort's gift shop. But Lilith's gift goes deeper: rumors say her predictions actually come true. Could she really be the genuine article? I've always mocked psychics, but damn if my skepticism isn't wobbling.

We hit the lobby and I'm ready to blast Serafina off my property like a pigeon. "Get the hell out," I growl, finger aiming at the front doors where her black Jag—she parks it smack in my loading circle—gleams like a trophy. "And don't fucking come back."

She only smirks. "Rome," she purrs, stepping closer, "hate and love are two sides of the same coin, remember?" Her fingertip drifts to my lips. Cold and feather-light. "We've always been fire."

My jaw clenches so hard I can taste blood. Fire—yeah, that scorching agony that burned me alive the last time we tangled. We were wildcats, slashing at each other, claws sunk into flesh we both refused to surrender. I won't let her venom seep into me again. She might've forgotten those nights of raw lust and ruthless fights, but I replay every scar in brutal detail. She needs off my turf, now.

"Out," I bark, jabbing again at the Jag. The nerve of

her—treating my circle drive like her personal valet zone. She could've handed the keys over, let my valet park it, but of course that would be an inconvenience. And inconvenience is a sin I know Serafina never commits.

She glides to her Jaguar, smooth and infuriating. "See you Saturday night," she calls over her shoulder. "At your gala."

Fuck. Who the hell put her on the guest list? Oh right—she's on the Kensington International board, having seduced granddad with her beauty and charm, so she's untouchable. Thanks, Granddad. I'm stuck with her forever.

I steel myself—yes, I'll go to the gala. My brothers have been hammering me with messages in our group chat at three in the fucking morning—Kalen's insomnia has him pinging everyone at ungodly hours. Every new message ping fuels my urge to tell them all to shove it. But there's a reason I'll drag my ass to that ballroom: Lilith will be there with Blake Walsh strutting by her side, and I'm not about to let them slip under my nose. That's the only reason.

Pathetic.

Chapter Thirteen

LILITH

That Serafina…now that was some bad energy. Not the dark, heavy vibe Roman gives off, and not unresolved trauma, either. Her aura was a slimy green—pure jealousy—and it was so strong it felt almost tangible. After she left my cabana, I burned sage, but her energy stayed stubbornly in the air.

My next client is the wife of a U.S. Senator. She's caught in a personal crisis over rumors that her husband, Senator Williams of Kentucky, is having an affair. With talk swirling that he's planning a presidential run, this scandal could be disastrous.

Kelly Williams is polite but guarded. The spread I lay out for her isn't catastrophic—it showed the scandal fading after a few news cycles and the mistress disappearing—but it did warn of some bumpy months ahead. Exactly the sort of balanced reading I like: not relentlessly dark, but not sugar-coated either—an opportunity for growth.

Once all the readings are done, I can't wait to get home. I've been spending every spare minute sewing my gala dress.

I grabbed that bolt of fabric yesterday after the shop closed, right after the courier delivered that rare, stunning crystal necklace, and I've barely put my sewing machine needle down since. I even have jeweled trim for the neckline. The design is simple—a scoop neck, sleeveless bodice, flowing skirt—but with that jeweled edging and the crystal resting at my throat, I just might blend in with the A-listers.

I find myself in the lobby, where Roman hunches over a stack of paperwork at the front desk. His eyes lift to mine, and something flutters beneath my ribs. My feet carry me toward him before I can think twice. "Rome," I say, my lips curving upward of their own accord, "that crystal you sent me... it's beyond perfect. I'm completely speechless."

He shrugs. "I saw it in the resort jewelry store and thought of you. I thought you'd like it. I read about it later—people say it's a powerful stone that opens all your chakras and aligns your energy centers. I don't really know what any of that means, but it sounded good."

Hmmm…resort jewelry store? Nope. That crystal is too rare and perfect to just be hanging around in a random jewelry store, even a random jewelry store in a place like this. He had to have had a supplier get it for him. So I wonder why he's lying about that? Why he's trying to make it seem so casual when he obviously put a ton of thought into it? Intriguing…

"Well," I say, "I love it." I don't ask the price tag, but a Painite of that quality—shipped by courier—could easily run a quarter-million dollars, plus thousands more for the platinum rope chain. I tell myself it's pocket change for him, but even so…such an extravagant, thoughtful gift.

He smiles. "Good. I hope you wear it to the gala." He clears his throat. "I'm really glad I ran into you. Serafina. She wasn't bothering you, was she?"

I replay her words in my mind. The warning about swimming in waters too deep for me. The snide suggestion I belonged on a late-night psychic hotline—which honestly wasn't the dig she intended, since those folks often have genuine gifts. Her casual mention of their former engagement, the implication they'd reunite. Her certainty that Roman could never truly see me, that our worlds colliding would leave someone—me—in ruins. Yet none of it landed where she aimed. Her venom revealed her fears, not my reality.

"No," I say honestly, tucking a strand of hair behind my ear. "She didn't bother me at all." I cock my head, studying the tense line of his jaw. "But maybe she bothers you."

He shrugs, his broad shoulders rising beneath his crisp white dress shirt. "She doesn't bother me. Well, that's not right to say. She literally bothers me, just because she won't leave me alone. But her presence in the world—" he pauses, his dark eyes narrowing, "—it annoys me, but doesn't bother me. Because if somebody bothers you, it implies that you care, which I don't."

I nod, my thoughts drifting to the half-finished silk fabric bolt waiting on my sewing machine at home, but something in his restless energy tells me he needs to talk about something else. His gaze sweeps the marble-floored lobby where guests in designer clothes mill about with Louis Vuitton luggage. "Can I see you in my office?" he asks, his voice dropping an octave.

I follow him to his office adjacent to the main lobby, and the sight steals my breath. Soaring thirty-foot ceilings crowned with a cascading crystal chandelier—thousands of teardrops of light that shimmer like stars caught indoors. The western wall consists entirely of floor-to-ceiling sectioned windows framing the Pacific's azure waves, white-capped and violent, crashing against jagged obsidian cliffs dusted with emerald vegetation. A massive twelve-foot slab of rare blue-veined Carrara marble forms his desk, polished to a mirror finish that reflects the California sunlight. Behind it hangs not one but three presumably authentic Renoirs—dancing girls in butter-yellow and blush-pink dresses, their porcelain faces flushed with youth and joy beneath dappled golden sunlight filtering through invisible trees.

I point to the largest painting, my fingertips trembling slightly. "Is that real?"

He nods, the corner of his mouth lifting in a rare half-smile that transforms his granite features into something almost boyish, revealing a dimple I hadn't noticed before. "Got it at Christie's in New York. $150 million. You like Renoir?" His voice is as casual as if he's discussing a cup of coffee, but his fingers drum once against the polished marble of his desk.

He's perched on the edge of his desk, one Italian leather shoe planted firmly on the plush carpet while the other dangles, the platinum cufflinks on his crisp white shirt catching the late afternoon sunlight streaming through floor-to-ceiling windows.

The look in his espresso-dark eyes is indiscernible, but there's something behind them—an intensity that makes my breath catch. And it's strange—right now, I don't feel the dark aura that usually surrounds him like a thundercloud. Instead, his energy pulses dark red, rich as burgundy wine—the color of vitality, strength, raw courage. The color of a heart beating beneath all that expensive tailoring. God, this man radiates passion like heat from a sun-warmed stone. I don't know why the stormy black aura has dissipated, but he seems to glow from within now, as if someone has finally switched on the lights inside a magnificent abandoned mansion.

"Oh, god, yes," I whisper, my voice thick with reverence as I drink in the master's brushstrokes—the dappled sunlight on silk dresses, the rosy flush on porcelain cheeks, the champagne glasses catching golden afternoon light. "The way he captured the upper class...it's like you could befriend them, talk to them. You can see the secrets behind their eyes, the whispered scandals on the tips of their tongues."

“He certainly does capture them well,” he replies. “Renoir has always been my favorite.”

I cock my head. “You’re different tonight, Roman. Less… tempestuous.”

He grins. “Tempestuous—that’s a perfect word for my usual self. But you’re right. I don’t feel stormy right now.” He arches an eyebrow. “There’s something about you that calms the chaos in me, at least in this moment.” He smiles softly. “Of course, I might see you later and all that turbulence will be back. I can’t control it. But right now, I’m… surprisingly peaceful. And I really shouldn’t be—thinking of Serafina normally kicks off a red haze.” He shakes his head.

I take a seat, my heart racing as he gazes at me—not with menace but with equal parts curiosity and desire.

“Lilith,” he says quietly, “I wanted to talk about my father and Max. You got caught up in that storm too.” He runs a hand through his hair. “It’s a mess—complicated and ugly—and I’m sorry you were dragged into it.”

“You don’t have to apologize, Roman,” I answer.

He shakes his head. “I just… I don’t want to pull you into my vortex. You strike me as someone upbeat, someone who hasn't been beaten down by life yet. And I worry that my drama is the last thing you need."

So that's why the crystal was a peace offering. He isn't necessarily chasing me—he just feels guilty for darkening my world.

"Roman," I say softly, "really, you don't have to say sorry." He may think my life is carefree, but he's wrong. I lost my mother, I never even knew my father—I've had my share of tragedy. I just choose not to let it define me.

He nods, still perched on the desk, looking at me with that tender ache that makes my chest flutter. "You're really going to the gala with Blake?"

I nod. "I promised." I let the words hang there, shutting down any chance for him to insist. I couldn't say no to Blake—and I won't put him in that position.

"Okay," he says. "Well, I wanted to see if you were okay after Sera came in and said those ugly things and also after seeing my brother and father with me. And I guess I'll see you at the gala."

"You will," I say with a smile. "And I really have to get home to get back to sewing."

He smiles. "You sew your own dresses?"

"Sure," I say. "I learned to sew when I was 10. I don't sew all my clothes, just the ball gowns and things that are beyond my financial reach."

"You'll wear the Painite to the gala?"

My fingers drift to the opalite crystal at my throat. "Of course," I say, drawing comfort from its cool smoothness. "I wouldn't dream of wearing anything else."

He tilts his head. "I don't think I've ever met someone who makes their own clothes."

"Well," I say, adjusting the handmade sleeve at my wrist, "when you're sixteen with champagne taste and a tap water budget, you learn to thread a sewing machine needle. My first major creation was my prom dress—necessity being the mother of invention. Now I do it because nothing in stores ever feels quite... me." I shrug. "Plus, it quiets my mind."

His smile reaches his eyes. "You're unlike anyone I've ever known."

"I hope that's a good thing," I say, returning his smile.

His gaze holds mine, unwavering. "It's the best thing."

Chapter Fourteen

ROMAN

I freeze at the entrance of the annual Kensington Gala. Asher's living art installation takes my breath away. Jellyfish-shaped chandeliers pulse with blue-violet light, casting moving shadows across the ballroom. The dance floor ripples with each step, sending circles of turquoise light outward. Waiters in silk capes that shift from green to gold carry trays of champagne, the glasses rimmed with edible silver. In the corner, a pianist in a silver suit plays a grand piano that seems to melt into the floor, the keys flowing downward in a way that makes me doubt my eyes.

On stage, four ballerinas in blue tulle pose under azure lights. Their bodies curve gracefully against a backdrop of autumn trees with vibrant leaves. Two yellow figures stand motionless in the background. The scene recreates Degas's "Dancers in Blue" so perfectly that, glancing between the reproduction displayed nearby and the living tableau, I struggle to tell which is more real. The slight trembling of the dancers' muscles as they hold their positions brings the masterpiece to life.

I spot Asher near the bar and make my way over. "The living art tableau? Pure genius, Ash. You've completely transformed the standard gala experience."

A smile breaks across his face as he punches my arm. "A Roman Kensington compliment? Mark the calendar." He takes a swig of amber liquid from his crystal tumbler. "The brothers are scattered throughout. And..." his voice drops, "Dad's camped at the northeast table with Patricia—Celeste's mother. They're looking rather cozy."

"Perfect," I mutter. "I'm sure he'll spare us both the awkwardness of a wedding invitation."

"No wedding plans yet," Asher says with a careful shrug. "But give it time. Maybe by then you might—"

My jaw clenches. "Don't. Not happening. Hell will need ice skates first."

Asher just nods, reading me like always.

Just then, Lilith shows up with Blake fucking Walsh. My lungs seize. She's wearing emerald silk that pools around her ankles, her dark hair loose with those new green streaks catching the light. The crystal pendant I gave her nestles at her throat.

She catches my eye across the ballroom, flashes that dimpled smile, then disappears into the crowd, arm linked through his. That five-foot-seven Irish elf with his perfect hair and designer suit. So he's got platinum records and a voice that's melted hearts. So what?

I watch his practiced laugh as he works the room, stopping to embrace Clooney while she stands beside him. Every A-lister gravitates to them. I watch them chat up Spielberg and make Dua Lipa laugh. My knuckles whiten around my tumbler as acid climbs up my throat.

If they could've only seen Blake the other night when he was threatening to fucking piss in my koi pond…

I feel Serafina before I see her. Something electric crawls across my skin. When she touches my arm, I grit my teeth against the familiar jolt. We're nothing but raw, animal chemistry—a goddamn biological mistake I kept repeating for two torrid and toxic years. But I'm done with the mindless fucking against hotel walls with someone who means absolutely nothing to me. And that's all she is, now. A temptation I could drag behind that stage, tear into like a starving man, and fuck into oblivion until we're both sweating and broken—only to hate myself with every fiber of my being the second it's over. Pure heroin rush followed by the most brutal comedown imaginable.

My eyes find Lilith across the room while Serafina's fingers slide up my arm. I shut down the sensation. All I see is Lilith—the tilt of her head, her smile as she laughs at something Blake says. My jaw tightens. She fits so naturally in this world that wasn't hers three weeks ago. Now she's chatting with Spielberg like they're old friends, and I can't look away.

"Roman," Serafina's voice slithers into my ear. "Pathetic, isn't it? Watching the help pretend she belongs. That little fortune teller is drowning in water too deep for her. Someone should remind her exactly what she is before she embarrasses herself further. Don't you agree?"

"What the hell do you want, Serafina?" My voice comes out like gravel.

"You. Us. I want what we had." Her lips brush my earlobe. "No man has ever made my body feel the way you did. You've ruined me, Roman. I won't let anyone else have you. Our wedding will happen this time. You loved me once—you'll love me again."

A bitter laugh escapes me. Love? What a goddamn joke. I spent two years mistaking non-stop fucking for something meaningful, and I won't make that mistake again. That raw, desperate connection was never love. Love is what Cameron had. Love is what Max has with Celeste.

I spot them across the ballroom—Max with his arm possessively around Celeste's shoulders, looking at her like she's the sun. And the moon and the stars, while we're at it. She just had their first child, so Max is really making her the center of his universe, even more than before. The intensity in his eyes makes my chest physically ache. I've never once looked at a woman that way. Not once. But Christ, I want to. I want that with a hunger that's eating me alive.

Serafina can go straight to hell.

The moment Blake gets dragged away by the paparazzi vultures, I pounce. Lilith stands alone—my target acquired. I cut through the crowd straight for her, my pulse hammering in my ears. Serafina's voice fades to nothing as I brush past her mid-sentence.

"Roman," Lilith breathes, her eyes widening. "You look devastating in that tuxedo. Not that you don't always look—God—but tonight you're just..." She catches herself, dropping her gaze. "Shut up, Lilith," she scolds herself. "Making a fool of yourself."

Something primal stirs in my chest at her words, but my face remains carved from stone. No way I'm letting her see one ounce of pleasure while Blake's cologne still clings to her skin. My jaw clenches so hard my teeth might shatter. One more time—just one more time I see that bastard's hand slide down her back—and I'll break every bone in it before he hits the floor. Make him regret the day he ever laid eyes on what's mine.

I stare at her, jaw clenched. "How's your date going with Blake? He planning to piss in the fountain next? Or maybe take a chainsaw to the ice sculptures? Hell, why not storm the stage during one of the tableaus and ruin a masterpiece while he's at it?"

"Very funny," Lilith says, her eyes flashing. "Your brother created something magical tonight. Those tableaus —God—especially Renoir's 'Luncheon of the Boating Party.' The way he captured those aristocrats... like you can see straight into their souls."

My pulse hammers in my throat. Asher's tableaus are fucking brilliant, and Renoir's my favorite too, but all I can think about is whether she's falling for that jackass. If Blake touches her again—if he so much as breathes near her—I swear I'll put that little elf through the nearest wall.

I step closer to Lilith, close enough to catch the scent of her jasmine perfume. "Is Blake your actual date or just a friend?" My jaw clenches as I wait for her answer.

She tilts her chin up defiantly. "What's it to you? Aren't you here with that goddess with legs for days? What's her name again—Jezebel or something?"

"Serafina." I almost tell her Sera means nothing, but stop myself. Let her wonder. Let her burn with curiosity the way I'm burning right now.

"Serafina," she repeats, her eyes flashing. "Ironic name for someone hanging off you all night. Isn't that some kind of angel?"

"Seraphim. Six-winged angels of purity." I can't help but smirk. "And yes, the irony isn't lost on me."

"So she is your date." Her voice drops, almost challenging me to deny it.

I don't answer. Instead, I reach out, almost touching one of the vibrant green streaks in her hair. "This is new."

Her hand flies up, fingers grazing mine for a split second that sends electricity through my veins. "It's temporary. I'll fix it before Monday. Jack thought—"

"Don't." The word comes out like a command. "It's perfect on you."

The blush that spreads across her cheeks hits me like a physical blow. My hands curl into fists to keep from grabbing her right here, surrounded by half of LA's elite. Christ, I've never wanted anyone like this.

Blake arrives back. His hand slides onto her lower back, his lips brushing her ear. Her laughter hits me like a fist to the gut. Something primal surges through my veins—hot, electric. My MMA training kicks in: target assessment, muscle memory, the sweet spot where his jaw meets his neck.

Before I can stop myself, I've ripped his hand away from her body. The bones in his wrist grind together under my grip. My vision narrows to a tunnel with only him at the end of it. "Try that again," I say, my voice dropping to something barely human. "Give me a reason."

Lilith's eyes widen to saucers as she takes in the scene—my fingers crushing Blake's wrist bones, his face contorting in shock. The fool should've known better. Lilith is MINE. Period. End of fucking discussion.

I register the glint of smartphone cameras in my peripheral vision, guests salivating over their next viral moment. Let them. They can plaster my face across every goddamn screen on the planet. My blood is lava in my veins as I stare down this pathetic excuse for a man—the same degenerate who tried to desecrate my koi pond—now daring to put his goddamn hands on MY woman. Something primal tears through me, a white-hot rage that obliterates rational thought. This. Ends. NOW.

Cameron's voice cuts through my rage like a knife. "Rome."

My brother. The peacemaker. Sent to stop me from

ripping Blake limb from limb in front of half of Los Angeles. But I'm not fucking moving. Not while that bastard's hand is still hovering near Lilith's waist.

"Asher needs you. Bar for the next tableau. Heavy as hell. You're the only one who can move it," he says, clapping my shoulder with a grip that could crush granite.

My pulse hammers in my skull, drowning out everything but the sight of Blake's fingers, five inches from what's mine. I want to tear his arm off and beat him with it.

"Lilith. Now." I seize her hand, and holy shit—lightning strikes my body, a white-hot current searing through me straight to my core. Her skin is impossibly soft against my calloused palm, delicate bones beneath my grip, and that goddamn jasmine scent of hers floods my senses, making my mouth go dry. My thumb brushes over her pulse point, feeling it flutter like a trapped bird. This is the first time I've ever touched her, and holy fuck. The electricity I feel could light up this entire room.

"I—" She glances at Blake, who's practically trembling with relief now that I've released his wrist. Coward. "I should stay—"

The rejection hits like a sledgehammer. My jaw clenches so hard I taste metal.

"Fine," I spit, dropping her hand. "Let's move the goddamn bar, Cam, before I decide to use it as a battering ram."

Cam's arm lands heavy across my shoulders as we head backstage. "Roman," he says, his voice dropping. "What the hell was that with Blake Walsh? You know he's practically royalty in this crowd, right?"

I roll my shoulders, waiting for my pulse to settle. "Yeah, whatever. So am I." Time to change the subject. "Where's the bar setup?"

"Just there." He points. "Next up is *Nighthawks.* They need muscle for that triangular counter—someone bailed last minute. And since you're built like a brick shit house..." He gives me a brotherly jab. "These art patrons couldn't lift their wallets without breaking a sweat. But you? You could probably deadlift that 2,000-pound monster solo."

My blood's still running hot enough that I almost want to try.

I grab my end of the bar, and together we hoist it onstage. The performers hover nearby—an older guy in crisp whites with that paper soda-jerk cap; a woman with finger waves and a crimson dress straight out of the '40s; two men in period suits complete with fedoras. The set materializes around us: storefront backdrop, diner façade, "Phillies" sign overhead, stools precisely arranged.

My mind jumps ahead to the Velázquez tableau—*Las Meninas* with its royal Spanish family, the intricate arrangement of courtiers, children, a dwarf, those paintings-within-paintings. And a dog.

I catch Cam's eye and laugh, the sound bouncing off the marble floors. "Hey Cam, one burning question about that Velázquez setup—how exactly is Ash planning to make a dog sit still for thirty minutes under these blazing studio lights?"

Cam runs a hand through his dark hair, the same shade all us Kensington brothers share - all but Ansel, who's hair is dirty blonde. "Oh right, that painting does feature a dog. Slipped my mind." His broad shoulders rise in a shrug. "Well, if Asher can somehow wrangle a fidgety six-year-old to stand still for a half hour in that ridiculous period costume, I guess he's enough of a miracle worker to hypnotize a dog into statue-like obedience." His mouth curves into that familiar crooked smile. "Just kidding. Even Asher's legendary charm has its limits. He probably commissioned some hyperrealistic canine replica for the tableau. The alternative—Asher slipping some poor mutt a Xanax—is too disturbing to contemplate."

I feel the tension in my jaw release as I laugh, grateful for this moment of lightness after the storm cloud that had been hanging over me minutes ago.

"Put nothing past that guy," I say, shaking my head. "But you're right. Even Asher isn't sociopathic enough to sedate a dog just to impress Los Angeles' champagne-swilling elite with his living art installation."

We push through the perfumed throng back to the main exhibition space, where the crowd buzzes with anticipation for the next unveiling. The first two installations had drawn gasps that rippled across the room like waves, followed by thunderous applause that made the crystal chandeliers tremble.

These Los Angeles and Hollywood socialites—draped in designer silks and dripping with diamonds—devour this living tableau concept with the same enthusiasm they reserve for the $300-per-ounce caviar served at my rooftop restaurant. I have to hand it to Asher; while the concept echoes Laguna's famous *Pageant of the Masters* with its breathing recreations of classical art, he's managed to distill that grand spectacle into something intimate yet equally captivating for this marble-floored country club gallery.

I scan the ballroom for Lilith. Every face that isn't hers might as well be a blank canvas. Then Serafina materializes, her fingers digging into my sleeve like talons.

"Roman," she says, crimson lips forming a perfect pout beneath the crystal chandeliers. "You abandoned me."

"We were never together to begin with," I say, shaking her off. My molars grind against each other as I picture

Lilith laughing with that Irish pop star—100 million albums be damned, he's just another drunk with grabby hands. I could break him in half without breaking a sweat. Or maybe I should just let Serafina hang on my arm all night, see if that gets Lilith's attention.

Listen to me. Plotting like some lovesick high schooler. This isn't who I am. I don't pursue—I'm pursued. Women line up for me, desperate for whatever scraps I'll toss their way. The gold-diggers want access to my empire. The shallow ones want this face, this body—which, objectively speaking, is exceptional. That's just genetics, not ego. And God knows I've got the IQ to match. Then there are the fixers, convinced they'll be the one to finally "heal" me. But I've never chased. Not once. Until Lilith. Now I'd set this whole place ablaze just to make her look my way. She's turned me into something wild and unfamiliar.

I despise it.

I crave it.

I clasp Serafina's hand as the first notes of a slow song drift across the ballroom. Sam Smith's voice fills the air with the ballad "Fire on Fire," and the lyrics hit too close to home—not for the woman whose waist I'm about to hold, but for Lilith. My eyes find her across the room, already swaying in Blake's arms, her gaze catching mine over his shoulder. Something electric passes between us.

"Excuse me," I mutter to Sera, not waiting for a response before releasing her and cutting across the dance floor.

I tap Blake's shoulder, not bothering with pleasantries. No asking if I can cut in. When he turns, I simply take Lilith's hand and pull her towards me. She comes willingly, her body melting against mine as if she belongs there. Blake might be glaring daggers at my back, but I couldn't care less. All that matters is Lilith's jasmine scent enveloping me, her warmth against my chest, her fingers intertwined with mine as we move in perfect sync to a song that feels written for us—two broken people (or maybe I'm the only broken one) finding salvation in each other's fire. As we turn beneath the chandeliers, I know with absolute certainty: this is where she belongs.

Her heart hammers against my chest, a wild rhythm that matches my own. She trembles in my arms, but those topaz eyes burn into mine with unmistakable hunger—she craves this as desperately as I do. Does she see it in my eyes? That I would raze cities to ash just to witness her smile? Each turn beneath these shadowed lights draws her body closer, and Christ, the torture of restraint is unbearable. I want to tear her clothes off and fuck her, right this second.

This song pulses through us like it was written in our blood. Her breath catches as she surrenders against me, her head finding sanctuary on my chest while my fingers finally—finally—tangle in that silken hair. I've been starving for this since the moment I first saw her. Her body melting into mine, my hands possessing her, our hearts crashing together until I can't tell where mine ends and hers begins. The heat between us could set this whole goddamn place ablaze.

Just then, somebody—some clumsy bastard in the crowd—accidentally dumps an entire flute of golden Moët & Chandon down the front of Lilith's emerald silk dress. The champagne darkens the fabric instantly, leaving a glistening stain from her collarbone to her waist. Dammit. The perfect moment shatters like crystal. But yet...

"Come on," I say, squeezing her hand. "Let's get to the dressing room where the performers are preparing. I'll find you something else to wear."

She nods, her kohl-rimmed eyes wide with disappointment. I guide her through the perfumed crush of bodies to the dressing area tucked behind heavy velvet curtains, where the actors for the next tableau are in their costumes and ready to go.

I scan the cramped backstage area, my eyes adjusting to the dim light. "Uh, I'll find something for you to wear." My fingers brush past the Victorian gown from the Renoir tableau—red at the neck, cream lace at the throat, blue bustle. Beside it hangs another period piece: a blue dress with Belgian lace collar, also from the "Luncheon of the Boating Party" tableau. Soon the "Nighthawks" actress will arrive with their cherry-red cocktail dress, padded shoulders and all, straight out of 1942.

Lilith's eyes light up as she spots a Victorian-era gown hanging on the rack. "Oh, this is exquisite," she breathes, fingers tracing the intricate lace collar. "Do you think it would fit me?"

I can't help but smile. The women I usually date would be texting their therapists by now, horrified at the suggestion of wearing something so outdated to the gala. They'd be tapping their Louboutins impatiently while I called Jacques, my personal shopper, to rescue them with something straight off a Paris runway.

"Lil," I say, the nickname feeling right on my tongue. "My personal shopper Jacques can have something delivered in thirty minutes if you'd prefer—"

"Absolutely not." She pulls the dress from the rack, holding it against her body. "This is pure magic. I'll be Winona Ryder in *The Age of Innocence*. A proper Edith Wharton heroine."

The dress transforms before my eyes as she cradles it. What I saw as an antique costume, she sees as a portal to another time—romantic and bold.

"You realize you'll stand out completely," I warn her.

She laughs, a sound like wind chimes. "Roman, I already do. Those people out there are your crowd, not mine. If I'm going to be the odd one out anyway, I might as well do it in something that makes me feel beautiful."

I start to argue that my people should be her people too, but stop myself. She's right, in her way. And watching her stroke that Victorian bustle with genuine delight, I wouldn't change a thing about her.

She looks at me with those wide topaz eyes, holding the shimmering midnight-blue silk dress against her slender frame as she gazes into the antique full-length mirror. "Oh, what are the chances this will actually fit?" She cocks her head, sending a cascade of dark curls tumbling over one delicate shoulder. "One in a million, I'm afraid. It's hard to find things to fit me because I'm, well, I'm pretty petite."

And that she is. Five-foot-four of pure fire, a goddamn lightning bolt in human form that couldn't weigh a buck ten soaking wet. Her wrists are so delicate I could snap them with a twitch, fragile as bird bones beneath my grip. Her waist—Christ—so small I could span it with my hands, crush it if I weren't careful. Then those breasts, full and heavy, straining against whatever the hell she's wearing, making my mouth go desert-dry every time she moves. She probably has plenty of clothing challenges.

I can relate to clothing struggles, but from the opposite end of the spectrum. At six-foot-four, with shoulders that barely clear doorframes and two hundred ten pounds of rock-solid muscle honed through countless hours of surfing and MMA training, I couldn't fit in most department store suits. That's why everything in my cedar-lined closet is bespoke, hand-stitched by artisans in a discreet Parisian atelier off the Rue Saint-Honoré. Even my weekend clothes—raw Japanese denim jeans and Egyptian cotton Henleys—are measured and cut precisely for my frame.

Now I'm standing here, watching her fingers trace the dress's lace neckline, wondering how women like Lilith navigate a fashion world that seems built for some mythical average that neither of us fits.

"Well," she says, her voice like honey dripping from a spoon. "I guess I won't know if it fits until I go and try it on."

"Lilith," I say, my voice dropping an octave lower than usual. "Let me call Jacques. He's used to fashion emergencies and he'll come out here and bring you the perfect dress in under a half hour. I just need to know your measurements."

Then I go up to her and place my hands on her waist, feeling the delicate curve beneath the silky fabric. She inhales sharply, her chest rising as my fingers spread across her midsection. "Waist seems to be about 25, give or take," I say, a jolt of white-hot electricity shooting from my fingertips up my arms and straight to my core. The scent of her perfume—something earthy with hints of jasmine—makes my head swim. I only wish she'd take off that dress so I could, uh, measure her properly. That's it. That's all I want to do.

She nods, a flush of pink spreading across her cheekbones. "24 1/2, actually," she says, with a slight tilt of her head, exposing the graceful line of her neck. "Bust around 36." She looks at me through thick lashes, her topaz eyes darkening at the edges like a forest at dusk. I'm not imagining the hunger there. But goddammit, there's all these people still around, shifting impatiently in their costumes, checking their watches, waiting for their turn in the spotlight. "Size 4 dress, actually," she adds, her lips curving into a knowing smile.

We're standing there, frozen in our own private universe, my hands still encircling her impossibly small waist, her staring at me with those mesmerizing pools of topaz with flecks of emerald dancing around the pupil. Eyes that would transform with anything she wears, from a ball gown to nothing at all.

I swear to god, I feel like I'm under some ancient spell as I stare at her, unable to look away. But then she shakes her head, breaking the trance, her dark hair, streaked now with light green, bouncing softly against her shoulders. "I'm going to try on this dress," she says, each word deliberate and teasing. "Excuse me."

When she disappears behind the heavy velvet curtain of the dressing room, I pull out my phone and text Jacques. Just in case. I ask him to bring me a green dress—emerald, the color of the ring around her pupil in otherwise topaz eyes—with a halter bodice that would showcase those delicate collarbones and those beautiful breasts, size 4 petite.

I can imagine Lilith in that dress, the silk fabric clinging to every curve, her sun-kissed skin glowing against the deep green. She would look so breathtaking she'll make me come undone and goddammit, I'm not fighting becoming undone with her anymore.

Jacques texts back within seconds, three thumbs-up emojis, and I know he's already making calls. The boutiques along Rodeo Drive closed hours ago, of course, but Jacques can have them reopened with a single mention of the Kensington name. He's pulled strings like this before, even though the sleepy-eyed shop owners and security guards absolutely despise being dragged from their beds at this hour.

Lilith emerges 15 minutes later, drowning in fabric that devours her delicate frame. The dress strangles her chest while the waist gapes open like a wound, the hem cascading in a waterfall around her ankles. Her eyes shimmer with unshed tears as she attempts a smile that cuts me to the bone. I rip my phone from my pocket and hammer out a text to Jacques: "ETA?"

Rodeo Drive isn't far. The boutiques will open early for me—Jacques knows everyone worth knowing there. He'll find something for Lilith, though watching her now, struggling with that ill-fitting dress, I'm not sure even Beverly Hills' finest could do her justice. My chest tightens as she tugs at the bodice again.

She twirls before the mirror, the fabric swishing against her skin. "Not perfect, but it'll do," she says, her reflection catching the light. She crinkles her nose, shaking her head with determination. "No. I need the 1940s red dress from the *Nighthawks* tableau. It has to be that one."

My phone vibrates. "Be there in 10," Jacques texts, the man who's saved my ass a thousand times. Then he sends a photo that makes my breath catch in my throat. Christ. Mermaid halter neck with a keyhole slit that will showcase the soft curve of her breasts, a thigh-high slit that will reveal those legs that haunt my dreams, all in a silk emerald green that will make her eyes burn like wildfire. No dress deserves Lilith, but this one might actually be worthy of her.

Jacques bursts through the door ten minutes later, a sleek box tucked under his arm, cheeks flushed from rushing. Lilith perches on the edge of her chair, still expecting the vintage dress from the *Nighthawks* display. I've kept quiet about my actual plan.

"Who's this?" Lilith asks, eyeing Jacques and the mysterious package.

I lift the lid, revealing a shimmer of emerald fabric. Lilith's mouth forms a perfect O.

"Roman, you didn't..." Her fingertips hover over the silk, barely making contact.

"Try it on," I urge, my voice lower than intended. "Everyone at the gala will be looking at you, not the art."

Her hands tremble slightly as she accepts my gift. Minutes later, she emerges in the gown. The Italian silk hugs her waist before flaring at her knees, emerald against her olive skin. The halter neckline frames her in a way that makes my throat go dry. Through the slit, I glimpse her leg as she moves. The back dips low, showcasing her spine. The color brings out flecks of gold in her eyes. She studies her reflection, catching her bottom lip between her teeth.

She stares at the dress, her fingers trembling as they trace the beadwork. "I can't accept this," she breathes. "It's—Roman, this must have cost more than my entire store makes in a month."

"I don't give a damn what it costs," I say, stepping closer until I can smell the jasmine in her hair. "All I care about is watching every man's jaw hit the floor when you walk in with me."

Her eyes lock with mine, doubt battling with desire. Then her lips part in a smile that hits me like a shot of whiskey—warm, intoxicating, dangerous. "You're impossible."

I grip her wrist, my thumb finding her pulse. "I'm your date tonight. Blake can go to hell."

She laughs—a sound that races through my blood. "And Jezebel?"

"She can burn there with him."

We go back to the gala, where a recreation of Velázquez's Las Meninas is being unveiled to appreciative murmurs. The guests in their designer wear settle at tables with crystal centerpieces glinting under the chandeliers. Dinner is served: wagyu carpaccio, lobster with risotto, and gold-flecked chocolate soufflé—exactly what you'd expect at an event where three Michelin-starred chefs are in the kitchen.

Lilith's eyes dart toward the crowded dance floor. "I should probably find Blake. I mean, I did come with him tonight."

Part of me wants to say forget him—she's with me now. But that would make her the kind of woman who abandons her date, and I wouldn't respect that. I clear my throat. "Go ahead and find him. Bring him over to our table." I shrug with practiced nonchalance. "Blake Walsh won't exactly be heartbroken. You're just friends, and let's face it—a guy like him always has options."

Caspian finally walks through the door. I lift my wine glass in his direction, nearly shattering the stem between my fingers when I see who's draped across him like a second skin. Violet fucking Monroe. The supermodel who's graced more magazine covers than I care to count, and who once told a reporter I was "nouveau riche with the manners to match." My jaw clenches so hard I taste blood, but Caspian—my supposed best friend—beams like he's won the goddamn lottery, blind to the viper he's brought into my house.

Casp and Violet join our table. Caspian's eyes dart around the hall before landing on mine. "Sera's meeting you here, right? That's what she said." His voice lifts at the end, hopeful as a kid on Christmas morning. My gut clenches. Oh, you sweet summer child…

Has it really been that long since I talked to him? No—we were throwing punches at each other just Tuesday. But apparently that was enough time for Sera to plant her little fantasy in his head. The one where his best friend and his sister get back together, making one big happy Blackwood family with me finally inducted as an official member. Christ. The guy can spot a feint from a mile away in the ring, but when it comes to his sister's games? Completely blind.

I lower my voice. "Listen, Caspian. Your sister isn't happening for me. Not ever. You know who I want."

The chair beside me—Lilith's chair—scrapes against the floor as Sera slides into it. "Found you," she announces, tossing her hair over one shoulder. "Hey Casp, Violet." She bumps her brother's arm with a smirk. "Told you he'd be with me."

Christ. I run a hand through my hair, watching three separate guys at the bar twist their necks to follow Sera's movement. Two wedding rings among them, glinting in the low light. Sera turns every men's head in this place, so why is she so fixated on me? Meanwhile, Caspian's expression has shifted to something dangerously hopeful, and any minute now, Lilith will walk by, see this tableau, and vanish before I can explain a damn thing.

I shoot Sera a death glare before excusing myself. Lilith's probably halfway to her car by now. Last time Sera showed up, she cornered Lilith in her own cabana, practically breathing fire as she warned her to "stay away from Roman." Sera has that effect on people—making them feel two inches tall with just a glance from those ice-blue eyes that have graced a dozen magazine covers. The woman's net worth rivals small countries, and she wields both her beauty and wealth like weapons. Her social media cult follows her every move; women want to be her, men want to possess her.

Christ. I need to find Lilith before she sees me with Sera and assumes the worst. Blake's probably already filling her head with reasons to bolt.

There she is. Standing alone, scanning the crowd with those wide eyes. I bulldoze my way through the mass of tuxedos and gowns, muttering half-hearted apologies. When she spots me, her face lights up and she throws her arms around my neck. The scent of jasmine and something earthy hits me, and my skin buzzes where she touches me.

Lilith's face lights up when she spots me. "Roman! There you are! Blake abandoned me for the woman I predicted he'd meet tonight—his Queen of Cups."

Talk about perfect timing.

"Queen of what?" I ask, moving closer.

"Cups. From the tarot." She gestures across the room where Blake stands enraptured by a brunette in blue. "I did a reading that said his soulmate was coming. Their eyes locked and—poof!—he forgot I existed." The way her lips curve upward with genuine delight rather than jealousy loosens something in my chest. She couldn't care less about Blake romantically. Thank God.

"I'll drive you home," I say, already fishing for my keys.

"Don't be silly. My Uber's coming at one—"

"Lilith." My tone leaves no room for argument. "I'm driving you."

She sighs. "But Venice Beach is completely out of your way. You're downtown, aren't you?"

I almost tell her about my place at the Four Seasons in Beverly Grove—barely ten minutes from here—but stop myself. She'd only protest more if she knew how close I lived, while her place is a good half-hour drive.

"Doesn't matter. You're coming with me."

"Roman," she says, smoothing the silk of her dress—the

one I had delivered this evening. "The crystal, the dress, now the ride home... A girl might think she's special."

What I want to say is that if she couldn't feel how special she was when we danced, I've clearly lost my touch. Instead, I just give her a slow smile that says everything I'm not ready to put into words.

Chapter Fifteen

LILITH

Roman is driving me home in his Bugatti. A Bugatti! Five million dollars worth of hand-crafted exclusive Italian engineering, and this is his car. The leather seats are butter-soft, and the engine makes this low rumble that vibrates through my whole body. I keep sneaking glances at him, then at my newly chipped nail polish, then back at him again. This man is the sun and I'm riding in his car, a car that is worth more than I could make in several lifetimes, literally. Pinch me now.

When he shifts gears, his knuckles flex, and I have to look out the window before he catches me staring. I've dated nice guys before—sweet baristas and one very earnest graphic designer—but Roman is something else entirely. He belongs on magazine covers, not driving me home after a gala that has his last name.

He looks over at me, his dark eyes lingering a moment too long. My stomach flips. Is that desire I see? The thought that Roman Kensington might want me—physically—sends a flush of heat across my skin. But that's all it could ever be between us, right? A brief collision of bodies, nothing more. Still, the idea that someone like him would find me attractive makes my pulse skitter wildly.

Sure, Jack tells me I'm gorgeous all the time, but best friends have to say that. They're contractually obligated to make you feel like a diamond when you see yourself as cubic zirconia. But even if Roman wanted a one-night thing... I couldn't. Not my style, not even for him. I shake my head, dismissing the thought. There must be some other explanation for his attention.

Roman's knuckles whiten on the steering wheel as he pulls into my driveway, killing the engine with a sharp twist. "Lilith," he says, his voice dropping to a near-whisper. "Those readings—you got inside my head. How the hell did you do that?"

I meet his burning gaze. "It's a gift," I say, my heart hammering against my ribs. "Are you finally admitting some people might have abilities you can't explain?"

He leans closer, the leather seat creaking beneath him. "I've spent my life dismissing all of it—the zodiac bullshit, chakra alignment, crystal healing—as expensive lies for gullible people." His jaw clenches. "But you..." His eyes lock onto mine, searching. "You're different. You saw things nobody could know." He exhales sharply. "Maybe there are forces in this world I can't control or understand." A dangerous smile cuts across his face. "Guess I need to revisit my non-belief in UFOs and Big Foot."

I inhale slowly to steady myself. "Would you like to come inside for some hot tea?"

"I'd love to," he replies without hesitation. I wait for the inevitable "but" that doesn't come. Roman unbuckles, steps out, then points a finger at me. "Don't move. That door mechanism is tricky as hell."

Glancing around the sleek interior, I realize there's no visible handle. Normally, being trapped would trigger my claustrophobia—I'm perfectly fine in small spaces until I can't escape, then panic sets in. Like when elevators stall or bathroom doors jam. But watching Roman stride confidently around the hood of his luxury car, I feel only anticipation. He'll open my door now, and maybe next time, he'll teach me how to do it myself. Next time. The possibility makes my pulse quicken.

He opens the door and leans down, his sandalwood and bergamot cologne hitting me as he points to a button tucked into the door frame. "Press here first, then push the door up slightly to clear the roofline." His smile catches me off guard. "You'll get used to it."

You'll get used to it. Four simple words that shouldn't make my pulse quicken, but they do. As if this isn't just a one-time ride. As if there will be a next time, and a time after that. He said it so easily, too—the way people talk about certainties, not maybes.

I get out of the car and then climb the steps to my little townhome. I push open my front door, conscious of Roman's presence behind me as we step into the darkened hallway. The clock on my microwave reads 2:17 AM. Not even six hours until I need to unlock Mystic Tides. My fingers brush the light switch, hesitating. Miranda's schedule flashes through my mind—no resort readings tomorrow or the next day, just two packed days next week. Back-to-back sessions for hours.

"Would you like some tea?" I ask, turning to find Roman closer than I expected, his frame filling my tiny entryway.

Two days a week. That's all I might see of him, and even then, he'd probably be tied up in meetings while I shuffle cards for wealthy strangers. My chest tightens at the thought. Sure, he'd joked about me getting used to his car, but reality is reality. I've seen Sera with her runway legs and practiced laugh hovering near him. That's his world. Not mine—with my secondhand furniture and a mortgage I can only afford because Jack splits it with me.

He sits on my couch, his tux pants against the cracked leather. "Sure," he says. Gracie winds between my ankles, meowing like she's starving though I fed her hours ago. The armrests bear her claw marks from when she was a kitten. I could replace the couch now that the bookstore's loan is paid off, but with rent hikes coming, that money's going to savings. Roman shifts, looking as out of place as a Rolex at a discount store. His world of penthouse views and private jets couldn't be further from my Costco mattress and the Prius outside that's pushing 150,000 miles.

I put the kettle on and turn to Gracie, who's circling my ankles with theatrical meows. "Drama queen. You'd think I've been starving you for days." I reach for the bag of Smalls—organic, wild-caught, worth every penny if it means keeping her healthy into her golden years—and fill her bowl. She attacks it like it's her last meal, then abandons it half-empty when she spots Roman.

Before I can even pour the hot water, she's made herself at home on his lap, her rumbling purr audible from across the room. His large hands look surprisingly gentle as they stroke her fur. I can't help but smile. If Gracie approves of Roman, that's worth more than any background check.

I return with two steaming mugs and set them on coasters atop my splurge coffee table—solid oak that cost a month's rent. Roman has transformed in the minute I've been gone. His bow tie dangles from one hand, his collar gapes open, and he's sprawled across my sofa like he owns it, one hand absently stroking Gracie's fur. Those dark eyes follow me, unblinking.

“So…” I break the silence, wrapping my fingers around warm ceramic. "The cards spoke to you after all?"

His lips curve slightly. "You could say that." Something flickers behind his eyes—vulnerability, maybe—before he continues. "Twenty-two years since my father walked out. After Mom died—refused treatment for her cancer because she was carrying Max—Dad crawled into a bottle and never emerged."

I sip slowly, letting the silence stretch. The cards had already shown me his fractured family tree, but this confession feels different—raw, unfiltered.

"He vanished," Roman continues, voice rougher now. "No goodbye, no forwarding address. My grandparents stepped in, raised eight boys without answers. Dad became this...forbidden topic. Like mentioning him might summon something worse than his absence."

I rest my palm on his forearm, and a shiver runs through me at the contact. His gaze drops to where I'm touching him, then lifts to meet mine. Something flutters in my chest.

"I can't imagine how hard that must be," I say softly.

His shoulders rise and fall. "After vanishing for two decades, he waltzes back expecting a hero's welcome. And my brothers? They rolled out the red carpet." The muscle in his jaw tightens. "It cuts deep, you know? Standing alone while my own blood acts like I'm the unreasonable one. I can't just hand over forgiveness like it's nothing. What he did..." His voice roughens. "My brothers keep pushing, like I'm the problem." He looks away, swallows. "Being the odd man out in your own family—it hollows you out."

I nod. "I understand it's still difficult for you. But—"

He drops his gaze to the floor before meeting mine again, his eyes clouded with something raw and unguarded. "I get it," he says, voice barely audible. "My grudge probably says more about me than him at this point. I just..." He pauses. "I'm not convinced he deserves forgiveness yet." His expression shifts, eyebrows lifting slightly. "Huh. 'Yet.'" A slow shake of his head. "Didn't realize that's how I actually felt." His throat works visibly. "Something about you makes me say things I didn't even know were inside me."

I smile and sip my tea. "And your youngest brother. Max." I remember now the card reading I gave him when I told him that he resented his youngest brother. Will he confess about that, too?

He shakes his head, his dark hair falling across his forehead. "That's another buried deep thought you managed to figure out." His eyes drift upward to the textured ceiling, jaw clenching. "God, what kind of person am I? But yes. I've always resented Max."

His voice drops to a whisper. "And no. I've never wanted to admit that, even to myself." His fingers curl into a fist against his thigh. "As if he had a choice in the matter, being born to a mother who needed cancer treatment but chose to have him instead." A muscle twitches in his cheek. "But I just think that his very birth caused the rest of us to not have a family. To become essentially orphans, even though our father was technically still alive." He swallows hard, Adam's apple bobbing. "We've all grown up with that open wound of our father's rejection and losing our mother so young. But goddammit, it's not Max's fault. It's not."

I can't look away from him— this beautiful, broken man drowning in rage and desperate to claw his way back to his family through the wreckage of his own heart.

I reach for him but don't quite touch him. "Roman," I

say softly, "you said 'yet.' That word holds possibility." My fingers hover near his clenched fist. "Your heart already knows there's a path back, even if you can't see it now."

The crystal pendant at my throat catches the light as I swallow what I really want to say about energy work and chakra balancing. Those suggestions would only make him retreat. What Roman needs is someone with credentials and letters after their name, someone who knows how to navigate the labyrinth of a man's grief. But suggesting therapy to Roman Kensington feels like offering swimming lessons to a drowning man who's too proud to admit he's in water.

He nods. "I know." His gaze drifts to the clock on the wall. "Damn. Three already? You must be exhausted." His fingers continue stroking Gracie's fur, but I notice the way his throat moves when he swallows. "Listen, Lilith... it's pretty late. I'm worried about driving home like this. Would it be okay if I crashed here?" He pats the sofa cushion beside him. "This looks comfortable enough."

My heart skips as I gather my courage. A billionaire Adonis in my bed? When would that chance come again? "You could use my bed," I offer, then feel heat rush to my cheeks. "That came out wrong—"

His expression brightens instantly. "I promise to be a complete gentleman," he says, tilting his head with that devastating smile.

"I think Jack left some pajama bottoms in the laundry," I say, trying to sound casual. They'll hit him mid-calf at best as Jack's barely six feet tall, but the mental image of Roman's sculpted chest above borrowed pajamas in my bedroom will definitely keep me warm on lonely nights to come.

"That'll be fine," he says.

So, I go to the laundry room and pick out some of Jack's

pajama bottoms out of the pile on top of the washing machine. Then I go back out and hand them to Roman. “Here," I say. "Jack's a few inches shorter than you so…”

He smiles at my plaid pajama bottoms. I’m sure it isn’t his usual bedtime attire—probably silk or some designer sleepwear—but he doesn’t complain. Then I realize I’ll need help getting out of this dress. Actually, the back zipper stops at the top of the rear end, so I could manage on my own. Still, picturing Roman tugging it down for me… I shake my head. I have to keep things in check tonight—and so does he. I barely know him, and if I let things go too far he might not respect me. I need to stand apart from the other women vying for his attention. No hanky-panky tonight.

After a few minutes behind my bedroom door, he reappears, shirtless and in too-short pajama bottoms. My breath catches. He’s perfect—no trace of fat, every muscle sculpted, an eight-pack framed by a lean waist. And there’s a tattoo on his chest: a rose wrapped in script. Somehow it suits him, a subtle rebellion against the pristine billionaire image.

I step closer and read the words: *Those who are hardest to love need it the most – Socrates*. A lump forms in my throat. He must’ve chosen it deliberately: to remind himself he deserves love, or that he needs it even if he pretends otherwise. He watches me with a small smile. “Got it one drunken night. Total cliché, I know. But don’t you think it’s true? Difficult people often…”

“…need love the most,” I finish, blinking. His dark eyes hold something—desire, compassion, all of it. I squeeze past him in the doorway and he doesn’t move, so our bodies brush together. My heart pounds as I stare into those obsidian eyes. Finally he shifts just enough to let me through, and I feel a pang of disappointment. I wanted him to kiss me—for a moment I think he almost did. But if he had, I couldn't have stopped myself. And that, I tell myself, would be a mistake.

My heart pounding, I unzip my dress and pull on my most modest pajamas—long pants with a matching button-up top. The silk nightie hanging in my closet calls to me in this heat, but I resist. Wearing that would be like hanging a neon sign over my head: "Take me now." And God help me, I want him to. But I can already see how it ends—me, completely wrecked over what he'd consider a casual fling. I'd never be able to show my face at the resort again. And I've grown attached to those weekday readings, surrounded by marble fountains and guests who arrive via helicopter. The money's good, the setting's divine, and there's always that moment when I scan the lobby, hoping to glimpse Roman's tall figure moving through the crowd, my stomach doing that ridiculous little flip that makes me feel sixteen again.

I slip into the softly lit hallway, my voice barely more than a whisper. "Um, the bedroom is ready." I shake my head, cheeks warming. That sounded way too suggestive. "I mean, it's late and we should really sleep. I have a queen-size bed—cozy, but not huge." My mind flutters: Should I shove a pillow between us like a barricade? No—that's ridiculous.

He gives me a gentle grin. "I promise I'll keep my hands to myself. We'll just lie down and sleep, side by side."

I force a nod, even though every nerve in me aches to press my skin to his. He's like a perfect marble sculpture come to life: flawless lines, warm skin. My heart hammers as I slip beneath the cool, cotton sheets, fluffing the pillow. He settles in next to me, breathing already deep and even. Within minutes, his soft snores drift through the stillness.

Morning light filters in at six-thirty. I need to shower before the store opens, but the world is muffled by the weight of him: his arms draped over my shoulders, a strong leg thrown across mine. He's sound asleep, hair tousled and thick, sleeping like a raven on my pillow.

I hesitate, reluctant to disturb him, but finally whisper, "Roman… I really need to get up."

He jolts awake, dark eyes blinking, hair a tousled halo. He glances at his watch, face crumpling. "Oh—shit. I have to get to the resort." He rises, fumbling into last night's tuxedo pants, his white shirt half-buttoned, designer shoes shuffling on the floor. His movements are hurried, awkward.

"Thanks for letting me stay," he breathes, stepping close to brush a quick kiss against my forehead. I close my eyes at the warmth of his lips. "Hope I didn't—put you out."

I shake my head, heart twisting. How can I tell him I don't want him to leave? He straightens his collar, half-smiles. "I'll see you next week at the resort, right?"

See you next week at the resort. The same thing as a dismissive "see you around." Or "I'll call you." My throat tightens. Guys like him don't ask girls like me out. Period. "You will," I manage, forcing a casual tone. He gives a small nod, then turns and is gone, the door clicking softly behind him.

I stand there, alone in the quiet room, and wonder why I bothered to hope.

Chapter Sixteen

LILITH

The night after Roman's sleepover, I find myself wide awake under a full moon. I grab a glass of merlot and slip out to my postage stamp-sized garden. Jack materializes beside me, right on cue—midnight is his natural habitat.

Jack prances over and hip-checks me with enough drama to qualify for a daytime Emmy. "Spill the celestial tea, Lili-pad! Which Hollywood demigods deigned to breathe the same oxygen as you mere mortals at the gala? I need names, faces, and any wardrobe malfunctions—preferably in that order."

I bite my lip, picturing Jack's meltdown if I mentioned brushing elbows with George Clooney, Leonardo DiCaprio, or—heaven help us—Chappell Roan. Some details are better left unsaid.

"Just the usual rich people," I shrug. "It was magical until someone baptized my handmade dress with champagne. Twenty-four hours of stitching, down the drain—though maybe it's salvageable."

"Disaster! You spent the whole night looking like a walking wine spill?"

My lips curve upward remembering Roman's rescue mission—his personal shopper arriving like a fairy godmother with a replacement gown. Each moment with him pulls me deeper under his spell. Yet this morning he'd vanished with a vague promise to see me at the resort, leaving me to decode what exactly we are to each other.

"No. Roman actually had his personal shopper deliver a dress to me. It was breathtaking—midnight green silk that caught the light when I moved. And it fit perfectly."

"Shut up!" Jack's eyes widened. "That man doesn't do anything halfway, does he?"

"There's more." I raised my palm when Jack's eyebrows shot up. "Not what you're thinking. Blake met someone at the gala—I think she might be the one for him—so Roman drove me home. It was after two, and his home is forty minutes away I guess, so when he asked about crashing on the couch..." I tucked my hair behind my ear. "I let him have the other side of the bed. We just slept."

"Lilith, you 'ho! This is major!"

"I know, and I'm..." I traced the rim of my teacup. "There's this electricity between us. Anyone would feel it—he's gorgeous. But it's more than that. He's like a storm barely contained in human form. Sometimes I think we recognize in each other what we're missing. I'm drawn to his intensity, that fire I've never let myself have. And I think he craves the calm he sees in me."

Jack squeezed my hand with a dramatic sigh. "Honey, I'm absolutely living for this romance novel you're starring in," he said, "but that man's emotional walls are thicker than my winter moisturizer layer. The way he eye-devours you? Chef's kiss. But sweetie, can Mr. Tall-Dark-and-

Emotionally-Constipated actually unclench enough to let you past the velvet rope? That's the million-dollar question."

"That is the million dollar question," I agree.

My phone vibrates against the table. Roman's name flashes on the screen. My heart slams against my ribs so hard I swear Jack can hear it.

Just wanted to check and see how you're doing. I don't remember if I thanked you for letting me stay last night

My fingers tremble as I type, deleting and retyping three times before hitting send.

Oh, thanks for checking on me! I'm doing great. And you did thank me for letting you stay. I don't remember if I properly thanked you for taking me home. If not, thanks! You're a lifesaver.

"Let me guess," Jack says, smirking. "Roman fucking Kensington is texting you."

"Is it that obvious?" I whisper, unable to look away from the screen.

"Honey, your face is practically radioactive. If we turned off the lights right now, you'd glow brighter than the goddamn moon."

Heat rushes to my cheeks as I press my palms against them. "I can't help it," I confess, my voice catching. "Just seeing his name—" Another ping cuts me off, and my stomach drops like I'm in freefall.

Hope I didn't wake you. Just got back from the resort and can't sleep...can't stop thinking about waking up next to you.

My cheeks flame hot as I read Roman's text. Jack peers over my shoulder, his smirk melting into wide-eyed surprise. "Well damn, Lil. The man's not exactly subtle about his feelings."

My fingers tremble as I type:

Actually, I'm wide awake too. For the same reason...

You at the shop today?

Yes. Readings scheduled.

Morning or afternoon?

Afternoon. Why?

Three dots appear, disappear, then reappear. Finally:

Just wondering if you'd play hooky with me. Another time. See you at the resort.

I groan and flop back against the pillows. I could cancel the readings. I could. But these clients book because they're lost, seeking guidance when they've run out of options. I can't disappoint them just because Roman Kensington—billionaire hotel magnate and ridiculous crush that he is—wants to see me.

"Another time," I whisper, clutching the phone against my chest. But I don’t say that.

See you then

Jack's eyes light up like sparklers as he practically bounces behind the counter. "Lilith! Playing hooky? Mr. Workaholic owner of elite resorts across the world wants to take the morning off to…" He wiggles his perfectly groomed eyebrows suggestively, his lips curving into a knowing smirk.

I feel heat rush to my cheeks. "Stop. He said nothing about-" I mirror his expression, raising my own eyebrows before dissolving into nervous laughter. "He just said play hooky. That could mean anything, you know."

"Say what you will," Jack says, leaning forward on his elbows, his voice dropping to a conspiratorial whisper. "But all the signs are there, Lilith. He's crazy about you."

He straightens up, counting off on his manicured fingers. "Let's see, Lilith. He played knight in shining armor when the pipes broke, wading through that disgusting water in his thousand-dollar shoes. He bought that crazy rare crystal for you that's worth a quarter mil. Played knight in shining armor again by bringing you that dress on the fly. He spent the night in your bed and then texted you to say that he can't stop thinking about waking up next to you. Now he wants to play hooky with you…." He shakes his head, a triumphant grin spreading across his face. "Girl. You have an admirer, a beautiful, wealthy, intelligent admirer with abs you could grate cheese on."

"You forgot complicated, stormy…" I close my eyes, feeling the flutter of butterflies in my stomach. "Intoxicating."

So, so, intoxicating.

Chapter Seventeen

ROMAN

Goddamn. How hard was it to just fall asleep next to Lilith last week? Hard enough that it's been a week since I left her tiny townhouse on the Venice Canal, and somehow she intrudes on my thoughts while I'm reviewing quarterly projections or approving the new sommelier's wine list.

I've hired two executive chefs since then, negotiated with a Saudi prince about his upcoming wedding reception, and spent three hours in a meeting about importing Italian marble for the spa renovation. But every time my phone stops ringing, every time I'm not placating some VIP guest or signing off on a seven-figure expenditure, I think of her. And of that night.

And, yes, I humiliated myself with that text asking her to skip work with me. Playing hooky? Me? I've never missed a day of work in my life. Thank Christ she had enough sense to turn me down. Between that and my pathetic "can't stop thinking about waking up next to you" message, I might as well have just sent her my bank statements and the deed to my soul. Everyone warns about drunk texting, but I was stone-cold sober when I sent those messages. No alcohol to blame—just pure, unfiltered idiocy.

I couldn't go further with her that night. Lilith isn't some disposable conquest. And Christ, even with every muscle fiber screaming for her, my chest feels like it might cave in as I think of giving her what she deserves. Not the platinum card. Not just another fuck. ME. Raw and unfiltered.

I've never handed those keys to anyone. That's why I kept it physical with women like Sera—that tawdry, torrid, toxic, tedious train wreck. God, she was perfect in her imperfection. I could slam her against a wall, burn through the sexual adrenaline, and walk away with my heart safely locked down. The mere concept of surrendering that to someone makes my hands shake. Control is oxygen to me. Without it, I suffocate. And Lilith? She'd own me completely. One taste and I'd give her everything—the empire, the broken pieces, all of it. The tattoo burning across my ribs says it all: those who are hardest to love need it the most. I'm a goddamn fortress of razor wire and land mines. But underneath? I'm starving for it. Desperate. Terrified.

So, even though I know that Lilith has been on the property twice this week, giving readings in her cabana and even started giving readings in the Poseidon suite for the first time, I have not gone near either place. I've been avoiding her. And I will keep avoiding her until I figure out exactly what I want to do. Until I know for sure that I'm ready to unlock that part of me that I have never unlocked for anybody. Goddamn, I just don't know if that's possible at this point.

I look out the window at palm trees bending almost

horizontal. The barometric pressure's dropping fast. The Weather Channel calls for a a very strong El Niño storm, perhaps the worst in decades, I call a mandatory meeting with my emergency team.

"OK," I say to Ned, Harry, Pete and George. "Phase One protocols. I want all outdoor furniture secured or moved inside. Pool areas cleared and locked down. Sandbags at every entrance point on the lower levels. Pete, coordinate with maintenance to check all backup generators and ensure we have three days of fuel. Harry, work with guest services—I want everyone moved from oceanfront rooms to interior accommodations. George, contact all scheduled arrivals and offer complimentary rebooking. And Ned, I need hourly weather updates and direct lines to emergency services."

I pull up the resort's storm contingency plan on my tablet. "If conditions worsen, we move to Phase Two—full guest lockdown in the Grand Ballroom with emergency provisions. I'll be leading this response personally."

I sit down and stare at the computer screen, my eyes tracking the angry red swirl of the massive storm as it barrels toward the California coast. The digital projection shows its massive eye, surrounded by violent bands of wind and rain.

Fuck!" The resort will survive, but Venice Beach is directly in the storm's path. My gut twists thinking about Lilith's shop—Mystic Tides—with its purple awning and crystals in the window, so close to the water. Just that old boardwalk between her and disaster. I remember her voice shaking when she talked about the seawall, fingers working that pendant she always wears. And Jack and Lilith in a crisis? They'd be useless.

"Uh, George," I bark into the walkie-talkie, my knuckles

white around its plastic casing. "I need to get to Venice Beach tonight. You can handle this, can't you?"

"Yes, boss," his voice crackles back, "but I thought you were going to lead the response."

My jaw tightens as I decide. George has military training and my emergency team backing him. Lilith has tarot cards and incense. Her eyes wouldn't see the danger coming until it's too late. And Jack with his designer boots? Useless.

I make my decision in a split second and slide behind the wheel of my black Rolls SUV—chosen this morning when I saw the storm clouds gathering. The first raindrops hit as I merge onto the 405 toward Venice. Within minutes, water floods the freeway. My wipers can barely keep up, giving me half-second glimpses of the road ahead. My knuckles go white on the steering wheel, but I push harder on the gas. All I can think about is Lilith's shop with its old foundation, sitting too close to what must be an angry Pacific by now.

I leave the Rolls in a flooded spot and run through the rain, my shoes and suit soaked through in seconds. The shop comes into view—Mystic Tides—with its front window broken. Through the gap, I see Lilith with wet hair stuck to her face, stacking tarot cards on a high shelf while Jack dumps crystals into bins. Water has already reached the bottom shelves, ruining books and submerging amethysts in the rising flood.

"Oh, Roman," she gasps when I burst through the door, her topaz-jade eyes wide with relief as she flings herself against my chest. Her body trembles violently against mine, her voice breaking. "Thank God you're here. Everything's ruined."

"We'll save what matters," I promise, already scanning the chaos for a solution.

For the next three hours, I direct the rescue operation. I haul soggy tarot cards and crystals to the shelves along the back wall, away from the flood. Lilith's dark hair with green streaks has frizzed into a halo as she moves her old leather-bound books, eyes wide.

Rain pounds the windows while I stack sandbags against the door, cursing when water seeps through anyway, ruining my expensive shoes. The smell of wet incense and paper fills the air. I climb a rickety ladder to patch the ceiling with duct tape and a garbage bag, wondering how I—a man who runs luxury hotels—ended up here during Southern California's worst storm in years.

The electricity snaps off, plunging us into darkness. The storm's roar is deafening, wind battering the storefront as we give up on the flooded floor. We load the last of her merchandise into my SUV—crystals, tarot decks, books, incense, candles, all of it wet. I wipe rain from my face. "You two have to get to my resort tonight."

Lilith shakes her head. "Roman, I can't leave," she says, gesturing at the mess around us. "Someone might break in." Her wet face catches the dim light. My chest tightens as I look at her standing amid the wreckage, water still seeping across the floorboards. She has insurance—she'd mentioned it when I replaced those old pipes last month—but that's hardly the point now.

"Lilith," I say, voice low and urgent. "What's a looter going to want? Piles of soggy tarot cards? Boxes of crystals? We've emptied the register, loaded everything we could into the SUV. There's nothing left to steal that's worth a damn. You can't stay here—and your house will be dark, too. You and Jack are coming to my resort. Tonight."

Lilith's gaze bats between me and the storm-lashed windows as if she might summon the courage to argue further. Before she can, Jack throws up his hands, soaked curls plastered to his forehead. "Roman, that sounds like literal heaven—luxury, warm beds, running water. I'm wiped out. Ready to collapse face-first into silk sheets and be waited on like the forgotten prince I am—since I'm still hunting my own Prince Charming."

I can't help the flicker of a grin. Lilith snarls at Jack over his "prince" quip, which only makes my heart pound harder. She's embarrassed for me, maybe scared I'll take him seriously. But I've wanted to hear those words from her lips for months. Prince Charming. For me, they feel like promise.

"That's settled," I say, voice firm enough to cut through the howl of wind. "You two pack what you have left. We're gone in five minutes. The Weather Channel says this storm's got us for two solid days—and nights. My resort has power, heat, hot showers. I'll see you there."

A flash of lightning splits the sky, illuminating our drenched silhouettes. I grab Lilith's arm. "Come on, before the storm decides to tear the roof off this place." With Jack at her side, she finally nods, and I lead them into the darkness—toward safety, comfort, and a flicker of hope amid the tempest.

Lilith shakes her head, her eyes wide with panic. "My Prius in this rain. I—"

Jack cuts her off with a dramatic eye roll. "What Lilith is desperately trying not to admit is that her front tires are practically bald. I've been begging her to get to the tire shop before she hydroplanes into the Pacific, but—"

"I haven't had the money," Lilith blurts, then quickly

corrects herself. "I mean time. And they're perfectly fine for most days. Just not in torrential downpours."

Fuck. My blood burns at the thought of her driving on dangerous tires. Mateo at Superperformance Foreign Auto Repair might laugh when I roll up with her beat-to-hell Prius instead of my Bugatti or Rolls, but he'll shut up when I slam my black Amex down. If our situations were reversed, I'd rather walk barefoot through broken glass than take my cars to whatever discount tire hell she uses.

I can't help the possessive smile that crosses my face as Lilith shrinks back, her cheeks flushed crimson. She thinks I'm judging her—first no insurance for the burst pipes, now this. What she doesn't understand is that I'm practically starving to take care of her. The fierce need to protect her hits me like a freight train, and I haven't felt this alive in years.

I arch an eyebrow. "So what I'm hearing is you want me to chauffeur you two in the Rolls."

Jack and Lilith exchange a glance, their heads bobbing in the slightest confirmation. Jack clears his throat. "Look, my Corolla and I have an understanding—we don't attempt hydroplaning stunts. And this one," he jerks a thumb toward Lilith, "once pulled over during a light drizzle and called me crying." He spreads his hands. "We're Venice Beach people. Rain happens to other zip codes. When water falls from the sky, we light sage and stay home with our kombucha and true crime documentaries."

I can't help but laugh. "All right, you two," I say, glancing between them. "Lilith, grab Gracie's carrier on your way out. Your cat's probably hiding under furniture with the power out. And both of you pack for at least two nights."

Relief washes over Lilith's face when I mention her cat.

Her eyes soften instantly. She probably thought I'd make her choose between safety and leaving her pet alone in a dark house. Not happening. She loves that cat too much. I've seen how she whispers to Gracie when she thinks no one's watching. With the way Lilith treats her cat, I wouldn't be surprised to catch them doing a tarot reading together.

Then, before Lilith can protest, I scoop her into my arms—keeping her shoes clear of the flood that's turned the boardwalk into a series of small lakes. She loops her arms around my neck and rests her head against my shoulder with a sigh. Her slight frame weighs almost nothing as I navigate through the waterlogged boardwalk toward the parking lot. The three of us reach my car and I help Lilith, opening the door and depositing her onto the front seat and then gently strap her in. Behind us, Jack gets into the back seat.

Jack sinks into the cream-colored leather of the Cullinan's back seat, running his fingers along the polished wood trim. "Lil," he says quietly, the engine purring beneath them. He fans himself with one hand. "Honey, this isn't a car—it's seduction on wheels. These massage seats are treating me better than my last three dates combined." He looks up at the starlight ceiling and gasps. "Roman, darling, if this is how rich people live, I've clearly been hanging with the wrong crowd. I might actually faint right now."

Lilith catches Jack's eye and smiles. "Jack," she says, widening her eyes dramatically. "Doesn't this remind you of my car?" She snorts, running her fingers along the pristine leather. "Just like my Prius with the Coke stains and sand that's practically part of the upholstery now." She pats the immaculate interior. "Practically twins."

I smile, watching Lilith next to me and Jack in the rearview mirror as they explore my Rolls. Jack keeps whispering "holy shit" while Lilith presses every button she finds. I've forgotten what it's like to be impressed by these things. The car cost more than most houses, but to me it's just transportation. Seeing their genuine amazement reminds me that none of this is normal. For a moment, I can almost remember when luxury still felt special.

I drive them home. The rain has turned Lilith's driveway into a miniature lake, so I scoop her into my arms again. Her body feels light against my chest as I navigate the flooded concrete and climb the short steps to her porch. When I set her down, our eyes meet for a moment. "Grab some clothes and your cat," I tell her, glancing at the darkening sky. "We need to leave soon. This storm's just getting started."

Back at Verde, I escort Lilith and Jack to their accommodations—the Azure Vista and Éclat de l'Onde suites, positioned side by side. I'd reserved them personally, no small feat considering we're running at nearly 95% capacity these days, up from 80% just a month ago. I find myself wondering if Lilith's presence has brought some mystical good fortune to the property. Her arrival coincided with an upswing, though Lars, my marketing manager, would argue it's his new marketing campaign we hammered out last quarter. Either way, the numbers don't lie.

I open the door to Lilith's suite. The Pacific stretches beyond floor-to-ceiling windows. Her eyes widen at the private terrace with its plunge pool, the silk rug underfoot, the marble catching sunlight. Champagne chills beside a platter of figs and cheese—standard for guests who don't blink at what this place costs per night.

I leave her alone in the suite, while I check on my team and she has a chance to shower. And damn, what I wouldn't give to join her in that shower…but, duty calls.

I check back in about an hour, after consulting with my storm team. They have everything in hand, as I knew they would. Greg is a great drill-sergeant - he actually was a drill sergeant in the military, so his role now as the head of my storm protocol team is natural for him.

I open the door and Lilith is now sitting in the living room, in front of the fireplace, where she's built a fire to warm her up. She's dressed in pajamas again, ready for bed, her hair wet again but wet from the shower, not the rain. She's fresh-faced, no makeup, and still the most beautiful woman I've ever seen.

"How is this suite for you?" I ask her.

Her eyes widen. "Oh. Can I move in here?" She laughs, but it fractures mid-sound, collapsing into a sob that wrenches through her entire body. I pull her against me, and she trembles violently, her tears soaking through my shirt. "God, I'm sorry," she chokes out, her voice raw. "It's all crashing down on me at once. My shop—it's gone, isn't it? The water damage alone..." Her fingers dig into my arms. "Insurance will eventually pay, but the paperwork, the inspections, the waiting—it's like drowning all over again. What the hell am I supposed to do until then? Where do I even start?"

I reach for my phone. "Let me make some calls. I know people—the best in the business—who can have your shop looking better than before. Carpenters, flooring specialists..." I scroll through my contacts. "Even that Persian rug supplier who did the Crete property. And the glass guys who installed those twenty-foot windows at this resort." I look up from my screen. "They all owe me favors. We'll stretch your insurance payout further than you'd believe."

Her lower lip trembles slightly, topaz eyes glistening. "Roman... why would you do all this for me?"

Her eyes widen with confusion, and I realize she truly has no idea how I feel about her. So I decide to show her. I cradle her face between my palms, my thumbs brushing the soft curve of her cheekbones. Time slows as I lean in, watching her eyelashes flutter closed, her lips parting slightly in anticipation. The first touch from my lips to hers is gentle —testing, questioning—but when she sighs against my mouth, I'm lost. Her lips are impossibly soft, tasting of cinnamon and that herbal tea she's always drinking. I tilt my head to deepen the kiss, feeling her fingers curl into the fabric of my shirt as she rises onto her tiptoes. The world narrows to just this—her warm breath mingling with mine, the silken slide of her hair between my fingers, the perfect pressure as she kisses me back with unexpected hunger.

She's breathing harder and so am I, my lungs burning like I've been underwater too long. My heart slams against my ribs like it's trying to break free and join hers.

This kiss—Christ—it's like being struck by lightning, like drowning and being saved at the same time. I've spent thirty-three years chasing a ghost, and here she is, flesh and blood, this wild-eyed tarot reader with her sun-kissed skin and untamed spirit. The parade of Victoria's Secret models, the actresses with their red-carpet smiles, the heiresses who could buy small countries—they've all turned to smoke in my memory. Erased. Meaningless.

Then my phone rings, cutting through the moment. Dammit. I want to keep kissing her, but she pulls back. Her amber eyes look down, lashes shadowing her cheeks as she takes a step away. I can feel her trembling slightly where our bodies still touch.

"You should probably answer that," she says, her breathing heavy, chest rising and falling in a rhythm that makes my heart race. "The storm..." Her voice trails off as thunder cracks outside, punctuating her words with nature's exclamation point.

I stare at my phone. Max. I let it ring twice before answering. "Hey."

"Rome," he says. "Been trying to reach you. You okay? Palos Verdes got hit hard—trees down everywhere. Malibu's fine, but Venice and Santa Monica are a mess. These storm paths are as unpredictable as you are."

I can't help but chuckle. Classic Max—youngest of us all with the biggest heart. Well, aside from Cameron, of course, the sainted brother. But Max is the kind of guy who'd give his custom-tailored Armani shirt off his back to a stranger in need. Something warm unfurls in my chest knowing I'm still on his priority list, especially after all the venomous words I've hurled his way lately.

"Thanks, Max, but I've got this under control," I say, glancing at the rain lashing against the floor-to-ceiling windows. "Need to get back to my storm crew before they think I've abandoned ship. I'll text you if anything changes."

"You do that," Max says, his voice softening. "Don't hesitate. Not even for a second."

I hang up and the realization hits me like a rogue wave —Lilith has completely derailed me. Outside, the El Niño storm of the century is battering my multi-million dollar resort, and here I am, daydreaming about a woman who reads tarot cards instead of supervising my emergency response team. Hell, Max seems more concerned about my property than I am. That ends now.

I turn around, scanning the empty living room. Following a hunch, I check the bedroom and find Lilith asleep on the bed, curled on her side. Her dark hair spreads across the pillow, and her lips are slightly parted as she snores softly. She shivers. I grab a throw blanket from the closet and cover her. Before leaving, I bend down and kiss her forehead, catching the scent of sandalwood in her hair.

"Bye, Lilith," I murmur, my voice barely disturbing the air. "I'll be back to check on you tomorrow."

With one last look at her peaceful face, I stride from the suite, already mentally shifting gears to rejoin my team.

Chapter Eighteen

LILITH

I wake up the next day after the nightmare at the shop in a luxurious suite with Egyptian cotton sheets and a view of the misty coastline. For a moment, I almost think I'm still dreaming.

Outside, a gentle rain taps against floor-to-ceiling windows, nothing like last night's howling tempest that had rattled the shop's windows and sent my crystals vibrating on their shelves. My muscles ache as if I've hauled sandbags for hours—which I practically did—and my fingernails are still rimmed with dirt despite my shower.

Bone-tired doesn't begin to describe it. Every time I close my eyes, I see my waterlogged tarot cards floating across Mystic Tides' wooden floors, and my stomach clenches with the sickening fear that my sanctuary might be beyond saving.

Last night, Roman promised to help rebuild the shop, his voice rough with determination against the backdrop of my ruined store.

Then he kissed me against the mahogany-paneled wall

—a kiss that scorched through my body like wildfire, that made my knees buckle and my mind go blank. I woke this morning in this ridiculous suite with its ocean view and Egyptian cotton sheets, still feeling the ghost of that kiss. My fingers keep drifting to my lips without permission, and every time the hotel phone rings, I nearly jump out of my skin, wondering if it's him calling from somewhere in this sprawling resort he owns.

Just then, I hear a knock at my door. I open it, and there's Roman on the other side. He balances a silver tray with crepes dusted with sugar, a small bowl of berries, bacon, a croissant, and orange juice. There's also—oddly—a small bowl of butternut squash soup. A single orchid stands in a vase beside the napkin. Somehow he's brought all my favorite breakfast foods, as if he'd been reading my mind.

"Thought you'd be hungry," he says as I open the door, his tall frame silhouetted against the misty gray afternoon, raindrops glistening in his dark hair.

"Actually, I'm starved," I say, my stomach growling in anticipation. "I don't think I ate yesterday. I was too busy trying to save my life's work."

"We can eat on your terrace," he suggests, gesturing toward the sliding glass doors. "It's still raining, but I'll enclose it so we don't get too wet. You can still see the ocean through the rain from here—all silver-tipped waves crashing against the cliffs."

We step onto the terrace. The infinity pool's blue glow meets the darkening sky at the horizon. Steam rises from the hot tub nearby. Bougainvillea and hibiscus frame the space, their colors vivid against white stone. In the center sits a marble table on iron legs. When the first raindrops fall,

Roman claps twice. Glass panels rise from the floor, sheltering us from the storm.

I smile as I sit down, trying not to stare at the croissants and bacon. My stomach growls. I imagine Roman, with his resort and fancy cars, expects women who know which fork to use without thinking. I can feel him watching how I hold my spoon —away from the bowl, not toward, the way my grandmother taught me. But part of me wants to be like Julia Roberts in *Pretty Woman*—kick off my sandals, climb onto the table, and eat those croissants with my fingers, crumbs falling everywhere.

Roman glances at me, his dark eyes softening. "How are you feeling today?" he asks, spearing a strawberry with his fork. Steam rises from his soup as he waits for my answer, the breakfast spread between us untouched.

"Better," I say, tucking a strand of hair behind my ear. "I slept really well. That bed is amazing—I didn't want to get up this morning." I close my eyes briefly, remembering. "I've never slept on anything that comfortable before."

"Grand Vividus mattress," Roman says with a hint of pride, his broad shoulders straightening. "$400,000 worth of Swedish craftsmanship, hand-stitched with horsehair and layers of breathable cotton." His lips curve into a rare smile. "I outfit all my rooms with them. Got them wholesale at half the retail price—an investment that pays for itself when sheiks and tech billionaires tell me they had the best sleep of their lives."

Half a million dollars for a mattress? No wonder I felt like I was sleeping on a cloud. My Purple mattress from Costco suddenly seems like a joke—like comparing a tricycle to a Ferrari. I can't let myself get used to this kind of luxury though. This billionaire fantasy world isn't meant for small-time psychic bookstore owners like me.

"Jack around?" Roman asks, scanning the room.

I roll my eyes. "Ten bucks says he's at the indoor pool right now, batting his eyelashes at some hedge fund manager. He's on a mission to land himself a wealthy husband and transform into the trophy spouse he was born to be."

Roman's laugh is low and warm. "Well," he says, his fingers threading through my hair as his gaze locks with mine. "I guess his best friend has caught herself a billionaire. Maybe he's hoping to do the same."

My pulse quickens beneath my skin. There he goes again, hinting at something lasting between us. I push the thought away. Men like Roman collect hearts like trophies. I've read enough cards to know when someone's playing a game, and I won't let my heart become another conquest on his shelf.

I look out the window at the ocean. The storm has passed, but the waves still crash against the rocks at the edge of the private beach. The water is gray and rough, sending up sprays of white foam when it hits the shore.

"I love the ocean," I say, pressing my palm against the cool glass. "There's something so timeless about it. Like the droplets of water in the ocean are some of the same ones that dinosaurs drank, that filled ancient seas, that have been part of this earth since before humans even existed."

Roman's eyes crinkle at the corners as he takes another bite of caramelized bacon. "You see magic in ordinary things, don't you?"

Heat rises to my cheeks. "I guess I do." I trace the rim of my water glass. "The ocean speaks to me. Those waves were rolling in before we even existed." I glance up to find him watching me intently. "And the redwoods up north—some are thousands of years old. Standing there, you feel time differently." I smile, suddenly self-conscious. "In my readings, I'm just trying to tap into something bigger than myself. Not forcing anything, just... listening."

Roman nods and looks towards the ocean. "I love the ocean, too, but for a different reason than you….It's where I belong." He smiles. "My dad taught us all to surf on our fourth birthdays. Had this thing about starting exactly then or you'd never master it." Roman shakes his head. "Dad was full of weird ocean superstitions. No wearing red on the beach—sharks. He had us thank the waves after surfing or he said we'd get bad ones next time. No eating oranges before paddling out or a tiger shark might get you." His smile softens. "Crazy stuff, but I believed every word."

I put my hand on his arm. "You speak of your father with a great deal of affection," I note.

He shrugs, gaze drifting somewhere past her shoulder. "He'd take all eight of us camping sometimes. Build these massive bonfires. Taught us to fish. Mom's birthday was always the hardest—he'd start the day determined to stay sober, cooking her favorite pancakes for us. By afternoon, he'd be three bottles in, crying over photo albums." He smiles and shakes his head. "One Christmas, he spent two weeks building us this elaborate treehouse, then fell off the ladder and broke his arm because he couldn't stay away from the whiskey. That was Dad—brilliant flashes of the father we needed, eclipsed by longer stretches of... absence."

Roman's face softens when he mentions his father. I notice, but stay quiet. Pushing would only make him shut down again.

"What about you?" he asks. "Your childhood?"

I sip my orange juice, the tartness matching the bittersweet memories. "Single mom raised me. Father was just a nameless one-night stand, according to Mom. But I had Cary Grant - always imagined he was my real father."

Roman's eyebrow arches. "The actor? Wasn't he—"

"Dead before I was born? Mere technicality." I laugh softly. "I was four when Mom introduced me to him through her old movies. We'd curl up on our threadbare couch watching *Bringing Up Baby* and *Arsenic and Old Lace. The Bishop's Wife* at Christmas, always." I trace the rim of my glass. "To little me, he was everything—charming, handsome, elegant, that mischievous sparkle in his eyes. I'd fall asleep imagining him swinging me up onto his shoulders. Easier than wondering about a real father who never bothered to exist in my life."

I cock my head. Actually, Roman somewhat reminds me of Cary Grant, just more beautiful. As if that was possible to my childhood self, because, in my eyes, nobody was more beautiful than Cary Grant.

Roman smiles. "So, you had your mother…"

I nod. "Mom just got me, you know? When I was twelve, I told her I could sense what the trees in our backyard were feeling. Not in a weird way—just impressions." I run my finger around the edge of my mug. "Instead of worrying, she bought me this journal with a tree on the cover and said, 'Write it all down. I'd love to hear what they're telling you.'"

The confession hangs between us. I've just handed this gorgeous man the weirdest piece of my history, yet something in his expression makes me keep going. He takes a slow sip of orange juice, those dark eyes fixed on mine—not with the polite tolerance I'm used to, but with a spark that feels like recognition.

He leans in, eyes soft. "What did the trees tell you?" Not a hint of mockery in his voice—just genuine curiosity.

I take a breath. "They weren't words exactly, but impressions. My mother noticed how I'd sit there for hours. On my tenth birthday, she gave me my first tarot deck." I smile at the memory. "She said the cards would help me understand what I was already sensing.The first time I laid them out, something clicked. Like finding a missing puzzle piece. That's when I knew someday I'd create a space where others could make those same discoveries."

"And your mother..."

"She was gone before I turned nineteen. Fifty-four years old. A stroke took her in the night." My voice catches. "The doctors said there were no warning signs. She carried a little extra weight, but nothing that should have..." I can't finish. The tears come despite my efforts to hold them back. Roman's thumb brushes them away, his dark eyes holding mine with such tenderness I feel my chest tighten. "The insurance policy she left—one hundred thousand dollars—felt like her final gift. Like she was still taking care of me somehow. I put myself through community college, earned my business degree, and when that little storefront on Venice Beach came up for lease, I just knew. Everything she'd taught me about following my intuition led me there. That shop became my sanctuary—built from her love, even after she was gone."

Roman shakes his head. "You're unlike anyone I've ever met. My life has been...different. Boarding schools. A Maserati for my sixteenth birthday. Ivy League education courtesy of my grandparents. Even this resort started with a loan from my grandfather—forty million dollars. Paid it back within a year with interest, but still."

My jaw drops. Forty million? I'd thought Mom's life insurance policy—a hundred grand—was life-changing money. The kind that let me open Mystic Tides. A million dollars in my account? That's fantasy territory. Something to daydream about between tarot readings and restocking crystal displays.

But now, with the shop...

Roman's eyes soften, reading my expression with unexpected precision.

"Lil," he says, his voice gentle. "The shop will be okay. I know the storm damage looks catastrophic right now. But I have connections—the best contractors in California. We'll restore everything, better than before. Mystic Tides isn't going anywhere. That place is your heartbeat. I won't let you lose it."

I narrow my eyes at him. "How did you know what I was thinking?"

He shrugs, the corner of his mouth lifting. "Maybe I'm catching your woo-woo vibes."

My hand finds his forearm, warm beneath my fingertips. "Your intuition is stronger than you think. Everyone has that inner knowing—that third eye. The universe whispers to us constantly." I lean closer. "Even science backs this up. Your subconscious processes millions of tiny details your conscious mind misses completely. That gut feeling? It's real. Your subconscious is basically a supercomputer compared to your conscious thoughts. So when something feels right or wrong here—" I tap just below my sternum, "—listen to it."

I close my eyes, hearing the rain softly patter against the window as my gut twists with certainty about Roman - that he's absolutely right for me. But my practical brain wages war against this feeling, like storm clouds gathering over the Pacific.

I hate when logic drowns out intuition. My brain keeps listing the reasons it won't work: Roman with his expensive suits and that jawline couldn't possibly want me long-term. He runs hotels where people worth billions relax by pools I could never afford to swim in.

But when he's with me, I notice things—the rough skin on his hands from years of surfing, the way his real smile changes his whole face. Something in me recognizes something in him, like finding a missing piece I didn't know was gone. It doesn't make sense on paper, but I feel it anyway.

Sometimes when he looks at me, I forget all the sensible arguments. Against all odds, this feels real.

I open my eyes to find Roman staring at me, something unguarded in his gaze that makes my breath catch. His lips are chapped from the salt water, and I remember their pressure against mine last night. I think about him sleeping in Jack's old pajama bottoms, how the morning light fell across his bare chest, how different he looked from the businessman in tailored suits. There's something almost startling about seeing someone so powerful half-dressed in borrowed clothes, vulnerable in sleep. Even now, I can hardly believe he's here with me.

He puts his calloused hand on my flushed cheek and caresses it with his thumb, rough skin against soft, as I can hear my heartbeat thundering in my ears like waves crashing against the Palos Verdes cliffs.

The storm returns. Rain hammers the windows. Outside, resort umbrellas strain against their anchors and the ocean crashes against the shore. Lightning flashes, followed by thunder that rattles the glass.

Southern California storms are deceptive that way—they quiet down, making you think they're over, then surge back. Wind finds the gaps in the building, whistling through palm trees. Another flash, another boom. My mother taught me how to count seconds between lightning and thunder to know how far away a storm was. I've forgotten the formula now, like I've forgotten so much about her.

Five minutes later, a sharp rap at the door cuts through our conversation. "Who could that be?" I ask as Roman unfolds his six-foot-four frame from the plush sectional, his bare feet padding across the Italian marble.

A familiar voice—high-pitched and dripping with affected charm—trills through the penthouse suite, and I groan, sinking deeper into the cushions. Serafina.

"What are you doing here?" Roman demands. The transformation is jarring—his voice hardens from the warm honey baritone that had just been whispering stories about his first surfboard into something cold and metallic. His jaw clenches as he stands in the doorway, blocking my view of the blonde goddess with her perfect manicure and designer everything.

Her stilettos click across the marble floor as she approaches. "I heard you were here." She tosses her rain-dampened hair over one shoulder. "I asked at the front desk." Her voice drops to a honeyed whisper. "And I have an emergency at my father's headquarters in Palo Alto. My plane is grounded in this weather, but I know that you have your pilot's license and you're not afraid of taking off in bad weather, so…"

"Sorry," Roman's voice cuts through the air like a blade. His jaw tightens, eyes cold as the storm outside. "Even I'm not fool enough to take off in this weather. You'll have to find someone with a death wish." He turns away, adding over his shoulder, "And that's no longer me."

Sera leans forward, her manicured fingers tapping the edge of the mahogany table. "Oh, come on," she says, her voice silky with persuasion. "You're the best pilot I know in bad weather. It's because you're remarkably void of fear. If anything, things that scare other people only make you sharper. Every other pilot would be so terrified of flying in this weather that they'll make a mistake and crash the plane. And I have to get to Palo Alto today."

"It's a six-hour drive," Roman says, his jaw tightening as he glances out the floor-to-ceiling windows at the charcoal clouds gathering on the horizon. Lightning flickers in the distance, illuminating his sharp profile for a split second.

Still, I wonder if he'll fly her to her father's office. Roman's the type who'd pilot through a storm just to prove a point. I've seen that look in his eyes before—right before he does something reckless that makes my pulse jump. And I can't help it—picturing his hands on the controls of that private jet makes me shiver in a way that has nothing to do with the weather.

Is there nothing this man can't do? He can apparently navigate a Gulfstream through stormy skies with the casual confidence of someone parallel parking. Yesterday, I watched him hoist my oak bookshelf—the one that took three delivery men to bring inside—with nothing but his own strength, veins mapping his forearms like rivers. And when he kissed me, those same powerful hands cupped my face with such tenderness that my toes curled against the hardwood, my body arching toward his like a flower seeking sunlight.

Roman's jaw tightens as he leans forward. "What's your father's emergency?" he asks, voice low and controlled.

"The storm's hammering Palo Alto right now. His tech headquarters lost power when lightning struck their backup generator. The server farm is overheating, and they've got millions in crypto assets that could vanish if the cooling systems stay offline much longer. His entire security team is trapped in the building because the electronic locks failed in lockdown mode, and now there's three feet of water in the parking garage."

Roman folds his arms across his chest. "And your presence is necessary because...?"

“I’m the only one who understands the proprietary storm-monitoring system my father installed last year - the one currently predicting catastrophic power failures within the hour. And it takes both of us to get it back online because of the way my father designed it.” She shakes her head. “Daddy didn’t have time to train somebody up there and I guess he didn’t imagine that a storm would hit of this magnitude so soon. Best laid plans…”

Roman's jaw tightens as he shakes his head. "I'll do this for Caspian and your father, not you. Got that?" He points at her, eyes narrowed, then looks up at the gray clouds. "Goddamn it, I don't know if I can get clearance to take off in this weather. Might have to override protocol." When he turns to me, his voice changes. "Lilith, I wish you could come with us, but I won't risk your safety like this."

“Oh, Roman, thank you so much!!!!” Sera is jumping up and down, but she takes a moment to give me a look of triumph.

“But Sera, I’m not stupid. I’m calling your father to make sure that the emergency is as you say it is.”

“You don’t trust me.”

“Your goddamn right I don’t trust you. So, I’m calling him right now.”

Roman takes his phone into the other room and five minutes later, he comes back out and looks at Serafina. “Let’s go. Not a moment to waste, it sounds like.”

He's risking his own life flying through this tempest for other people—including this woman with honey blonde hair cascading down her back, pouty crimson lips, and a designer outfit that probably costs more than my monthly store rent. A woman he obviously doesn't care about anymore. But he does apparently care for her father and this Caspian person, whoever that is.

My fingers instinctively touch the rose quartz pendant at my throat as I watch him. The crystal warms beneath my fingertips, and I know as sure as I'm sitting here that he'll successfully navigate through this weather, his capable hands steady on the controls. I have complete faith in this. And I also have complete faith in something else—that I can trust him.

Yes, Sera might look like a Barbie Doll come to life with her perfect figure and flawless complexion, and her father is apparently a tech billionaire who no-doubt has a mansion overlooking the Pacific, and she's an heiress and probably brilliant if her father relies on her like this, but no matter.

Roman is meant for me. The universe has aligned our paths for a reason. Of that I'm sure.

Time to listen to my gut for once, to trust the intuition that's been humming through my veins since the moment our eyes first met.

Chapter Nineteen

ROMAN

Home at last. The flight to Palo Alto with Serafina was worth it, even if her father's headquarters was a complete disaster zone when we arrived. I didn't do it for her—I did it for her and Caspian's old man.

When my father vanished, Fritz Blackwood stepped in. Not in the day-to-day way, buried as he was in building his tech security empire, but in the ways that mattered. He'd call from Lake Como: "Roman, get your ass on a plane." Next thing I knew, I'd be carving through waves behind their boat. Christmas in Crete. Spring break on Swiss slopes. Hell, he even showed up to watch me play hockey sometimes.

For him, I'd walk through hell. For Sera, I wouldn't fucking get out of bed if she called me from a burning building.

The loyalty to Fritz is why I flew through what felt like the apocalypse yesterday. For sixty minutes, I fought to keep that Gulfstream level while lightning cracked close enough to smell. The rain hammered us like we were in God's shooting gallery. I violated direct ATC orders not to take off —the FAA paperwork alone might cost me my license.

But what kept flashing through my mind during each violent drop wasn't the turbulence—it was the cosmic joke of finally finding love, only to nosedive into oblivion before I could actually enjoy it.

Flying back was a cinch, as the storm had passed, leaving behind only a few scattered clouds painted pink and gold by the setting sun. I spent one entire day at the Blackwood, Inc., HQ helping out with their storm protocols. In the meantime, the storm had completely passed and I flew back in a clear blue sky.

Unfortunately, since I wasn't white-knuckling the polished titanium controls of the Gulfstream G650 during our turbulence-free hour back to LAX from San Francisco International, it gave Serafina permission to do everything she could to try to seduce me. Her manicured fingers kept "accidentally" brushing my thigh, her Chanel No. 5 perfume deliberately wafting my way each time she leaned too close to whisper something inconsequential into my ear.

When she first showed up, I ignored it. Now I notice things—how her smile tightens when I lean close to Lilith during readings, the way she shifts when Lilith laughs at my jokes. She's always counted on me being available. My past relationships were placeholders, and she knew it. But Lilith is different. I catch her watching us like a hawk eyeing prey, and I know she wants to destroy this before it becomes something real. I need to be careful.

I shut down Sera's flirting with a curt "no thanks," and mercifully, the flight from San Francisco landed in LA before she could try again. Now I need to swing by the resort—though my storm response team has probably already handled everything—before racing to Mystic Tides.

Lilith texted me that she and Jack took an Uber back to her shop because she couldn't stay away another second.

I can picture Lilith now, standing amid the wreckage of her shop, eyes red-rimmed. I'll tell her not to worry. One call and I'll have carpenters building better shelves, flooring specialists laying hardwood that'll outlast the next storm, and someone replacing that window. She can handle inventory—that's her thing—but she'll need backup with insurance. Those companies design their claims process to wear people down. Not happening. Not to her. Not on my watch.

I swing by the resort. George meets me in the lobby, silver hair slicked back, suit pressed despite the chaos around us. He briefs me with the same unflappable confidence that made me hire him, assuring me everything's under control.

Workers in blue coveralls hammer away at the east wing's torn roof, the steady rhythm competing with the crash of waves. At the Verde water park, men in safety vests swarm over the Typhoon Twister slide, torches cutting through twisted metal. Sparks rain down into the empty pool below. El Niño had peeled back the fiberglass like a banana skin, leaving it curled and broken.

Across the grounds, more crews replace shattered glass in the oceanfront bungalows, Spanish tiles torn away by 80 MPH winds. I step carefully around palm fronds scattered across the same paths where I'd walked with Lilith under moonlight.

I know I can leave my billion-dollar baby in George's capable hands and go to where I'm really needed – Mystic Tides, where Lilith is waiting.

I drive there fast, taking the corner hard enough to make the tires complain. Through the broken shop window, I see Lilith unpacking boxes of books and crystals, her green-streaked hair falling across her face as she works. Her hands aren't steady. Jack stands nearby in his usual dramatic outfit, watching her with concern.

"We'll have to stack these on that shelf over there," she says, her voice soft but strained.

Jack plants a hand on his hip. "But Lil, darling, that shelf is practically disintegrating. One good sneeze and those books will avalanche to the floor."

"No choice." She blows a curl from her flushed face. "Until my insurance check materializes from the bureaucratic ether, I can't afford new shelving."

I feel the corner of my mouth curl upward. This is where I thrive—in moments of chaos that need order. I'm like all men in that I love to feel useful, to fix what's broken. And something about Lilith's gentle resilience awakens a fierce protectiveness in me I've rarely felt before. It's not that she's helpless—I've seen her stand her ground—but right now she's drowning in problems I can easily solve with a series of phone calls.

“You called?” I ask her, even though she didn’t actually call me.

She yanks the door open. "Rome!" She crashes into me, and I catch her at the waist. The scent of jasmine. My fingers in her hair, her feet lifting off the ground as I kiss her—quick but certain. Then it hits me: I've kissed her like this is normal, like I belong here, like I'm the guy who shows up when she needs someone.

“This place-” She shakes her head, tears spilling down her cheeks. “Ruined. Everything’s ruined.”

I meet her gaze. "It's all handled. Jake's crew arrives this afternoon for the flooring. Brazilian Walnut instead of pine this time—it'll hold up better against flooding. And I've ordered a new marble counter with display cases for your crystals."

She wraps her slender arms around herself, those gemstone eyes wide with worry, her whole body trembling beneath her soaked lavender sundress. Raindrops still cling to her dark curls. "Roman, please, I can't let you—"

I cut her off, my voice firm but gentle. "Nick's the best glazier in the county. You'll have a new window by sundown—double-paned, hurricane-resistant." I run my hand along the water-damaged shelving. "Patrick's crew will replace these with Brazilian Rosewood. The grain patterns are incredible—warm, rich, with swirls like caramel in coffee. It'll showcase your books and crystals perfectly." I tap the polished sample in my pocket. "Better than oak. This is right for Mystic Tides."

Lilith's eyes widen. "Roman, I can't possibly—"

"The Persian rug arrives today," I say, cutting her off. "Midnight blue with silver constellations woven through it. Museum quality, but sturdy enough to withstand another El Niño." I tilt my head, already picturing it. "And what about a stained-glass door? A celestial design to catch the morning light would be perfect." Before she can object, I'm texting Theodore. His response is immediate. "He'll be here tomorrow."

Lilith runs her fingers through her hair, tugging at the ends. "It sounds beautiful, but my insurance..." She gestures helplessly at the wreckage. "They'll only cover what was here before—pine floors, basic shelving, that cheap window. These upgrades..." She bites her lip. "I can't."

"Jack," I say with a subtle nod toward the door. "Got a minute outside?"

Jack practically dances out the door, his eyes sparkling with mischief. "Planning the honeymoon already? And do tell—any eligible bachelors in that famous Kensington lineup?"

I laugh despite myself. "None that bat for your team. Sorry to disappoint. But if I meet someone worthy, you'll be first to know." I lower my voice. "About Lilith..."

"Ah." Jack's expression softens. "Our girl doesn't take handouts—from anyone. She's got this whole independent goddess thing going on." He sighs fondly. "Put her in front of a tarot spread or a meditation circle, she's brilliant. But the business side?" He makes a crashing sound. "Double-orders inventory, mixes up the books constantly. And crises? Well, you've seen it. She needs someone, but she'd rather drown than admit it."

Roman runs a hand through his hair. "I want to help her, but she's so damn stubborn. I could transform that shop into something spectacular without even touching my main accounts."

"Let me handle this," Jack says with a wink. He sashays back inside, his voice carrying through the open door. "Lilith, honey, do you have any idea what most women would give for this kind of attention? And it's nothing to him—financially speaking." Jack's tone softens. "Look, I may not be a straight man, but I'm still a man with brothers, so I understand them. They need to feel useful. When you keep refusing his help, you're rejecting more than his money."

Her eyes widen as she gives a barely perceptible nod. "God, everything you're describing sounds like fantasy. Brazilian Rosewood shelves, hand-woven rugs, Brazilian Walnut flooring, and a stained glass entrance? I've spent nights scrolling through design sites, knowing I'd never afford a fraction of what you're offering. And we're practically strangers." She shakes her head, tucking a strand of hair behind her ear. "I can't imagine how to repay this kind of generosity."

"Lil," I lean forward, my voice softening. "Your repayment is making this the most extraordinary metaphysical bookshop anyone's ever seen. I've already visualized it in my mind—hell, I might be more excited than you are. That's all the payment I need—watching your place outshine every other shop in Los Angeles."

Her smile finally breaks through, a flash of light that hits me like a punch to the gut. Jack twirls her across the hardwood, but when he spins her toward me, I seize her waist and pull her against me. Sam Smith's "Fire on Fire" floods the room, the same damn song from the Gala—the one about two broken souls finding each other in the wreckage. My pulse hammers as her body melts into mine.

Jack clears his throat with theatrical flair. "Well, well, well," he drawls, but I barely hear him. Her eyes—those impossible topaz-jade eyes—lock onto mine, burning through me. We're just in jeans, nothing like that night at the Gala, but Christ, the electricity is the same. Maybe stronger. "I'll just... skedaddle to the boardwalk for some carbs," Jack stage-whispers, waggling his eyebrows. "Though clearly you two are about to devour each other like it's an all-you-can-eat buffet of sexual tension, so... toodles!"

But, of course, we're interrupted again. The contractors arrive right on schedule. Jake, my flooring specialist, walks in first with his crew trailing behind him. "We need to clear everything out," I tell him, gesturing at the cluttered space. "Let's load the shelves and inventory into your truck before you tear up this disaster of a floor."

For the next few hours, we form a human chain, passing books and fixtures from hand to hand until Jake's truck is packed. While his team begins demolition, I review tomorrow's schedule: Nick for the new windows, Theodore for the custom door with its stained glass celestial design that will complement my specially ordered rug. Patrick will come in with the bookshelf installation. And, last but not least, Shane will install a new marble check-out counter and marble display case, where Lilith will sell her crystals and assorted sundry items such as her Buddha statues.

When the renovations are complete, Lilith will walk through those doors and her jaw will drop. The marble, the chandeliers, the ocean view—it'll all come together perfectly. Still, even the most exquisite resort in California can't hold a candle to the way her eyes light up when she laughs.

But I can't stop thinking about those death traps she calls tires. "Lil," I say, trying to sound casual, "those tires of yours are balder than my Uncle Thomas." She rolls her eyes, but I press on. "I know a guy who can replace them today."

What I don't mention is that Mateo usually has his hands full with vehicles worth more than most people's homes. The kind with Italian names that purr like satisfied cats. Not exactly in the same league as Lilith's rust-speckled sedan. But Mateo owes me one, and besides, I'd rather replace her tires than watch her slide off the road in the next rainstorm. A new car would be ideal, but I can already picture her face if I suggested it—like I'd just proposed she grow a second head.

I pull Lilith's car into Superperformance, and Mateo's shoulders start shaking before I even cut the engine. By the time I step out, he's doubled over with laughter.

"Laugh it up, fuzzball," I say, channeling my inner Han Solo. "This is my girlfriend's ride. Show some respect." I slide my black Amex across the counter, which only makes his lips twitch harder as he tries to compose himself. Part of me wants to join in—the car is ridiculous compared to what I usually drive—but I keep my face neutral. "New tires, oil change and check her out, top to bottom, and fix anything that's wrong. And stop laughing. Not everybody drives a Rolls."

"My bad," Mateo straightens up. "Just never thought I'd see Roman Kensington step out of a decade-old Prius with tires balder than Dwayne Johnson. But we'll treat her right. Ready by closing."

"Perfect. Need to get back to Venice."

Mateo murmurs something to George, who disappears and returns with a gleaming Rolls, which I'll use to get back to the shop. As I settle into butter-soft leather, I call back, "Check everything—brakes, fluids, the works. Can't have her stranded somewhere at 2 a.m. or hydroplaning off a road."

I steer the Rolls back toward Venice, where Lilith still needs my help during her recovery. The thought hits me somewhere on the 405—I've fallen hard for this woman. Today, I drove her beat-up Prius to my mechanic, who couldn't stop laughing at the sight of me behind its wheel. The tires were so worn you could see the steel belts peeking through. And I didn't care one bit.

If that's not love, I don't know what is.

Chapter Twenty

LILITH

After two weeks of construction, my bookstore is finally finished, and I'm speechless. I run my fingers along the Brazilian Rosewood shelves, feeling their smooth grain beneath my touch. My shoes make a satisfying click against the Brazilian Walnut floors as I walk the perimeter, admiring how the midnight blue Persian rug anchors the space with its hand-stitched stars and moons. Sunlight streams through the stained-glass celestial bodies embedded in the new front door, casting colorful patterns across the marble checkout counter.

I blink back tears. Roman still hasn't seen it—he's been trapped at the resort attending to actual Danish royalty who specifically requested his personal attention. While I've been here supervising repairs and replacing inventory lost in the flood, he's been checking in daily.

This morning, as workers packed up for good, a delivery arrived—a bouquet of rare black dahlias, black Baccara roses and midnight orchids, their petals edged in silver, nestled among sprays of baby's breath and eucalyptus.The blue matches my Persian rug perfectly. Somehow, without seeing the renovations, he knew exactly what would belong here.

Jack's eyes widen as he spins in a slow circle, taking in the gleaming Brazilian Rosewood bookshelves, the Brazilian Walnut hardwood floors, the celestial stained glass mural in the middle of a new solid door, and the crystal chandelier that casts rainbow prisms across the newly polished hardwood floor.

"Oh, lady," he says, his voice dropping to a reverent whisper. Jack fluttered his hands dramatically. "Honey, this man is capital-S Smitten with you! Only a billionaire who's gone completely gaga would zhuzh up this place like a fairy godfather on steroids and send those black Baccara roses—which, FYI, cost more per stem than my first Prada knockoff. Congratulations, sweetie, you're now the proud owner of the most fabulous New Age bookstore this side of Sedona. The spirits are smiling!"

I laugh, fidgeting with the sleeve of my gauzy lavender blouse. "Oh, Jack, let's not get ahead of ourselves. Like you said, this renovation was pocket change to Roman and he seems like he wanted a project. And that project is me. That's all."

Jack rolls his eyes dramatically, his chunky silver rings catching the light as he gestures wildly around us. "Say what you want, but this is the kind of thing a man in love will do. And what are you talking about, the man needs a project? As if running a string of elite resorts that host royalty, celebrities and billionaires on the regular isn't enough of a project? Not to mention training for that MMA charity tournament in December where he's getting those gorgeous cheekbones pummeled for a good cause. No. That man needs a project like a hole in his perfectly chiseled head,

Lilith." Jack's manicured fingers curl into exaggerated air quotes when he says "needs a project." "Stop denying it. He's head over Gucci loafers for you. You're one lucky bitch, I'll give you that."

My breath catches when I spot the man of the hour coming through the door, his six-foot-four frame filling the entryway, dark hair slightly tousled from the coastal breeze.

God, every time I see him, my lungs seize, butterflies swarm like a hurricane behind my ribs, and goosebumps race across my skin. His jawline could cut glass, those piercing obsidian eyes scanning the room with the intensity of a predator.

He's devastatingly beautiful, but it's more than his chiseled features or the way his tailored navy suits hug his broad shoulders. It's more than his razor-sharp intelligence or how he shows up for me when I need him the most. It's more than how he carried me through rain-soaked streets when my shop flooded and took care of me afterwards. There's something electric between us—like two puzzle pieces clicking into place after being lost for centuries.

I doubt Roman, with his pragmatic business mind, believes in soul connections, but my tarot cards have never lied. Even as my logical side whispers it's impossible for this billionaire who commands luxury resorts across continents to choose ME, my heart recognizes the truth in how his gaze softens when it finds mine across the crowded room.

Jack is right—I'm one lucky bitch.

I gasp as we step inside. "Roman, this place is incredible!"

He surveys the space with a casual glance and the corner of his mouth lifts. "It'll do." His eyes soften when they land on me. "You look exhausted. We both deserve a break after these past two weeks. Come surfing with me today."

Surfing? My heart skips. Roman doesn't invite just anyone to join his sacred ritual. That last day over breakfast, his voice had dropped to a reverent whisper describing those Saturday mornings with his brothers—the only moments when his notorious temper truly subsides.

I've barely managed to stand up on a board twice in my life. But the thought of Roman showing me his private stretch of beach, away from the chaos of my flooded bookstore and his emergency flights to San Francisco...I can already feel the salt spray on my face, see his rare, unguarded smile.

"I'd love that," I tell him, meaning every word.

Roman grinned. "Perfect. I've got everything ready—board, wetsuit, the works. You'll meet Silas and Ansel today. Just two of the brother horde, not the whole Kensington circus at once." He pauses, then shrugs. "Though honestly, they're all pretty decent guys. I'm the family terror." A self-deprecating smile crossed his face. "Or as I prefer to call it, the one with standards. We'll swing by the resort first so you can change, then hit the waves." His eyes brightened with genuine excitement. "God, I can't wait—ocean, surfing, you."

I nudge his shoulder playfully. "The family terror? Clearly they've got the wrong Kensington brother."

Roman's eyes darken slightly. "Trust me, they don't." He runs a hand through his hair. "But around you...I don't know. I'm different." He glances away, as if embarrassed by the admission. "Even my brothers noticed. They've all stopped by since the storm to check on the resort, and every single one asked what's gotten into me." His mouth quirks up. "Connor actually checked my coffee for mood stabilizers." He reaches for my hand, his thumb tracing circles on my palm. "Turns out I don't need medication. I just need you."

I don't know what to say. I'm floating on a cloud of bliss as I walk next to him toward yet another gleaming luxury SUV—a Lamborghini Urus that sits like a crouched panther in the California sunshine, its obsidian paint job reflecting the swaying palm trees above. The curves of its aerodynamic body catch the light in a way that makes my breath catch.

I never knew Lamborghini made SUVs. I'd only seen those flashy sports cars hugging the road, driven by men with something to prove. This one's different though—practical but still impressive. I glance at Roman as he reaches for the door handle, hoping this is his only Lamborghini.

But anyhow, I wish I could tell him that he fundamentally changed me the way he says I changed him, but I really can't. My heart has always been full of light, brimming with the kind of contentment that made friends call me their "sunshine girl," but what I feel now is different—it's as if someone turned up the saturation on my already colorful world. While Roman tells me I've transformed him from stormy to serene, I can only think that he's taken my everyday joy and amplified it into something that makes my skin tingle and my chest ache with its intensity.

The door of his sleek black Lambo SUV closes with a satisfying thunk. "So," he says, his tanned fingers drumming against the leather steering wheel. "I didn't even ask you if you surfed. If you don't, that's not a biggie. I'm a great teacher." His smile reveals perfect white teeth against sun-bronzed skin.

"I have, actually," I say, adjusting the hem of my floral

sundress over my knees. "I know the fundamentals at any rate. I'm not good, though. I hope that's not a problem."

“Not at all." He chuckles, his deep voice filling the luxury car's interior as he turns the key in the ignition. "My brother Max sometimes brings his wife, Celeste, surfing with us. And she, for lack of a better word, sucks. Can't read a wave to save her life. Last time, she nose-dived three boards in a row and still insisted on paddling back out like a half-drowned cat with something to prove. Of course, that’s all moot now as Celeste has apparently given up surfing for now because she’s bonding with their baby, but she’ll be back once she actually gives up some control to the nanny.”

"So, I guess I don't need to be perfect out there, then."

"Christ, Lil, if you can paddle that little ass of yours out past the break and stand up for five seconds without eating shit, you're already outperforming my sister-in-law." I run my hand through my salt-stiffened hair, squinting against the glare bouncing off the Pacific. "Max is so goddamn gone for her that he'll waste a perfect swell playing lifeguard while the rest of us are shredding. Used to give him hell about it—called him every name in the book." I feel my jaw tighten, watching the waves curl and crash. "Now I wonder if he wasn't the smartest Kensington all along."

We get to the resort, and I go to the changing room for the beach. Polished teak doors open to a space more day spa than beach hut. Marble floors gleam under soft lighting, with plush robes hanging from wooden pegs. The showers have rainfall heads and fancy toiletries. Even the air smells expensive.

I think about the beach restrooms I knew before. The metal toilet seats that burned your thighs in summer. The cement floors always flooded with dirty water. The graffiti-covered benches. This place is definitely for the one percent.

I always hated public restrooms. The fungus in every corner, the bleach that never quite worked. Toilets without seats, or worse—with seats but covered in stains. You'd hover, trying not to breathe. But here? Clean marble, soft lighting, and actual flowers. Like everything else in this place.

Roman provided me with a wetsuit, of course—a sleek black Neoprene second skin that hugs my curves while promising to shield me from the Pacific's bone-chilling embrace. Even in summer, these waters never warm beyond a teeth-chattering sixty degrees, nothing like the bathwater waves I'd once floated in off Myrtle Beach, where the Atlantic caressed rather than shocked. But those warm southern seas come with their own price tag—monster hurricanes that could flatten a coastline in hours. Fair trade, perhaps.

I meet Roman on the private stretch of beach hidden from prying eyes, just around the rocky bend from his resort's manicured shoreline—a pristine half-mile crescent of platinum sand nestled between jagged cliffs that rise like sentinels against the horizon.

He has a beginner's surfboard just for me – a nine-foot foam monstrosity in a garish shade of aqua blue that makes me think of kiddie pools. It's nothing like his sleek six-foot fiberglass shortboard with its custom black and gold design that gleams like obsidian under the California sun. I know enough about surfing to understand why mine needs to be longer – for stability – while his shorter board lets him carve through waves with the precision of a surgeon's scalpel. I've watched enough surf competitions to not be a total novice, but my wobbly knees and uncertain balance will never match the fluid grace that seems to run in the Kensington DNA.

I see Ansel and Silas striding toward us like twin luxury yachts parting ocean waves. Both of them so gorgeous my mouth actually waters—the Kensington DNA should be studied by scientists. Ansel, the musical genius behind Kensington Recordings' global empire, tosses his sun-kissed dirty-blonde hair back from his face, revealing those hypnotic aquamarine eyes dancing with secrets and promises. His full lips curl into that trademark smirk that's launched a thousand Instagram fan accounts. Beside him, Silas exudes the quiet intensity of old money—fitting for the CEO of Kensington Jewels who personally negotiates with royalty for their precious stones. His raven-black hair, identical to Roman's, contrasts dramatically with those electric sapphire eyes framed by lashes so thick and dark they look almost artificial against his golden California tan.

Roman pulls each brother into a bear hug, then turns toward me with a hand at the small of my back. "Lilith from the Gala," he says, by way of introduction. Before I can extend my hand, they're both wrapping their arms around me like I'm a long-lost cousin. Something inside me melts a little. Growing up in a house where we greeted the mailman with hugs, this feels like the Kensington version of being handed a key to their fortress.

Ansel's eyes dance with mischief. "So you're hanging out with our very own Sonny Corleone?"

Roman's jaw tightens. "Sonny got a bad rap. Sure, he had a temper, but the man was loyal to his core. Died for it, even." He leans forward, voice dropping. "Sonny would've given you the clothes off his back. Michael would've ordered your execution without blinking. Hell, he had his own brother whacked."

"I hope Lilith's brushed up on her mob movie references," Silas says with a smirk.

Roman turns to me. "Have you?"

I offer a noncommittal shrug. Pop culture osmosis has taught me enough—the hotheaded Sonny with his fists-first philosophy, calculating Michael who'd sacrifice anyone for the family business, and poor Fredo, forever seeking approval until that final fishing trip. I study the brothers' faces, wondering which one might be their Michael. Probably none. I bite back a smile. Roman's nothing like Sonny anyway. The comparison doesn't fit him at all.

I scrunch my nose. "Mob movies aren't really my thing." The mere thought of violence flickering across a screen while I'm nestled under my hand-crocheted blanket with a bowl of lavender-salted popcorn makes my stomach twist into sailor's knots. War films with their earth-shattering explosions that make my teeth vibrate, survival stories where some poor soul always ends up as another creature's dinner, dusty westerns with their inevitable shootouts leaving crimson blooms on cotton shirts, zombie movies with intestines glistening like wet ribbons—they all leave me white-knuckled, my fingernails creating half-moon indentations in the armrest, my heart hammering against my ribcage as I dread the inevitable moment when a character I've grown attached to collapses into a lifeless heap before the credits mercifully appear. Needless to say, slasher movies with their butcher-knife gleam are the absolute last thing I'd ever voluntarily subject my sensitive soul to.

“Uh oh,” Ansel says. “Roman knows every single movie Scorsese has ever directed. You might be in trouble, Lilith. I just hope he doesn’t force you to watch a trilogy of *Goodfellas, Casino* and *The Irishman*, with *The Departed* thrown in for good measure.”

Oh. Watching a lineup like that sounds like absolute hell to me. Then again, if Roman’s by my side while I watch them, I might…be okay. Then I shake my head. No. I won't be that girl. I won't pretend to like things I abhor just because my totally hot boyfriend? Can I call Roman that yet? No. Too soon. Totally hot crush. That's it. A totally hot crush likes something and if I just say "me too," I'll lose myself. Not doing that.

"Stop," Roman says, watching my face. "If she doesn't like mob movies, she doesn't like mob movies. But you might like other Scorsese movies, like *The Wolf of Wall Street* or…"

"No, not *Wolf of Wall Street.* That one has some violence. *Hugo,*" Ansel says helpfully. "That's a pretty tame movie, set in 1931."

"*The Age of Innocence,*" Silas says. "That's based on an Edith Wharton book set in the Gilded Age. I'll bet you'd love that one."

The Age of Innocence. That reminds me of that Gala night when I thought I'd have to make do with a Victorian-era dress, before Roman came to my rescue with that glorious green halter dress that absolutely took my breath away.

Yes, I do love that movie, actually. Period dramas like that usually sweep me away, as do historical fiction and any kind of biopic or biographical fiction. Give me the lush orchestral swells of *Amadeus*, the haunting piano melodies of *Immortal Beloved*, the sweeping landscapes of *Gandhi*, the frenetic mathematical scribbles of *A Beautiful Mind*, the glittering sequins and soaring vocals of *Bohemian Rhapsody*, the grainy black-and-white footage of *A Complete Unknown*, or the kaleidoscopic Elton John spectacle of *Rocket Man* over any smoke-filled, bullet-riddled mob movie, any day of the week.

Roman's smile softens his usually sharp features, the dimple in his left cheek appearing like it does in those rare magazine photos where he's caught off-guard. "Something tells me I'll have to keep enjoying watching mob movies with my brothers or Caspian," he says, his deep voice carrying that hint of gravel that makes my skin tingle. He leans forward, the expensive fabric of his wet suit stretching across his broad shoulders. "But that's okay. I like other kinds of movies, too. All different kinds of movies, actually," he adds with a playful glint in those obsidian dark eyes, "so I'm sure we'll agree on something."

“Okay,” Ansel says. “Let’s get out there.”

My hands tremble slightly on the board as we paddle out. I catch Roman's eye, and he gives me a reassuring nod before Ansel splashes water directly into his face.

"First one to wipe out buys dinner," Ansel announces, ducking Roman's retaliatory splash.

Silas snorts. "If we went by that rule, Roman would be bankrupt by now."

Roman's scowl breaks into a reluctant grin as we position ourselves beyond the break, waiting for the perfect wave. My shoulders loosen as I watch them, these powerful men transformed into boys by the ocean.

Silas, his sun-bronzed face creasing with mischief, calls over the crash of waves. "Hey, Roman! Remember when you insisted on surfing in Puerto Rico during Hurricane Marie?" He shakes his head, salt water droplets flying from his dark hair. "Only Roman would be crazy enough to think he could conquer fifty-foot monsters in winds that could tear the roof off a house."

Roman's jaw tightens as he runs a hand through his own wet, tousled hair. "I wasn't actually going to surf that day, you moron. Max was being a complete ass, getting everyone worked up about nothing." His voice carries over the roar of the ocean. "I just needed to shut you all up. One mention of surfing during a hurricane, and suddenly everyone forgot their petty arguments."

"Yeah, but Roman," Ansel chimes in, his lean body balanced perfectly on his board, "the fact we believed you'd actually do it says everything about your reputation."

Silas paddles closer, his muscular shoulders glistening with seawater. "And then you actually took that Gulfstream out in near-tornado conditions with lightning splitting the sky. If I'd known what you were planning, I would've drugged your morning espresso until that suicidal impulse passed."

Roman's eyes darken like the gathering storm clouds on the horizon. "You know exactly why I did that."

"Noble intentions," Silas concedes with a solemn nod before his expression lightens. "Noble but certifiably insane. If you'd crashed, we would've had your Darwin Award framed next to Mom's photo."

A massive wave begins to swell behind them, a wall of blue-green glass rising from the depths. Without another word, all three brothers pivot their boards in perfect synchronicity, powerful arms cutting through the water as they catch the wave's momentum, carving elegant lines down its face while I watch, breathless with admiration.

They all paddle back, their muscular arms slicing through the glittering turquoise water. Roman turns to me, droplets cascading from his sun-kissed skin. "I'll stay behind on the next one and make sure you can get up on your board."

I smile, my heart fluttering beneath my soaked rash guard. The pressure weighs on me like the ocean itself. When the next wave swells—a towering wall of blue-green glass—I gather my courage, push up from my stomach, and wobble to my feet. My legs tremble like palm fronds in a storm as I ride the churning foam for about ten breathless feet before the board slides out from under me. The ocean swallows me whole, salt burning my nostrils, my limbs tumbling in the frothy chaos.

Meanwhile, Roman and his brothers cut through the wave, their boards gliding smoothly as they trace clean lines across its surface, riding it until it breaks on the shore.

Roman says "Good job" when we've paddled back to the lineup, his voice deep against the rhythm of the waves. Sunlight catches in his wet eyelashes. "Now, for the next wave, keep your feet shoulder-width apart, back foot angled slightly. When you feel the wave catch, pop up in one motion—don't hesitate—and bend your knees more than you think you need to." His strong hands demonstrate, one palm flat like a board while the other makes a quick, decisive hop. "Weight centered, eyes forward, not down. The board goes where you're looking."

I nod nervously, salt water dripping from my chin as I try to commit Roman's instructions to muscle memory. When the next wave swells beneath me—a glassy blue-green wall of water—I pop up to standing just as he showed me, knees bent, arms out for balance. The board glides beneath my feet, and for a glorious moment, time slows. I'm flying, cutting across the face of the wave for a good fifty feet before my ankle wobbles and I tumble sideways into the churning foam. I surface with a gasp and a grin. Progress.

Roman paddles back out to me, water streaming from his tanned shoulders. "Great job!" he calls over the crash of an incoming wave. "Next time, try to pop up faster—knees to chest in one motion. And keep your weight centered over the board. When you see a good wave coming, start paddling earlier so you catch the momentum before it breaks."

I nod. The next wave rises on the horizon. I paddle hard like Roman showed me, arms burning through the salt water. The board lurches, and I push up to my feet, balancing on the slick surface. Then I'm moving across the face of the wave, spray hitting my skin, morning light everywhere. The wave curls behind me as I ride it all the way in. My heart pounds, and I can't stop grinning, my cheeks aching. I feel the triumph in my blood. I actually did it!

Roman high-fives me when he paddles back, droplets flying from his bronzed forearm. "You were amazing!" he exclaims, his dark eyes crinkling at the corners. "You're a natural out there. A water baby."

I smile, tasting salt on my lips. For the next three hours, the four of us ride the swells. I catch three more waves, each one a rush as the board skims across the water.

Roman moves with confidence, reading the ocean's patterns perfectly. His shoulders work as he maneuvers, cutting through the foam with precision. The sun catches on his wet skin.

When he grins at me between waves, I can't believe he's looking at me—the same woman who's endured countless boring first dates—now surfing alongside a man who handles both business and waves without breaking a sweat. I'm still waiting for the catch.

Finally, the guys collapse onto their towels, breathing hard, hair wet and tangled. Roman, though, still looks ready for more. When his dark eyes meet mine, I catch a glimmer of something playful there.

"There's a secluded cove just beyond those jagged rocks," he says, pointing to where the shoreline curves out of sight. "Crystal clear water. No tourists. Let's go over there." He nods toward my faded canvas tote with its embroidered celestial symbols. "And bring your bag along."

My fingers brush the worn edges of my tarot deck inside my bag. Mom's gift, always with me. I wonder if the cards will reveal anything between us today.

I peel off my wetsuit, shivering as the damp air hits my skin. I pull my sundress over my bikini and wrap myself in my oversized sweater that smells like sunscreen.

Roman steps out of his wetsuit, water beading on his chest. He pulls on a gray hoodie, his dark hair sticking up. Though it's July, the "June Gloom" hangs over us -the locals know better than to expect true summer until mid-July, when the sun finally burns through the morning fog and stays until October's crisp evenings arrive. The June Gloom turns the Pacific slate blue beneath pewter clouds. True summer won't arrive for weeks, as any local knows.

I follow him to the cove, my sandals slipping on mossy rocks as we find a hidden strip of sand. In the tide pool between black stones, clear water reveals an underwater garden. Roman crouches down, pointing to purple sea anemones swaying with each ripple.

"Look at those," he says softly. "Aren't they beautiful?"

And they are—pulsing with life, both fragile and resilient against the constant push and pull of the ocean. I stand there watching the creatures sway delicately in the water.

My heart pounds as Roman and I find ourselves truly alone for the first time since that morning in his suite. No staff, no guests—just us. I remember the sunlight through those windows, the taste of espresso on his lips, the rough texture of his jaw under my fingertips. I'd wanted more then, and the thought that tonight I might get it makes my stomach flip.

He takes my hand, his grip warm and sure, and leads me to a cashmere blanket spread out on the sand. The sun is setting, turning the Pacific into a canvas of gold and amber.

I nestle against him and tell him about the green flash—that elusive emerald burst that appears for a split second as the sun's final curve disappears beneath the waves. "Most people go their whole lives without seeing it," I whisper, my head finding the perfect spot on his shoulder. "The atmosphere has to bend the sunlight just right, splitting it like a prism." I trace my finger along his jawline, feeling the slight stubble beneath my fingertip. "Finding you was my green flash, Roman—that one-in-a-trillion moment that happens when you've stopped looking for it."

Roman's smile crinkles the corners of his eyes. "I don't think the green flash is necessarily one in a trillion. But it's a very rare sight for sure. I've never seen it." He walks to the rocks and pulls out a bottle of champagne and two glasses from where he'd hidden them earlier, the sunset glinting off the crystal.

"I tucked this away last night, because I knew I would be spending the sunset here with you." He raises one dark eyebrow, his chiseled face softening. "Yes, I planned this whole evening down to the minute."

I can't help but laugh, the sound carrying on the salt-tinged breeze. Of course Roman has something meticulously planned. That's quintessentially him—the man who anticipates every possibility, who leaves nothing to chance.

We recline on the cashmere blanket, propped on our elbows, our shoulders nearly touching. The champagne bubbles in my glass, golden and inviting. I take a sip, tasting apple and something like toast. It hits my empty stomach fast, warming me from the inside out. One glass in and I'm already feeling it—my worries washing away with each swallow.

"So," Roman says, his voice low and intimate as he swirls the champagne in his glass, the dying sunlight turning the liquid to amber. "Would you like to do another spread for me?"

I reach for my silk-wrapped deck, which I'd tucked into my bag earlier with a strange certainty I'd need it. The cards feel warm against my fingertips, almost vibrating with potential. My heart flutters with anticipation—I can sense the universe aligning for us.

I shuffle the cards, their edges catching the sunset as I arrange them on the blanket. The reading unfolds better than I expected. The Ten of Cups shows fulfillment in our future, while The Sun promises joy ahead. In the past position sits the Three of Swords—conflict and heartbreak. Looking at the figure gathering abandoned weapons on the card, I realize this represents Roman's past, not mine. The Two of Cups forms our foundation—a soul connection. This spread tells me what I've suspected: Roman's romantic history is marked by struggle, but something better waits for us.

I trace my finger over the three of swords card, its pierced heart gleaming under the soft light. "Roman, these cards suggest you've experienced deep heartbreak. You've kept your soul locked away."

Roman's jaw tightens as he nods once. "It's not what you're thinking."

"Tell me what I'm thinking," I challenge.

"That I'm damaged goods." His voice drops lower. "That I push women away because my mother died when I was four and my father abandoned us. That I'm just another rich guy with daddy issues." He meets my eyes. "Maybe that's part of it, but there's more."

I tilt my head. "What more?"

He looks past me, his gaze distant. "I've dated incredible women—beautiful, brilliant, kind. Perfect on paper. But something was always...missing." His fingers drum against the blanket and he takes another sip of his champagne. "I could never shake the feeling that my perfect match was out there somewhere. And I refused to settle for almost-right, only to meet her later when I'd built a life with someone else." A muscle in his cheek twitches. "I couldn't bear creating that kind of mess—hurting someone who deserved better than to be my placeholder. So I waited."

I smile, my lips curving upward involuntarily. What he's trying to express through his careful, measured words—without dipping into what he'd dismissively call my "Woo-woo language"—is that deep down, he's always believed his perfect match existed somewhere in this vast world, breathing the same air, gazing at the same stars, waiting for their paths to finally cross. He refused to compromise his heart for anything less than that cosmic connection.

The realization washes over me like a warm wave—I've held that exact same belief, cradled it close through every disappointing date and lonely night. Finding your soulmate must be as miraculous as catching that elusive green flash at sunset, that split-second emerald burst when the sun kisses the horizon.

My fingers hover over the tarot spread, touching the edges of each card—The Lovers, The Sun, The Star, The Ten of Cups. I glance at Roman beside me, his profile lit by the candle between us. His breathing has slowed, and I wonder if he feels it too. Something clicks when we're together, like finding the right key for a stubborn lock.

The cards only confirm what I've suspected since that first day at the bookstore: this grumpy, beautiful man with his unexpected moments of kindness wasn't a random encounter. Some part of me has been waiting for him.

“What about Serafina? Were you serious with her?"

Roman's shoulders lift in a casual shrug. "Caspian's sister was off-limits from the start. Should've known better." He meets my eyes, his voice softening. "Never told anyone this stuff before you. It's... different with you. I can tell you things I wouldn’t tell anybody else." His fingers drum against his thigh. "Serafina and I burned hot—all chemistry, no substance. When she said 'I love you,' I couldn't say it back. Not gonna lie to a woman about that." He exhales slowly. "Marriage was on the table. Thank Christ it fell through." A shadow crosses his face. "Started thinking maybe scorching sex was all I'd ever get from a woman, you know? But something felt wrong about settling." His mouth quirks up at one corner. "When she cheated, I felt nothing but relief. Gave me the perfect exit without Caspian coming after my head." He taps his temple. "Dodged that bullet."

A contented sigh escapes me as I nestle against Roman's chest, the rhythm of distant waves rolling in. Something shifted in the air between us when he just confided in me—his voice lower, more vulnerable than I've ever heard from the infamous Kensington temper. He's letting me see behind the walls, and my heart flutters at the privilege.

Twilight deepens around us, the last traces of sunset having faded into memory. Roman's gaze finds mine, his dark eyes revealing what words cannot. A current passes between us—recognition. The missing piece found.

My voice quivers slightly as I ask, "You wanted something deeper than just physical attraction, and..."

"I searched for it with Serafina and every woman before her. Never found it. I'd stopped believing it existed at all." His eyes lock with mine. "Until you."

I close my eyes as warmth floods through me, from my chest to my fingertips. This man—this powerful, complex man who could have anyone—has never felt this way before? The connection between us vibrates like a plucked string, resonant and true. I can't find words for the symmetry of it, how perfectly our broken pieces align.

His fingers thread through my hair, and when his lips claim mine, the kiss resonates through me like a struck bell, the sensation spiraling from my lips down my spine to the soles of my feet, each nerve ending humming in perfect harmony.

His mouth is soft yet demanding, tasting of salt and something darker—whiskey, perhaps, or just the essence of him. My fingers clutch at his shoulders, feeling the heat of his skin through the thin fabric of his shirt, and when his tongue brushes mine, I can't help the small sound that escapes me, a surrender and a demand all at once. The sweetness of it borders on pain, a delicious ache blooming in my chest as if my heart has forgotten how to beat properly.

Roman draws me onto his lap, his mouth never leaving mine. I feel his strong hands slip beneath layers of fabric, finding the ties of my bikini with practiced ease. My breath catches as he deftly unties the knot. With quiet confidence, he helps me out of my sweater and coverup before laying me gently on the blanket. Despite the cool coastal air, I'm flushed with warmth—his body heat radiates between us like a living thing.

His lips trace a path downward, and when his mouth finds my breast, I arch toward him instinctively. The precise circles his tongue makes send currents of pleasure through me, first one side, then the other, each touch deliberate and knowing. Heat pools low in my belly, and I close my eyes, surrendering to the sensation, hoping this moment stretches into forever.

His voice drops to a reverent whisper. "Your breasts are so beautiful." His fingertips trace the curve where they swell from my ribcage, eyes drinking in what I've hidden under baggy cotton for most of my life. At five-foot-four and 110 lbs, my DD cup size has felt like a cosmic joke. I remember the burning shame of eighth grade gym class, layering three compression sports bras until I could barely breathe, the elastic cutting angry red lines into my skin. I remember the whispers in hallways, the leering gazes of fathers picking up their sons after school. His palms cup their weight now, thumbs brushing across my nipples as he murmurs, "They're absolutely perfect." I almost believe him.

His voice is dreamy, reverent—a low, honeyed rumble that vibrates against my flushed skin like the first tremors of an earthquake, making the fine hairs on my neck stand at attention. He kisses a slow, deliberate path down my stomach, his five o'clock shadow grazing the sensitive hollow beneath my navel, each press of his full lips leaving a trail of silvery goosebumps in its wake.

When he reaches the apex of my thighs, his warm breath fans across my most sensitive flesh, the scent of his cologne—sandalwood and something uniquely him—mingling with our shared arousal before his tongue finds my core—tentative at first, then bold, tracing intricate patterns that make my toes curl.

His fingers, calloused from years of surfing, slip inside me, curving upward with knowing precision against that perfect spot, and the dual sensation sends electric sparks racing up my spine, igniting every nerve ending until I'm arching beneath him, fingers clutching the blanket beneath me, my body a live wire of pleasure that threatens to short-circuit my very consciousness.

He peels off his sweater in one fluid motion, revealing the sculpted bronze torso that made my breath catch in my throat the other night. The moonlight traces the ridges of his abs, highlighting the thin scar that runs along his left side —a surfing accident from his youth. When he spent that night in my bed, his fingertips had hovered just above my skin, never quite touching, respecting the invisible boundary I'd drawn. But tonight, his midnight eyes hold mine with an intensity that sends shivers down my spine.

Waves crash as my heart pounds. We're tucked away in this cove, black rocks curving around us like a shield. Salt hangs in the air, catching on his lashes, dampening the sand under our feet. The ocean matters to both of us—to me, it's rhythm and connection; to him, it's where he and his brothers played before everything changed. The tide moves in and out, like the pull between us that won't let go.

I swallow hard and close my eyes as he hovers over me, his breath scorching against my core. My heart hammers wildly as the velvet steel of his manhood burns against my inner thigh. God—the sheer size of him. I knew from the way his tailored suits strained across his body what waited beneath, but feeling him now, thick and pulsing against me, sends electricity crackling through every nerve. His muscles lock tight above me, a predator barely restraining himself from devouring his prey. I gasp, unable to breathe, unable to think, my body trembling with desperate need.

He's breathing harder and harder as he goes back to the hole in the cliff, where he brought out the champagne and glasses, and comes back with a condom, which he slips on deftly. I cry out as he enters me, white-hot pleasure searing through my body like summer lightning across a midnight sky. My eyes squeeze shut as his mouth—tasting of salt —crashes against mine, tender for only a heartbeat before turning ravenous, his stubble rough against my flushed skin.

He moves with a rhythm that makes me lose track of time, sometimes fast, sometimes slow, drawing out sounds I didn't know I could make. When I call his name, it echoes against the cliffs above us. His hands—rough from saltwater and sun—grip my hips and flip me over in one smooth motion. I find myself on top, fingers pressed against his chest, moving with an urgency I can't contain.

We crash together like waves breaking against rock, my body arching, trembling, as he he's hovering over me again, driving deeper and deeper. I'm no longer just myself—I'm pure sensation, pure need. His grip bruises as he lifts me, my weight nothing to him, and when he fills me completely I cry out, my voice unrecognizable.

Our bodies crash together again and again. His breath is hot on my neck, each exhale rough against my skin. I taste iron—I've bitten my lip. The world shrinks to just us, to this heat between us that wipes my mind clean of everything but now, but him, but this need I can barely contain.

We finally explode together in a supernova of sensation, my entire body convulsing with wave after merciless wave of the most violent pleasure I've ever experienced. His release floods me, scorching and primal, marking me from within. I collapse against him, utterly devastated, every muscle trembling uncontrollably as he gasps for air against my neck, his powerful frame quaking beneath me like the aftershocks of an earthquake.

His mouth finds mine, then moves across my face, my neck, my collarbone. We lie on the blanket under the night sky, skin against skin. My fingers thread through the coarse hair on his chest as my lips brush his nipple. My body still hums with pleasure, yet I want more. This need for him has settled into my bones—a heat that won't fade. I want to be closer, to dissolve the space between us until we're one.

His breathing turns ragged against my neck, his chest heaving after that bruising kiss. I feel him hard against me again, insistent. "I'm going to make this last," he whispers as he slips on another condom, his voice dropping to that place that makes my skin prickle. He enters me with excruciating deliberation, claiming territory inch by torturous inch until I'm gasping, clawing at his back. The world narrows to just this—just us—as he fills a void I've carried my whole life without knowing. My body arches, desperate for more, for all of him. This isn't just sex. With each touch, Roman finds something in me I didn't know was there. I close my eyes and feel myself changing, opening, becoming someone new.

Each time I shatter beneath him, our bodies slick with sweat, we're barely given a moment to catch our breath before his mouth crashes back onto mine, hungry and demanding. The cycle begins again—his hands everywhere, my nails raking down his back, both of us trembling and desperate. For hours, we make love under the silver glow of stars, the ocean's roar matching the blood pounding in my ears. This primal need burns hotter with every touch, consuming us both until there's nothing left but Roman and me and this insatiable fire.

We finally lie still, catching our breath. Roman pulls the blanket over us as night gives way to morning. Right next to us, the waves break against the shore. The sky lightens as dawn is breaking - light pink, rose,violet. "Lilith," he whispers into my hair, his voice different somehow. "I've never felt this way before. Not with anyone."

I'm nestled against him, the cashmere blanket soft against our skin. "I know. Soul mates aren't just something from fairy tales," I whisper, tracing the line of his collarbone with my fingertip. "Some souls find each other lifetime after lifetime. Most people never experience it—they find someone wonderful, someone they truly love, but there's... something missing." I watch his eyes as they follow my touch. "When it's real, though, you recognize it instantly. It's beyond love—it's like finding a piece of yourself you never knew was lost." My voice catches. "That's what I felt the first time you kissed me. Like something clicking into place after being wrong my whole life."

Roman looks at me, his dark eyes penetrating like the midnight waves of his beloved Pacific. "Yes," he says, his voice a low rumble that vibrates through my chest. "As silly as I always thought something like soul mate sounds before, I know what you mean now." He leans in, his sandalwood cologne mingling with the salt air as his lips brush against my ear. "As crazy as this sounds, after we haven't known each other that long, I know this is the truth."

I smile. There's a mirror in his eyes, reflecting exactly what I feel. We've found each other in a way that defies explanation. I'll carry this certainty with me through whatever comes next—that for one night, at least, the universe aligned perfectly. Even if dawn breaks this spell, no one can take away these hours when two strangers became something impossible to name.

Chapter Twenty-One

LILITH

The next day, I'm still shaking. Every cell in my body vibrates with aftershocks from that night with Roman on the beach. Sand still clings to my hair, my skin raw where his stubble burned against my neck. I close my eyes and feel the weight of him again, pressing me into that blanket, the roar of waves drowning out everything but our breath. My soul recognized his before my mind could catch up—how else to explain the way my body arched toward him without thought?

Six times we made love, and each time I shattered completely, rebuilt only by his hands. The hunger between us was primal, violent even—teeth and nails and promises. Even now, hours later, I taste salt on my lips and don't know if it's the ocean, his skin, or my own tears when he finally broke something loose inside me that I never knew was caged.

I keep quiet about my night with Roman. It feels too private to share, especially with Jack, who'd want every detail. When he asks about the surfing and why I didn't come home, I lie through my teeth.

"We fell asleep under the stars," I say, fighting the wild flutter in my chest, desperate to keep my face neutral even as my skin feels electric with the memory of Roman's touch. If Jack catches even a hint—God, he'll pounce. He'll ask intrusive questions about every detail—how did he kiss, was he good, how big is his manhood—reducing something magical to a vulgar checklist.

I can already hear him: “Rate him on a scale of one to ten. Did he make you scream?” I can't bear it. I won't let last night become another of Jack's brunch anecdotes. What happened between Roman and me detonated something inside me. It's mine. Mine to protect. Mine to cherish. Mine to understand before the world tries to diminish it.

Jack's eyebrows shoot up. "Spill it, honey! You two finally sealed the deal, didn't you? I'm dying for details."

I swallow hard. My palms dampen as I search for a convincing lie, and I try hard to dig deep and summon any acting skill I have. Which isn’t easy, considering the last time I acted was as Tree Number Three in *Our Town* and I got stage fright.

"Jack," I say, forcing my lips into what I hope is a casual smile. "Nothing happened. After surfing, we had this amazing picnic right on the sand. We talked for hours—I mean, really talked—and I guess I dozed off against his chest. The night was so perfect, all warm breezes and stars overhead. We just... stayed there."

Jack's face falls. "Hold up. You're telling me this is the second night you've been with Mr. Tall-Dark-Handsome-and-Loaded and he hasn't made a move?" He squints at me. "Maybe my gaydar's on the fritz. I was positive he was into you."

I see the trap he's laying—trying to get me to blurt out

some steamy confession to defend Roman's masculinity. Not happening.

"He's perfectly fine," I say, meeting his gaze. "He's just... respectful. And when something does happen, you'll be the first to know."

He narrows his eyes, leaning in so close I can smell his cologne. "Bullshit," he whispers, then slaps his hand on the table. "You're lying through your teeth. That man rocked your world, didn't he? You had the kind of sex where you saw capital-G God, honey—and I'm talking full-on divine revelation, hallelujah, speaking in tongues—and would've seen stars if you weren't already seeing actual stars because, let's be honest, that man dragged you outside for some al fresco action, didn't he? The SCANDAL of it all!"

I shake my head ineffectually and go to the kitchen to make some tea. Jack follows me in there, his eyes eyes gleaming with mischief. "Fine. Keep your secrets." He leans back, a knowing smirk spreading across his face. "But I see right through you, Lilith. You're already picturing white picket fences with this guy, and God forbid I reduce your future husband to a piece of ass." He winks. "Don't worry. Your dirty little secret's safe with me."

I smile. Jack knows me so well. Too well. "Thank you," I simply say. "Now, I have to get to work and I think you do too. You're on the schedule for today after all."

Jack's eyes roll dramatically. "I come in at 11, you know that. So I'll see you there, slut." His giggle erupts, infectious, and I can't fight mine either. God, if he only knew. The truth burns inside me like a supernova—Roman didn't just make me see stars; he ripped open the cosmos.

My body still trembles with aftershocks. But what's destroying me, what I absolutely cannot confess to Jack, is how Roman detonated something in my soul. The vulnerability terrifies me. Jack's staring now, wounded by my silence, hungry for details I'm clutching to my chest like precious contraband.

I get to the shop and get busy. It's August on Venice Beach and the crowd's in full swing. One person after another comes in, looking for crystals, books, cards, candles. I have three readings scheduled, all of which will take place once Jack gets here at 11 so he can man the shop while I do my readings.

Jack gets in at 11, just like clockwork. He looks at me with side-eye, but nods. "Lilith," he says. "I'm sorry about this morning. I was thirsty, I'll admit it. But if you don't want to tell me about your soul-shattering sex with Roman, then I know you're serious about him. And all I can say is…" He smiles and mimes popping a champagne bottle. "When's the wedding?????"

I shake my head and then see a familiar face - Max. I smile at him and he comes in and gives me a hug. "Max!" I say. "What brings you here?"

He smiles. "I needed to talk to you about a few things." He points to my back room. "Can we?"

I nod, feeling apprehensive, not knowing what this is all about.

We go back to my reading room, which is private and away from the shop. "Some tea?"

He shakes his head. "No, that's okay." Then he smiles. "I see the look on your face, and it looks like you're scared that I'm here. Don't be. I don't bite." Then he grins. "Well, I won't bite you at any rate."

I laugh, too, and wait for him to tell me why he's here.

"I heard about your surfing date with my brother," he

finally says. “My other brothers, Silas and Ansel, tell me that they think Roman is gone for you. Said that he’s never looked at a woman the way he looks at you. Said that they’ve never seen Roman so patient with a woman. And just the fact that he invited you surfing at all says everything. He’s never, ever invited a woman surfing.”

My heart is pounding with every word Max is saying. If the brothers think Roman is serious about me, then…Well, they’re Roman-whisperers, at least I assume they are, so they must know.

“That’s…” I want to tell him that I feel the same about Roman, but the words escape me.

Max clears his throat. "Look, the brothers sent me as their spokesperson since we've met before—when I was hunting for those healing crystals for Celeste, remember?"

I shift in my seat, trying to read his expression. Friend or foe? Too soon to tell.

"I'm not here to give you Roman's whole biography. But there's something about our dad you should know. Whatever Roman's told you...well, it's probably not the complete picture."

"I figured as much," I say. "I'm listening."

Max's eyes soften. "Dad's actually incredible. But the addiction controlled him for years. Mom's death destroyed him. He's staying in my guest house now, and honestly? These past six months I've finally gotten to know him as an actual person, not just this...shadow from my childhood. I was barely seven when he disappeared, and our grandparents basically made him a forbidden topic."

My pulse quickens. This could be exactly what I need—a window into Roman's father that isn't clouded by Roman's anger.

"The truth is," Max continues, twisting his wedding band, "Dad chose the bottle over a noose. Jameson was his lifeline when everything else felt hopeless. He left because he knew staying would damage us all." Max rubs his temple. "Roman can't forgive him for not fighting the alcoholism, but it wasn't just about drinking. It was grief tangled up with something much darker." He pauses. "Dad recently told me something none of us knew—he battled severe depression long before meeting our mother. Multiple hospitalizations."

The pieces click together in my mind. A man already fighting his own demons, then losing his wife while raising eight boys? No wonder he drowned himself in whiskey. The alcohol wasn't weakness—it was survival.

Max's eyes drift to the window. "Turns out Dad's been fighting depression his whole life. Started on medication when he was just a kid—thirteen. Mom was the one who made sure he took his pills every day." He rubs his jaw. "None of us had a clue. Dad thought it would make him look... I don't know, broken somehow." His voice drops. "After Mom died, he just... stopped. Not on purpose. He was drowning in grief, couldn't remember to breathe, let alone take medication." Max pulls out a silk handkerchief, working it between his fingers. "The meds withdrawal hit while he was already at rock bottom. Missed doctor appointments. Told Granddad and Nana he was fine, still taking everything. But he couldn't even see straight enough to save himself with the very thing that had kept him going all those years. Just kept falling."

“So, your father…”

Max nods. "The drinking controlled him, not the other way around. Dad said he needed alcohol to blur out reality

—everything hurt too much when he was sober. There were stretches when we were kids, when he'd stay clean for a while, months at a time. We thought those were the good times." Max's voice drops. "For him, they were hell. He'd white-knuckle it for our sake, but after tucking us in, he'd sit alone with that revolver in his lap, just... contemplating." Max rubs his face. "That's why he left instead of getting help. He was convinced the booze was keeping him alive. When he wasn't drinking, death felt like his only other option—every single day, every waking moment."

I nod. "And now?"

"He's thriving. Got a job at Whole Foods while developing this passion project he's been dreaming about since getting back on his feet." He shakes his head with a grin. "And get this—he's about to propose to my mother-in-law. Celeste and I are going to be step-siblings."

I can't help but laugh. "That's wild."

"Right? We joke about it, but honestly? I'm rooting for them. It's not just that he's functioning again—he's genuinely happy. Taking his medication consistently for the first time since we lost Mom." His expression turns earnest. "Look, I'm sure Roman's painted his own picture of our father. I just wanted to offer another perspective." He hesitates. "Maybe you could help soften Roman's stance? Dad adores him—adores all of us—and this estrangement is crushing him."

"I'll try my best."

"Thank you. Silas and Ansel tell me Roman's completely smitten with you, which is uncharted territory for my brother." His smile returns. "The women who've pursued Roman—you wouldn't believe it. These accomplished, gorgeous socialites completely unraveling when he ended things. Showing up uninvited, blowing up our phones

- not just Roman's phone, but all of us brothers' phones too - tearful confrontations—the works. And Roman? Completely unmoved. But with you? Different story entirely. That's why I think you might be the key to healing this rift between him and Dad."

Oh, just hearing that fills my heart with so much joy… Roman's never been serious about a woman, but these guys think that I might be different? Me? Talk about feeling like Cinderella.

"Well, Max, I'll do what I can."

"Thanks." He looks at his watch. "Well, gotta get back to the studio. Take care, Lilith."

I go home after a long day at work and freeze in the doorway of my apartment. Roman Kensington is in my kitchen, dishing out Chinese food onto my mismatched plates while my cat Gracie winds between his legs, purring for scraps.

"There you are," he says, looking up with a rare, genuine smile. He gestures to the spread on my tiny table where two candles are already lit. "Jack said orange chicken and moo shoo pork would win you over. And this..." He holds up a bottle of Fetzer Sundial Pinot Grigio like it's a prized vintage. "Jack says it's your favorite wine."

The sight of a billionaire who probably has sommeliers on speed dial and no-doubt has an entire wine cellar at home pouring twelve-dollar wine makes my chest tighten with something unexpected.

"Speaking of Jack," I say, dropping my bag, "where is my roommate hiding?"

Roman's smile turns sheepish. "I might've financially encouraged him to visit Steve and Benji tonight."

I bite my lip. Those three together means chaos somewhere in Venice Beach tonight, but for once, I'm grateful for Jack's absence.

We devour orange chicken, moo shoo pork and lo mein from white paper cartons, chopsticks clicking against cardboard as we pass the bottle of cabernet back and forth, not bothering with glasses. We eat the food on the coffee table in front of my couch while binge-watching *Friends*. When the last noodle is gone and the wine bottle stands empty on my coffee table, I find myself leaning toward him, my fingers brushing against the silk of his hair as our lips meet, tasting of soy sauce and something sweeter.

Before I know it, we're in my bed, my skin tingling where his calloused fingertips trace invisible figure-eights across my collarbone, down the ladder of my ribs. Roman's dark eyes, flecked with subtle green in the dim lamplight, lock with mine as he moves inside me—not with last night's wild beach frenzy that left sand in the sheets, but with a deliberate, measured rhythm that makes my breath catch in my throat. Each slow, deep thrust makes me see stars, my body a live wire reaching ground. His solid weight above me is both anchor keeping me from floating away and wings lifting me higher, and when his warm lips brush the sensitive hollow below my ear, tasting faintly of salt and whiskey, I arch into him, feeling the vast universe contract to just this singular moment—his thundering heartbeat against my flushed chest, the cool midnight-blue silk of his sheets against my damp back, and the exquisite coiling tension building between us like a powerful tide rushing inevitably toward shore.

Again and again, we make love like this, his calloused hands tracing fire across my skin, my fingernails leaving crescent moons on his broad shoulders. The sheets tangle around our ankles as we move together, the moonlight casting silver shadows across the planes of his face. Until finally, around 2 in the morning, after making love for six hours, we collapse in a tangle of limbs, skin glistening with sweat, breath coming in ragged gasps. He lays next to me, his muscular arm a warm weight across my waist, while I trace lazy patterns through the dark curls on his chest, feeling his heartbeat gradually slow beneath my fingertips.

I take a deep breath as I hear his heartbeat, strong and steady beneath my ear like waves against the Palos Verdes cliffs.

"Lilith," he says, his voice a low rumble that vibrates through his chest into mine. "I've never felt like this before. This sense of peace. Somehow, being with you tames the chaos in my head."

I sigh against his warm skin, breathing in his scent of sandalwood and salt. Max's words echo in my mind—their father, battling the dark clouds of depression since he was barely a teenager. The weight of this secret presses against my ribs, begging for release.

But the confession crystallizes in my throat, sharp and immovable.

We collapse into sleep, limbs entwined, my cheek pressed against the thundering drum of his heart, his arm locked around my waist like I might vanish if he loosens his grip. Dawn explodes across the room, setting fire to the sheets as his hardness burns against me again. He claims me in one desperate thrust, swallowing my gasp with a savage kiss that bruises my lips. Our bodies collide—slick skin, ragged breath—as he drives deeper, harder, until I'm clawing the sheets, crying his name. Then he dresses with furious reluctance, his goodbye kiss tasting of promises and possession.

As he leaves, pressing a lingering kiss to my temple, the

truth about Max remains trapped behind my lips. A premonition shivers down my spine—this unspoken secret will return like a boomerang, cutting through whatever fragile peace we've found.

As much as I pray, fingers clutching my moonstone pendant, that it won't.

Chapter Twenty-Two

LILITH

I go home after a long day at work and freeze in the doorway of my apartment. Roman Kensington is in my kitchen, dishing out Chinese food onto my mismatched plates while my cat Gracie winds between his legs, purring for scraps.

"There you are," he says, looking up with a rare, genuine smile. He gestures to the spread on my tiny table where two candles are already lit. "Jack said orange chicken and moo shoo pork would win you over. And this..." He holds up a bottle of Fetzer Sundial Pinot Grigio like it's a prized vintage. "Jack says it's your favorite wine."

The sight of a billionaire who probably has sommeliers on speed dial and no-doubt has an entire wine cellar at home pouring twelve-dollar wine makes my chest tighten with something unexpected.

"Speaking of Jack," I say, dropping my bag, "where is my roommate hiding?"

Roman's smile turns sheepish. "I might've financially encouraged him to visit Steve and Benji tonight."

I bite my lip. Those three together means chaos somewhere in Venice Beach tonight, but for once, I'm grateful for Jack's absence.

We devour orange chicken, moo shoo pork and lo mein from white paper cartons, chopsticks clicking against cardboard as we pass the bottle of cabernet back and forth, not bothering with glasses. We eat the food on the coffee table in front of my couch while binge-watching *Friends*. When the last noodle is gone and the wine bottle stands empty on my coffee table, I find myself leaning toward him, my fingers brushing against the silk of his hair as our lips meet, tasting of soy sauce and something sweeter.

Before I know it, we're in my bed, my skin tingling where his calloused fingertips trace invisible figure-eights across my collarbone, down the ladder of my ribs. Roman's dark eyes, flecked with subtle green in the dim lamplight, lock with mine as he moves inside me—not with last night's wild beach frenzy that left sand in the sheets, but with a deliberate, measured rhythm that makes my breath catch in my throat. Each slow, deep thrust makes me see stars, my body a live wire reaching ground.

His weight pins me down yet somehow lifts me up. When his lips touch below my ear, tasting of salt and whiskey, I arch against him. The world shrinks to just this—his heartbeat on my chest, my sheets cool against my back, and the tension building between us like a tide coming in.

Again and again, we make love like this, his calloused hands tracing fire across my skin, my fingernails leaving crescent moons on his broad shoulders. Until finally, around 2 in the morning, after making love for six hours, we collapse in a tangle of limbs, skin glistening with sweat, breath coming in ragged gasps. He lays next to me, his muscular arm a warm weight across my waist, while I trace lazy patterns through the dark curls on his chest, feeling his heartbeat gradually slow beneath my fingertips.

I take a deep breath as I hear his heartbeat, strong and steady beneath my ear like waves against the Palos Verdes cliffs.

"Lilith," he says, his voice a low rumble that vibrates through his chest into mine. "I've never felt like this before. This sense of peace. Somehow, being with you tames the chaos in my head."

I sigh against his warm skin, breathing in his scent of sandalwood and salt. Max's words echo in my mind—their father, battling the dark clouds of depression since he was barely a teenager. The weight of this secret presses against my ribs, begging for release.

But the confession crystallizes in my throat, sharp and immovable.

We collapse into sleep, limbs entwined, my cheek pressed against the thundering drum of his heart, his arm locked around my waist like I might vanish if he loosens his grip. Dawn explodes across the room, setting fire to the sheets as his hardness burns against me again. He enters me in one desperate thrust, swallowing my gasp with a savage kiss that bruises my lips. Our bodies collide—slick skin, ragged breath—as he drives deeper, harder, until I'm clawing the sheets, crying his name. Then he dresses with furious reluctance, his goodbye kiss tasting of promises and possession.

As he leaves, pressing a lingering kiss to my temple, the truth about Max remains trapped behind my lips. A premonition shivers down my spine—this unspoken secret will return like a boomerang, cutting through whatever fragile peace we've found.

As much as I pray, fingers clutching my moonstone pendant, that it won't.

Chapter Twenty-Three

ROMAN

It's been a week since those magical nights with Lilith, and reality has come crashing back. Cameron's summoned another "mandatory" Kensington Brothers meeting. Since us brothers are in the same town for an extended period of time, Cameron, ever the opportunist, is making damn sure we suffer through family bonding. Lucky fucking me.

At least the powwow will be taking place at Max's cliff-side estate. I've always loved Max's palatial retreat—terra-cotta tiles warming under the California sun, bougainvillea cascading over whitewashed walls, and floor-to-ceiling windows that frame the Pacific like priceless artwork. The infinity pool seems to melt into the horizon, creating that perfect illusion of endless blue that only twenty million dollars can buy.

It's the kind of place—with its sprawling backyard and those sturdy oak trees perfect for treehouses—that I'll probably buy once I settle down. My steel and glass penthouse high above Los Angeles has its charms, but it's no place for sticky fingers and hide-and-seek. And now I can suddenly picture Lilith there—in that hypothetical backyard, maybe with a curly-haired toddler on her hip. The thought doesn't terrify me like it should.

When I arrive at Max's sprawling Malibu estate, the circular driveway already lined with my brothers' luxury vehicles, I discover the real purpose behind this gathering. The mahogany conference table in Max's home office—a room we only use for serious family business—has been set with eight identical leather portfolios, each embossed with our initials in gold.

Of course there's a formal agenda; there always is with us Kensingtons. We're not the type to spontaneously grab beers and pizza on a Tuesday, save for birthdays or holidays when obligation dictates. No, when all eight of us are commanded to appear, something significant is brewing. And as I flip open the leather folio with "RK" gleaming on its cover, I finally understand why we've been summoned today.

And there's Serafina, perched at the table like she belongs here. I shake my head. Of course she'd show up—minority shareholder on Granddad's Kensington International board and never one to miss flaunting it. No one bothered to mention this was a goddamn boardroom ambush rather than the casual sit-down I'd been promised.

Goddamn it. This little meeting is a set up, plain as day. I suspect this when I see Sera. My suspicion is confirmed when my father's weathered face appears in the doorway of Max's mahogany-paneled office, those familiar crow's feet crinkling around eyes that mirror my own.

I shake my head, my fingers curling into fists against the polished conference table. How dare they? Cameron invited me with his usual cryptic text—just a time and place, no details—and sure, with eight Kensington brothers under one roof, shit always goes down. But this? This crosses a line.

My jaw locks tight enough to crack a walnut, teeth grinding as I stare at the man who walked out twenty-two years ago. The familiar rage bubbles up like lava, hot and destructive.

I'm going to need Lilith's cool hands on my temples tonight, her lavender scent washing over me as she whispers ridiculous affirmations that always seem to work. And Caspian—I'll text him for an emergency session at the gym, where I can pummel the heavy bag until my knuckles bleed through the wraps. We've been sparring twice weekly, but with the tournament looming, I'll need more mat time anyway.

Still, I plant my Italian leather shoes firmly on Max's herringbone floor. The old Roman would've already slammed the door hard enough to rattle the hinges. But after those magical nights with Lilith, something shifted. I'm still seething, but I remain seated, white-knuckling my way through civility.

I shoot a death glare at Cameron, who shifts uncomfortably in his Italian leather chair, his tanned face flushing. His eyes drop to the polished mahogany table between us. He knows exactly what he did.

Cameron clears his throat, the sound echoing in our father's cavernous study. "We all know why we're here. Everybody but Roman anyways."

Everybody but Roman? The familiar acid burn of betrayal rises in my chest. This just gets worse by the second, like watching a five-star resort crumble in slow motion.

So, the rest of my brothers—all seven of them sitting around me with their identical Kensington jawlines—have been privy to information I haven't. And of course I'm the last to know. *Way to go guys, make me feel like I'm even more on a deserted island.* I cross my arms over my chest, the fabric of my shirt pulling tight across my shoulders, and continue drilling holes into Cameron with my glare.

Cameron leans forward in his leather chair, fingers steepled under his chin. "Roman," he says in that practiced compassionate voice—the one with the slight vocal fry at the end that makes my jaw clench and my temples throb. "The reason why you have not been in the loop on this is because all of us brothers have been trying to get something together before including you, because we know that you're going to be a hold out. We didn't want you to get in on the ground floor of this, because..." His voice trails off, Adam's apple bobbing as he swallows hard.

Connor jumps in, his square jaw set with determination. "What Cameron's trying to say is that we all knew that you would try to sabotage it from the beginning, so we wanted to get the details worked out before we included you in it."

My fingers curl into fists against the mahogany table, knuckles whitening. I can't wait to find out what they're talking about. Whatever it is, it's clearly something that's going to make me want to flip this entire conference table and pummel all of them with my bare hands until their designer clothes are stained with blood.

I level a gaze at them that could freeze hellfire. "Go on," I say, my voice dangerously quiet. Everyone except my father. Him, I refuse to acknowledge. One glance in his direction and I might snap completely. The Verde board of directors wouldn't appreciate having to explain a homicide to their shareholders, so I keep my eyes fixed elsewhere, jaw clenched so tight my teeth might crack.

Cameron clears his throat, his Adam's apple bobbing

nervously beneath his crisp collar. "As you know, Roman, our father has been recovering from a decades-long alcohol addiction and has been stocking organic produce at Whole Foods while he tries to rebuild his shattered life. And our father now considers himself fully recovered—he still attends his twice-weekly meetings in that dingy church basement, but swears the burning urge to drink has finally subsided. He's practically glowing with Patricia Jenkins, and there might even be wedding bells on the horizon. He's currently occupying the poolside guest house at Max's Malibu estate..."

Oh, really? Dad is lounging at Max's oceanfront paradise now, is he? Complete fucking news to me. Then again, anything involving Dad would be news to me considering my brothers tiptoe around the subject like it's a sleeping bear with a hangover.

"Well," Cameron continues, fidgeting with his platinum wedding band that he still wears years after his wife was killed in that car accident, "Max thought it would be healing for Dad to bond with his first grandchild," which explains the guest house situation. "The point is, Dad is finally stable, sober, and eager to channel his energy into a meaningful project." Cameron's steel-blue eyes lock onto mine with laser focus, and suddenly I feel seven pairs of Kensington eyes burning into me from around the table. They're all holding their breath, waiting to see if Mount Roman will erupt or stay dormant. And, truth be told, I'm wondering the same fucking thing.

I tilt my head back, staring at the ornate crown molding of the ceiling, and Lilith's face materializes in my mind—those topaz eyes, that crooked smile. *Yes.* The tightness in my chest loosens, like a fist unclenching. When I lower my gaze back to my brothers, they're frozen in a tableau of caution

—Cameron's jaw clenched, Ansel's fingers drumming silently on his thigh, Max shifting his weight from one Italian leather shoe to the other.

"Go on," I say, my voice deceptively calm. Then I lock eyes with Cameron, my stare as sharp as a surgeon's scalpel. "And if you want me to say yes to any fool thing you're going to present to me, you better not have him present it." No need to specify who "him" is. The temperature in the room drops five degrees at the mere suggestion of our father.

Cameron's shoulders tense as he inhales deeply, his knuckles whitening as he nervously clenches his fists. "Now, as you probably know, Roman, our father has been living for years on Uncle Thomas' farm in England—that sprawling estate with the stone cottage and rolling green pastures. What you don't know," he continues, voice dropping to nearly a whisper, "is that between milking Holsteins and tending those prized heirloom tomatoes, Dad's been obsessing over blueprints for a chain of eco-friendly hotels. Twenty years he's hunched over Thomas' antique oak desk, sketching solar panels and rainwater collection systems. Thomas—with his Greenpeace t-shirts and that compost heap bigger than my first apartment—sparked something in Dad. It started as late-night conversations over home-brewed ale, but now?" Cameron's eyes meet Roman's. "Dad's got detailed renderings that would make your architects weep."

I can feel my jaws clenching so hard my molars might crack. The vein in my temple throbs like a countdown timer. "Let me fucking guess." My voice drops to a dangerous whisper. "You want to brand this chain of eco-friendly resorts as Kensington Properties, so that Dad's concept can capitalize on the Kensington name. So that people will flock to his resorts thinking that I'm behind it."

Heat crawls up my neck, my skin tight as a drum. "Absolutely fucking not. No fucking way." I finally look at my father, whose watery green eyes dart away like frightened fish. "Dad, how dare you? How fucking dare you?" My fist comes down on the mahogany table, rattling the crystal water glasses. "You leave us for over two decades, no word, now you're here and you want to ask me to help you launch a resort chain? Goddamn, that's probably the richest thing I've ever heard."

I slam back into my chair, knuckles white against the armrests. Cameron's lost his goddamn mind. He knows—KNOWS—how I feel about that bastard who calls himself my father. Twenty-two years. Twenty-two FUCKING years he was gone, and now he wants to ride my coattails?

My blood is practically boiling under my skin. They're trying to hijack everything I've built, every sleepless night, every deal I clawed my way through. The Kensington name on my resorts means something because I MADE it mean something. And they want to slap that prestige onto his properties? I'd sooner burn my entire empire to the ground. Cameron, my brothers, my father—they can all go to hell if they think I wouldn't see through this pathetic scheme.

Cameron leans forward in his leather chair, his expensive watch catching the sunlight streaming through the floor-to-ceiling windows of Max's office. "Now, Roman," he says, his voice taking on that placating tone he's used since we were kids. "Hear me out. You have a name in the resort business. One of the most prestigious names, if not the most prestigious. The guests you host are royalty with their private jets and entourages, business titans who close billion-dollar deals in your conference rooms, A-list celebrities hiding behind designer sunglasses. They'll still flock to your marble-floored lobbies."

I narrow my eyes. "Cut the crap, Cam. I can see right through your sweet talk. Whatever bad news you're about to drop, no amount of flattery is gonna soften the blow. Just saying."

He nods. "Noted." And then goes on with his fool idea. "Dad's new concept won't interfere with your brand at all. He'll be chasing a completely different clientele—the kind of wealthy eco-conscious elites who glide through Malibu in matte-black Teslas and custom Lucid Airs with sustainably harvested walnut dashboards. The type who host charity galas for endangered butterflies while wearing vintage Rolexes, who demand their five-star luxury be wrapped in reclaimed bamboo and organic linen. They'll pay triple for bedding hand-stuffed with ethically sourced Mongolian cashmere, expect their heated infinity pools to run on rooftop solar arrays, and won't touch a morsel unless the menu specifies which local farm grew each microgreen garnishing their plates. And we'd like to fold it into your Verde resorts, so it could be a subsidiary or an off-shoot of the Verde name. It'll be called 'Sunstone by Kensington.'"

I narrow my eyes, feeling the muscle in my jaw twitch the way it always does when Dad comes up. "So, Dad will steal Leonardo DiCaprio from me, then." My fingers tighten around my water glass. "Because Leo's passion is saving the planet. Right now, he stays in my presidential suites when he visits overseas. But Dad will snag him right out from under my nose, along with his Hollywood entourage and all that influence."

I slam the glass down, clear liquid sloshing over the rim. "No. I won't have Dad riding my coattails after twenty-two years of nothing. Dad can build his eco-resort empire, but the Kensington name stays with me. If he tries to use it, I swear to God, I'll drain every account I have fighting him in court. And as for this concept being folded into Kensington Properties as an off-shoot of Verde, cold day in hell comes to mind."

"Roman," Max pipes up, leaning forward in his Italian leather chair, his Rolex glinting under the chandelier. "I've been working with Dad on this concept for several months. He had everything meticulously mapped out—blueprints, sustainability reports, projected financials—when he arrived in Malibu. He was trembling when he first showed me, afraid we'd slam the door in his face. But once I saw what he'd created..." Max's eyes light up like emeralds catching sunlight. "I absolutely love it. Every A-lister from Malibu to Beverly Hills would kill to stay there. The solar panels alone are revolutionary, and the water reclamation system would cut usage by sixty percent. If Dad launches his flagship here in California, the waitlist will stretch to next summer before we even break ground." He runs his manicured fingers through his sun-kissed hair. "But yes, we need the Kensington name. That five-star reputation you've built. One word—Kensington—and investors will be throwing money at us."

Max fixes those infuriating green eyes on me, the same eyes that have graced magazine covers and closed million-dollar deals. His chiseled jawline tightens as he waits for my response. The golden boy. The Ken doll with perfect teeth and dimples that could charm the devil himself. But now I see past the polished veneer to the snake beneath.

I grip my water glass until my knuckles turn white.Yes, I've secretly always blamed him for the disintegration of our family, which is totally unfair. Now I have legitimate grounds for loathing him. He's been conspiring with our father behind my back, plotting to leverage my ten years of sleepless nights building this empire, all so Dad can slap our name on his eco-fantasy and pretend he didn't abandon us when we needed him most.

Acid rises in my throat as I clench my jaw. *Don't lose it, Roman. Don't fucking lose it.* I squeeze my eyes shut and reach for the memory of Lilith—her sun-dappled skin against mine on the beach, the salt air in her hair when I thought about those three words I'd never given anyone. But the image shatters. Even she can't calm the tremor in my hands.

I force my voice into something controlled, each word precise as a knife. "Max. You went behind my back with him? Developed this whole concept in secret and then what—thought I'd just smile and nod?" My gaze sweeps across my brothers' faces. "Who else was part of this little conspiracy?"

"No one else," Cameron says, shifting his weight. "Just Max. He and Dad have been holed up planning this for months since Dad moved into the guest house. They brought it to us after everything was finalized. And now—"

"And now I'm supposed to just roll over and accept it?" I cut him off. "This won't touch any of your businesses. But mine? Dad's trying to piggyback on everything I've built. Not happening. And for the record, I find it fucking laughable that any of you thought I'd lift a finger to help the man who walked out on all of us twenty-two years ago."

“Rome,” Max says.

I slam my fist on the mahogany conference table. "Don't. Just fucking don't." My voice echoes off the floor-to-ceiling windows overlooking the Pacific. I rise slowly, my six-foot-four frame casting a shadow as I lock eyes with each brother—Cameron's resigned gaze, the twins' matching scowls, Ansel's downturned mouth, Max’s practiced innocent look. I deliberately avoid the weathered face at the end of the table and I also avoid looking at Sera.

My jaw clenches so tight I taste blood. "Now, hear this, every last one of you. It will be a cold day in hell before I let Dad piggyback off what I've built. Ten years. Eighty-hour weeks. My resort empire, constructed brick by bloody brick while he was God knows where." My voice drops to a dangerous whisper. "Blood, sweat, and tears doesn't begin to cover it." I lean forward, knuckles white against the polished wood. "Cold day in fucking hell before the man who couldn't send so much as a birthday card for over twenty years uses my reputation." I turn to Max, whose defiant expression falters. "And you. Try launching that eco-resort using my name, and I'll bury you in litigation. I'll drain every account I have fighting you in court. Don't.Even.-Think.About.It."

I get up out of my chair, the mahogany legs scraping against Italian marble as I push back with enough force to nearly topple it. My jaw clenches so tight I can feel a vein throbbing at my temple. There's only one person I want to see right now—Lilith. But the click of Sera's heels echoes behind me as I storm through the grand foyer.

Sera's heels click rapidly behind me as I stride toward my Aston Martin. The gunmetal finish catches the sunlight under the resort's terracotta-tiled portico.

"Roman, wait!" Her voice rises with desperation. "That ambush wasn't my doing, I swear."

I keep walking, keys already in hand.

"Please," she persists, "let me make it up to you. Dinner at Adelaide's—my treat."

I know her game. Adelaide's isn't just any five-star restaurant—it's the crown jewel of her Beverly Hills hotel, The Blackwood.

"Sure, whatever," I mutter, hitting the unlock button.

"Saturday at eight, then!" She sounds triumphant as I slide into the driver's seat.

I nod curtly and pull away, my tires squealing slightly against the pavement. Twenty minutes later, I'm pushing open the door to Mystic Tides, the scent of sandalwood incense hitting me immediately.

Jack glances up from behind the counter where he's wrapping crystals in tissue paper for a customer. "Well, hello there, Mr. Gorgeous," he calls out with a wink.

My leg bounces nervously as I drop into one of Lilith's worn leather chairs—one of the few pieces that made it through the flood. Jack finishes with his customers before practically skipping over to join me.

"So," he says, leaning forward conspiratorially, "Lilith's thinking about bringing Gracie in as our shop cat. Thoughts? I told her I'd consult the Roman oracle before she makes any decisions. Cat allergies and all that."

A smile tugs at my lips despite my mood. There's something disarming about how Jack treats my opinion like gospel. I'm accustomed to deference—it comes with the territory—but this feels different. Genuine. Even Lilith seems to value my input, though she rarely asks directly. Maybe she doesn't need to.

"Cameron was just telling me about this," I say, leaning back. "Cat allergies can trigger serious asthma attacks in some people. Not life-threatening usually, but definitely lawsuit material. She might want to reconsider, much as she loves that furball."

Jack sighs. "That's exactly what I said to her. But she's been moping around about leaving Gracie by herself all day. I suggested getting another cat to keep her company, and I think she's warming up to the idea." His manicured fingers squeeze my forearm. "What's your vote for Gracie's new playmate? You've seen Gracie—mostly white with those black patches. I'm leaning toward a calico or maybe one of those all-black ones. Black cats get passed over at shelters, you know. Could be Lilith's good deed for the month."

I exhale slowly, fighting back a smirk. Cat color coordination—what a luxury to have such trivial concerns. "I'm sure Lilith will be happy with whatever she chooses."

"Obviously," Jack's eyes roll dramatically. "But what would you pick?"

"Calicos have always caught my eye," I admit, glancing at my watch. I'm dying to know how much longer Lilith's reading will take, but barging in and demanding her attention would be tactless. That brand of rudeness I reserve for my brothers. Lilith deserves better—she gets the version of me that remembers his manners.

Jack gives a knowing nod. "Calicos. I'll let her know you're a fan. So you're into the lady cats too, huh? That's Lilith's preference. I keep telling her it's all the same—I mean, who can even tell without looking under the hood?" He waves his hand dismissively. "But she swears the males get aggressive and spray everywhere. Between us, I think it's just her imagination. What's your take?"

I shrug in agreement. Biology dictates that calicos are almost always female, same with tortoiseshells, while orange tabbies skew male. Not that I've ever paid attention. If Lilith has her preferences, that's her business. But Jack's right—I couldn't spot the difference between a male cat and a female one if my life depended on it. Cats have never been my thing, but for Lilith? I'll learn to appreciate the furry little creatures. Small price to pay.

My fingers tap a staccato rhythm against the leather

armrest as I check my Rolex for the third time in five minutes.

"Just a few more minutes," Jack says, nodding toward the vintage wall clock. "Though fair warning—you might want to brace yourself when you see who's in there with her."

"Let me guess. Walsh?" The name tastes bitter on my tongue.

I get my answer with the unmistakable lilt of an Irish accent as Blake emerges from behind the beaded curtain. He wraps Lilith in a lingering embrace, his lips brushing her cheek. My knuckles go white. The muscles in my jaw twitch. After that ambush from my brothers this morning, my self-control hangs by a thread.

Blake spots me first while Lilith turns away to straighten her reading room. His eyes widen in recognition before he quickly adopts an innocent expression, gliding past as if we're strangers. The look I return could freeze hell itself.

I push through the beaded curtain into Lilith's reading room. The scent of sage hits me first, then I see her—back turned, arranging crystals and shuffling cards on the velvet-draped table. When she spins around, her face brightens. "Roman! What a nice surprise!"

My jaw tightens. The image of Blake's arms around her, his lips pressed to her cheek, flashes through my mind. Add that to the ambush my brother just pulled, and I'm a powder keg with a lit fuse.

I came here thinking she'd calm me down. Big mistake. Now jealousy's crawling under my skin like fire ants.

She moves in for a hug. I stand there, arms dead at my sides. Something flickers in her eyes—hurt, confusion—before she retreats to her side of the table. "So," she says, matching my frost with her own. "How are you?"

I drop into the red velvet chair across from hers, forearms on the table. "I wanted your take on something, but now..." I exhale. "Hell if I know why I'm even here."

She nods. “Take?”

I sigh, rubbing the tension at the back of my neck. "Yeah. My father wants to use my name to launch his own resort chain. It'll be one of those eco-friendly resorts—you know the type. Gleaming solar panels catching the California sun, reclaimed water trickling through designer fountains, recycled wood polished to a high shine. They'll serve overpriced locally sourced cocktails with those soggy paper straws that dissolve before you finish your drink. The bathrooms will have those frustrating low-flow toilets you have to flush three times. Oh, and get this—" I lean forward, voice dripping with sarcasm, "—mattresses stuffed with cashmere that cost more than most people's monthly rent. Rainwater harvesting systems visible through glass floors, cleaning staff armed with biodegradable products, and entire structures built from imported bamboo. Every ingredient on the menu will be sustainable and local, with the farm's entire life story printed on recycled paper menus that feel like sandpaper."

Lilith's face brightens. "Oh wow, that's wonderful news! Your father's really turning things around. I mean, the Whole Foods job was a good start, but this—this shows real commitment to rebuilding. Men often need these tangible projects to process their emotions, you know? This could be exactly what he needs."

My jaw tightens. "Wait—how exactly do you know where my father works?"

“Oh. Right.” Then she pauses for a few seconds, seconds that seem to drag on forever. “Uh, Max stopped by yesterday," she says with a shrug that’s supposed to look casual, but is masking her fear. "I think he was doing the protective brother thing, scoping me out." Her smile widens. "He filled me in about your dad. The parts you've been... skipping over."

Something hot and dangerous unfurls in my chest. Not jealousy—I don't think there's anything between them—but betrayal. My own brother and Lilith, comparing notes on me.

I rise to my feet, hands clenching involuntarily. "What else did Max tell you about me?"

"We weren't discussing you," Lilith says quickly, then hesitates. "Well, not directly. He just thought I should understand the full situation with your father. He mentioned that you might be..." She trails off, shaking her head. "Look, he was just concerned I wasn't getting the complete picture."

I turn away, my jaw clenched. "So you're siding with Max? Is that it, Lilith? My own brothers won't back me up, and now you're joining their little mutiny? Shipping me off to Elba like some fallen emperor?"

"Roman, I don't even know what Elba is," Lilith says, her voice steady as still water. "Listen to me. Everyone processes loss in their own way. Your father—he got lost in his grief. The drinking made it worse, kept him away longer. I'm not saying what he did was right." She leans forward, her eyes searching mine. "But holding onto this anger—what's it giving you? What purpose does it serve?"

My teeth grind together. "So when exactly did my brother stop by?"

Her gaze meets mine for a flash, then drops to the floor like a stone. "Roman, I tried to bring it up, but the timing never felt right."

Son of a bitch. Max was here before I showed up at her townhouse last night, and she kept it from me. I study her face, searching for other secrets. If she hid this, what else lurks beneath that innocent expression? What other truths will she decide I don't need to know?

I feel my upper lip curl into a sneer, my jaw clenching so hard that a dull ache spreads through my temples. The bitter taste of betrayal coats my tongue. "Crystal clear whose team you're on." My voice drops to a dangerous whisper, each word sharp as broken glass. "Guess I misread everything about you. Was it all just a gold-digger's long game? Did our night on the beach and the night in your bedroom mean anything at all?"

The words leave my mouth like poison darts, and I instantly want to snatch them back. My brain screams at me to stop, that Lilith has never once shown interest in my wealth, that I'm only lashing out because her honesty feels like betrayal. But the damage is already done.

She bows her head, hair falling like a curtain between us. "Lil," I choke out, the apology burning my throat like acid.

"Just go," she whispers, but the tremor in her voice screams louder than any shout. When she turns away, I clench my fists so hard my knuckles crack. Every cell in my body screams to grab her, to crush her against me until neither of us can breathe. I don't. I'm a fucking lightning strike searching for ground. One touch and I'll incinerate everything. The image of her with Blake branded into my retinas. Max's betrayal pulsing in my veins. Her defending my father—my FATHER—hammering in my skull like a death sentence.

I slam the door hard enough to splinter the frame on my way out.

Chapter Twenty-Four

ROMAN

Two nights later, I meet Sera at her restaurant, Adelaide's. The valet whisks away my Aston Martin as I approach the gleaming glass entrance, where a doorman in crisp black livery holds open the door.

Inside, Sera's Beverly Hills flagship glows with amber light reflecting off polished marble and brass accents. The air carries notes of saffron and truffle, while crystal stemware tinkles amid the hushed conversations of Hollywood elite and tech billionaires. This crown jewel of her Blackwood chain could put any five-star hotel restaurant to shame.

I'm here at her request—and honestly, she's the only one who's shown any sympathy for how pissed off I am that my dad wants to slap my name on his new eco-resort. Everyone else seems fine with him co-opting my identity for a project, especially after he bailed on me and my brothers twenty-two years ago, but Sera gets how shitty that is.

She makes her entrance in her typical grand style—after all, she owns this restaurant and has every A-lister from

Hollywood to the C-suites on first-name terms. That translates to a solid thirty-minute parade of handshakes and hugs before she finally reaches our table.

When she slides into the chair across from me, I can't help but notice how different she looks. Gone is her signature plunging neckline—her usual attention-grabbing style that highlights her ample curves. There's no short hemline flaunting legs sculpted by a thousand lunges. Instead, she's chosen a modest green sweater dress that picks up her eye color exactly, with soft makeup—no fluttery falsies or scarlet lipstick. She's dialed way down, and somehow, she's more magnetic than ever.

It hits me: she must've figured out I'm all about that natural beauty—like Lilith, who barely ever wears makeup or high-end labels, yet to me, outshines anyone. Tonight, though, Sera is giving Lilith a run for her money.

Next, I realize she's skipped her usual perfume bomb. Instead there's just a whisper of jasmine drifting off her.

I close my eyes. There's no doubt she's modeling herself after Lilith. It's strangely flattering to Lilith—a tarot reader in a modest Venice Beach flat with her best friend, who has zero influencer clout—that a billionaire hotel mogul with millions of Insta followers would steal her vibe. Then again, maybe Sera just figured that's the only way to sway me. Newsflash: I'm drawn to Lilith for her heart, not her handbag.

I cut straight to the point. "What's your angle here, Sera?"

"Just offering some solidarity," she says, placing her hand on my forearm. "Not many people understand what you're going through with your father." Her nails—shorter now, painted in a subtle beige—rest against my skin. Part of me wants to call her out for this Lilith-lite transformation, but damn if she hasn't found my weak spot. My instincts scream that she's playing me, but the hunger to have someone in my corner keeps me rooted to my seat.

"Right," I say flatly. "The real reason?"

She leans in. "It's about Lilith and Blake Walsh. They've been spending time together. I think something's happening between them."

"How do you know this?"

"I hear things, Roman. I listen to the gossip amongst the A-List crowd and people are buzzing about it."

I shut my eyes as the words land like a sucker punch. My gut knows she's feeding me exactly what will hurt most —she was at the gala, saw how I nearly demolished Blake for touching Lilith. What Sera doesn't realize is how her manipulation hits its mark. The image of Blake embracing Lilith a few days ago flashes through my mind, his lips against her cheek, and my blood simmers despite the innocence of the gesture.

"Roman," she says, her voice softening with concern. "I'm worried she's playing you. And that's not like you—you're brilliant with people. Always have been."

"Playing me how?"

"Come on. Your face has been splashed across every business magazine worth reading. *Forbes, Architectural Digest,* all those hotel industry bibles." She ticks them off on her now-subtle fingers. "A woman like that sees dollar signs, connections, status. So she orchestrates getting hired at your resort, puts herself in your path." Her lips purse as she shakes her head. "And while you're falling for it, she's using your attention to make Blake Walsh jealous. It's classic—attach yourself to someone important, wealthy and devastatingly handsome, and suddenly everyone else sees you differently. Like you're wearing designer clothes instead of knockoffs."

She's a master at this game. Always has been. The way she tilts her head, times her smiles, chooses her words—it's like watching a chess grandmaster who's already planned ten moves ahead. And I know exactly what she's doing. So why can't I look away?

My fingers tap against the mahogany, betraying my unease. When the waiter appears, I order a steak, bloody. She requests salmon, delicate. I ask for Macallan, neat. She echoes my choice with a knowing smile.

"Tell me," I say, fighting to keep my voice neutral. "About my father's situation—you think I'm right to keep him at arm's length?"

"Absolutely," she purrs, leaning forward. "What kind of man abandons his children for decades, then waltzes back expecting a welcome? He deserves nothing." Her fingers brush my forearm, lingering. "But you? You deserve everything." Her voice drops to a whisper, eyes never leaving mine. "Remember how we were together? No one's touched me since that compared. At night, I still feel you—like a ghost against my skin. We could have that again, Roman. Forever this time."

Her words break the spell I'm falling under. "I've changed my mind," I say, pushing back from the table. "Tell the kitchen to cancel my order. Coming here was a mistake."

I stand abruptly. The ease with which she watches me leave unsettles me—like she anticipated this reaction, like it's part of some calculated game.

I can't breathe in here anymore. Minutes later I'm gripping my steering wheel, tires squealing toward Venice

Beach. Toward Mystic Tides. Toward her. Whatever's unfinished between us ends today.

Chapter Twenty-Five

LILITH

After Roman left a few days ago, I lit a bundle of dried sage, watching the tendrils of smoke curl upward from its smoldering tip. The earthy, herbaceous scent filled the room as I waved it in slow, deliberate circles over the cushion where he'd been sitting, his energy still lingering like a shadow. With eyes closed, I whispered my prayer to Brigid—my copper-haired Celtic goddess with eyes like emerald fire, who cradles a flame in one hand and a sword in the other. I could almost feel her presence as I asked her to mend the jagged pieces of Roman's heart, those fragments I'd glimpsed behind his steel gaze when he thought no one was looking.

Now, two days later, I'm still immersed in healing rituals for Roman as often as I can. Whenever I get a few minutes to myself at the store, I'm meditating, praying to my goddess and fingering my crystals.

Jack leans against my doorframe, arms crossed. "A healing ritual, Lil, huh?" The corner of his mouth twitches. Despite being my best friend and fiercest defender for years, he still raises an eyebrow at my crystals and candles. I arrange my rose quartz and Rhodonite in a circle, their pink surfaces catching the afternoon light.

"Roman doesn't trust me," I whisper, more to myself than Jack. "That's the real wound." My fingers trace the smooth stone. "But I still love the stubborn fool enough to try healing him from afar."

The singing bowl recording fills my store with resonant tones as I close my eyes, picturing Roman's heart mending under Brigid's care.

"Don't hover," I say without looking up. "I need complete focus for this. I'll find you when I'm done."

“Okay,” he says and then leaves.

A half-hour later, I emerge from the back room, my hands still trembling from Roman's energy. I have more readings scheduled for today - just normal people, no royalty or billionaires come to this store of course - but all I can think about is escaping to my bathtub later and submerging myself until the day dissolves like bath salts. Candles, a bubble bath and a good novel sound like heaven right now.

"Lass!" Blake's voice cuts through the shop as he bursts through the door.

"Blake!" My face ignites with relief. God, I need his light right now. Roman's darkness still clings to me like smoke, suffocating my spirit, while Blake radiates pure sunshine. "What brings you back?"

"Desperate for another reading." His eyes flash with urgency. "I'm turning into one of those psychic junkies. My manager's breathing down my neck about the tour—wants me back on stage by December. But Christ, I'm burned out. Need to know if taking a real break will kill my career."

I can't help but smile at this man—platinum records

lining his walls, stadiums screaming his name—still riddled with doubt: "The world won't forget Blake Walsh any more than they'd forget Taylor Swift or Ed Sheeran. But come on back."

The cards reveal that he should indeed take a break and if he does, he'll come back better than ever and his fans will anticipate his return and not forget him. As we return to the shop floor, Blake wraps me in his signature bear hug and plants a kiss on my cheek. That's when the door explodes open.

"YOU!" Roman roars, a feral sound that freezes my blood. His body becomes a weapon—a blur of calculated fury as his foot connects with Blake's jaw with a sickening crack. Blake crumples to the floor like a marionette with cut strings. Roman towers over him, chest heaving, veins throbbing at his temples, eyes wild with primal rage. I stand paralyzed. My scream dies in my throat as reality fractures around me. This isn't happening. This can't be happening.

What kind of monster lurks beneath that Armani suit?

The initial shock fades when I see Blake sprawled across the floor tiles. He staggers to his feet—relief floods through me—and massages his jaw before giving his head a little shake. "Seems we've got a pattern forming here, lad," he quips as I steady him.

Jack remains frozen behind the register. I glance around, grateful the store is empty of customers. No witnesses means no smartphone footage of Roman Kensington demolishing someone in a bookstore. His reputation for having a temper is one thing, but actual evidence of him channeling his inner MMA fighter would send his investors running. The billionaire hotelier who punches first and negotiates later isn't exactly the financial partner most people are looking for.

I rush to Blake's side. "Are you hurt?" Jack tries to get between Blake and Roman but he's like a sparrow trying to fend off a hawk. His slender frame barely covers half of Roman's muscled silhouette.

Blake works his jaw back and forth. "My poor face. Thirty years of pristine condition, ruined in seconds. How bad is it?"

I probe his jawline with gentle fingers. The skin's already warming, but nothing shifts under my touch. "You'll live. Just expect some colorful bruising." I glance at Roman, whose controlled stance reminds me he could have done much worse. Those MMA sessions with Caspian taught him precision—even in rage, he holds back just enough to avoid hospital visits.

I jab a finger toward Jack. "Go down the boardwalk to the ice machine." Then I whirl on Roman, my voice rising to a pitch that makes the crystal pendants near the register tremble. "And you! Get out before I call the police!"

Roman blinks rapidly, the veins in his neck no longer bulging. His shoulders drop as he looks from Blake's crumpled form to me. "Lil," he whispers, "I'm so—"

"Out!"

Jack bursts through the door, ice cubes rattling in a plastic bag. I kneel beside Blake, whose jaw is already purpling. "My silk scarf, Jack. The indigo one." I keep my eyes locked on Roman, who hovers by the bookshelf, fingers twitching at his sides. When Jack hands me the scarf, I wrap the ice carefully, pressing it against Blake's swelling jaw. "I'm so sorry. Please don't tell anyone about this."

Blake winces as he touches his face. "I guess we're even. I made quite the scene at his resort." His eyes meet Roman's across the room. "No, Lil, like Vegas, whatever happened here stays here. We've all been there—rage so blind you can't see." He rises unsteadily, crosses to Roman and places a hand on his shoulder. "I'll pray for you, brother." Then to me: "Lil, I'll see you."

I lunge for the door and wrap my arms around Blake, clinging to him like a life raft. "I'm so sorry about this," I repeat fiercely against his ear. The moment he steps away, I feel it—the suffocating darkness Roman has brought crashing into my sanctuary. The crystals on the shelves seem to dim, the incense smoke curls away from him like it's afraid. Jack's aura, usually a brilliant sapphire, has faded to a trembling, anxious gray. And Roman—God—he's a black hole standing among my books, his rage still pulsing like a heartbeat, threatening to devour everything I've built here. I feel my own light being violently ripped from my chest, my energy draining into his bottomless fury until my knees nearly buckle.

"I'll call you tomorrow, okay?" I gasp to Blake, already feeling myself drowning.

Blake nods and disappears into the evening crowd.

The door clicks shut. My shoulders slump. Three tarot readings to get through tonight, and then—my bubble bath, candles, meditation chants, and novel.

I've never needed them more.

Then, my vision blurs at the edges, turning crimson as rage floods my system. Roman's toxic energy has been suffocating me since he walked in, yet he's still planted by the register like some entitled god, oblivious to the hurricane building inside me.

"Jack," I snarl. "Door. NOW."

Jack scrambles to comply while I lunge at Roman. Something primal takes over—my hands slam against Roman's chest with such force that his six-foot-four frame actually staggers. "GET OUT AND TAKE YOUR DARK ENERGY WITH YOU!"

The scream tears from my throat, raw and feral. His eyes widen in shock as I keep coming, fingers curled like claws, shoving him again and again. Each impact sends jolts up my arms but I don't stop, driving him backward until he's teetering at the threshold. With one final violent thrust, I expel his massive body onto the boardwalk like exorcising a demon. The door slams shut with a satisfying crash, lock clicking into place as I slap the "Closed" sign against the glass, my hands trembling with adrenaline.

I cancel every reading with shaking fingers. That bubble bath can't come soon enough—I need to wash him off my skin.

Chapter Twenty-Six

ROMAN

The next night after the fight with Lilith, I storm through the door of the Blackwood gym, the heavy metal hinges groaning in protest. The familiar scent of sweat-soaked leather and antiseptic cleaner fills my nostrils as I slam my duffel bag onto the polished concrete floor.

My veins throb with molten rage that's been building since my dinner with Sera, where she planted that poisonous seed about Lilith and Blake's "friendship." The memory of my roundhouse connecting with Blake's jaw in Lilith's crystal-filled shop flashes behind my eyes—the satisfying crack followed by the horror on her beautiful face. Her delicate hands, adorned with those silver rings she always wears, had somehow found the strength to shove my six-foot-four frame backward, again and again, then out her door, her caramel eyes flashing like lightning as she banished my "dark energy" from her sacred space. The humiliation burns in my chest like acid.

Before Caspian's arrival, I circle the punching dummy like a predator, its worn leather surface already bearing the scars of countless fighters before me. I unleash a barrage of blows—jabs that make my knuckles sing, hooks that wrench my shoulders, and kicks that send shockwaves up my shins. Sweat drenches my compression shirt, plastering it to my heaving chest, but the black rage remains coiled inside like a venomous snake.

Only Caspian, with his steady gaze and calming baritone, can draw out this poison. He knows the exact pressure points of my psyche, the perfect words to make the crimson fog recede from the corners of my vision.

Caspian drops his gym bag at the door, already dressed to spar. His eyes narrow as he studies my face.

"Rome," he says, voice low. "Talk to me. You've always got that edge to you, but tonight..." He crosses his arms. "That's the same look you had when your old man walked out. Twenty-two years ago, and I still remember it."

That day. My fist connecting with drywall, feeling nothing until I looked down at the blood. The ER doctor's face when he saw the X-ray. Broken in three places, but my right hand—not my dominant one. Even in my rage, some survival instinct had protected my left.

This thing with Blake is different. Pure blind fury that's been building since my brothers ambushed me. Then Serafina fanned the flames with her insinuations, and when I saw Blake's hands on Lilith—I snapped. Lost it completely. But it wasn't just that - it was that I also saw him at her store days before I stormed in there and put my boot to his face. The pieces fitting together: Blake constantly visiting Lilith, Sera whispering that she's seen them together.

Sera wants me back—I know that—but what if she's right? What if I'm the fool in Lilith's game?

My head's a storm cloud. This fight isn't just training. It's oxygen. "Talk later. Let's go."

So, for the next two hours, Caspian and I spar in the gym's octagon, our bodies slick with sweat that stings my eyes and leaves salt trails down my back. My lungs burn like I've swallowed fire while my quads tremble, threatening to buckle as we trade combinations—his lightning-fast jab catching my shoulder, my counter hook grazing his temple.

The rhythmic thud of four-ounce gloves against skin echoes off the chain-link fence surrounding us, punctuating our ragged breathing as we prepare for my MMA bout coming in December. My ribs throb with a deep purple ache from a particularly brutal side kick that'll leave a boot-shaped bruise by morning, but I push through it—pain is just weakness leaving the body, and I need to be anything but weak when I step into that cage for real.

Finally, we collapse on the mat, sweat-drenched and gasping. Caspian props himself up on one elbow, fixing me with that look he always gives when he's about to drop some wisdom.

"Your technique is solid now," he says, wiping blood from his lip. "UFC caliber, even. I should know—half my clients fight professionally." He taps my temple with his gloved fist. "But this? Still your weakness. You fight like a man on fire. Learn to burn cold instead, and nobody will touch you."

I shake my head so hard my neck cracks. "I'm a fucking wreck tonight."

"I can tell. What's going on?"

I suck in air like I'm drowning. "Lilith and I had a fight. I can't trust her." My fist slams into my thigh. "Goddamn it, I thought she was different. I even thought—"

Caspian grips my shoulder, steadying me. "You thought?"

The words burn in my throat. I almost tell him everything—how after that first night with her on the beach, I saw my future flash before my eyes. But the humiliation scalds worse than any punch I've taken in the ring.

What kind of pathetic fool calls someone The One when she's playing him like a goddamn fiddle? There is no "One"—that's fairy tale bullshit. There's just bodies colliding, sweat, heat, sex that makes you forget yourself. I gambled that Lilith might be more than that. I lost. And I would rather get my teeth knocked out than crawl back begging.

“Nothing.”

Caspian leans forward. "Level with me, Rome. Since when do we hold back with each other?"

I slam my fist against the table. "My goddamn brothers started it." The memory makes my jaw clench. "They ambushed me with this proposal about Dad opening some hippie eco-resort chain using our name. 'Sunstone Retreats by Kensington,' if you can believe that bullshit." I mime the words in the air like they're a marquee. "And get this—they expect me to absorb it into my company. Like the man didn't walk out on us for two decades and now deserves the keys to the kingdom."

Caspian's expression doesn't change. "And after this meeting?"

"I needed Lilith." My voice softens despite myself. "Around her, I can breathe. It's like... this rage I've carried since I was a kid just evaporates. I become someone I actually like." I rub my temples. "Or I did, until I walked into her shop and saw Blake fucking Walsh with his arms around her. I nearly put him through a wall, but somehow I kept it together."

“Okay. Then what happened?”

I glance up from my water glass. "Had dinner with Sera last night."

Caspian's face brightens with that familiar look—like a puppy who thinks you're about to throw his favorite ball. I cut him off with a raised palm before he can start planning our wedding reception.

"Not happening. Ever. But she mentioned something about Blake and Lilith spending time together. Said people are buzzing about it." I rub my jaw, the stubble rough against my fingertips. "Look, I know she's your sister and you worship the ground she walks on, but Sera lives to stir shit up. I'd ignore her stories about Blake and Lilith completely if I hadn't already been wondering the same thing myself."

“So you don't trust Lilith because...?" Caspian asks, eyebrow raised.

The question hits like a sucker punch. Truth is, Lilith's given me zero reason for suspicion. She and Blake are friends—end of story. If she meant nothing to me, I wouldn't give a damn who she hangs out with.

But she does mean something.

Christ, she means everything.

“I swung by her place after Serafina mentioned they'd been hanging out. I just—I needed to hear it from her. And also, when everything's red and I can't think straight, she's the only one who brings me back. She makes the world...I don't know, bearable. And there he was again. Twice in three days? What are the odds? Either I've got the worst fucking timing in California, or he's practically living there. Something in me snapped. I threw a roundhouse—pulled it just enough not to do real damage. You know how I can control it. I just wanted him to feel it, you know? To feel a fraction of what's burning in my chest every time I think about them together."

"Anything else bothering you?"

I shake my head. "Yes. Max." My jaw clenches. "You already know the deal with him. I've got this...this thing where I blame him for our family falling apart. Makes no sense—not his fault—but feelings aren't exactly logical, are they?" I run a hand through my hair. "And now? Max rolls out the red carpet for Dad, puts him up in the poolside guest house, then sits there at dinner playing cheerleader. From him, of all people? That's just—" I make a twisting motion with my hand near my chest. "That's just twisting the knife."

Caspian nods. "Okay, I see what's going on. Let's go through all this piece by piece. Now, your brothers..."

"Yes."

"Rome, I see how you stand apart at family gatherings —watching from the edges, jaw tight. You think you're the odd man out. But they're not pushing you away; you're the one who keeps backing up," Caspian says. "I've known your brothers for years. When Cameron talks about you, there's the same pride in his voice as when he mentions his other brothers. The difference isn't in how they see you—it's in that fire you carry.

Look at them: Kalen selling out stadiums, Connor dominating awards seasons, Ansel signing some of the biggest music stars in the world, Max producing billion-dollar blockbusters, Asher planning events for royalty and billionaires alike, Silas working with crown jewels and rare precious stones around the world. And they each, to a man, talk about you just as reverently as they talk about every other brother. So they've all got that Kensington drive, just filtered through different lenses. Your flame just burns more visibly. Those resorts you've built across four continents? That's your intensity finding its purpose. But when it's not channeled, Rome—that's when it consumes you instead."

I shake my head. "No, you're missing the point. Everyone's turned on me. I'm stuck on this goddamn island because I refuse to play nice with my father, and they're either waiting for me to cave under the pressure of their little fan club, or they're perfectly happy keeping me isolated out here."

Caspian exhales slowly. "Rome, forgiveness doesn't mean telling someone what they did was okay. You never have to say that to your father. Forgiveness is something you do for yourself. It's about letting go of the poison eating you from inside and making room for something better. It's unlocking those chains you've wrapped around your own heart so you can finally breathe."

I don't interrupt him. This isn't the first time I've heard this speech, but somehow, today, the words are finding cracks to seep through.

"As for Max—your feelings toward him aren't logical, and you know it. You need to extend that same grace to him. Whether he needs your forgiveness or not isn't the point—you need to give it."

"Yeah," I say. "I've got to let go of this thing with Max." I can't bring myself to use the word 'forgive,' because Max doesn't need forgiveness, but the meaning's clear enough. I know what needs to happen.

Caspian leans forward, elbows on his knees. "Your old man bailed when things got messy. When emotions ran high. And what are you doing with Lilith? Same damn playbook." His eyes narrow. "This Blake thing? That's your exit strategy, man. Just like when Serafina cheated—yeah, she screwed up, but you were already halfway out the door, weren't you? You just needed the excuse." He pauses, watching me. "The difference is, you actually care about Lilith. I see how you look at her. Never saw that with my sister, much as I wanted to. But now you're torching something real because it scares the hell out of you. Tell me I'm wrong."

I shake my head. "You're not wrong," I say. "I just didn't think of it that way."

Caspian adjusts his stance. "One more round. Use that anger—make every hit count."

The knot in my chest has loosened since I arrived. After hours of pummeling both Caspian and the practice dummy, that crimson fog has mostly burned away. Between jabs and hooks, I'd unloaded about Dad, the resort, my brothers, Lilith—and Caspian had nodded, asked the right questions, known exactly when to push.

We circle each other on the mat. This time my body moves with precision, not rage. Left hook. Roundhouse. Grapple. Each connection feels clean, deliberate.

"There it is!" Caspian blocks my combination, grinning through his mouthguard. "Now you're fighting smart, not just hard."

The final training round leaves me drained. My muscles quiver with fatigue, anger replaced by a hollow ache in my chest.

In my car, Sam Smith's "Fire on Fire" floods the speakers—our song. My forehead drops to the steering wheel while my fingers hover over my phone.

I need to call Lilith, but shame—unfamiliar, suffocating shame—stops me. The memory replays: my caveman rage, Blake crumpling from my kick, and worst of all, Lilith's small body somehow shoving me backward out of her shop, her eyes wide with rage as she locked the door.

The kind of strength she mustered to shove me out of her store like that only comes from pure adrenaline—like mothers lifting cars off trapped children. That's how angry she was, and to make a sweet, pure woman like Lilith that angry…goddamn, it makes me ashamed that I'm the one who brought her to it.

She deserves better. Her smile ignites a wildfire in me that burns through every defense I've built. And now I've snuffed it out. I murdered that light when I went after Blake, and it's another sin branded onto my conscience—one I'll carry like an open wound that refuses to heal.

Bringing out my phone, my thumb hovers over her name.

Why can't I just press call?

Chapter Twenty-Seven

LILITH

The night after my confrontation with Roman has given me some distance—I'm calmer now, and things look a bit clearer. Yet what I really need is more clarity. I can't read my own tarot cards—like I've told Jack over and over, my personal bias always seeps in. If I laid out a spread with the Ten of Swords, The Tower, Three of Swords, Five of Swords and The Devil, I'd twist even those dark cards into something hopeful, simply because I'm desperate to hear what I want.

Jack offered to do the reading for me. "Lilith," he said once Roman stormed off, "I don't know what set him off, but I'm not judging him. I know you love him, whether you admit it or not. Let me read the cards—we can sort this out together."

I appreciated his offer, but I needed someone truly objective. Jack wants that fairy-tale ending for us just as badly as I do—even after seeing Roman's rage explode, the moment he kicked Blake and Jack witnessed every dreadful second, Jack's hope for us is as strong as mine. I still believe

Roman is hurting, and part of me thinks I'm in his life to help him heal.

That's why I've reached out to my mentor, Elinor Jacobs, in Malibu. The Ethereal Veil sits right in downtown Malibu and is probably the most frequented psychic bookstore in L.A. Elinor is sixty, has read for everyone from royalty to Hollywood stars, and when I was launching my own shop she guided me with nothing but good advice. I trust her completely—and still, I'm jittery about what she'll reveal. What if the cards don't show what I'm hoping for? Then again, tarot readings aren't set in stone. They just map out possible futures if I take no action. And I have the power to change the outcome.

"Hello, Elinor," I say, breathing in the familiar scent of lavender and sage that always clings to her flowing silk kimono.

"Lilith!" She glides across the room in her bare feet, silver anklets tinkling, and enfolds me in a hug that smells of jasmine oil. "I saw you made an appointment, and I was so excited. You've been on my mind lately for some reason."

Though her silver-streaked auburn hair is twisted into a loose bun atop her head, wisps of it frame a face remarkably free of wrinkles. Her emerald eyes sparkle with the vitality of someone decades younger than her sixty-something years. She always credits her ageless appearance to a regimen she follows religiously: organic vegetables from her own garden, gallons of green tea instead of wine, sunrise yoga on her amethyst-crystal mat, and daily "grounding" sessions where she presses her bare feet into dewy morning soil to absorb the earth's energy. The smooth bronze of her skin and the easy way she moves make me wonder if maybe she's onto something.

"You probably knew I'd be coming in," I say, watching

her fingers—adorned with silver rings on every digit—arrange her tarot cards with practiced precision. After all, Elinor actually is psychic, not just a tarot reader.

"Well," she says, her bracelets clinking softly as she gestures toward the velvet-cushioned chair across from her. "Let's do your reading."

I follow her into the reading room. Lavender incense perfumes the air, mingling with the warm glow of flickering candles. Behind the reading table, a crystal tree clings to the wall, its branches illuminated with delicate white lights. The brilliant red walls—the color of passion and vitality, connected to the root chakra that grounds our spirits to earth—make me reconsider my own reading space at Mystic Tides. The front of my store got its dream makeover; perhaps my consultation room deserves the same attention.

Sinking into the plush velour chair, I watch Elinor's nimble fingers shuffle the deck. Her eyes meet mine with knowing mischief.

"Love question today, isn't it?" she asks with a mischievous glint in her eye.

My cheeks warm, the flush spreading across my face like spilled wine. Usually, I come to Elinor with business concerns—when I first considered opening my shop in that crumbling Venice Beach storefront with the leaky ceiling, and several times since for guidance on expanding my crystal collection or redesigning the window displays. But today feels different. My shop is thriving, shelves stocked with leather-bound journals and amethyst clusters that catch the California sunlight, and my position at Roman's resort—with its panoramic ocean views and clientele dripping in diamonds—fulfills me professionally. It's my heart, fluttering like a caged bird whenever he enters a room, that needs navigation now.

Since meeting Roman, I've realized how shallow my past relationships were—boys playing at being men, none worthy of even a moment's reflection. None ever affected me deeply enough to seek the cards' wisdom.

Only Roman.

She shuffles the cards with practiced hands, cuts the deck, and waits for me to select a half with trembling fingers. The Celtic Cross appears before me, card by card. Her brow furrows.

"This man of yours," she murmurs, tapping the King of Wands, "carries storms inside him. See how Temperance lies reversed across his path? Peace eludes him." Her fingertip traces the edge of another card. "Yet Strength paired with The Star suggests determination to evolve. But childhood shadows him—the Six of Cups upside down tells me he clings to old hurts."

She settles back, studying the pattern. "He stands at a threshold, though there's much to clear away first. As for your future together..." She indicates a card showing a flower-adorned structure. "The Four of Wands promises eventual harmony, but the journey there won't be simple."

"Worth pursuing, then?" I ask.

"The cards suggest so." Her eyes meet mine, suddenly penetrating. "The Seven of Swords reveals what truly troubles you—not his volatility or chaos, but his inability to trust you. That's the heart of your concern."

I nod. Nailed it on the head, of course.

I twist a strand of hair around my finger. "But how does he move past it? The trust issues?"

My chest tightens. If Roman can't learn to trust me, we're

done before we've really begun. Yet here I am, already drowning in feelings for him—like I've sunk to the bottom of some impossibly deep ocean trench with no way back to the surface. Maybe I could still swim away now, save myself from completely shattering later. But I need to know if there's hope.

Elinor shuffles the cards again, laying them out in a deliberate pattern. "The cards suggest healing will come," she says, tapping one. "Temperance, upright now. And here—Judgment indicates a personal breakthrough awaiting him, something separate from you that will ultimately bring down his walls." Her fingertip rests on a bright card. "The Sun promises joy when that happens." She meets my eyes. "These spreads are swimming in love, Lilith. He's worth the fight."

Later on, at my house, I sit cross-legged on my meditation cushion, journal open in my lap. My pen hovers over the page as I write about Roman's jealous rage, the way his foot connected with Blake's face when he saw us talking. The candle beside me flickers as I pour my confusion onto the page.

By the final paragraph, clarity emerges like moonlight through clouds. Roman's wounded soul is the question mark in our story. A man whose heart is barricaded behind walls of hurt can't truly love. I need someone whose spirit is open to connection.

I close my eyes and send one final wish into the darkness.

Chapter Twenty-Eight

ROMAN

It's been three days since my fight with Lilith. I snap my fingers at a bellhop whose tie is crooked by two millimeters. "Fix it." My voice comes out like gravel. When the hostess at Oceana sets water glasses with fingerprints on the tables, I dump them all in the kitchen sink myself. My assistant flinches when I enter the office. The resort gleams under my inspection, but I still can't sleep at night.

I storm through my resort like a man possessed. The Carrara marble reception desk shows a hairline crack beneath its polish. A guest's Louis Vuitton weekend bag sits unattended for seventeen seconds before a bellman materializes. The Krug champagne being poured at the bar isn't quite at the perfect 47-degree serving temperature. In the reflection of the gilt-framed mirror, I spot a cushion on the custom Fortuny-upholstered sofa that hasn't been plumped since breakfast. Each microscopic flaw enrages me to the point that I can't see straight.

I can't help it. After the ambush from my brothers and the fight with Liilith, the red haze has taken over my psyche like California wildfire. My jaw clenches so tight I can hear my molars grinding. I bark orders at the resort staff—demanding the lobby flowers be replaced because they're "two shades too pink," insisting the beach towels be refolded with precisely seven-inch corners, snapping at a bellhop for breathing too loudly. I see the fear in their eyes, the way they scatter like seagulls when I approach, but the burning in my chest won't subside.

Except Miranda, ever my North Star, asked to see me for lunch today. So, we meet at the Bone and Brass, our flagship resort restaurant with its soaring thirty-foot ceilings, polished copper fixtures that catch the California sunlight, and floor-to-ceiling windows overlooking the cerulean Pacific. The place has been written up in everything from *Food and Wine* to *Bon Appétit* and just earned its third Michelin star.

I actually poached Philippe Benoit—the Food Network's golden boy with his trademark handlebar mustache and tattoo-covered forearms—to head this place. *Architectural Digest* featured the restaurant's cantilevered glass dining terrace and hand-carved mahogany bar in their spread on architectural masterpieces. That's my thing, really, architecture. If I hadn't become a hotelier, I would've designed buildings, translating the clean lines and perfect proportions I see in my mind into physical reality.

I slide into the white leather chair across from Miranda in the resort's private dining room, the floor-to-ceiling windows framing the Pacific behind her. The waiter brings our lunch—my swordfish seared to golden perfection with Philippe's signature lemon-caper sauce glistening on top, and Miranda's plump scallops arranged like pearls on a bed of saffron risotto. I check my Patek Philippe watch, a gift to myself after the Tokyo acquisition. "Twenty minutes, Miranda. That's all I have."

"Roman," she says, her crimson lips pursing as she sets down her fork with a delicate clink against fine china. Her British accent always becomes more pronounced when she's annoyed, which she is right now. "I've been your right hand since you were a cocky 22-year-old with more ambition than experience. I watched you transform that $40 million loan from your grandfather into a multi-billion empire with properties on four continents. So I've bloody well earned the right to tell you when you're being a proper ass."

I clench my jaw, feeling a muscle twitch beneath my three-day stubble. "Miranda, this resort has been absolute hell today. The air conditioning in the east wing, the double-booked wedding pavilion—"

"Oh?" Her eyebrow arches perfectly, like a drawn bow. "So you have a knock-down, drag-out fight with Lilith and suddenly everything in your immaculate resort is falling apart? That timing doesn't strike you as suspicious, Roman?"

I exhale slowly, knowing Miranda has a point. If I keep breathing fire at my staff, even the veterans who've weathered my tempests before will eventually reach their breaking point. Then I'll be left with nothing but rookies who flinch at my shadow.

"Take off," Miranda says, her voice gentler now. "Go see Lilith at Mystic Tides. That woman has a way of clearing the storm clouds from your head."

I nod, drinking my water. "After lunch, I'll go over there."

"Please do," Miranda says. "I've been talking staff down off the ledge all morning. Please stop making so much work for me."

After lunch, I head to Mystic Tides. Jack's at the register when I walk in, but the moment he spots me, his eyes slide away. Gone is the flirtatious "Hey handsome!" I've grown used to. Gone is the rapid-fire commentary on everything from celebrity gossip to astrological forecasts. Instead, he finishes ringing up his customers, fixes me with an arctic stare, then pivots and busies himself reorganizing a display of tarot decks.

"Jack," I venture. "How's it going?"

Jack flutters his fingers in the air like he was shooing away gnats and gives a theatrical shrug. "Was going fine until about thirty seconds ago when you arrived, darling. Lilith called it—you're toxic with a capital T-O-X-I-C. Like Britney, but without the bops. Funny how I never saw it before, but honey, the scales have fallen from these fabulous eyes."

I scan the room, but Lilith is nowhere to be found. "Jack, I'm sorry—"

Jack whips around, one hand slicing through the air. "Save it, honey." His eyes won't meet mine. "Christ on a cracker. I've been all 'cosmic soulmates' this and 'written in the stars' that to Lilith. Drove the poor girl absolutely batshit with my—" he adopts a singsong voice, fingers wiggling dramatically, "—visions of your genetically blessed babies and Lake Como nuptials. God, Como! Like I'll ever see it on my pathetic retail wages." His laugh sounds like glass breaking. "Such. Ridiculous. Fantasies." He deflates, examining his cuticles. "Meanwhile, Lil's all practical Patti: 'Jack, please,'" he mimics in a softer voice, "'I barely know the man.'" His shoulders cave inward. "Should've listened. Girl's got the sight, you know?"

Each word hits me like a physical blow. Lilith didn't feel what I felt. Didn't sense what seemed so obvious to me—

that connection. While I've been walking around feeling like I've known her my entire life, she's been... what? Just humoring me?

I scan the empty shop. "Lilith's not around today?"

"Nope." Jack arranges crystals in the display case. "She's at some retreat in Big Sur. Something about purifying her energy field from toxic billionaires." He shoots me a pointed look.

My mind drifts to those rugged cliffs where I caught the best wave of my life last summer. The urge to jump in my Aston Martin and race up the coast hits me like a rogue swell. But I can already imagine her face—those topaz eyes narrowing with irritation at the billionaire who can't take a hint.

I just nod and Jack's face softens. "Look," he says, the edge gone from his voice. "Between us? Lilith is crazy about you. Won't say it outright, but she's hurting bad. And it's not about you roughing up Blake—that's whatever. There's zero happening between them anyway. Blake's already seeing someone new—some Pisces writer Lilith calls his 'Queen of Cups.' Winifred something. Lilith's already playing match-maker, had them over for dinner, the whole thing." He lets out a sigh, running a hand through his hair. "So no, we're not pissed you went caveman on Blake. We're pissed because after everything, you still don't trust her."

His words slam into me, knocking the air from my lungs. I remember what I told Lilith—that perfect bullshit about waiting for "the right woman." How I'd recognize her instantly. How I'd never let her go. Yet here I am, having met her, having held her, and what did I do? Pushed her away like all the others. Maybe it was never about finding the right woman. Maybe it's about me—about the ten-year-old boy who woke up one morning to find his father gone, about the three-year-old who couldn't understand why his mother would never come home. Maybe those ghosts have been chasing me all along.

I clear my throat. "Appreciate it, Jack."

"What exactly?"

"Not punching me in the face. Not dialing 911 when I appeared at your door."

"Please. My fist would shatter against that jawline of yours. Besides, emergency rooms? Hard pass. Everyone coughing and sneezing in those waiting areas—I'd walk in with fractured knuckles and leave with the plague." He waves dismissively. "Anyway, what would I tell dispatch? 'Help, there's an annoyingly attractive man standing in my store behaving himself?'"

I force a smile and make my exit. The resort will have to wait. If I go back now, I'll have the entire staff updating their resumes by morning. On impulse, I find myself steering toward Max's beach house, just thirty minutes away. Six o'clock—he might actually be home for once. Fatherhood has a way of reshaping priorities.

Through the window, I spot him on the floor with Violet, making her giggle as he dangles a stuffed animal just out of reach. My chest tightens. Their pit bull Piper is running around the room while Celeste throws a plastic chicken for her. This is such a domestic scene that my heart aches just a little.

When did my baby brother—the one I've silently held responsible for our family falling apart—become this man with a child of his own? I stand frozen on the path, hands jammed in my pockets. Inside, Celeste will soon be feeding the dog and setting the table, or maybe their housekeeper Rosa is preparing dinner. Either way, I'm the intruder here. I turn and walk back to my car without knocking.

I get back to my penthouse and pull out the tarot card Lilith pressed into my palm before I left. The Tower. Lightning strikes a stone structure, sending figures tumbling through the air. I run my thumb over its worn edge, remembering her words about foundations crumbling to make way for something stronger. Something truer. The card feels heavy in my hand—heavier than it should—like it's carrying the weight of everything I need to let burn down before I can rebuild.

The doorbell rings and my heart leaps. Lilith? No—she's six hours north in Big Sur. I swing the door open to find Silas, his hands jammed in his pockets.

"Hey, Rome," he says, shifting his weight.

I step back. "Family sent their diplomat, or is this a personal visit?"

"Bit of both. Was nearby and thought I'd roll the dice."

I gesture toward the bar. He follows. Two fingers of Macallan, no ice. The amber liquid catches the light as I slide his glass across.

Silas clears his throat. "Look, about the family meeting—"

"Let me guess," I cut in. "The brothers took a vote on whether I need a straitjacket, brain surgery, or just heavy pharmaceuticals. The trifecta, perhaps?"

Silas laughs. "Still the dark humor, I see. No, we don't think you need an intervention. But there's something you should know."

I nod. "Go on."

Silas clears his throat, his eyes meeting mine. "The family has your back, Roman. Always. We think maybe you've got this idea we're pushing you away because you won't forgive Dad." He leans forward, voice dropping. "That's bullshit. We're Kensingtons, man. Same blood." He taps his chest twice with his fist. "I'm here because I need you to hear this—your place is with us. Your feelings about Dad? They're yours. We might see it differently, but that doesn't change a damn thing about how we feel about you."

I nod, my chest constricting. "Thanks," I rasp, swallowing hard.

"There's something else. When Dad first showed up, I felt exactly like you did. I just... kept quiet. You had the balls to speak up when I didn't. The others welcomed him with open arms, and I just went along with it. But between us? I was on your side the whole time."

"I knew it," I say, biting back the "soy boy" comment hovering on my lips. For a split second, I want to rip into him for not having the spine to stand with his own brother. Instead, I exhale slowly. The guy drove all the way here just to check on me. That counts for something.

"Roman, listen to me." His voice dropped to a raw whisper. "I sat across from Dad last night. Just us. And I made myself really hear him. He broke down—completely shattered—admitting he should've gotten help. But God, Roman, he was planning to kill himself. Planning it. The drinking? That was the only goddamn thing keeping him from pulling the trigger. He was drowning. Nothing made sense anymore. Eight children to raise alone when Mom—his everything—was suddenly gone. He told me when she died, he'd stand in the shower each morning and scream until his throat bled, just to feel something besides the emptiness."

Huh. I know a thing or two about that—about letting the shower drown out your screams, about craving any sensation that isn't the hollow ache inside your chest.

"Look, after actually giving Dad a chance—really listening instead of just waiting for my turn to talk—I get it now. He recognized he was poison as a role model. He was afraid we'd become his mirror image—the bottle, the darkness, the weakness. Now he sees eight successful men and thinks, 'I did the right thing by leaving.' And maybe there's truth there, Rome. Even if he'd gotten sober, gotten help, the reality is he couldn't handle raising eight boys alone. Our grandparents could. If he'd stayed... broken as he was... who knows what kind of damage we might be carrying now."

"But look at the damage we *are* carrying now," I counter, my voice rougher than I intended. "We're all broken to a certain degree." I run my hand through my hair, feeling that familiar tension in my jaw. "Maybe none of the brothers are as fucked up as me, but they've got their own shit—they just don't explode like I do."

I tick them off on my fingers. "Connor developed such severe social anxiety that he could barely speak without stuttering. Those little bastards at school tormented him until I had to beat the living hell out of them. Asher's obsessive-compulsive disorder got so bad he'd wash his hands until they bled. Kalen's agoraphobia kept him trapped in the house for three years straight—he'd have panic attacks so bad he'd pass out if we tried to get him outside. You developed selective mutism and didn't speak a single goddamn word for two years—not one."

I shake my head. "Even the ones who look fine aren't. Ansel puts on that sunshine act, but I used to hear him crying in his room. Cameron escaped to Africa to save everyone but himself. And Max—Christ, Max grew up with such fears of abandonment. He couldn't trust anyone to stay. Every time someone got close, he'd sabotage it because he was convinced they'd leave him like Dad did. If

Granddad hadn't shoved Celeste at him and forced them together, Max would still be alone."

I press my palms against my eyes. "But I'm the only one still bleeding. Connor is an A-List actor who has no problems speaking. Kalen travels the world, touring. You won't shut up. Max has Celeste. Asher's OCD makes him a fortune planning events. They all got better. I'm still just... broken." I drop my hands, suddenly exhausted. "That's why I feel so fucking alone, no matter how much you insist that you all love me."

Silas nods, his fingers drumming against his knee. "Look, I get it. We all carry scars from back then." His voice drops. "Cameron used to wake up screaming for her. I couldn't speak. You broke your hand punching that wall when you were twelve." He leans forward, eyes locked on mine. "But imagine if Dad had stayed—bringing whiskey bottles to our baseball games, passing out during parent-teacher conferences. Seven more years of that darkness. Ten more. Would any of us be standing here now?"

I shake my head. Silas is making sense.

Silas leans forward. "So what's the deal with Lilith? Ansel can't stop talking about her. We both think she balances you out—all that sunshine to your storm clouds.

Something catches in my throat. "It's over," I manage. "I stormed into her shop like a complete jackass. Now she's in Big Sur and I doubt she'll ever want to see me again." The admission costs me. "I'm starting to see how this thing with Dad—this anger I can't let go of—it's like poison. Everything good I touch turns toxic. Lilith was..." I can't finish.

Silas gives me a long look. "Then fix it, Roman."

"I wish I could. But I don't know where to start."

Chapter Twenty-Nine

ROMAN

At my next sparring session with Caspian, I step onto the mat carrying every scrap of tension, grief, and anger I've been hauling around—and I'm determined to turn it all into focused power. The gym's air hangs heavy with the smell of sweat and leather, punctuated by the metallic clang of weights dropping and the steady thump of gloves on heavy bags.

I breathe deep, tuning out the chatter, centering myself on each jab, each kick, until, by the end of our drills, I feel a calm I haven't known in weeks. Silas's words—that my brothers truly have my back—echo in my head, soothing like warm sunlight on chilled skin. Caspian catches my eye as I wipe sweat from my brow. He can sense it too: I'm not scattered anymore.

"So, Rome," he says later, as we lean against the juice bar counter, cold plastic bottles of protein shakes sweating between us. The bright blender lights flicker behind the counter, illuminating rows of fresh fruit and green powders.

"You were laser-focused in training today. What's behind your newfound… serenity?"

I shrug, twisting the cap off my coconut and banana protein shake. I know he expects me to credit some truce with Lilith, but that's not it. It's simpler—and bigger. I'm beginning to believe my brothers will stop harassing me about Dad. If I can keep my heart open, maybe they'll stop viewing my refusal to forgive as betrayal.

"I—" I start to explain the shift in my head and heart, but then I spot Max weaving between treadmills, his running shoes squeaking softly against the belt. I'd assumed he only ever trained at the Patrician Country Club gym—emerald walls, polished marble floors, strict dress code. Seeing him here, in the grit and grind of Caspian's place, surprises me. He tenses when our eyes meet, like he's bracing for another blast of my anger from our last conversation—when he sided with Dad and I took it as a personal attack.

I force a grin and open my arms without thinking, and he relaxes into a hug. "What are you doing here?" I whisper, pulling back to search his face. "I thought you always worked out at the country club with Gianni."

He lets out a soft laugh that rumbles in his chest. "I am —mostly. But I'm training for a triathlon now, and my coach is based here." He glances around at the punching bags and mats. "I'm raising money for breast cancer research, in honor of Mom."

His voice catches on that last word, and I feel my chest tighten. My little brother, lifting weights for a breast cancer, the same thing that took our mother and the reason why all of our family's fundraisers - our galas, our charity matches and races - center on that disease. "A triathlon?" I echo, stepping back to take in his lean frame, the sinews in his forearms. "Where?"

"In Hawaii. The Ironman World Championship." He flexes a bicep and grins, the veins popping beneath his sun-bronzed skin. "26.2 miles running under that brutal Kona sun, 112 miles biking through black lava fields that shimmer with heat, and 2.4 miles swimming in the Kailua Bay. They call it the ultimate endurance test for a reason. Celeste thought it'd be a meaningful way to honor Mom. All I have to do to qualify is complete a different Iron Man this spring and pay a fee and I can get in through the Iron Man Executive Challenge."

A swell of pride warms me. "If anyone can complete an Iron Man, it's you." I rest a hand on his shoulder. "But how do you sleep? You're running a movie studio, there's a new baby at home—Celeste—"

He shrugs, eyes bright. "I make it work." He puffs out his chest and lands a playful punch on my arm. "Hey, you want in? I was planning to ask one brother to train with me—and you're the obvious choice. You're doing that MMA charity tournament for breast cancer research too, right?"

My throat goes dry, and I swallow hard. Max wants me by his side in Hawaii, not Ansel. After all the harsh words I've spat or nearly said to him, here he is offering me a place on his team. My heart stutters in my chest as I look at him—his hopeful smile, the steady confidence in his stance—and wonder how I ever doubted his loyalty.

I shrug. "Sure." Like I'm agreeing to grab a burger instead of committing to the most grueling triathlon on earth. The Ironman. I've got this. While my brothers all maintain decent physiques—Connor for his shirtless scenes, Kalen for his stage presence—Max and I take it to another level. He's the only one who matches my 5 AM workouts, my protein-obsessed meal prep, my constant tracking of metrics. Swimming 2.4 miles in Kona Bay? Thank god it's not open ocean. Biking 112 miles under the Hawaiian sun before running a full marathon? It'll be hell. But I've never met a challenge I didn't want to conquer. And if it means more time with Max, even better.

Max's face breaks into a smile and he embraces me again. "Well," he says. "Let's coordinate our schedules. I mean, maybe you'll start training after your MMA tournament. I won't be participating in this year's triathlon, of course, because it's in a matter of months - this October. So it'll be next year. Plenty of time for you to transition from MMA to triathlon training. I'll be looking forward to doing this with you, Rome."

At that, Max goes back to what he was doing - running on the treadmill. I turn back to Caspian. "Well, what do you know? Max wants to train for a triathlon with me. Not Ansel, but me." This gives me a strange sense of pride, like a brother finally chose me for something as opposed to somebody else. And not just a brother, but Max, the guy I've been resenting my whole life, a fact that I never acknowledged until Lilith brought it out with one of her tarot spreads.

"See," Caspian says. "And they all got your back as much as Max does. You just have to open your eyes." He looks at me meaningfully. "Now, to tackle your feelings about your father and Lilith…"

"One thing at a time," I say with a smile.

Chapter Thirty

ROMAN

I decide to go ahead and do something I've been avoiding like the plague - review my father's proposal for the eco-resort project. The thick manila folder sits on my glass desk, its edges worn from where his hands touched it. When I finally crack it open, the business plan inside is immaculate - crisp white pages with precise charts and projections.

While I'm not shocked that my father remembers how to put together a proposal - he ran Kensington Pictures' international distribution with an iron fist before he vanished into the misty English countryside to milk Holsteins and down pints with ruddy-faced farmers for twenty-two years - I'm caught off guard by how meticulously he's thought through every detail.

I call Cameron, my phone pressed between ear and shoulder as I flip through the glossy appendices. "Cam," I say, my voice echoing in my cavernous office. "I read Dad's proposal. It's actually quite good. I'm thinking I'll test some concepts at the Verde, see if they hold water. No pun intended."

"That's great, Rome," Cameron says, his voice warm through the speaker. "You should call Dad and meet with him."

"Not quite ready for that," I reply, mentally noting the "quite" slipping into my vocabulary - a hairline crack in my resolve.

For the next two weeks, I implement Dad's ideas at the Verde, after lengthy consultations with my sustainability team - three earnest engineers with identical wire-rimmed glasses. And throughout those two weeks overseeing the resort's eco-friendly renovations, Lilith keeps slipping into my thoughts. She wouldn't know the first thing about sustainable HVAC systems or gray water recycling, yet I find myself wanting to tell her about every solar panel we install. I catch myself imagining her smile when I mention I'm taking Dad's proposal so seriously. Or how her eyes would light up hearing that Max convinced me to sign up for the Ironman after my MMA tournament wraps. The timing works perfectly—I need this muscle mass for the cage, but distance training will strip me down to something leaner, more efficient. Different bodies for different battles.

She hasn't been at the resort in weeks. Miranda tells me she's taken some time off. I remember Jack telling me about Lilith taking some time off for a retreat in Big Sur, so that's probably where she is.

But I can't take another day of this. Before I can talk myself out of it, I'm behind the wheel of my Range Rover, cutting through Venice Beach traffic toward Mystic Tides. The steering wheel feels slick beneath my grip. What the hell am I doing? We haven't spoken in a month, yet here I am, desperate to loop her into every detail of this project like she's already mine.

She might not even be at Mystic Tides yet—might still

be on the winding coastal drive back from Big Sur. But I need to see her. Need to hear her voice, before I lose my goddamn mind.

The great Roman Kensington, racing through the streets because some tarot-reading hippie hasn't called him in a month. My brothers would never let me live this down.

Chapter Thirty-One

LILITH

Jack leans against the counter as I unlock the store Monday morning. "So? Big Sur? Spill."

I smile, still feeling the lingering peace from my impromptu two weeks away. LA's version of nature—the manicured paths of Griffith Park, the carefully arranged stones in the Van Nuys Japanese Garden—had started to feel like museum exhibits of the outdoors. Big Sur was different. There, the redwoods don't just grow; they command. Waves don't just roll in; they explode against ancient rocks. Waterfalls don't trickle; they plunge straight into the churning Pacific. A week there and I'd remembered what wildness actually feels like.

"Oh, Jack," I say. "There's nothing like Big Sur. I actually was in nature up there. I can't describe the peacefulness I felt in seeing those trees. Trees that have been around since the birth of Christ. Can you imagine them back then? Just little tiny sprouts, determined to grow? And then at some point, they become little twigs. And now they're two hundred feet tall and blanket that forest into darkness. The things they've seen...and I felt the universe talking to me in that forest. And in the surf. It all just felt so untouched."

"And the retreat itself?"

"It was wonderful. It was one full week of mindfulness meditation practice. And then one week of ancient wisdom practices and how to incorporate them into our daily life. I never felt more at peace than I did there."

Jack nods. "Well, Lilith, I-"

The shop bell chimes. I glance up and freeze. Roman. Standing in my doorway, backlit by afternoon sun. My pulse quickens instantly. We haven't spoken since the Blake incident weeks ago, but something's different about him. His energy has shifted—his aura is not the stormy black cloud I'd grown accustomed to, nor the fierce crimson intensity, but something warmer, more balanced. Orange. Creative. Thoughtful. Emotionally centered. I can't help the small gasp that escapes me.

"Lilith," he says gently.

"Rome," I say, staring at the oak floors under my bare feet, my toes curling against the smooth wood. My face grows hot. My heart pounds like it did when I was sixteen in Ms. Harmon's biology class, drawing star signs instead of labeling frog parts. I can almost smell the chemicals again, feel my heavy thrift-store skirt with the little mirrors I'd sewn on it, hear people whispering about my purple-streaked hair that hung to my waist.

Roman would've been the popular guy back then—wearing his sports jacket over wide shoulders, walking confidently through hallways as other students moved aside, wearing a crown at the dance while I stayed home reading cards.

I shake my head, my amethyst earrings swinging against my neck. That old insecurity still follows me—the feeling I don't belong around rich boys in expensive suits. High school never really ends, does it? The feeling clings to me like the sandalwood scent that fills my shop. And now here's Roman, standing between my bundles of sage and old spell books, the incense smoke wrapping around him as if I'd planned it that way all along.

Roman shifts his weight from one Italian leather shoe to the other. "Uh," he says, his jaw working. The man who commands a billion-dollar empire can't string two words together in my little shop. "Lil, I—"

"It's okay," I say softly. The dark cloud that usually surrounds him has lightened, no longer the threatening storm that once made me fear he'd roundhouse kick Blake into next Tuesday. I can breathe easier now, even if I'm not quite ready to trust the calm.

"You know how we talked about my father designing that eco-friendly resort?" he finally manages. I nod, remembering that conversation. "I've started incorporating elements at Verde," he says. His eyes find mine, unexpectedly vulnerable. "Sustainable materials, solar arrays, rainwater collection—the whole package. I thought... with your connection to nature... maybe you'd want to see the plans?"

I nod, inhaling the scent of sage from a nearby bundle. He stands perfectly still, hands in his pockets, but I sense the wildness beneath his tailored suit—a tiger temporarily at rest. Will we end up back where we started, with him snarling at any man who glances my way?

"Sure," I say. "I don't have any more readings scheduled for today. They were all this morning."

He nods. "You haven't been at the resort lately."

"I haven't. I've been away. In Big Sur."

"Right," he says shyly. "Well, if you don't have any

readings, would you like to come to the resort to see the changes?"

I smile. "Let's go."

We get in Roman's car—his Range Rover, which has a handle inside so I can get out of it easily, thank God—and the engine roars to life like a caged beast.

"Lilith," he says, his knuckles whitening on the steering wheel. "I'm really sorry about Blake."

I dig my nails into my palm. "Are you apologizing for kicking him and losing your temper?"

He slams his fist against the dashboard. "Yes, that. And for not trusting you."

My pulse quickens. That's what I needed to hear. The violence isn't what burns me—it's what it reveals: his refusal to trust me. The fact he sees it now makes my blood sing.

I lean in, close enough to feel his heat. "And why don't you trust me? What have I ever done to make you think I'm not to be trusted?"

He whips his head toward me, eyes blazing. "Nothing. That I don't trust you is my shit, not yours."

I jerk away, staring at the blur of trees outside. He still doesn't trust me. Every cell in my body screams to escape, but I remain frozen, my breath shallow. His gravity is crushing, inescapable. I'm drowning in him, helpless as a ship being devoured by Charybdis. My brain shrieks warnings, but my heart pounds a different rhythm entirely. I've survived by following nature's law: when heart and head wage war, the heart must triumph. And God help me, my heart is chained to this man, unbreakable.

I lower my voice, eyes on the floor. "You still don't trust me."

"What makes you say that?"

"Present tense." I look up. "Not 'didn't trust me.' You

said 'don't trust me.'" My chin lifts slightly. "You might backpedal now, but those exact words just came out of your mouth. And I've always believed what slips out unplanned is what someone truly means, no matter how much they deny it afterward."

He exhales sharply, his jaw clenched. "I won't lie to you. I don't trust you." His voice drops to a ragged whisper. "But it's my demon to slay, not yours." He seizes my hand, pressing it against his thundering heart before bringing it to his lips. His eyes burn into mine. "I swear to you, I'll tear this darkness out by its roots. Whatever it takes." His grip tightens. "I can't lose you. I won't."

We arrive at the resort as the sun dips low over the Pacific, casting a golden glow across the infinity pool. Roman's calloused fingers intertwine with mine as he guides me through the property, his voice softening with pride as he points out the solar panels disguised within the Spanish tile roofing, the living walls of succulents that reduce cooling costs, and the elegant rain catchment system that feeds the lush native gardens. His thumb absently strokes my knuckles while he explains how each change preserves the luxury experience while reducing the resort's carbon footprint.

"The pools are now all solar-heated," he says, pointing to the various infinity pools and salt-water lap pools around the property. "And these enormous terra-cotta vases are rain barrels that capture rainwater that we can use to water our gardens and even our lawns. And I've put some plans in the works for some more bungalows that will have mattresses filled with cashmere, a natural fiber. I've already implemented this idea in some of the more upscale suites and they've been really popular."

I nod, the ocean breeze tousling my hair as I inhale deeply. "These are beautiful changes," I say, tasting salt on my lips as the late afternoon sun bathes the cliffside in amber light. "You could add those massive driftwood sculptures I saw in Malibu—bleached bone-white and twisted like ancient spirits—in the marble lobby. Or install those heavenly rainfall showers where guests feel embraced by warm, purified ocean water cascading over river stones. Maybe glass-floor sections where they can watch purple starfish and emerald anemones swaying in the tide pools below, or sleek solar panels that catch the light like sequined waves along the winding cliffside path. Your guests would fall in love with this coastline while feeling virtuous about preserving its wild magic."

"Let's go into my office," he says. "I'd like to write down your ideas so I can implement them."

My heart pounds like a tribal drum as his warm fingers close around mine, sending electric currents up my arm. He leads me through the sleek corridor to his corner office—a vast space with floor-to-ceiling windows that frame the glittering Pacific. Roman settles into his ergonomic leather chair, the material sighing beneath his weight as he pulls up to his gleaming glass desk. His fingers hover over the keyboard of his state-of-the-art computer. "Okay," he says, his deep voice resonating in the quiet room. "Now what were your ideas again?"

I take a deep breath, trying to ignore how his cologne—notes of sandalwood and something distinctly masculine—makes my thoughts scatter. "Rainfall showers crafted from purified ocean water," I begin, watching his intense eyes focus on me. "Glass floor sections suspended over natural tide pools where guests can watch the mesmerizing dance of sea anemones and starfish. Driftwood sculptures carved by local artists that tell the story of the Pacific." I tuck a strand of hair behind my ear. "And, I don't know, maybe one of those underwater restaurants like in the Maldives? Or even a luxury underwater suite? I remember reading about them in a travel magazine—how the walls are transparent and schools of tropical fish swim by while you're eating or sleeping."

Roman's eyes widen, dark lashes framing his surprised expression. He snaps his fingers, the sharp sound cutting through the air. "Oh my god, Lilith," he exclaims, leaning forward so suddenly I can see the flecks of amber in his brown irises. "I can't believe you said that. I never even considered underwater luxury suites or restaurants until this moment."

His fingers fly across the keyboard, bringing up dazzling images on his triple monitors—underwater dining rooms where jellyfish float past like living chandeliers, and submerged glass bedrooms where the ocean becomes both ceiling and walls. "The luxury suite has an infinity pool that seems to melt into the sea," he points out, his voice quickening with excitement, "butler's quarters with private access, and enough space for six guests to live like aquatic royalty."

He swivels toward me, his smile transforming his usually stern face. "This is a fantastic idea," he says, his gaze holding mine. "I'll need specialized architects and marine engineers, but these would be perfect for our ultra-high-net-worth clients who've seen everything else."

A smile tugs at my lips. Leave it to Roman to casually drop millions on something as extravagant as underwater dining rooms and bedroom suites. The renderings are breathtaking though—I can almost feel myself drifting off to sleep beneath schools of tropical fish dancing overhead.

Roman pushes away from his chair and perches on the edge of his desk, those mile-long legs dangling. It's a habit I've noticed he reserves for our meetings—this casual posture that seems at odds with the buttoned-up billionaire everyone else sees. I doubt anyone else gets to witness this version of him.

"Lilith," he says, his voice softer than usual. "Your perspective on this is invaluable. What made you think of it? How did you know about these underwater structures in the Maldives?"

"I stumbled across it in Big Sur," I explain. "During a meditation retreat—nothing fancy, just simple bungalows and lots of silence. I was thumbing through a travel magazine in the lobby, waiting for my instructor, when I saw the article. The concept just stuck with me."

His throat bobs with a swallow as he shuffles papers on his desk, not meeting my eyes. "These weeks without you... I've been miserable," he admits. "I know I fucked up."

"You did," I say, my lips curving despite myself. "And I've been counting the days too. But if you can't bring yourself to trust me—"

Roman slides off the edge of his desk in one fluid motion and draws me to my feet. His fingers thread through my hair, his voice dropping to a murmur against my temple. "Trust takes time with me. I'm trying."

And then he's kissing me, his mouth crashing against mine with such force I stumble backward, my spine meeting the cool plaster wall as his calloused hands find my flushed face, my tangled hair, the sensitive hollow of my neck—anywhere to hold me closer. I taste cherries and ocean salt and raw need on his tongue as it slides against mine, three torturous weeks of absence dissolving in the molten heat between us. His strong fingers dig into the curve of my hips, lifting me effortlessly until my feet dangle above the hardwood floor, and I wrap my trembling legs around his solid waist, not caring about that stupid fight anymore, only that now we're breathing each other's ragged air, desperate and starving like survivors of some emotional shipwreck.

His calloused hands claim my feverish skin with desperate hunger, strong fingers pressing into my soft flesh as if trying to reach the very marrow of my soul. I cry out —a high, broken sound—when Roman's perfect white teeth graze the sensitive hollow of my neck, the sharp sting melting into liquid pleasure as he growls my name —"Lilith"—like a sacred prayer and a forbidden curse tangled together in the humid darkness between us.

Then he carries me to his couch and the solid weight of his muscled body crushes me into the vicuña wool, anchoring me to earth while my dizzy mind threatens to shatter into a thousand glittering pieces.

We're soon naked and when he slips on a condom and drives into me with one powerful thrust, I claw at his broad, sweat-slicked back, feeling the electric connection between us ignite like summer wildfire. His midnight eyes burn into mine, pupils blown so wide with desire that only a thin ring of amber remains, a possession that mirrors my own consuming, ravenous need.

I lock my trembling legs around his narrow waist viciously, demanding more, branding this incandescent moment into memory—the corded muscles of his shoulders straining beneath my crimson nails, the primal sound torn from deep within his throat when I command him harder, deeper. When release finally detonates through every nerve ending, it ravages me like his beloved Pacific ocean during a violent storm—powerful, merciless, and absolutely devastating in its intensity.

Afterward, lying on his black leather couch, the Pacific churning and frothing right outside the floor-to-ceiling windows, I watch moonlight glint off the whitecaps while he holds me against his warm chest. His fingers trace lazy patterns on my bare shoulder, his lips occasionally brushing my temple.

My body feels languid, satisfied, yet my mind races with uncertainty. His espresso-dark eyes still hold that guarded look when they meet mine, and he admitted he still doesn't trust me - for no good reason. But I have to follow my heart, which has tangled itself in Roman's presence like sea kelp wrapped around an anchor.

Chapter Thirty-Two

ROMAN

When I spar with Casp next, I notice sweat already on his shoulders as his eyes track me across the mat. "You're lighter," he says, circling with his hands up. My kick catches his ribs—not hard, but he grunts approval. I land three more combinations cleanly, countering his takedown and landing a knee when he gets close. When we break, Caspian wipes his split lip. "That's what I'm talking about, Kensington. Focused." He studies me. "What's with the new attitude?"

A smile tugs at my lips as I picture Lilith's face when I see her tonight. Things with Max have been better too, and I've even caught myself considering Dad's eco-resort pitch more seriously than I'd care to admit.

"Just doing some mental housekeeping," I tell Casp.

He nods approvingly. "Whatever it is, don't stop. You're looking sharp for the tournament."

That evening, I drive to Lilith's place, a bottle of Château Margaux tucked under my arm. I'd grabbed it without thinking—just something from the back of my collection. Only when I'm at her door do I remember it's worth more than her monthly store rent.

The door swings open and there's Lilith, launching herself at me with a squeal of "Roman!" Her legs lock around my waist, and I'm kissing her before I can think, careful not to drop the Cabernet in my right hand. She's practically weightless against me, all warmth and softness.

I set her down gently and place the wine on the kitchen island. The apartment glows with dozens of candles, and the air is thick with jasmine incense—her scent.

I scan the shop. "Jack around?"

Lilith's eyes light up as she shakes her head. "Has a date! Can you believe it? Some A&F model with a billboard on Sunset. Jack's practically vibrating out of his skin over this guy and they just met yesterday. But sometimes lightning strikes—he might be The One!" She clutches her crystal pendant. "God, I hope so!"

Sweet Lilith. Ever the fucking romantic, that one is. Which is why I love her. Oh, god, do I? Yes. Yes I do. My chest constricts at the realization hammering through me for the first time—I love her. The thought slams into me like a tsunami, drowning me in panic while simultaneously anchoring me to earth with absolute certainty.

"I had an idea," Lilith says, twirling pasta onto my plate while I uncork the bottle. "Something to try tonight." One eyebrow arches playfully. "A ritual that might help us avoid another Blake situation at the shop."

"I'm listening," I say, swirling the wine in my glass. I've come around to most of Lilith's spiritual practices—except that panchakarma cleanse I read about. No. Just no. But about the other practices? Open mind. Max has been doing some research on his own because Celeste dabbles, and he assures me that what we think as “alternative” are actually traditions that have survived millennia. "What did you have in mind?"

We finish eating, do the dishes, and then she brings out a velvet pouch, untying its golden drawstring to reveal a collection of gleaming crystals that catch the light.

"These are all blessed by a local shaman, Orion Torres," she says, her eyes brightening. She places a translucent pink stone in my palm, smooth and cool against my skin. "Rose quartz. For harmony and emotional comfort."

Next comes a deep purple crystal with jagged edges that sparkle. "Amethyst for calm and stress relief." A silvery lavender stone follows. "Lepidolite, for anxiety relief and emotional balance."

She adds a delicate pale blue stone with swirling patterns. "And Blue Lace Agate, for better communication and to soothe your mind." She cups her hands around mine, pressing the stones into my palm with gentle pressure, her touch lingering as she nods. "One more." A glossy black stone, sleek and substantial, joins the others. "Black tourmaline - protective and absorbs negative energy."

I smile, half-ready to humor her by accepting these crystals as if they might magically grant me the inner peace I've chased my whole life. Only she's ever given me that—well, except when I see her with another man and my vision goes blood-red. But Lilith has a different angle.

"The crystals don't have to be magic," she says, her eyes earnest. "Think of them like... mental speed bumps. Like when people wear rubber bands to snap whenever they crave sugar or alcohol. It interrupts the automatic response. So next time you feel that anger building, you could touch these—" she nudges the stones toward me, "—and give your brain a chance to step in before your temper takes over."

I smile and finger the crystals—cool, jagged amethyst

and polished rose quartz—and nod. "Well, it's worth a shot," I say, my voice rougher than intended. "If nothing else, they might be placebos." Then I reach into the pocket of my tailored slacks, fingers brushing against warm metal keys before finding what I'm looking for. "And I'd like to give you this," I say, extending my palm to reveal a piece of sea glass—smooth as silk, the color of absinthe, worn by countless tides into the size of a large pebble. "It's from our day of surfing."

The memory returns—her hair stiff with salt, her skin warm and sweet-smelling, her laugh as the waves broke around us. I feel my face flush. That night on the empty beach, just us under the stars. I've carried this piece of glass with me since then, something to hold onto during difficult moments at work. Now I want Lilith to have it.

Her eyes go wide when I hand her the green shard, and she holds it up like it's a million-dollar gem, not something I picked up on the beach. "Oh, Roman, it's beautiful!" she breathes. The sea glass catches the light against her palm, and I find myself watching her face instead of the glass. "Sea glass represents resilience—broken pieces transformed by the ocean into something precious."

Of course she knows the spiritual meaning of random beach debris. She traces its edge with her fingertip. "This could've been battered by waves for centuries. Maybe from an ancient Roman vessel." When she smiles at me—those little crinkles by her eyes, cheeks flushed—something in my chest shifts. Christ. The woman gets more joy from beach trash than the wives of my investors get from their ten-carat diamonds.

I nod. "That sea glass must have some real power. Ever since that night on the beach, I've found myself reaching for that memory whenever things get rough." I sigh, my fingers curling into a fist at my side. The red haze still comes, still blinds me sometimes. But I'm fighting it.

What helps most is her—Lilith. When she's near, my mind quiets. The storm inside me calms to stillness. Unless I see her with another man. Then it's like watching someone else hold my oxygen tank while I'm drowning. That's why Blake gets under my skin so badly. I've come to need her peace, and seeing her offer it to someone else makes the chaos roar back with a vengeance.

We sit down on the couch and listen to some music - Tori Amos, the singer-songwriter that Lilith loves the most when she's relaxing. Especially this particular album, *Little Earthquakes,* Tori Amos' very first. We're sipping on wine and I'm studying the crystals Lilith gave me. And, for some odd reason, an image of my mother - beautiful, blonde, way too young to die - comes into my mind.

I was barely three when we lost her. Strange how memory works—I still see her lying there, skin stretched too tight across her bones, head bare where her blonde hair used to be. She'd finally agreed to treatment after Max was born, though the doctors had already given their grim verdicts.

I remember us gathered around her bed that last day—all eight brothers, with tiny Max cradled in Rosa's arms. Rosa, who'd become more mother to us than housekeeper by then. Through her room's silence came this very song playing softly on her CD. The lyrics about standing alone when your protector's gone—they weren't just words. Even at three, something in me recognized that this song would dictate my life.

I stare at the ceiling, the melody washing over me. "'Winter,'" I whisper. "This song..." My throat tightens. "They played it in her room that last day." Mom died at home, in a hospital bed, surrounded by machines, IV drips and her family.

My fingers tremble slightly as I remember Cam's hand gripping mine as my mother took her last breath—three years old and terrified, but Cam was there. Always there. While Connor and Kalen had each other, while Asher shadowed Silas and Ansel trailed after Max, Cam chose me.

I rub my face. Christ, I've been an ungrateful bastard to him.

"What is it about this song?" Lilith's voice is gentle, patient.

"The lyrics," I say. "When I hear it, it's her voice. Mom loved Tori Amos." I close my eyes. "It's about finding your way back to yourself. About standing proud when the person you love is gone. Forgiveness. Peace." I touch one of the crystals, cool against my fingertips. "Growing up, I'd see mothers with their children in restaurants and this... rage would build inside me." I inhale deeply. "And I'd blame Max. We all did, once we were old enough to understand that she died for him."

Lilith nods. "She did it because she loved him, not because she had to."

"Why do you think that?"

"Well," she says, her eyes softening. "People don't jump in front of bullets because it's on their list of things to do that day. They do it because they care about someone more than they care about themselves. The love is so strong it pushes the fear away. It makes their own life feel small next to the person they're saving."

I swallow hard, my voice barely above a whisper. "Why couldn't she choose us? Choose to stay alive?" I run my hand through my hair, searching for words. "It reminds me of that trolley problem. You know the one—train's coming, can't stop. Eight people tied to one track, one person tied to another. You're standing at the switch. Do you let it keep going, kill the eight? Or do you pull the lever, divert it, kill the one? Either way, you've got blood on your hands."

Lilith's eyes soften. "Utilitarian theory - the greatest good for the greatest number," she murmurs. "But Roman, what if she couldn't bring herself to flip that switch? What if she already felt that baby's heartbeat as part of her own?"

I lift one shoulder in a half-hearted shrug. "Some things just don't have good answers." My chest feels heavy, and I need to steer us away from this topic. "What are your thoughts on the eco-resort concept?" Lilith saw some of the concepts integrated into my resort. I wonder what she thinks about the entire project.

Lilith's eyes light up. "Like I said, it's brilliant! And I'm so excited about some of the alternative spa therapies your father might provide that are based on ancient practices. But what really excites me is the sustainability aspect. Reducing the carbon footprint while connecting hospitality to nature's rhythms? That's exactly what the industry needs. Is the location near any natural spaces?"

I drum my fingers against the edge of the desk. "Laguna Beach. Prime location—ocean views with the canyon right behind it." My jaw tightens. "That is, once it's built. Dad's eyeing one of my existing properties. A boutique hotel I acquired last year but never personally managed. His big plan is to buy it from me, convert it into complete eco-friendly and rebrand it as his signature resort."

"Laguna is perfect!" Her smile widens. "Forest bathing is transformative—barefoot on the earth, pine-scented air filling your lungs, leaves crunching underfoot. And with ocean access too..."

I manage a tight nod, my thoughts drifting elsewhere.

She studies my face. "Are you considering reaching out to your father about collaborating on this?" Her hopeful expression makes me want to promise her I'll call him immediately. But I can't bring myself to offer false assurances.

I hold up a hand. "Let's not get ahead of ourselves." Then I pause, realizing something. My father's face flashes in my mind, and my jaw doesn't clench. My fists don't ball up. The thought of him doesn't trigger that familiar surge of heat behind my eyes. I still don't want to see him, but the murderous impulse has faded to a dull ache.

Is it Lilith's presence? Something about her melts the ice in my veins. Or maybe it's the work I've been doing, the mental reps of imagining a conversation where I don't launch myself across the table at him. Baby steps.

I lean in and kiss her. That same jolt runs through me. Strange how just talking with her calms me down, like sitting by the ocean. But when her lips part, that calm vanishes. My heart pounds, and I want more of her.

I lift her into my arms—Christ, she weighs nothing—and carry her to her bed, sheets already a mess from earlier. She smells like that hippie shop of hers, jasmine and salt air, and I can't get enough. As I devour her mouth, worship between her thighs, and finally drive into her with savage need, I burn every curve into my memory like a man possessed, mapping uncharted paradise. She rakes her nails down my back, drawing blood, marking me as conquered territory—her territory—and I surrender completely to her claim.

Hours blur. Moonlight cuts across her back while she rides me and I drive into her again and again…Dawn's coming, but I don't give a damn. I want her again. And again. And again. Like some addiction I never saw coming, this need to taste every inch of her skin.

We finally lay in her bed, both of us sated for now, her in my arms as I stroke her hair and kiss her forehead lightly.

Lilith's dark hair spills across my chest, the green streaks catching the moonlight that filters through her bedroom windows. Her skin is warm against mine beneath the sheets.

"You know what I learned in my retreat in Big Sur," she says, tracing circles on my bare shoulder.

"What's that?" I watch her lips move, still swollen from our kisses.

"Well, there's a way to heal intergenerational trauma. It's something that anybody can really do, even people who don't believe in the things I believe in."

"And what's that?" I brush a strand of hair from her face, my dark eyes meeting hers.

She takes a deep breath, her chest rising against mine. "Visualization. Meditation. You focus on the trauma as if it's alive, breathing..." Her fingers dance in the air between us. "Then you surround it with white light until it turns to black smoke that just... disappears."

I smile as I thread my fingers through hers, feeling the delicate bones beneath her soft skin. "I could try that," I say. I'm humoring her, but not really - I'm willing to try anything and if it helps to picture the trauma of losing my mother so young and having my father bolt for so many years as something bathed in white light until it turns to black smoke and disappears into the ether, then why not?

"I hope you do," she says, looking at me with those topaz-jade eyes that seem to shift color in the sunlight streaming through her windows.

"And there's always something else that helps, too," I say, tracing the curve of her collarbone with my thumb.

"My MMA training. What do you say about coming to my charity match? I'll be raising money for breast cancer research, the same thing our family always raises money for."

I take a deep breath, inhaling the scent of her lavender shampoo. This isn't something I share with just anybody. I've been in charity tournaments before, and I've never once thought about inviting whatever woman I happened to be dating at the time. But this is different. I'm realizing that I need Lilith like I need air.

"I'd love to go," she says, kissing me, her lips tasting faintly of the herbal tea she'd been drinking.

We make love again, slower this time, my hands mapping every curve and hollow of her body as if committing it to memory. Neither of us have anyplace to go today, as it's Saturday and I always take Saturdays off to surf. Surfing will happen today, of course, as usual, the Pacific waves calling to me like an old friend. But later on today.

For right now, there's just the two of us, drowning in each other in Egyptian cotton sheets that feel like clouds against our skin.

Chapter Thirty-Three

ROMAN

I'm meeting my father at Sea Foam Brew on Monday to discuss the eco-hotel project. After twenty-two years of silence, I'm as ready as I'll ever be—which is to say, not ready at all. That's why I chose this particular coffee shop on Venice Beach. It's only a block from Lilith's store, where I can escape afterward when my nerves are shot to hell.

When my father walks in, I rise to my feet, jaw clenching when I see Max trailing behind him. Why is my youngest brother so invested in this project? The man has a newborn at home and runs a freshly-merged studio that's been churning out blockbusters like a factory. Plus, he's training for the Iron Man next year. He shouldn't have time to breathe. Yet here he is, playing mediator.

Smart move on my father's part, bringing backup, in case Hurricane Roman turns into a Cat 5. Maybe the old man knows me better than I thought.

I clear my throat. "Dad." The word feels like a stone in my mouth. Sure, I agreed to this meeting about his proposal, but that doesn't mean I'm rolling out the welcome mat.

"Rome." His voice breaks, eyes glistening with unshed tears. Classic Michael Kensington manipulation. All I see is the same weakness that infected half my brothers. "Thank you for coming."

I tap the proposal on the table, pages bleeding with my red ink corrections and other ideas I wrote in the margins. "It has potential." My attention shifts. "Max. Didn't expect to see you here."

Max straightens his tie. "I've been studying up on resort development. Thought I could contribute something valuable."

I arch an eyebrow. "Between running your company and changing diapers? Does Celeste know you've taken on another project?" I shake my head. "She must be thrilled."

"It's just something on the side," he says with a shrug.

I study him, seeing him differently now. Another brother falling into Dad's orbit, willing to sacrifice precious hours with his family to chase approval from a man who abandoned us all. And for what? To dabble in something he knows nothing about.

Still...I can't help but admire Max's loyalty, misguided as it is. The fact that he's here, and he's sacrificing precious moments to help Dad with this project - it's all so transparent. He thinks if Dad stays busy with blueprints and investors, there won't be time for whiskey and disappearing acts.

My chest tightens watching him shoulder a burden that was never his to carry. I want to grab him by those tense shoulders and tell him what took me years to learn: Dad's demons are his own. We didn't pour the drinks then, and we can't stop them now. Max needs to loosen his white-knuckle grip before Dad inevitably does what Dad's always done—choose his own path, consequences be damned.

I glance at Max. "With your schedule, I'm surprised you even have time to hit the bathroom. Your call, though. Just don't get your hopes up." I arch one eyebrow, and his slight nod tells me he understands.

Dad clears his throat. I've been staring at everything but him since he took a seat. "Rome, you have no idea how much it means that you're considering my eco-resort concepts. I could really use your guidance on making something like this work."

Something in my chest constricts like a fist closing around my heart as my father—his salt-and-pepper hair catching the late afternoon sunlight—seeks my expertise. I blink hard against the sudden burn behind my eyes and remember when our roles were reversed: me, a gap-toothed kid with scraped knees, hanging on his every word, thinking he hung the moon. The way his calloused hands guided mine around a fishing hook slick with worm guts.

I think about him teaching me to ski in Switzerland. His hands were steady on my shoulders while I stood there shaking, convinced the bunny slope was actually a death-defying cliff. His voice broke through my terror as he repeated our code: "Pizza to slow down, French fries to go, Roman. I won't let you fall." I was only 4 then—the same year he taught me to surf. Years later, we'd race each other down black diamonds, shouting like maniacs the whole way. The bastard always won, which drove me crazy, but damn if it wasn't a good time.

I think about his steady grip on my surfboard as I wobbled atop my first wave. The sharp scent of fresh-cut pine as we hammered together a lopsided treehouse that felt like a mansion. I was barely ten, voice still high and clear, when he vanished—but not before he'd leaned close one evening, bourbon on his breath, to give me advice about girls, specifically one girl I was crushing on and wanted his advice about how to approach her.

I shake my head, trying to push away memories that hit me like a rogue wave. My throat tightens, and I notice my hands trembling against the table. Shit. I walked right into this trap. I'm not as bulletproof as I thought.

"So, Dad," I manage, reaching for my phone. "I implemented similar sustainability measures at Verde." I swipe through photos of the resort renovations. "Lilith actually suggested—" I stop cold. He's going to ask who she is and what do I tell him - what is she to me? The word "girlfriend" feels both too juvenile and too significant. "Partner" sounds like we share a law firm or we're gay. "Significant other" is what guys who drink kombucha say. And "friend" doesn't begin to cover what goes on between us as often as we can see each other.

Dad's eyes light up like I just offered him a winning lottery ticket. "Lilith? Who's that?"

Great. I just handed him the perfect opening. Now he'll try to extract personal details, thinking if I talk about my woman, he can mention Patricia, and suddenly we're bonding like he didn't disappear for two decades. Like we're normal. Like we're actually father and son.

Max is practically vibrating in his seat, his eyes lit up like it's Christmas morning. I know that look—he's itching to spill everything about Lilith to Dad. Our eyes lock across the table. His excitement dims as he reads the warning in my eyes - I'm giving him the same look I gave Blake right before I roundhouse kicked him to the floor. That's how it's always been—seven brothers who know exactly where the line is with me, and how quickly I'll cross mine if they step over theirs.

I open my mouth, but something makes me stop. "She's..." The syllables of Lilith's name sit heavy on my tongue. I work my jaw. Fuck that. This man standing in front of me—he doesn't get access to her. That's not something he's earned.

My jaw tightens. "Never mind." Max's face falls. I catch his eye, my expression hardening into a warning. Dad shifts in his chair, his gaze flicking between us. At least he has the decency to stay silent.

Dad nods, his green eyes dimming like lights in a power outage. Did he honestly think I'd roll out the red carpet to my inner world after all these years? That I'd pour him a scotch and tell him about Lilith, about the nightmares that still wake me? This meeting has an agenda, typed and printed: business only. Nothing else is on the table—certainly not the father-son heart-to-heart he seems to be fishing for.

Then I look at Max and feel that familiar burn rising in my chest. My fists clench at my sides. Max—all of them—have welcomed him back like some prodigal father. I can picture it now: Dad sitting on Cam's leather couch, nursing a beer while my oldest brother passes him photos of Alecia cradling baby Stephanie. That little face he'll never actually see. That tiny coffin he wasn't there to carry. His own granddaughter, gone before he bothered to return. His daughter-in-law, who he'll also never know. I hope whatever he found out in England was worth missing all this.

I slam the folder down on the desk. "Your proposal shows promise. But there are things I'd change."

Dad leans forward. His knuckles whiten as he grips the chair's armrests. Behind his eyes, I see it—that desperate hunger to breach my defenses, to force his way back into my life with his goddamn apologies for vanishing when we needed him most. Does he actually think the word sorry fixes anything?

"Son," he says, voice cracking. "Whatever you say. You're the expert."

I lock eyes with him, jaw clenched. "I'm an expert at running resorts that don't give a shit about carbon footprints. Not eco-friendly designs. But I've got sustainability architects and engineers—absolute geniuses—who tore your proposal apart and found every weakness. Things you never even considered."

Dad's eyes light up like he just won the fucking lottery. "Go ahead," he says, and I can read his thoughts without Lilith's tarot cards. He's practically doing backflips in his head because I'm talking to him instead of hurling him through the plate glass window.

Max has that same puppy-dog hope plastered across his face. I shake my head hard. Goddammit. I'm sending the wrong message. I want to cut this man out of my life like a tumor. But I can't let him crash and burn—he'd crawl right back inside a bottle and end up at Uncle Thomas' farm again, leaving my brothers shattered. Christ. They'll break in ways worse than if this walking disappointment had stayed dead to us all along.

"Let me summarize just some of the changes my experts suggest." Then I go through some of the suggestions with my father, whose eyes widen at my red-inked changes.

"Roman, Jesus—I can't believe you actually took this seriously." His voice cracks slightly. "What did your sustainability team say? Can we make this happen?"

I lock eyes with him. "It'll work. But you need serious capital—fifty million, minimum." I slam my palm on the table. My jaw tightens. The truth burns in my throat: with the Roman Kensington name attached, investors would be climbing over each other, throwing cash at his feet. Without me, he won't get funding. But I'm not ready to help him—not yet.

He nods. "I'll talk to Dad."

Max leans forward. "Roman. If you put your name behind this, Dad wouldn't have to get a loan."

My molars grind together so hard I taste enamel dust. Blood rushes to my face, pounding in my temples. I slam both palms on the table and stand, sending my chair crashing backward.

"This meeting is over." I lock eyes with Max, daring him to say one more goddamn word. The little shit ambushed me in front of my father, put me on the spot, and he knows he's wrong.

I storm out without another word. Outside the coffee shop, I pause and glance back through the window. Dad's head is bowed, shoulders shaking slightly. Max has his arm around him. My chest tightens and my throat burns. Damn it. Am I the asshole here? I take three steps back toward the door, then stop. I turn away, then back again. My fist clenches, unclenches.

Twenty-two fucking years and he ambushes me with Max like this. I reach for the coffee shop door handle, then jerk my hand away like it's electrified. I exhale slowly, run a hand through my hair. Max catches my eye through the glass, nods once. Whatever. Max will handle it. He always does. That's his thing, not mine. Isn't it?

After swinging by Mystic Tides and finding the CLOSED sign hanging in the window, I drive straight to Lilith's place. It's just past seven when Jack swings open her front door, his eyebrows shooting up.

"Well hello, gorgeous! Perfect timing. Lilith's wrapping up her meditation circle—first one in ages. The ladies are about to hit some fancy cocktails. Well, except our girl. She'll nurse some mocktails, as she don't drink so much, as I'm sure you've noticed."

"They're still at it?" I ask, glancing toward the living room.

"Just finishing. She used to host these weekly before your resort snatched up all her free time. Tonight's the big comeback—five of her closest girlfriends in there getting their zen on."

I stare down at my calloused knuckles and exhale slowly. What am I even doing here? Her world: crystal healing and group meditation. Mine: boardroom battles and buried rage. I'm a walking disaster with daddy issues and a mean right hook. Someone like her—all light and genuine goodness—deserves better than getting dragged into my darkness. And how long until I take away all her light with my vortex?

Goddamn it, I'm a fucking parasite for being with her. She's like oxygen to me—the only thing that silences the goddamn hurricane raging between my ears. But what the hell does she get? A quarter-million crystal pendant? A store makeover I threw money at? That's not love—that's just me buying the right to drain her light until there's nothing left. Christ, I'm no better than my father.

I shake my head. "Uh, I shouldn't have come here. Don't tell Lilith I stopped by, okay?"

Jack knits his brows. "Okay, but-"

I clench my jaw. "Got an early meeting tomorrow and I haven't been sleeping much lately." My body aches with exhaustion, but I'd sacrifice every minute of rest to feel Lilith writhing beneath me again. For three straight nights,

I've stayed over with her and devoured her until dawn, pinning her against the headboard, the wall, the floor—anywhere I can claim her. The sound of her gasping my name has become an addiction I can't shake. She probably hasn't closed her eyes for more than an hour at a time either.

I drive back home with a jackhammer pounding behind my eyes. What a goddamn train wreck I am. Just thirty minutes with my father and my mind's a war zone again—worse than before. How do you forgive someone who taught you that trust is for suckers? The old man's like a virus in my system—infecting everything from how I run my hotels to how I look at Lilith when she smiles at me. She's the only person who's ever made the noise in my head quiet down, who's made me feel... Christ, I don't even have words for it.

But I'm damaged goods. Period. And Lilith? She's got her little bookshop, that Jack guy who makes her laugh, those crystal-clutching friends who probably chant under the full moon. She radiates light. Meanwhile, I'm over here dragging around twenty-two years of daddy issues like a ball and chain.

I've got to end this. Cut her loose before she drowns with me. It'll gut me, but she deserves better.

Chapter Thirty-Four

LILITH

My friends from the psychic fair spread their colorful cushions across the living room floor, folding their legs into lotus positions around me. Sage, Luna, Aurora, Hazel and Indigo—it's been months since we've gathered like this. Between running Mystic Tides, helping at the resort, and spending time with Roman, I've barely had a moment. Incense burns in the corner while our tea cools, and someone's put on Enya in the background.

We spill into my living room where Jack stands at the bar cart, stirring drinks. He's already made virgin margaritas for the girls who drove here, and one for me too—I'm more of a occasional-glass-of-wine person anyway. Something about tequila feels too much like an escape hatch, and I've never needed one of those.

"Well?" Jack asks, dipping his pinky into his own very-much-not-virgin margarita. He winces. "Needs more agave."

Aurora beams at him, her face still flushed from meditation. "Divine. There's nothing like riding that collective energy wave. These women are magical."

Jack squints. "Remind me what TM stands for again?"

"Transcendental meditation is just sitting quietly for twenty minutes, twice a day, repeating a personal mantra in your mind while letting thoughts drift by without judgment —no complicated poses or breathing required. It's like mental flossing that helps clear out stress," Indigo explains. "It could be any mantra, something that means something to you at that moment, for instance."

"Like Lilith might chant something like 'tall, dark, handsome and complicated' over and over again?" Jack asks, teasing me.

I laugh. "Yes, that definitely describes Roman."

"Oh, Roman?" Hazel asks. "Do tell."

I don't know what to say. Roman consumes me like wildfire, burning through every defense I've ever built. My heart hammers against my ribs at the mere thought of him. What we have feels almost dangerous in its intensity—like staring directly at the sun. "He's..." My voice catches. I swallow hard, trying to contain the trembling in my hands. "He's unlike anyone I've ever known," I finally whisper, the inadequacy of these words crushing me. "He's a very special guy."

"A very special guy who was here tonight," Jack says with a grin.

My heart beats out of my chest. "Here tonight? What happened to him?"

Jack shrugs. "Said he had something to do. Said he was tired or something."

Just then, my phone buzzes. Roman's text.

> Lilith. I can't do this. I'm texting because I'd shatter if I heard your voice. I'm drowning in my own darkness and I refuse to pull you under with me. You deserve better than the fucking chaos I bring. We'll cross paths at the resort, but that's it. Don't try to fix this. Don't try to fix me. I'm sorry.

And that was it. He didn't even sign his name.

Indigo's gaze locks with mine, her pupils dilating slightly. Among my spiritual sisters, she's always had the strongest connection to the other side. "I sense something about Roman," she murmurs, her voice dropping an octave. "There's a shadow following him tonight. A deep, dark shadow." She extends her palm. "I need something with his energy on it."

I slip into my bedroom and return with the crystal he gave me for the gala and the sea glass he picked up from the beach on the first night we made love. When Indigo's fingers close around them, her body goes rigid, shoulders tensing. "He's drowning in darkness tonight, Lilith. Absolutely drowning."

Oh. I need to get to him, then. His text notwithstanding, if he's in trouble, I need to be there. In the kitchen, Jack's laughter mingles with the clink of wine glasses as Luna arranges cucumber slices around the edge of the hummus bowl. The scent of warm pita fills the apartment.

I glance at my phone again, then back at my friends who've barely settled in for our catch-up. My stomach knots. They'll understand, won't they? I grab my keys from the hook. I have to get to Roman.

But where does he live? I have no idea. Never been there before. So I text Max, ask him for Roman's address, which he readily gives to me. He says he's concerned about his brother, too.

> Roman met with Dad earlier. Coffee shop meetup ended with him bolting out the door. I've blown up his phone for hours—nothing. Classic Roman shutdown mode. To get into his apartment, he needs to meet me in the lobby and escort me or give me special permission and when he's in one of these moods, nobody's getting through. The doorman at his Four Seasons building just shrugged when I showed up. Can't help worrying about what's going on in his head right now.I keep picturing him up there alone, probably putting his fist through something expensive. Can' t shake this knot in my stomach.

I flash an apologetic smile at the women gathered around my tarot table. "I hate to cut this short, but Jack can finish your readings." My pulse hammers against my throat as I gather my cards with trembling fingers. Somewhere across town, Roman might be smashing glassware against walls or emptying a bottle of whiskey. The vision of either scenario sends me straight to my car, my hands shaking on the wheel.

I get to Roman's apartment building, The Four Seasons private residences, and my jaw drops. The gleaming glass tower pierces the sky like a diamond-tipped spear, doormen in crisp uniforms standing sentinel beneath a massive portico. Fountains dance in synchronized patterns across the marble courtyard. Holy shit, this isn't just luxury—this is wealth so excessive it feels like stepping onto another planet.

I approach the doorman, his white gloves pristine

against the navy uniform, his posture military-straight beneath the gleaming brass buttons of his jacket.

"May I help you?" His voice is clipped, professional, with just a hint of judgment as he takes in my home-sewn wrinkled sundress and windblown hair.

God, do I feel out of my depth. The marble lobby stretches behind him like an ocean I could drown in. "Roman Kensington. He lives in the penthouse suite. I need to see him." My voice comes out smaller than I intended.

"Do you have special permission to see him?" One eyebrow arches slightly.

"I don't." I clutch my purse strap tighter, feeling the leather bite into my palm.

He nods, lips pressed into a thin line. "Mr. Kensington is our most treasured guest." Then he sees something in my eyes—raw desperation, probably—and his expression softens. He nods again. "I'll contact him and see if he can meet you here."

I practically bounce on my toes. "Thank you!" My arms twitch with the urge to hug him, but I keep them at my sides. People at the farmers market always joke that I'd hug a cactus if it looked lonely enough, but I won't hug him, even though I'm dying to.

My stomach knots as I follow him. Max couldn't even get Roman to see him—his own brother. What chance do I have? Some hippie girl from Venice Beach who drove forty minutes up the coast on nothing but a hope and a prayer. But I had to try.

To my relief, he comes right back. "Mr. Kensington will be down shortly."

The urge to embrace him overwhelms me again, and before I can stop myself, my arms are around his broad shoulders, my eyes stinging with the threat of tears. "Thank you," I whisper.

His smile tightens at the edges as he stands there, wooden and uncertain. I've made him uncomfortable. I should probably regret my impulsiveness, but I can't bring myself to. In my world, unexpected hugs are like those little kindnesses strangers sometimes offer—small but necessary gifts. Everyone craves that connection, that momentary shelter of another person's arms. At least, I think they do.

It seems like forever, but Roman soon appears in the lobby. He nods at the doorman. “Thanks, Henry,” he says. “I’ll take it from here.”

We rocket upward in the elevator to the twelfth floor. The doors slide open directly into his penthouse, and I gasp. Moonlight pours through floor-to-ceiling windows, revealing a view that steals my breath. The Los Angeles skyline stretches before me, countless lights twinkling against the night. Marble floors lead past a floating staircase to multiple living areas I can barely take in at once. Through another glass wall, I glimpse a rooftop garden and infinity pool that seems to spill right into the city below.

From here, you can see everything—downtown's skyscrapers to the east, the Hollywood Hills dotted with homes to the north, and to the west, past the grid of streets, the dark expanse of the Pacific, where distant ships' lights blink like stars fallen to earth.

I stand frozen in the doorway, my lips forming a stunned "Oh my god." The glossy pages of *Architectural Digest* hadn't prepared me for this reality—twenty-foot ceilings with exposed beams, floor-to-ceiling windows framing the Pacific, furniture that probably costs more than my entire shop inventory. This isn't just wealth; this is obscene, beautiful wealth. I run my fingertips along a marble countertop that stretches longer than my apartment.

Is this really the home of the man whose beautiful body I've memorized these past weeks? The man who texts me at 2 AM not for booty calls but because he's thinking about something I said? Whatever we are—lovers, dating, something undefined—I know one thing: my heart has already claimed him, and I'm not backing down now, no matter how intimidating his world might be.

His lips twist into something that might be a smile but never touches his eyes. "I wanted you to come over," he says, voice dropping to a growl. "But I've dreaded you coming over, too." He slams his fist against the doorframe, making the hinges rattle. "I knew you would come over, though, after my stupid text." His knuckles whiten as he clenches his fist so hard it trembles. "I wanted to rip that phone apart the second I sent it."

“I know,” I say. “Tell me what’s going on.”

He shakes his head, his jaw clenched so tight a muscle jumps beneath his skin. "Lilith, this is tearing me apart." His voice breaks. "You're this—Christ—this radiant fucking miracle. Pure sunshine burning through everything. And I'm what? A black hole. A goddamn supernova of rage that's been collapsing in on itself for twenty-two years."

His fist pounds against his chest. "I can already see it happening—you trying to save me, letting my poison seep into your veins because that's who you are. You'd set yourself on fire to keep someone else warm." He grabs my shoulders, fingers digging in. "I can’t watch you dim yourself for me." His breath comes ragged now. "Because I love you." The words rip from him like a confession. "There. I said it. I fucking love you. I’m fucking *in* love with you.” He runs his hands through his dark hair and starts pacing the floor. “I’m drowning in you. I wake up choking on how much I need you. And that's exactly why—" his voice cracks open, "—why I have to walk away before I destroy the only thing that's ever mattered."

My heart doesn't just leap—it explodes into a thousand sparks when he confesses he loves me. Because I don't just love him too—I crave him, need him, worship him with a desperation that terrifies me. God, I would tear open my chest and offer him my still-beating heart if he asked for it.

The words burst from me like they've been trapped for years. "Oh, Roman, I love you too!" My voice breaks, my whole body trembling. "I can't believe you feel the same way. I thought..." The confession dies on my lips. How could I tell him I'd been terrified this was just another conquest for him? That every night I'd lain awake wondering if I was just a warm body while my heart was being ripped apart by wanting him so completely? My eyes burn with tears as I grab his shirt. "I've been drowning, Roman. Drowning in you. And now—" My voice catches. "Now I'm not alone anymore."

He shakes his head violently. "No. Don't you fucking see? Because I love you so goddamn much it's tearing me apart inside, I have to let you go. It's survival for you, Lilith." His voice breaks. "You'll drown in my darkness. You'll suffocate under the weight of my demons. I can't—" He slams his fist against the wall. "I can't destroy the only pure thing in my life. Your light. Your heart." His eyes burn into mine. "If I didn't love you, I'd take you right here against this wall until neither of us could stand. Because Christ, Lilith, looking at you right now is like dying of thirst in front of an ocean I can't drink. But I won't be that selfish monster. Not with you."

I grab his face between my hands, forcing him to look at

me. "Roman, stop. Just stop." My voice cracks. I grab his wrist, my nails digging into his skin. "Yes, you're damaged. God, we both know that." My voice drops to a whisper, eyes blazing into his. "But you're like lightning striking sand—violent, scorching everything it touches, yet creating something so exquisite it takes my breath away every time I look at you." My fingers dig into his skin as tears burn in my eyes. "Your father abandoned you, your mother died, and you've been carrying that rage like it's the only thing keeping you alive. But he's back now, don't you see?" I'm almost shouting, desperate for him to understand. "He's back, and you're talking to him, and it's only a matter of time before—"

His eyes flash like a predator's. "Don't. Finish. That. Fucking. Sentence. Lilith," he snarls, each word a bullet. "There is no 'matter of time' before I reconnect with that bastard. I saw him today for one reason—I refuse to watch him crash and burn."

When he catches my hopeful expression, something raw twists across his face. He slams his palm forward. "You don't get it. I need him successful because my brothers are my goddamn heartbeat. If he fails, he'll crawl back into a bottle because he's pathetic. Then he'll drag himself to Uncle Thomas, bleeding shame, and destroy every one of my brothers' souls. And what's left of mine will be obliterated." His voice drops to a dangerous whisper. "So yes, I need him sober. Clean. Functional. But for them—never him. For Cam, Silas, Asher, Kalen, Connor, Ansel and Max. Especially Max." His fist clenches white-knuckled. "That kid would shatter into dust. He's carried the blame like a fucking cross his entire life."

I nod. “Can I read some cards about this situation?”

He jerks his head violently, veins bulging at his temples.

"No. Fuck the cards, Lilith. This isn't about tarot—it's about you accepting that my father destroyed something in me that can never be fixed. Never." His jaw clenches so tight that I can hear his teeth grinding. "You deserve the goddamn world, Lilith. Every. Fucking. Thing. A man who falls to his knees for you. Who trusts you completely." His voice breaks. "And the second part's not me. I don't lie—I can't trust you because I can't trust anyone." He slams his fist against the wall, leaving a dent. "But as for the first part…" He shakes his head. "Christ, I worship you. Take a bullet for you. Burn alive for you. I'd let the flames consume me until there's nothing left but ash."

My throat constricts like someone's tightening a noose around it, but I force the words out anyway, my voice raw. "Roman." I grab his arm, my nails digging into his skin. "I will not let you throw everything away. Not like this." My voice breaks, tears streaming down my face. "There's a light inside you—something good and pure that burns brighter than all this darkness. I've seen it. I've felt it." I press my palm against his chest, feeling his heartbeat hammer beneath my fingers. "It will win, Roman. I swear to God, it will win."

He slams his fist against the wall, his voice a raw scrape. "How can you be so goddamn certain about everything, Lilith? The world isn't this fantasy place where light conquers darkness every time!" His eyes burn into hers. "Sometimes darkness devours everything. It consumes until nothing's left. How can you look at me and not see that happening?" His hands tremble. "I'm drowning in it." He drags in a ragged breath, voice dropping to a whisper that cuts like glass. "My mother's death ripped the light from me when I was three. Then my father—" His throat constricts. "That bastard extinguished whatever flame was left.

Twenty-two years later, I'm still choking on that smoke. This isn't darkness that just lifts, Lilith. Maybe there's a spark inside me somewhere. Maybe. But the rest? It's a fucking abyss."

I sit down on his couch and pat it. He reluctantly sits next to me.

I reach for Roman's hand, my fingers trembling. "Roman," I whisper, my voice barely audible over the thundering of my own heart. "You have to have faith." I squeeze his hand harder, willing him to understand. "Faith. It's invisible, untouchable—I know that terrifies you—but I swear I have enough for both of us." My eyes lock with his, and I can see the storm brewing there. "Your father—" His jaw clenches instantly, a vein pulsing at his temple. God, I'm playing with fire. One wrong word and he'll explode, banish me from this penthouse forever. But the cards showed it so clearly, and something deep in my soul knows it's true. "You're right at the edge of something transformative with him." I press my palm against his chest, feeling his heart race beneath my touch. "I can feel it here, Roman. Not psychic mumbo-jumbo—this is pure, raw intuition screaming at me. You and Michael—you're going to heal. It's already happening."

He looks at me and his expression slams into me like a tsunami. I brace for rage—those obsidian eyes turning to volcanic glass, veins bulging in his neck, his massive hands seizing me and hurling me toward the elevator while his roar shatters the air between us. But no.

What I see instead rips through me like shrapnel—he's shattered, gutted, a man drowning in his own wreckage, yet... God help me... there's a desperate flicker in those eyes. Hope. Raw and bleeding hope. It's carved into every line of his face, a silent, primal scream asking if I truly believe he could forgive his father. Because beneath all that armor, beneath the fortress he's built around himself, he's desperate for that reconciliation with Michael. I can see it in his eyes.

He breathes my name—"Lilith"—and closes the space between us. His mouth finds mine with a tenderness that makes my knees weak, his lips a whisper against my own before deepening into something that makes my pulse quicken and my thoughts scatter.

I don't want this. I want to rip him open with words, force him to bleed out every dark secret, every buried pain. I need to drain his rage like venom from a wound before it kills us both. But his mouth crushes mine, and my body betrays me—electric, desperate. My fingernails dig into his shoulders as his teeth graze my neck. Words evaporate. They always do. And God help me, I'm already addicted to this cycle of silence and skin.

Roman grips the doorframe until his knuckles blanch white. "Lilith," he says, his voice raw. "I fucking love you. Christ, I'm drowning in it. I'd tear my own heart out if it meant keeping you with me. When you're gone, I can't breathe—can't think—but when you're here..." His eyes burn into mine. "You're the only goddamn peace I've ever known. I'm too selfish to let you go, even knowing I'll destroy us both. I swear on my mother's grave, I'd put a bullet in my head before I'd hurt you. But this—us—it's like playing with fire in a room full of gasoline."

He scoops me up like I weigh nothing, his muscles flexing against my body as he carries me toward the spiral staircase leading to his loft bedroom. Each step upward punctuated by his mouth crashing into mine, his teeth grazing my bottom lip, drawing a gasp from deep in my throat. My skin burns everywhere he touches, electric currents racing through me. "I can't breathe without you," he growls against my neck, his voice raw with need. The words echo my own desperate hunger—he's become as essential to me as my next heartbeat.

His bedroom is magnificent—a sprawling sanctuary where floor-to-ceiling windows frame the Pacific like living artwork. Minimalist furniture in muted grays and blues complements the view rather than competing with it, while the California king bed sits on a raised platform, its crisp white linens practically glowing in the golden hour light that streams across the polished marble floors. My entire apartment could fit into this bedroom.

For the next three hours, we make love with a desperate hunger that leaves us gasping and trembling. The world outside this room ceases to exist. There is only his skin against mine, the thundering of our hearts, the taste of salt on his neck. We crash together like waves against rock, over and over, until neither of us remembers where one ends and the other begins.

Chapter Thirty-Five

ROMAN

God, it feels so fucking good to be waking up next to Lilith in my bed. My eyes snap open at 5 AM, my body still crackling with electricity from last night—every nerve ending raw, every muscle humming. I'd sworn to myself I'd cut her loose. Had rehearsed the speech a hundred times. Can't drag her down into my darkness. But the second I saw her standing in that lobby, something primal in me shattered. She's a goddamn force of nature—a hurricane I want to run straight into. When I'm with her, I'm both on fire and completely still for the first time in my miserable fucking life. She's rewired me from the inside out.

I brew a cup of coffee, planning to head to the resort by 7—later than my usual arrival, but I'll compensate with evening hours. When I return to the bedroom, Lilith's side of the bed lies empty. Following a hunch, I climb the stairs to my rooftop sanctuary and spot her by the infinity pool.

She sits cross-legged on the Carrara marble, fingers resting on her knees, eyes shut in perfect stillness. I hang back, coffee warming my palms, not wanting to disturb her meditation or whatever ritual she's performing. Instead, I simply drink in her beauty. As the first rays of dawn break across the horizon, highlighting the green streaks in her hair - she has no idea how much I love those green streaks because they're so her - she opens her eyes, rises fluidly, and stretches skyward, unaware of my presence in the shadows.

She spins around, her smile radiating warmth across the terrace. "Roman, I couldn't resist this view! The sunrise called to me—perfect for my morning devotions to the goddess. And this rooftop garden is beyond belief!"

She's not wrong. My rooftop terrace spans six thousand square feet of curated paradise—Japanese maples casting dappled shadows over custom limestone pathways, a glass-bottomed infinity pool suspended over the Pacific, three separate lounging areas with handwoven Moroccan daybeds, and a living wall of rare orchids that cost more to maintain monthly than most people's mortgages. I have a full-time gardener, Hans, who comes in just to maintain the orchids. I flew in Hiroshi Yamamoto from Kyoto to design the rooftop garden and paired him with Isabelle Duchamp from Paris—they'd never collaborated before my project.

But…goddess? Then I shake my head. Of course, goddess. This is Lilith. I need to know everything about this woman who's hijacked my entire existence. I realize that beyond the tarot cards she clutches like weapons and her claims about seeing auras—which I'd normally dismiss as complete bullshit—I know nothing. Nothing except that when she walks into a room, the chaos in my brain goes dead silent. Not even the strongest sedatives have ever shut down my demons that effectively. Christ, I'm drowning in questions about who she really is, what she believes, what drives her.

She sits down on one of the outdoor sofas—teak wood

frame with cashmere cushions—and pats the space beside her. I join her, though my watch reminds me I should be halfway to the resort by now. My phone buzzes in my pocket—probably Miranda with another crisis only I can solve.

For 10 years, I've been the first to arrive, last to leave, six days a week. Before that? Seven days, sometimes sleeping on the office couch. The strange thing is, I never resented a minute of it. The resort was my oxygen. But watching Lilith's hair catch the sunlight, feeling that unfamiliar lightness in my chest—I suddenly see my schedule for what it is: not dedication, but hiding. Running from the emptiness waiting at home. Miranda's been ready to step up for months. She knows the operation inside out, commands respect from the staff. Maybe it's time I trusted someone else to carry the weight. Maybe it's time I had something to rush home for.

I grab my phone and fire off a quick text to Miranda: "Taking today off." Her response pops up almost immediately—a heart-eyed smiley face followed by:

> About time! Looks like that tarot reader is working her magic on you. Don't worry about anything here—I've got it all covered. Stay away as long as you need. God knows you deserve a break.

I smile to myself, thinking how perfect today could be. I could spend the whole day pinning Lilith to the bed, watching her face as pleasure overtakes her again and again. But first, I need some answers about this goddess business she mentioned. I've always been skeptical about that spiritual stuff—when someone talks about praying to goddesses, I usually picture either someone dancing around a cauldron in the woods or someone who should probably be talking to a psychiatrist instead of burning sage.

"So," I say. "Goddess."

She smiles. "Yes, goddess." Her eyebrow arches playfully. "Look, if this thing between us is going somewhere, we should be honest with each other. I could hide the fact I start each morning with goddess prayers, but eventually you'd catch me with my altar out—or worse, I'd pack it away and lose a piece of myself. And trust me," she adds with a soft laugh, "you don't want a watered-down version of Lilith Sydney. Better to lay all my crystals on the table now."

I laugh, but it's raw, almost desperate. "Lilith, you could tell me you sacrifice virgins under a blood moon while chanting in tongues, and I'd be there holding the knife for you. Nothing—nothing—would make me love you any less." I nod.

Love. The word burns through me like lightning striking dry timber. It sears my throat, ignites my chest. I never believed I'd say it to anyone, let alone mean it with every atom of my being. Thank Christ Granddad kept his manipulative claws out of my life the way he sank them into Max, forcing him to marry Celeste. Lilith is everything the old bastard would despise—wild, untamable, spiritual. Everything that makes my heart slam against my ribs when she walks into a room. Perfection. Mine.

She laughs. "No virgin sacrifice here. But I participate in solstice and equinox celebrations."

Roman arched an eyebrow. "You celebrate solstices and equinoxes?"

"Mmm," Lilith nodded, her silver moon earrings catching the light. "You do too if you celebrate Easter and Christmas."

“What do you mean?”

Her lips curl into a smile, her eyes catching the light. “You know how we decorate eggs and fill our homes with flowers at Easter? The ancients did the exact same thing for Spring Equinox celebrations. And Easter’s date? First Sunday after the first full moon after the Equinox—pure lunar calendar stuff. Total pagan playbook. Christianity just came along later and sprinkled some Jesus over traditions that had been around for centuries.”

She's practically glowing, thinking she's blown my mind with this revelation. I've heard it before, but watching her excitement, I realize I'd never connected those dots about the lunar calendar. Should've been obvious to a science guy like me.

She goes on. “And Christmas? Those evergreen decorations, gift exchanges, feasts, even the yule log burning in the fireplace—all borrowed from Winter Solstice traditions.” She tilts her head, a playful challenge in her voice. "When early Christians were converting the masses, they weren't fools. They knew people wouldn't abandon their harvest festivals and winter solstice celebrations overnight, so they simply rebranded them. Easter eggs became about resurrection rather than fertility. December feasts celebrated a holy birth instead of the return of the sun."

I nod along, even though I could recite these winter solstice and spring equinox rituals from memory. Something about the way Lilith's eyes light up when she shares her "secret knowledge" makes me bite my tongue. Her hands flutter like birds as she speaks, punctuating each revelation. I find myself leaning closer, not to hear the facts I already know, but to watch her animation. Now, this goddess business she's getting into...

“Now, you were praying to a goddess this morning?”

Lilith's eyes lit up. "Yes. The goddess Brigid." She traces the silver pendant at her throat—a triple spiral etched into hammered metal. "She's the Celtic goddess of healing, inspiration, and protection. Her sacred flames were tended by nineteen priestesses in ancient Ireland." She smiled, a soft blush coloring her cheeks. "I really don't do anything elaborate, just meditate on her presence each sunrise while thanking her and asking her to watch over me and my loved ones through the day." She nods. “I built a small altar for her in my garden. I've got these red candles for fire—Brigid was the goddess of blacksmiths, you know. Then white ones to honor her connection with dairy farmers, and yellow for spring and renewal. There's this little statue of her too, right in the center. It's nothing fancy, but it feels right to have her there, watching over my herbs and flowers."

I shrug. Whatever works for her. People file into pews every Sunday seeking the same thing Lilith finds at dawn with her crystals, candles, statue and incense. Different deities, different rituals, same human need. As long as it brings her peace, who am I to judge?

“And what do you get out of praying to Brigid every day?”

"When I commune with Brigid, I feel... anchored. Like there's this invisible thread connecting me to something ancient and powerful." Her eyes meet mine. “And I feel that she watches over everyone I care about." A soft smile. "Especially you, Roman."

I sink into the sofa cushions, my eyes fixed on her. She prays for me. Something shifts in my chest at the thought—warm, unfamiliar. Part of me wants to dismiss her faith in some ancient goddess watching over us as childish fantasy. Yet I can't. There's something about her devotion that disarms me completely.

I change the subject, though. “I’ve decided to play hooky from the resort today. What do you say we disappear together?"

Lilith's eyes light up, then dim slightly. "I'd love that, but I have readings scheduled. My clients—"

"Say no more." The disappointment stings, but I push it aside. "When's your next free day?"

She scrolls through her phone calendar, brow furrowed. "Tuesday and Wednesday next week. I always block those off—keeps me sane."

"Tuesday and Wednesday it is, then." I step closer, claiming those days with my tone. "They're ours now." I kiss her until we're both breathless. "I should go. Tonight, though?"

"Tonight?" Her smile turns playful.

"Jack's with the Abercrombie model, right?"

She laughs. "He practically lives there now. Yes, come over. I'll cook."

"Eight o'clock." I brush my lips across her forehead. "Lock up when you leave?"

"Of course."

Driving to work, I message Miranda about my changed plans. My thoughts drift to Lilith. We're from different universes—me with my billion-dollar empire, her with her tarot cards, crystals and goddess-praying. Yet somehow she's become essential to me.

And that terrifies me in the best possible way.

Chapter Thirty-Six

LILITH

Time melts away as Roman and I fall into a delicious rhythm—he arrives each night after his shift at the resort, just after I turn the key in my shop's lock. Six consecutive nights of passionate bliss until dawn. Jack's been scarce, wrapped up in his Abercrombie & Fitch model fling. I laid out cards for them at Jack's insistence—the spread suggested a passionate but ultimately temporary connection. Jack seems perfectly content with this forecast.

"Seth's gorgeous but a bit of a himbo," Jack confided over mimosas yesterday. "Though what he lacks in conversation, he makes up for elsewhere." He paused, watching me with knowing eyes. "But what you have with Roman? That core-shattering deep earthquake kind of love? Me too. Want that too. So still on the lookout."

Tuesday finally arrives—two whole days just for us. Gracie will be fine in Jack's care - he's promised to stay with her for the next two days and have Seth over instead of him going to Seth's. And I've got a surprise for Roman he'll never see coming.

The purr of his Aston Martin announces him outside my door. Of all his luxury cars, this sleek beast makes my heart race the most. He kisses me as I slide into the buttery leather seat.

"Where to, my little witch? The world awaits." His eyes dance with possibility. "Paris is just a private jet away. Or Lake Como—my resort there makes the one here look pedestrian." His hands paint pictures in the air between us. "Picture my Parisian penthouse: top floor of a pre-war masterpiece, Eiffel Tower framed in every window. September in Paris means golden leaves. We could walk through Luxembourg Gardens barefoot—I know how you love feeling the earth. We'd dine at Bellanger, dance under moonlight, and fall into bed until dawn breaks... though that last part's becoming our specialty anyway."

I bite my lip. "So I can choose anything?"

"Whatever your heart desires," he says, bringing my fingers to his lips.

I meet his eyes. "I want to visit your mother's grave. I had a dream about it last night—something tells me it's important."

Roman's Adam's Apple bobs visibly. "Let me get this straight. I offer you the romance capitals of the world, and you want to spend our getaway at a cemetery?" His brow furrows, then softens. "But who am I to argue with your sixth sense? You've always been better at reading the universe's signals than I am. And here I thought you'd jump at the chance to see the Eiffel Tower."

"Paris will still be there," I say, squeezing his hand. "This feels more urgent somehow." I keep to myself the rest of what the dream revealed—how this visit might open a door between him and his father. How the little boy who lost his mother at three never properly grieved. The cards had been showing me this path for weeks, but now I was certain.

So, we drive south to Newport Beach to Pacific View Cemetery, where famous people like Kobe Bryant and John Wayne are buried. The cemetery has neat green lawns that go downhill toward the ocean, which you can see past the cliffs. You can smell the salt water and trees in the wind that moves through the palm trees along the walkways.

Catherine's memorial takes my breath away—an angel cradling a heart-shaped marble stone. Her name and dates frame the inscription: "Those we love don't go away...they walk beside us every day." When I glance at Roman, his eyes have darkened to obsidian. The shimmer around him —the aura I rarely see anymore except when he's experiencing overwhelming emotion—pulses violet. The color of transformation, one that appears when someone begins healing from their deepest wounds.

Roman bows his head and I put my hand on his shoulder. "I'm going to go and take in the scenery," I say, sensing that he needs to be alone.

He nods, his jaw clenched so tight I can see the muscle twitch. The cemetery air feels electric around him. He hasn't been here—I'd stake my life on it. His grief isn't just unprocessed; it's radioactive, burning him from the inside out. Roman's rage has been his heartbeat since childhood—bloody knuckles in school hallways, savage tackles that made coaches wince, a ruthlessness that bulldozed competitors when he built his empire.

I discovered his Harvard Westlake yearbook that sleepless dawn at his place—quarterback with a reputation for playing through injuries, swim medals won while practically drowning competitors with his wake. His grief transformed him into something unstoppable, something terrifying. It made him rich. Made him powerful. Made him feared. But it's hollowed him out completely, leaving nothing but scar tissue where a soul should be. Standing at his mother's grave might be the first time he's faced something he couldn't beat into submission.

I perch on the jagged edge of the cliff, my bare toes curling around sun-warmed rock as the Pacific stretches endlessly before me. Salt-tinged wind whips my hair across my face as I close my eyes, visualizing tendrils of rose-gold light flowing from my heart toward the cemetery where Roman kneels.

He stays there for what feels like forever—the sun arcing visibly across the sky. When he finally appears on the path behind me, his footsteps are steady, unhurried. He lowers himself beside me, our shoulders barely touching. His eyes, those stormy dark pools, are rimmed with red but hold a stillness I've never witnessed. The crackling energy that normally surrounds him—that volatile crimson haze—has dissolved into a luminous cobalt blue that pulses with each of his now-even breaths. I can feel the transformation in the air between us, like the moment after a thunderstorm passes.

He shakes his head. "That was..." His voice catches. "I needed that more than I realized." He draws his knees to his chest, arms draped over them as we sit on the grass watching the Pacific roll in. "I was barely three when she died. Never been here before—not that I remember, anyway. Don't think we came to the gravesite back then." A sigh escapes him. "And after that? Nobody ever brought us. Dad was too wasted most days. My grandparents..." He stares at the horizon. "Old-fashioned thinking, I guess. Thought it would traumatize us or something. Years just slipped by, and eventually, I stopped thinking about coming at all."

I reach out my hand and he takes it, gripping it tightly.

Roman looks at me, his voice softening. "We don't always see eye to eye on everything, Lilith. I still can't wrap my head around those crystals you keep by the bed, even if your cards did nail my situation with Dad." He runs a hand through his hair, a half-smile playing at his lips. "You pray to your goddess, I'm still figuring out what's up there—if anything. But you get me. When I mentioned Paris and you chose this place instead?" He gestures around them. "Any other woman I've dated would've had my assistant booking the jet before I finished the sentence. They always took everything I offered and asked for more. But you…" His voice catches. "You actually thought about what I needed. That's new for me."

I can't help but smile at the change in him. "There's something different about you today. Your eyes seem clearer."

"Let's fly up to Carmel," he says, twisting his watch around his wrist. "My helicopter's fueled up. We could be at L'Auberge by sunset." His voice softens. "I was barely three when she died, but I remember her hand in mine at that beach. The way the foam tickled our toes. Then the redwoods at Big Sur..." He trails off, staring past me. "I just need to go there now. After all this."

"To say goodbye," I whisper, completing his thought.

The cards had shown this—his journey through grief, the sacred ground he needed to stand on before he could face his father. The Tower followed by The Star. Destruction before healing. I'd seen it in his reading, but he needed to discover it himself.

On the drive back to his estate, Roman surprises me

again. He opens his walk-in closet to reveal a section with women's clothes—my size. “I bought these just in case you need them, which you do since we’re going on an impromptu trip that you haven’t packed for,” he says with that half-smile that makes my stomach flutter. I run my fingers over the soft fabric of a bohemian tunic, the premium denim jeans. Even the lingerie is tasteful. I choose some jeans, underwear, tunics and lingerie and pack them up for our little trip.

Within the hour, we're at Hawthorne Municipal Airport where his private Airbus helicopter waits. I've never been in anything like it—all buttery leather and polished wood. Roman slides the headset over his dark hair and speaks to the control tower, his voice dropping an octave. The same voice that commanded a jet when he rescued Serafina's father last month. My pulse quickens watching his capable hands move across the controls. Is there anything this man can't master?

The sun hangs low in the sky as Roman's private chopper touches down at Monterey Regional Airport. A sleek Jaguar waits on the tarmac.

"My guy always comes through," Roman says, tossing our bags in the trunk. The engine purrs to life beneath us as we wind our way down to Carmel.

At L'Auberge, we barely pause in our suite before Roman pulls me toward the beach. His steps slow as we reach the shore, his gaze fixed on some invisible point beyond the waves.

"She was dying," he says quietly. "But this place made her happy. Even at three, I sensed it was her last goodbye to Carmel." His voice catches. "Crazy that I remember it so clearly."

I touch his arm. "Children absorb more than we realize, especially during moments that shape us."

"The home videos help," he admits. His jaw tightens. "Her silk scarf, her smile watching us play..."

He walks to a gnarled cypress at the shoreline, silhouetted against the sapphire water. I hang back, giving him this moment with his ghosts.

Roman's voice falters. "This trip has hit me harder than I expected." His gaze drifts to the gnarled oak, its branches casting dappled shadows where they stand. "Right here. This is where she'd rest after chasing us around all day. Dad would just sit beside her, their fingers laced together." He drags his teeth across his lower lip, jaw tightening. "The way he looked at her... Christ. He loved her so much. No wonder he broke when she—"

He nods, his eyes softening at the edges. The rigid line of his jaw relaxes. I watch understanding of his father's grief bloom across his face like the first light of dawn breaking through storm clouds.

"Let's head home tonight," he says, voice gruff with emotion. "I've had enough of hotel beds. I want my bed." His fingers find mine, squeezing gently. "With you in it."

The helicopter ride back feels different somehow. Roman stares out the window, silent but no longer brooding. This pilgrimage accomplished exactly what I'd hoped—forced him to confront the empty spaces grief had hollowed out inside him.

And perhaps more crucial than that, showed him how to reclaim the piece of his heart he'd walled off from his father all these years.

Chapter Thirty-Seven

ROMAN

Standing at my mother's grave in Carmel cracked something open inside me. Twenty-nine years of grief exploded through that crack like a geyser. I'd been drowning it in violence since I was a kid—bloodying noses at Harvard Westlake until my knuckles split, my grandfather's checkbook the only thing keeping me enrolled - 10 near-expulsions, all of them covered up by Granddad's money.

On the football field, I was a fucking demon—breaking tackles, breaking records, breaking jaws when I could get away with it. I'd slam my helmet so hard it cracked, scream until veins bulged in my neck, but nobody cared because I delivered two state championships and I was awarded All-California honors.

In the pool, I'd swim until my lungs burned like they were filled with acid, pushing through pain that would make normal people quit. I played the enforcer on my hockey team—the goon who'd slam opponents into the boards when they got too close to our star players. My teammates knew: mess with them, deal with me. My knuckles stayed split open all season, but that raw edge I couldn't control off the ice? On the rink, it made me valuable.

That same fury built my hotels, crushed my competitors, made me a goddamn billionaire before thirty-three. The grief wasn't a weakness—it was rocket fuel. It burned hot enough to launch me into the stratosphere, even if it left nothing but scorched earth behind me.

But now...I'm not exactly at peace, except when Lilith's around—which she isn't at the moment. What I do have is focus. Not the kind that comes from pure rage, but something more controlled—like I've taken those flames and channeled them into a blowtorch.

I'll need that precision today when I meet some investors who could potentially back my father's venture. I haven't mentioned to my father yet that I arranged this meeting. I'm still working up to facing him properly. Baby steps.

These investors represent the first move in my long game—eventually folding Sunstone by Kensington into my existing portfolio. When I shared this with my brothers last night—sworn to secrecy from Dad, of course—they practically vibrated with excitement. Max nearly hit the ceiling. But first things first: I need to sell these investors on the concept.

I clear my throat. "Let's begin." The investors settle into their ergonomic chairs, arranged around the Brazilian Rosewood table—Finn Juhl's masterpiece that took six months to source. Sunlight streams through the floor-to-ceiling windows, catching the textured swirls of the Pollock behind me. That painting was worth every penny of the $150 million I paid at Christie's. These men need to see success before they'll invest in it. Nothing communicates that message like sitting in the shadow of a nine-figure artwork while discussing projected returns.

The investors glare at me over my father's proposal—the one I gutted and rebuilt with cutting-edge sustainability specs that cost me three sleepless nights and a small fortune in consulting fees. The boardroom reeks of cologne and hostility.

"Green deals are financial suicide," Harrington slams his palm on the table. "A goddamn liberal fantasy bleeding money we don't have for a climate crisis that doesn't exist."

"Four Seasons isn't doing this. Ritz-Carlton isn't doing this," Matthews sneers, jabbing his finger at the page. "There's a reason."

"And this New Age horseshit?" Blackwell's face contorts with disgust. "Reiki? Meditation? Chakra balancing? You want to turn a luxury resort into some kind of hippie commune?"

Their objections hit like machine-gun fire. I feel my jaw clench, but I've prepared for this ambush. I have ammunition for every single attack.

I slam my palm on the table, making the water glasses jump. "Gentlemen, let me be crystal fucking clear." I lock eyes with Harrington. "You think climate change is liberal propaganda? Fine. But the ultra-wealthy—our target clientele—they're watching their children develop allergies and autoimmune disorders at record rates. They're having their blood tested for microplastics and finding poison coursing through their veins. They're paying top dollar for organic tomatoes because they're terrified of what conventional agriculture is doing to their bodies. These same people will pay a fortune for what we're offering. Read the market research - Chapter Two."

Harrington looks skeptical, but opens the proposal and

reads the market research, nodding. I make a good point and he knows it.

I pace the floor and look out the window and then spin around to address the second concern. "Matthews. You think being the only eco-friendly resort in America is a problem?" My voice rises with each word. "It's a goddamn gold mine. The eco-resorts in the Maldives and French Polynesia are booked solid two years out. Two. Years. So don't tell me there's no market, Matthews. There's a market. And we're about to own it."

I fix Blackwell with a hard stare. "These so-called 'New Age' practices date back millennia. The Four Seasons in New York—hardly some backwater motel—offers what they market as 'wellness services.' Hypnosis. Aura readings. Chakra balancing. Energy work. Crystal therapy. Spiritual guidance." I tick each one off on my fingers. "If the most prestigious hotel in Manhattan sees the value, I fail to understand your hesitation. The Four Seasons sets industry standards—we'd be foolish not to follow suit." I clear my throat. "Our tarot service has become one of the resort's most sought-after experiences. My reader, Lilith Sydney, has a three-week waiting list that includes European nobility, political elites, and tech moguls. Turns out crystal energy and chakra alignment pair quite well with champagne and caviar."

I slam down into my seat. What the fuck am I doing? Every ounce of sweat, every vein throbbing in my forehead—all for him. This is his goddamn baby. We build this thing, and he's the one running it, cashing in while I'm just the bank.

No—that's bullshit. My resort would be the parent company, so I'd rake in profits too. Plus, it would be my Laguna hotel he'd be buying for his flagship project. So I'd be intimately involved. But it would be his victory lap. His redemption story. And yet here I am, bleeding myself dry for these jackasses, fending off their pathetic objections like I'm his personal attack dog. For what? For fucking what?

For him.

And what does that say about me?

Chapter Thirty-Eight

ROMAN

Later that afternoon, I finally escape the investor meeting from hell. Despite the chaos, I'm pretty sure I convinced everyone to back this project, though only Sam Thierry committed on the spot—ten million dollars, no hesitation. Figures. The guy's environmental portfolio makes this a no-brainer for him. I've barely settled back at my desk when my phone lights up with Max's name.

The phone slips in my sweat-slick palm. "Rome," he says. "Dad's in the hospital."

Hospital? My heart doesn't just seize—it fucking implodes. Shouldn't matter. I've told myself for twenty-two goddamn years that I don't care about my father. Then I shake my head, knuckles white around the phone. Who the hell am I kidding? If I lose Dad now—

"What's wrong?" My voice scrapes out, barely recognizable.

"Went into cardiac arrest at work. His heart stopped beating for three minutes. Thank God Whole Foods had an AED or he'd be dead right now."

My throat closes like someone's strangling me. The room spins. Dad's heart stopped. He was clinically dead. I grip the edge of the table, knuckles white. "Jesus Christ. What caused it?"

"They're running tests, but they think it's Long QT Syndrome. His heart's electrical system is fucked up. He's been killing himself—working full shifts at Whole Foods, then staying up until 3 AM every night on that resort proposal. Doctor said if he doesn't get a pacemaker immediately, the next time will be his last."

"Where is he?"

"Cedars."

Lilith's waiting for me tonight. But Dad's heart stopped. They had to shock him back to life. I've been clutching this grudge for twenty-two years, and for what? If that AED hadn't been there, if his heart had given out in some random grocery store aisle—that would've been it. No more chances. No more time.

The realization hits me hard and fast—beneath all this anger, I've loved him. Always have. And I almost lost the chance to tell him so. One cardiac event, and suddenly all you're left with is regret, that hollow echo of "too late" that follows you to your own grave.

I'm halfway to Cedars Sinai before I realize what I'm doing. My fingers find Lilith's number while I weave through traffic. When I push through the hospital doors, Max, Ansel, and Silas are already pacing the waiting room floor. Celeste, Max's wife is here, too, looking terrified.

The revolving door keeps spinning. Cam bursts in wearing scrubs, stealing minutes from his ER shift downstairs. Connor follows with makeup still on his face, straight from set. Kalen slides in next, guitar calluses visible as he runs a hand through his hair. Just as I think we're missing one, Asher appears, completing our reluctant brotherhood tableau.

I scan the room—eight mega-successful sons huddled under fluorescent lights for a man who walked out on us. Connor's face has launched a dozen blockbusters. Kalen's fingers have strummed to millions. Each of us commands empires from different corners of the world. Yet here we sit, brought to our knees by our father's failing heart—the same heart that had no trouble leaving us all those years ago.

The doctor emerges, his face a mask of professional concern. "We're prepping your father for emergency surgery to install a pacemaker," he says, before leaving again, and my stomach drops. Emergency surgery. The words echo in my head.

I nod mechanically, aware of my brothers' pale faces around me. A thought slices through my worry—Dad's eco-resort project. Can he handle the stress during his recovery? If he can't, I'll have to step in, on top of my own properties, just when I'd promised Lilith more of my time.

Christ, listen to me. My father died and was brought back and I'm thinking about business logistics. But isn't that part of it too? Giving him something to be proud of? Maybe after recovery, he could run one resort, at least. Not multiple. Not now.

The doctor comes back out. "Is there a Roman Kensington here?" he asks, looking around the waiting room.

I stand up and nod.

"I'm Roman Kensington."

"Mr. Michael Kensington would like to see you."

So Dad asked for me specifically. I swallow hard and trail behind the doctor, my pulse hammering against my collar.

The room—private, of course—screams Granddad's

influence. No shared accommodations for a Kensington. Polished hardwood instead of linoleum. A deep burgundy quilt that definitely didn't come from hospital supply. Plush armchairs that could belong in a luxury suite. I step through the doorway and there he is, propped against pillows, his expression shifting from expectation to genuine surprise, like he'd issued the command but never actually expected me to obey it.

"Roman!" he says, his green eyes lighting up like candles.

I don't say anything. I just sit in the soft chair by his hospital bed. I'm surprised by how nice this room is. Most hospital rooms I've seen have those ugly green or white walls, cheap floors, thin blankets, harsh lights, a basic TV, and that weird hospital smell. I've been lucky enough to never stay in one myself, which is probably why I'm so impressed right now.

It's always seemed strange to me that hospitals don't make their rooms more comfortable for healing. If you're sick, you should be in a nice room. That's why I make sure every room in my resorts feels like a sanctuary—the kind of place that soothes you the moment you walk through the door. Hospitals charge $2,000 a night for a crappy shared room—they could at least make them look decent.

I stalk into the room. "You asked for me."

"I did." He nods, extending his hand. My pulse hammers as I grip it—harder than I should. His eyes ignite, not just brightening but blazing like a man seeing salvation. "Roman—"

"Dad," I cut him off, my voice like gravel. "Save it. We both know what happened. You had choices. You chose the bottle over your sons. Over me." My jaw clenches so tight my teeth might crack. "I will never—never—forget watching you walk out that door. It wasn't okay then. It's not okay now." My chest heaves with each breath. "But goddammit, I love you. That's the tragedy here. I never stopped, not through twenty-two years of birthdays, milestones and graduations you missed." Something breaks in me. "If I didn't love you so much, your betrayal wouldn't still be burning a hole through my chest."

Tears gather at the edges of his eyes, threatening to spill over. Twenty-two years have passed since those three words crossed my lips to him. After today's close call, I can't bear the thought of him not knowing—that despite everything, my love for him remained, buried but unbroken all this time.

Dad's hand trembles in mine, but I don't pull my hand away. "Roman," he says, his voice cracking. "The regret I carry—for leaving you boys—it's..." His Adam's Apple bobs as he struggles to continue. "Stephanie. Alecia. A granddaughter and daughter-in-law I'll never know." He looks down, shaking his head. "Connor's Oscar speech. Kalen clutching those Grammys. Your championship game when you made All-California." His breathing grows uneven. "Every graduation. Every sporting event. Every piano recital for Ansel and Kalen. Every play Connor starred in. Every milestone. Gone." His chest rises and falls heavily. "If I could rewind time... But that's not how it works, is it? While I was drowning myself in booze and self-pity, your lives kept moving forward. The world didn't stop because Michael Kensington checked out. I just... missed everything that mattered."

I nod, my eyes stinging. When's the last time I let myself cry? After he walked out, I put my fist through drywall instead of shedding a tear. Decades of his absence, and all I've done is throw things, punch walls, and scream. Even when I thought Lilith was gone for good after the Blake incident, I just hit the gym with Caspian until my knuckles bled and my muscles screamed.

My brothers, though—Cameron with his song writing, his cooking and his do-gooderism, the twins with their heart-to-hearts—they've probably all had a good cry. Hell, even Ansel and Max, tough as they try to be, probably let it out sometimes. Maybe that's why they can move forward while I'm stuck in this loop of rage. Maybe there's something to this vulnerability shit after all.

"Dad," I say. "I'm not quite ready to forgive and definitely not ready to forget. But I am ready to talk. I guess that's all I can ask from myself that I can be in the same room as you and we can be friendly again." I nod. "But, for the first time in a long time, I think I might get there - be ready to forgive. At some point in time. Baby steps."

Dad's face breaks into a smile. "That's all I can ask," he says.

I hold his hand a little longer, feeling the chill of his skin against mine, the bones too close to the surface. In our home videos, Dad was a 6'3" mountain of a man with shoulders that filled doorways.

Now his hospital gown hangs loose, and his eyes hold a sorrow I can't bear to name. During his sober stretches, he was the father who taught me to carve through powder, who showed me how to read waves before I could read books, who stood behind me with steady hands as I baited my first hook—and that man seems impossible to find in this bed. I remember being nine, racing him down the Streif in Kitzbühlen, that insane Austrian slope with its 85% gradient where we hit 120 MPH, and I wasn't scared because he was there. Where did that father go?

I'm mourning a ghost. The man who lays in that

hospital bed isn't my father—he's just wearing his face. The guy who used to storm into boardrooms and close million-dollar deals without breaking a sweat is gone. In his place is this... shadow, fumbling with his eco-resort blueprints and second-chance romance.

During those brief windows of sobriety in my childhood, I caught glimpses of who he could be. Now I have to accept what remains: a man hollowed out by two decades of regret and the crater my mother's death left behind. He'll never be whole again. But maybe I can stop being an asshole long enough to let him piece together whatever life he has left.

My hands grip the edge of the table, knuckles white. "Dad," I finally say, my voice like gravel. "Mom's death destroyed you. Broke you. And you just kept drinking. You never even tried to get help—not rehab, not AA, nothing." I look him straight in the eyes, my jaw clenched so tight it aches. "You could have fought for us. Your sons. But you didn't even try."

He shakes his head. "Son, there's something I never told you boys. Well, Max knows. I've battled depression my whole life." His eyes drift to some middle distance. "Growing up was hell. My folks thought depression was just weakness. 'Man up, Michael. Stop your bellyaching.' When I was fifteen, I attempted suicide - swallowed a whole bottle of my mother's sleeping pills." He swallows hard. "After my attempt, doctors recommended medication, but my parents shipped me off to military school instead." A heavy sigh escapes him. "It wasn't until college—sitting in Psych 101—that everything clicked. Got myself to a doctor, started meds. My physician finally called my parents, broke it down for them. 'Michael's brain chemistry is off. He needs these pills like a diabetic needs insulin.' That's when they finally got it."

I bow my head. This is the first I'm hearing this. "So, when Mom died...."

Michael's hands trembled as he spoke. "After Catherine passed, I...I stopped taking care of myself. My medication—I just couldn't remember to take it. Or maybe I didn't want to." He swallowed hard. "The dark thoughts came every day after that. Every single day. It wasn't just grief—it was the SSRI withdrawal, the drinking. God, I convinced myself the whiskey was medicine - why did I need Prozac when I had Jack Daniels?" His voice softened. "Patricia saved me. She understood what it means to stare death in the face—her battle with breast cancer taught her that. She connected me with her therapist." A fragile smile crossed his face. "For the first time in decades, I can see daylight breaking through."

I stare at him for a moment. "Oh." My jaw tightens as I consider what I really need to know. "So, Dad," I finally say, my voice steadier than I feel. "What happens if Patricia leaves you? Or if she—I don't know—gets hit by a bus tomorrow? Are you going to crawl back into a bottle and disappear for another twenty years? Because that's your pattern. That's what you did when things got hard before. Why should I believe anything's different now?"

Christ. How am I supposed to trust him again? If I let him back in and he bails a second time, I won't just feel like an idiot—I'll be destroyed. He needs to give me more than some bullshit about how he's a changed man. Uncle Thomas's farm is still running, and I'd bet my flagship resort that Thomas would welcome him back tomorrow without a single question. And there's no way my brothers haven't grilled him about this already. Especially Silas.

He nods. "Trust isn't something I expect from you, Roman. Not after I vanished for twenty-two years." He rubs his thumb against his sobriety chip. "You deserve concrete reasons to believe I'm different now. And here they are - I've got a therapist who doesn't let me hide from myself—three sessions every week. Never bothered with that before." His voice softens. "My sponsor answers my calls at three in the morning when the old demons visit. The whole AA group —they see me clearly and still choose to stand beside me." He sighs. "Patricia and I are good together. She fills some of the emptiness your mother's death left. But you're right to question that too. Life offers no certainties. The difference is, this time I've built myself a lifeboat before sailing into rough waters."

I nod. The therapist and AA—that's new. My jaw clenches. If he'd gotten help twenty-two years ago...but that's not how it went down. The past is the past. Now I'm staring at two doors: behind one, I believe he's changed, that he won't detonate our lives again. Behind the other, I let him back in without promises. I run my hand through my hair, suddenly realizing there's no third door anymore—the one where I keep telling him to go to hell and never look back. Somewhere along the line, I've already made the choice to have him in my life, one way or another.

Dad's eyes find mine. "Roman, I've noticed something. You hold Max responsible, don't you? For everything that happened."

I don't bother denying it. The truth sits between us like a third person.

"I want to show you something I never leave behind." Dad gestures toward a battered leather satchel in the corner. "Would you mind?"

The bag feels heavier than it should as I pass it to him.

He reaches inside and withdraws a journal bound in faded burgundy leather, its spine cracked from years of handling. My breath catches—Mom's handwriting on the cover.

Dad's fingers move with practiced precision to a dog-eared page. "This part," he says, tapping a paragraph. "You need to see this."

I trace Mom's handwriting with my fingertips, a knot forming in my throat...

I've chosen my path. This choice will take my life, but I've already bonded with the miracle growing inside me. Another boy—my little Max. Last night I dreamed of him, a perfect reflection of Michael, my North Star, the man who's held my heart since the moment we met.

The weight of leaving behind seven other sons without their mother crushes me, but I cannot sacrifice my unborn child so that I might live for my seven other sons. Each of my boys carries a piece of my soul, though Roman—my stormy, complicated three-year-old—concerns me most. He reminds me so much of my father: brilliant and kind, yet harboring a tempest within. Dad found salvation in running endless miles; I hope Roman discovers his own sanctuary from the chaos in his mind. Above all, Roman needs reassurance of his worthiness of love, though he resists it fiercely.

Sweet Cameron wears his heart openly—may he never change. The twins, Kalen and Connor, are barely toddlers; I pray they find their way without memories of me to guide them. Little Ansel remains a beautiful mystery. As for six-year-old Asher, our prodigy who devoured Great Expectations at four and truly comprehended it—brilliance awaits him. And serious Silas, so thoughtful and deep even now…I hope they can all forgive me for the choice I made. And it is my choice. I love them all.

I read her words and my head drops like it's been cut from my body. She chose to die for Max—a choice I've crucified him for all these years. But now I understand. She did it for love of Max and, goddammit, she worried about me the most. She saw the hurricane raging inside me even then, and with her dying breath, begged me to find peace. And what have I done? Spat on everything she wanted. She'd be gutted if she knew how my temper has burned every bridge, poisoned every relationship.

The first tear hits my hand like acid. Then another. Then a flood breaks through a dam I built thirty years ago. I grab for the Kleenex on Dad's nightstand, but it's useless against this deluge.

Dad pats the bed, and something primal in me responds. I climb into his bed and collapse beside him, my body convulsing with each sob. And suddenly I'm drowning in a memory—I did cry once, didn't I? We all did, crawling into Dad's gigantic bed, all of us seeking shelter. His arm wrapped around me then as it is now, and the fortress I've spent my life building crumbles to dust. I'm three years old again, my soul being ripped in half as I realize my mother is gone forever.

Dad grips my shoulder, his fingers digging in. "Roman," he says, voice breaking. "I love you. She loved you. She loves you still. I believe that with everything I am. When you die, that love burns on like a supernova—and right now, she's watching us." His eyes glisten. "She's finally at peace. Because her son came back to me."

My throat closes completely. I can only nod as twenty-two years of rage and grief collapse inside me. I'm back with him. Finally. The weight of his arm across my shoulders anchors me to this moment—this is where I belong, where I've always belonged. And somewhere beyond this world, Mom is watching her broken men finally heal, her son allowing her husband to hold him together when he's been shattering apart for so fucking long.

The doctor comes in, interrupting this father-son

bonding that's finally happening. "We need to prep Mr. Kensington for surgery," he says gently.

I nod, getting out of the bed and giving his hand a firm squeeze. "Dad, kick some ass in there," I tell him, my voice gruffer than I intended. "I'm not going anywhere. Well—" I clear my throat. "I mean, I won't be sitting in this exact chair the whole time, but when you open your eyes, you'll see me. Count on it."

He nods, tears in his eyes. "Roman, I can't tell you how much this means to me that you're here."

I nod back, swallowing hard against the lump in my throat. "I am, Dad. And I always will be." The unspoken thought hangs between us: *Don't disappoint me again.* My fingers flex involuntarily, muscle memory from years in the ring. A realization washes over me like the tide at Palos Verdes—I'm not powerless anymore. If he vanishes like before, I have the resources to find him, the strength to confront him and I'll bring his ass right back. I'm not that abandoned ten-year-old anymore. My shoulders relax slightly as this understanding settles in my chest, a strange comfort in this fragile reconciliation.

Chapter Thirty-Nine

LILITH

Roman's text about his father didn't reach me until after my last tarot reading of the day. Six back-to-back sessions had left me emotionally spent—the disappointment in a client's eyes when the cards reveal unwelcome truths always takes something out of me. My phone stayed buried in my bag until evening, when I finally saw Roman's hospital updates followed by a message saying he'd be at my place by 8.

Part of me wishes I could have sat beside him in that sterile waiting room, but what comfort could I really offer? Something tells me he and Michael needed that time alone anyway. As I unlock my townhouse door, a warm certainty fills me—father and son have crossed some invisible threshold today. I can't explain how I know, but I do. The fortress around Roman's heart has been developing tiny fissures for months now, barely visible but significant. Like cracks in a dam that start as whisper-thin lines before the whole structure gives way to the pressure behind it.

The doorbell chimes at 8 sharp. Roman stands in the doorway, all six-foot-four of him filling the frame. Jack circles him like a hummingbird to nectar, his attention to Seth apparently forgotten. I can't blame him—Roman draws people in without even trying, something magnetic in the way he holds himself.

"You made it," I say, ushering him toward the kitchen where the scent of melted mozzarella and marinara hangs in the air. My chicken parm isn't fancy—just breaded cutlets, jarred sauce, and cheese that bubbles golden at the edges—but it's honest comfort food, paired with asparagus spears and a simple salad.

His lips brush my cheek, but his eyes are somewhere else entirely. After we eat, instead of joining Jack for movie night on the sofa—tempting as that sounds—I lead Roman to the balcony. We stand side by side under the night sky, his silence a tangible thing between us. I let it be.

Roman's eyes lock with mine, his voice raw. "Lilith, my father's heart stopped today. For three minutes, he was gone." His fingers tremble slightly. "If Whole Foods hadn't had that defibrillator..." He trails off, jaw clenching. "When I was thirteen, my swim teammate Dave just... collapsed after a meet. Perfect health, stronger than me even." Roman's voice catches. "Long QT Syndrome—his heart couldn't recharge between beats. That school had no equipment. Nothing." He shakes his head. "Goddamn school, not having basic life-saving equipment. Our school had one, of course, but not this Holy Cross school who hosted our meet. If our meet was at home, he would've lived a long life."

"What kind of equipment?" I ask softly.

"AED. Automated external defibrillator." His eyes darken with memory. "One shock could have saved Dave. Given him a chance at a pacemaker, medication, a future." Roman's knuckles whiten. "My father got that chance today. But for those three minutes..."

I reach for his hand, my stomach plummeting. His text had only said his father was in the hospital—not that Michael's heart had stopped beating before doctors brought him back.

"Oh, Roman...how terrifying."

"Yeah." His voice catches. "Knowing your dad flat-lined, even for a few minutes..." He shakes his head. "Changes how you see everything." He squeezes my fingers. "I'm not saying all is forgiven. But I'm ready to let him back in."

"I know," I whisper. The investor's meeting for Michael's resort project had already told me that much, but hearing Roman say it aloud makes something warm unfurl in my chest.

Roman's eyes meet mine, vulnerable in a way I've rarely seen. "But I realized something. I'm still waiting for him to disappear again. And that's why—" he swallows hard, "—why I've tried to keep you at arm's length too. Once you've been blindsided like that...you start expecting everyone to vanish. You build walls. Prepare for the worst. Because nothing hurts more than being caught completely off guard by someone walking away."

I nod. "Since we're sharing our deepest fears, I should probably tell you mine."

"I'm listening."

"I worry about what happens when the fairy tale ends. Right now, everything's magical—the way you look at me, the electricity when we touch, those late-nights where we're discovering each other. But someday the magic fades." I pause, my fingers fidgeting with the edge of my sleeve. "On nights I'm alone in my bed, I stare at the ceiling thinking about the moment you'll finally see the reality—a billionaire hotel king and a woman who reads tarot cards for a living.

When that day comes, what's stopping you from walking away?"

His smile vanishes, replaced by a look of raw hunger. "Lilith." Her name sounds like a prayer on his lips. "When the honeymoon ends—when we're stripped bare of pretense—I'll still be here, clawing my way back to you every damn day." He grips the edge of the table until his knuckles whiten. "My entire life has been warfare inside my skull. A fucking bloodbath. I've channeled it—through the hotels, through beating Caspian to a pulp in the ring, through pushing my body until it breaks." His voice drops to a growl. "But the chaos always returns. Always. Except with you." He reaches for my hand, his touch desperate. "You silence the screaming. You're not just a want, Lilith. You're oxygen. You're salvation. And I will burn this world to ashes before I let you go."

I nod, relieved. "Well, since you put it that way…."

His eyes lock with mine, burning with raw intensity. "You don't have to worry about me leaving. But you—" his voice breaks, "if you bolt when things get tough..." He grabs my hands so tightly it almost hurts. "I'm not there yet, but goddammit, I'm trying. Because losing you would destroy me. I'd shatter like my father did."

His breath catches as realization floods his face. "My father—" he whispers, voice ragged. "My mother wasn't just someone he loved. She was his fucking oxygen. Just like you're mine." His voice drops to a dangerous whisper. "That's why he broke. He couldn't breathe anymore."

A muscle jumps in his jaw as he swallows hard. I grip his arm, feeling the tension vibrating through him. He's finally seeing the truth about his father. About why his father left. And when he fully understands, fully absorbs it, that forgiveness will break like a dam.

I can already feel the flood coming.

Chapter Forty

ROMAN

Fight day. My heart hammers against my ribs as I stare down Phoenix Fraser across the locker room. Bastard's built like a brick shithouse—same height, same reach, but his eyes are dead cold. Silicon Valley hedge fund prick with something to prove. I catch him looking at the ALS Research logo on his shorts—his father withered away from it. I touch the pink ribbon on my own gear, feeling Mom's absence like a phantom limb. Fraser wants this win? He'll have to pry it from my bloody hands.

The arena for our charity match gleams under spotlights that catch on the eight-sided cage, its black padding worn at the corners from previous fighters' grips. The canvas floor, stretched taut and painted with sponsor logos, gives slightly under my feet as I pace the perimeter. Around us, tiered seating climbs toward a ceiling hung with banners from past tournaments—almost indistinguishable from the professional octagon where I've watched countless UFC championships.

Caspian is talking to me, making sure I have the Eye of

the Tiger out there in that ring. "You've been more focused lately than I've seen you. Remember your arsenal—those lightning jabs that come out of nowhere, that vicious leg sweep that took down Dominguez last month, and especially that guillotine choke that makes even the veterans tap out in seconds. You've got the killer instinct of a shark that smells blood in the water. You got this."

The crowd blurs until I spot my family—all seven brothers, Dad, even my grandparents. Nana's going to clutch her pearls when Phoenix and I start throwing hands in the cage. My gaze finds Lilith, leaning toward Max, her hands animated as they talk. Max has my face plastered across his chest, my tournament number bold beneath it. On his other side, Celeste—Max's wife—shadow-boxes with surprising intensity, jabbing and hooking at invisible opponents. I've never given her much time, writing her off as bland after a few polite conversations. Watching her now, mimicking fight moves with such enthusiasm, I feel a twinge of regret for keeping her at arm's length.

The referee goes through the rules, raises his hand, and the match is on. I feel a focus I haven't felt before as I circle Phoenix, gauging distance. When he telegraphs a jab, I slip left, countering with a leg kick that connects with a satisfying thud against his calf. He winces but recovers, pressing forward. I sprawl instinctively when he shoots for a double-leg takedown, driving my hips down and framing his head with my forearm, the charity match crowd roaring their approval.

Phoenix's right hook catches me square in the jaw. My vision blurs as I stumble backward, my gloves instinctively rising to protect my face. The canvas shifts under my feet. Sweat and blood sting my eyes. Through the chain-link fence of the octagon, I glimpse Lilith's face among the crowd—her hands pressed against her mouth, eyes wide—flanked by Max, Celeste, and my brothers. The ref hovers nearby, watching for signs to call it. I spit my mouthguard into my glove, reposition it, and nod at Phoenix. The buzzer marks the end of round two. In my corner, Caspian whispers urgently as he presses ice against my swelling eye. "He's dominating the ground game. Keep it standing."

The first two rounds are a brutal dance of near-misses. His jab grazes my chin; my hook catches nothing but air. Sweat stings my eyes as we circle each other under the glaring lights. By the end of round two, the electronic scoreboard flashes his advantage: 5-4. The crowd's roar fades to white noise. Three rounds is all we get in these charity amateur matches—one last chance.

Round three. My muscles burn, but I find something primal inside me. I feint left, then slam a right cross that connects with a satisfying thud. The buzzer wails. Final score: 6-5, my favor. I raise my taped fists as my chest heaves, utterly spent but triumphant. Half a million dollars for breast cancer research. Worth every bruise.

After the match, I towel off, throw on fresh clothes, and head out to find Lilith and my family waiting in the main part of the arena, by the glass entrance doors. And—Serafina? Didn't spot her in the crowd earlier. I slide my arm around Lilith's waist while my brothers circle me with backslaps and congratulations.

When I catch my father's eye, something unexpected happens—I step forward and hug him. We've been reconnecting since his pacemaker surgery, both of us hoping that little metal guardian keeps another cardiac episode at bay. Something clicked for me recently. The way Lilith breathes life into my world, makes everything brighter—Mom must have done that for him. Losing her stole his air, left him fumbling in darkness. I get it now. If Lilith vanished from my life? Christ. I'd be worse than the monster I was before I met her.

Serafina comes up to me after I'm done hugging my father. "Congratulations, Roman," she says. "You did fantastic out there."

I nod at Sera. "Thanks." My voice comes out even, neutral. A month ago, I would've brushed past her without a word, but lately, things have shifted. Dad and I managed a whole dinner without raising our voices last week. And waking up next to Lilith each morning feels like the anchor I never knew I needed.

"Can I talk to you?" Sera gestures toward the exit, where the crowd streams out into the night.

"Sure." I turn to Lilith, press my lips to her cheek, breathe in that hint of sandalwood she always carries. "Be back in a few minutes."

Lilith's smile reaches her eyes—that calm, knowing look that tells me she's not worried. And why would she be? Next to Lilith's quiet fire, Sera is just... background noise.

I follow Sera into the night, the night chill raising goose-bumps on my arms. "What's up?" December's here, and with it comes the Winter Solstice—not Christmas, mind you, but the actual Solstice. Funny how I've adopted Lilith's vocabulary. My phone buzzes with her latest text: elaborate plans for honoring the Sun God's return instead of Christ's birth. She wants us to light a yule log, feast together, and tell ancient tales of the Oak and Holly Kings. There's even this ritual called Wassailing where we'll pour spiced cider on saplings and serenade them for good health.

Six months ago, I'd have rolled my eyes at all this. Now? I'm actually looking forward to it. Picking up mulled cider on the way home. Besides the tree-blessing part, it's not so different from the Christmas traditions I grew up with anyway.

A part of me wants to Google the whole Winter Solstice thing to see if any of it makes scientific sense. But I've seen how Lilith's eyes light up when she talks about these rituals. So I'll nod, I'll participate, I'll respect what matters to her—even if I can't bring myself to believe.

Sera clears her throat. "Well, Roman, I was wondering about Lilith. I hear you're pretty serious about her."

"I am. Why?"

She shrugs. "Well, I'm wondering if you don't know how it looks to the outside world for you to be dating a witch."

I burst out laughing at her characterization of Lilith as a witch. That's not accurate at all. Lilith doesn't even identify as Wiccan. She simply embraces alternative spiritual practices. Her beliefs involve tarot readings, goddess worship, crystal healing, Reiki energy work, and aura perception. She celebrates the same holidays everyone else does—Christmas, Halloween, Easter—just under their traditional names: Winter Solstice instead of Christmas, Samhain instead of Halloween, and Spring Equinox instead of Easter. In many ways, her approach is more authentic than most people's. She honors the ancient Celtic Druid traditions that gave these celebrations their original purpose—Winter Solstice marking the sun's rebirth and longer days ahead, Spring Equinox celebrating the earth's renewal after winter's dormancy.

I roll my eyes. "Come on, Sera. Lilith isn't brewing potions at midnight. She's just into alternative spirituality."

Sera leans forward and raises an eyebrow. "Listen, Roman. Modern witches don't fly on broomsticks. They burn sage, collect crystals, read tarot cards, and commune with nature—exactly like your precious Lilith." She smirks.

"Though the way you've been following her around like a lovesick puppy, maybe she does have magical powers after all."

I cross my arms. "Fine." My voice lowers to a growl. "Call her whatever you want. If she's a witch, she's my witch, so tread carefully." I narrow my eyes. "And how exactly do you know all this about her?"

"My friend sees her regularly for readings. Lilith doesn't exactly keep her beliefs private. According to my friend, she prays to goddesses, bathes in forests, heals with sound bowls, burns sage everywhere, and owns enough crystals to rival a museum. You can sugarcoat it as 'alternative spirituality' all you want, but everyone else calls it what it is—witchcraft." She gives me a pointed look. "I'm just saying, be careful. Your investors talk, Roman. They might start wondering if you're burning sage in the boardroom next."

I shake my head. "Mind your own business, Sera." Through the doorway, Lilith's laughter rises above the conversation, my brothers leaning in like plants toward sunlight. They're under her spell—though not like me. For them, she's a charming addition to family gatherings. For me, she's essential.

Let the industry gossips whisper about how the cutthroat hotel magnate fell in love with some crystal-loving hippie. In the boardroom, I'm still the same calculated predator who built an empire of luxury properties across four continents. If anything, since Lilith, my deals have gotten sharper. She grounds me, clears the static that used to cloud my judgment.

So Sera can take her concerns about Lilith being "bad for business" and shove them.

Chapter Forty-One

LILITH

I reach across the counter, my bangles jingling against my wrist. "Jack," I say. "Hand me those crystals." My fingers wiggle impatiently as I survey the cluttered shelves.

The afternoon sun streams through the window, painting rainbows across the floor. I've spent the morning making space for my newest finds—red beryl, glowing like liquid fire, and alexandrite that shifts between green, purple and blue depending on the light. I can't wait to display them with my usual collection: amethyst clusters, jasper, tiger's eye, lapis lazuli, quartz points, black tourmaline, citrine, labradorite, selenite wands, and obsidian—glossy black mirrors that remind me of Roman's eyes when he looks at me.

I'm excited to be offering these new stones. The business has been picking up, I've been lining up readings at my shop at a brisk pace of at least 5 a day, and I'm still working my side-hustle at the resort, which has padded my bank account, too. That means that I can afford the beautiful Red Beryl and Alexandrite stones, which sell for $1,000 a carat. Such good things have happened for me since Roman came into my life. Such abundance! But I know that I willed it all into existence - my positive thoughts makes energy that attracts like energy from the universe. The law of attraction at work.

I'm humming Fleetwood Mac's "Rhiannon" under my breath as Jack practically dances between the bookshelves, breathlessly detailing his conquest of Angus Phillips, some cater waiter from one of the Hilton Hotels.

Seth—the "Abercrombie & Fitch model" he swore was his soulmate last month—has apparently been kicked to the curb. But the way Jack is graphically oversharing every intimate detail makes it crystal clear Angus isn't The One either. Jack only broadcasts bedroom skills when he's treating someone like a trophy, not a partner.

"God, Lilith, his tongue—that piercing!—holy shit," Jack's eyes roll back dramatically. "The things that metal stud can do should be illegal in at least thirty states. You haven't truly lived until someone with a pierced tongue has made you see actual stars. You should convince Roman to get one immediately."

I force a tight smile. "I'll add it to his suggestion box."

What I don't say: Roman's mouth is already devastating perfection. The way his tongue moves against my skin makes me forget my own name—no hardware required.

Jack throws his hands up. "Right, I forgot. Roman Kensington, billionaire sex god extraordinaire. Perfection incarnate."

I've never shared a single explicit detail about Roman with Jack. And I never will. What happens between us in the dark feels too sacred, too raw—like telling would break some unspoken spell.

"And what are you humming there?" Jack asks, leaning

against the counter, his turquoise rings catching the morning light.

"Rhiannon," I say, the melody still dancing on my lips. "You remember that song."

"Right. The song about the witch, right?" Jack's blue eyes sparkle with amusement beneath his perfectly arched eyebrows.

"Yes. But Rhiannon wasn't actually a witch. She's a Welsh goddess of fertility and the moon, with flowing black hair and the power to grant wishes." I twist a strand of my own hair absently. "But I think she's a witch in the song."

"Any reason why you're humming that particular tune today?"

I shrug, my gauzy sleeve slipping off one shoulder. "No. It's weird - I wake up with a song in my head every single morning and it's often a song I haven't heard in awhile. No rhyme or reason." I'm now arranging the purple hydrangeas in the bay window, their sweet scent mixing with the shop's sandalwood incense. "This morning it was Rhiannon."

Just then, I look up and see Serafina coming through my door, her stiletto heels clicking aggressively against the hardwood floor, designer sunglasses perched on her perfect button nose. I roll my eyes. Well, maybe that's why I have the song “Rhiannon” in my head - because I wish I were an actual witch and could concoct a spell with my mortar and pestle that would keep Serafina out of my shop. But here she is, so I have to be nice to her even though I'd love to bounce her right out my door and onto the sun-drenched Venice Beach sidewalk.

“Hello,” I say brightly. “Can I help you?”

“Yes,” she says, looking right at Jack, as if she’s willing him to leave. Jack actually does get the hint and comes up to me. “Going for a coffee break. Want anything?”

I shake my head and keep arranging my flowers, tucking each hydrangea stem precisely two inches from the last, their powder-blue blooms like little clouds against the crystal vase. I glance at Sera, whose glacial blue eyes flick over my work with the barest hint of a sneer tugging at her coral-glossed lips. She's probably thinking these flowers are as common as dandelions, as prosaic as daisies, as boring as baby's breath.

As ever, the woman looks like she stepped out of the glossy centerfold of *Vogue Italia*. Her blood-red Birkin bag —crocodile, of course—dangles from the crook of her elbow, worth more than my Prius and six months' rent combined. Those Louis Vuitton sunglasses perch atop her head like a crown, while her thigh-high boots of butter-soft calfskin hug legs that stretch for miles. The leather skirt clings to her narrow hips, and her black cashmere sweater drapes just so across collarbones sharp enough to cut glass.

Her body is all natural curves, her face a symphony of high cheekbones and full lips, her blonde hair cascading in a waterfall of honey-gold, wheat, and copper—the kind of dimensional color that costs other women $500 at Drybar but somehow, infuriatingly, grows that way from her perfect scalp. Every time I see this woman, I think about how much she won the lottery—the genetic lottery and the old-money lottery—for she's a walking billboard for both, right down to the tiny diamond stud winking from her perfect, shell-like ear.

She enters my shop like she owns it. "Lilith. We need to discuss Roman."

I keep my eyes on the lavender sprigs I'm arranging, avoiding her ice-blue stare. "I bet. What about him?"

"It's just infatuation for him." Her heels click as she

circles my display table. "Did you bewitch him? That's your specialty, isn't it?"

"Absolutely." I can't help but smirk. "Eye of newt, toe of frog—you know the drill. Though in *Macbeth*, those were actually code names for herbs, not literal animal parts."

"I'm well aware," she snaps, tossing her perfect hair. "I didn't earn my Cornell PhD in hospitality management by being ignorant. Roman has the same degree—finished his doctorate by twenty-two, actually. Genius runs in that family." She pauses, examining me like I'm a curious specimen. "Where did you attend university?"

My shoulders tense as I shrug, hating how easily she's making me shrink. The question dangles between us—exactly as she intended—making me feel smaller with each passing second. "I went to LACC," I say.

"Los Angeles City College," she says, wrinkling her nose. Then she shakes her head. "You're after him for his money, aren't you?"

I shake my head, trying to hold my temper. "No. I couldn't care less about his money." Truth bomb, there. Roman is just somebody who I feel is meant for me, money or not. If he would've come into my shop after surfing the day and informed me that he was driving Uber for a living or waiting tables or whatever I'd still be in love with him because I'm in love with the person. Not the money. But I'm not going to explain all that to Serafina because she wouldn't believe me anyhow, so why waste the breath?

Serafina's eyes narrow. "Let me get this straight. You're just some nobody with a community college degree selling crystals on the boardwalk, and somehow you've convinced Roman Kensington—a man worth billions, who's graced the cover of *Forbes* 5 times, who warranted a five-page *Vanity*

Fair spread just two years ago—that he's in love with you? What kind of voodoo did you work on him?"

I tuck a strand of hair behind my ear, my voice steady despite the heat rising in my cheeks. "I'm sorry, was there an actual question hidden in that insult, or were you just looking for an audience while you judge my life choices?"

Her scarlet lips curl into a sneer. "I want to know what witch spell you put him under."

I roll my eyes until I can almost see my own brain. "Sera, you might not understand this with your platinum-encrusted worldview, but Roman loves me and I love him and there wasn't a spell involved. I'm not a witch. I don't know how to draw pentagrams or brew potions in cauldrons or whatever you're imagining. And anyway, I do know some women who wear pentacle necklaces and celebrate the solstice, and they tell me their core principle is respecting free will. Their magic can't force someone to do anything against their nature. So even if I dance naked under the full moon—which I don't—I wouldn't use that power to manipulate Roman's feelings."

"Oh, witches have a code of honor, do they?" Her diamond tennis bracelet catches the light as she flicks her wrist dismissively. "Fascinating."

I roll my eyes again, feeling the beginnings of a headache pulsing behind my temples. "What do you want, Sera? You're here cluttering my aura with negative energy for some reason, and I'd really like to know what it is."

"Brass tacks," she says, leaning her Pilates-perfected body toward me, wafting a cloud of something French and expensive. "I want you to break up with Roman."

"Oh, okay. Sure." I snap my fingers sarcastically. "You tell me to break up with him and I guess you think I'll just do it." I shake my head, my handmade rose quartz earrings swinging against my neck. "I know your type. I went to school with girls like you—girls with Daddy's credit card and designer handbags. They drove Porsches to school. They all thought they were entitled to things without working for them. They all felt that because they're beautiful, popular, and trust-fund rich, that they could just bat those extension-enhanced eyelashes and make everybody cater to their every whim."

I smile, remembering myself in high school—my lavender-streaked hair smelling of patchouli oil, my thrift-store denim covered in hand-embroidered stars, my silver nose ring catching the light, my tarot cards worn at the edges from daily use. Women like Serafina would've bullied me. Did bully me.

But I never surrendered my crystal pendant to their Tiffany charm bracelets, because I knew, even then, that my worth wasn't measured in carats or brand names. I knew it then, standing in bathroom stalls wiping away tears, and I know it now, facing down this couture-clad mean girl. I won't give in to this overgrown bully now, no matter how many zeros are in her checking account.

Sera's crimson lips curl into a serpentine smile. "Break up with him or else."

"Or else what?" My voice catches in my throat.

"Or else his father's resorts will be dragged through the mud." She raises one perfectly arched eyebrow, her diamond studs catching the light. "You don't think I have connections in the media world, do you? My father is a tech billionaire in Silicon Valley with a mansion overlooking the Pacific and he knows everybody in the new media landscape. And once I tell my father about Roman dating a witch—" she spits the word like venom "—he'll blast it far and wide until Roman's reputation crumbles like sand. Old school investors with their Brooks Brothers suits and country club memberships don't look too kindly to actual witches. They don't burn them at the stake anymore, pity that, but they don't exactly invite them to their yacht parties, either."

I stare at her blankly, but she continues

"Roman has a very particular image to convey - successful, brash, handsome, uber-wealthy," she says. "And I can't believe that you can't look in that cracked mirror of yours and see how pathetic it looks for him to be with you." Then she narrows her eyes. "Imagine the headline: 'Kensington Heir Courts Crystal-Gazing Hippie.' The investors would run screaming. Then add Michael's whiskey breakfast habit?" She leans closer. "Those Wall Street types, they want stability. Not a billionaire who spends his nights with tarot cards and his mornings bailing Daddy out of the drunk tank. The Kensington empire would crumble faster than those ancient ruins in Greece."

"Get out!" I scream, my finger trembling as I point at the door, the amethyst ring my grandmother gave me catching the afternoon light.

She doesn't leave, but just stands there in the doorway, tossing her honey-blonde hair and shaking her head. "Read this story," she says, thrusting her manicured hand toward me, a tablet displaying a mock article. "As soon as I snap my fingers, it'll be all over social media and in every glossy industry magazine from Los Angeles to Dubai. I've already contacted the editor of *Forbes* about this juicy piece of gossip."

My heart pounds against my ribs as I read the story that Sera had concocted. The story paints a picture of Roman's new lady, a practicing Wicca who dances barefoot around crackling bonfires for Samhain and the winter solstice, who reads worn tarot cards by candlelight, who believes that rose quartz crystals heal broken hearts and who prays to an ancient Celtic goddess with outstretched arms. All true, so I can't very well sue for libel. Well, I'm not a practicing Wicca, but my belief system with its herbs and incantations aligns with theirs, so that's a grey area for suing.

And then I see the pièce de résistance—the story also goes into depth about Michael's alcoholism, detailing every bottle he emptied, every family dinner he ruined, every promise he broke. The article even includes a photo of him passed out on a front lawn, his tie askew and his expensive suit stained with what could have been whiskey or vomit. The caption reads, "Michael Kensington: The Fall of a Would-be Hotelier." My jaw clenches so hard I can hear my teeth grinding.

I want to tell her that I don't care about this story. That I love Roman—the way his eyes crinkle when he laughs, how he holds my hand under restaurant tables—and he loves me and that's all that matters. That he's too well-established in his five-star resorts so that anything these tabloids and social media vultures might say about me wouldn't affect him.

But that's not true and I know it. Roman's trying to get his father's new eco-resort idea off the ground right now. It's a revolutionary concept and he's been lining up skeptical investors in boardrooms across the world. What would happen if these new investors get spooked because they think that Roman's gone completely bonkers because he's dating me?

And this story about Michael's alcoholism…that will kill the project for sure. Roman told me that the investors don't know about his father's problems. They have no reason to know, really. But with this article published, that will change. Those investors will get spooked for sure.

Oh, God, I can't be selfish here. Roman's face had lit up like a child's on Christmas morning when he told me about reconciling with his father—the deep crease between his eyebrows smoothing out for the first time since I'd known him. His hands had gestured wildly as he described helping Michael establish his own luxury resorts.

What would happen if the investors for Michael's new project get spooked by me being in the picture? The fact that Roman's dating me—a woman who reads tarot cards for a living, burns sage bundles in her apartment, and only has an associate's degree from City College with its peeling paint and flickering fluorescent lights—how could I possibly be anything but a detriment to Roman's polished *Forbes* magazine image? And if I am a detriment, how would that affect his father's fledgling resorts?

I bow my head, my hair falling forward to shield my face as hot tears threaten to spill. The Tiger's Eye crystal pendant at my throat—the one Roman said matched my eyes—suddenly feels like it's choking me.

I can't believe I never saw this coming, even with all my tarot cards and intuition. I've been living in a fairy tale bubble all this time, floating on incense smoke and wishful thinking, where love conquers all like some cosmic force. But it doesn't, does it? The real world, with its marble-floored boardrooms and judgmental stares, dictates that barefoot bookstore owners with healing crystals do not end up with billionaire hotel magnates. Period, end of story. And in that same cold, hard reality, women like me, with our thrift-store dresses and New Age philosophies, do nothing but tarnish men like Roman's polished reputations just by standing at their side.

My fingers curl into my palms, nails digging half-moons into the flesh as I finally speak. "If I break up with him, you'll leave him alone, then? You won't drag his name through the mud with this story? You won't tell people about Michael's alcoholism?"

Serafina's lips curve into what might pass for a smile in certain predatory species. "Of course not. You break up with him, there's no need to run that story, is there?" Then she cocks her head. She leans in, voice dropping to a whisper. "You have two choices. Either you walk away from Roman now, or I run this story and personally visit every investor backing his father's project. I'll make sure they know all about the witch who might curse their fortunes while they sleep. I'll let them know exactly why dear old Dad disappeared for so long." Her lips curved into a cold smile. "Watch how quickly they disappear. And Roman will know exactly who to blame."

I exhale slowly, feeling something crack inside my chest. My heart will shatter like sea glass, but I have to do this.

Later on, Jack comes back to the shop, the little bell above the door announcing his arrival with its familiar silver tinkle. I'm already planning my exit strategy, my fingers absently rearranging the same stack of amethyst crystals for the third time today.

I'll move to Northern California where I don't have to see Roman's fancy cars pulling up outside my shop, because I know that with those penetrating dark eyes and that stubborn Kensington jaw, he won't understand and he'll continue to come here until I take him back. I can't do that. I love him so much that my chest physically aches when I think of him, and I know I'll crumble like sea salt if he asks me to come back.

Jack sashays in, peacock-blue scarf fluttering, and

freezes mid-stride. "Oh honey," he says, voice dipping low with concern. "Who do I need to destroy today?" He plants his hands on his narrow hips, head tilted. "Was it that plastic surgery nightmare? Just say the word and I'll channel my inner drag queen rage."

I manage a weak smile. Jack's always had this radar for my moods—probably why we've stayed friends since college. My crystals are still vibrating from this morning's energy shift; I can practically feel my aura pulsing purple and gray around me. Even Jack, who rolls his eyes at my "woo-woo stuff," seems to sense it.

I sigh. "No, Jack, I'm okay. And trust me, Sera isn't some plastic princess. That woman was born perfect and damn well knows it." I've seen enough fake faces in this city to spot silicone from across a crowded room—this is LA, where people sacrifice at the altar of cosmetic surgery daily. But Sera? Her jawline could cut glass, her skin glows like she bathes in liquid gold, and those breasts defy gravity without a surgeon's help. The bitch literally emerged from her mother's womb as if she'd stepped off a Chanel runway, Venus incarnate with a platinum card instead of a seashell. No wonder she struts around like she owns the oxygen we breathe. Her daddy's billions just poured gasoline on an already raging fire.

"You're not fine. Tell me what's going on."

I shrug, tucking a strand of hair behind my ear where it's escaped my messy bun. "I didn't tell you this before, because I just figured I didn't want to do it. But when I was in Big Sur, with those dramatic cliffs overlooking the Pacific, which is by Carmel-by-the-Sea, you know, I received an offer to open another shop in Carmel. This woman named Raven Thornheart really befriended me in Big Sur and told me about the opportunity to franchise the shop up there." I sigh, gazing out the window at the Venice Beach crowds. "It's so beautiful up there, Jack. Fog rolling in over pine trees, the scent of salt and earth. I know I could be happy there. That place is calling to me like a siren song."

Jack's perfectly groomed eyebrows shoot toward his hairline as he tosses his head back dramatically. "Honey, what are you even talking about?" He waves his hand dismissively. "Roman's resort is here. What am I missing? Unless—" he leans forward, voice dropping to a theatrical whisper, "—he's opening up a branch up there that he'll be running? In which case, spill the tea immediately."

I sigh and tell him about Sera's ultimatum, watching his expression darken with each word. Jack listens, drumming his manicured fingers against the counter, and shakes his head. "Sweetie, I'm gagged—positively gagged—that you're letting Miss Thing with her off-the-rack personality and that smile that cost more than my rent boss you around. These trust fund princesses with their Louboutins and their 'Daddy's special girl' black Amex? They're used to people rolling over faster than I do at Tinder notifications." He leans in, eyes sparkling. "But honey, you? No ma'am. I'd tell her to sashay away so fast her hair extensions would need therapy. And I'd do it," he snapped twice, "fabulously."

"Not that simple," I say, running my fingers over the worn tarot cards I've been using all morning. "Roman's trying to start a new eco-resort hotel chain for his father. It's a delicate time for him right now, and a whiff of scandal might do him in like a house of cards. And dating me, the quirky tarot reader with crystals in her bra, just might qualify as a scandal, don't you see? Everybody will assume I'm a witch, and the word witch is still a dirty word with those conservative money men. And if my being a so-called witch doesn't do Michael's resort in, the stories of his alcoholism will. So, I have to bow out of his life. For his sake."

"So what are you going to do, then? Just move up there without telling him?" Jack's perfectly groomed eyebrow arches as he leans forward on my shop's velvet couch.

I nod, twisting my crystal pendant between my fingers. "Yes. I can't face him. I wouldn't be able to do what's right, which is to break up with him. It'll be easier if I just move up there without the big scene between us." I sigh.

I thrust a small canvas tote bag of cat toys into Jack's hands. "So you'll watch Gracie while I'm gone? I leave tomorrow, and I'll be there about a week—just long enough to feel if the energy's right for me. If the universe wants me in Carmel, I'll know." I twirl a strand of hair around my finger. "Gracie would hate the drive. You've seen how she gets in the carrier—all claws and drama."

"You're leaving him without a word. Scandalous," Jack says, shaking his head of glossy chestnut hair. "And what about the townhouse? What about me?" His voice cracks slightly on the last word.

"Oh, Jack," I say, and hug him, the tears streaming hot and salty down my flushed cheeks. His familiar scent of sandalwood cologne envelops me. "You're really my soul mate, do you know that? You wouldn't want to come up there with me, would you? I mean, there won't be any AF models up there for you and it's a small town so there might not be much action for you at all, but it's a beautiful, peaceful place with misty mornings and you might like it."

Jack laughs, his azure eyes crinkling at the corners. "Oh, honey, I thought you'd never ask! I need you like Linus Van Pelt needs his security blanket. That's pathetic, isn't it?" He adjusts the silk scarf around his neck.

"Okay, then, it's set!" I'm suddenly much happier, a

warm glow spreading through my chest. I can't have Roman, which is an absolute tragedy, but if Jack's with me, that'll give me some degree of comfort. "I'll go up there and stay a week and get a feel for the place before I sign any lease. I need to feel the place is right, feel it in my bones, see if it calls to my soul. And if it does, I'll sign a lease and we can move up there together!"

Jack shakes his head, his lips pursed. "And when Roman god comes to the store looking for you, all broody six-foot-something of him?"

"We'll cross that bridge when we come to it." I whisper, staring out at the Venice Beach sunset painting the sky in shades of amber and rose.

Chapter Forty-Two

LILITH

I leave for Carmel the day after Sera's unwelcome visit, tearfully bidding both Jack and Gracie a bittersweet goodbye. But perfect timing, really. Roman's calendar has been packed lately—juggling resort operations, investor meetings, and those long sessions with his father about the eco-resort chain.

One night at the resort, when I got off work there, I found him in his office, blueprints spread everywhere, his father leaning over his shoulder pointing at something while Roman nodded and smiled. Twenty-two years of absence, and now they speak a shared language of sustainable materials and energy-efficient designs. When Roman texted me at midnight—"Still working with Dad. Miss you."—I hugged my phone to my chest. For a man who once swore he'd never forgive Michael Kensington, those late nights planning together say everything words cannot.

I get to Carmel-by-the-Sea about six hours after I left LA. My car's engine quiets as I slow to the town's mandated 25 mph. The village looks like something from another century—cottages without street numbers, shingled roofs at odd angles, streets with names instead of numbers. Cypress trees twist overhead, and salt air mixes with wood smoke from stone fireplaces. Ocean Avenue slopes toward the white-sand beach and the Pacific.

The new shop space sits in one of those storybook cottages Carmel is known for. It has a steep roof of cedar shingles weathered to silver, leaded glass windows that catch the morning light, and curved eaves. Stone chimneys rise from either end, and a rounded wooden door sits beneath an oak archway. Cypress trees surround the property, filtering sunlight onto a path lined with lavender and roses.

I can't help but look around at this new space and think that it's absolutely perfect for my new shop. After all, I'll be opening a New Age shop, a place where you could find everything from spell books to tarot cards to crystals to books about subjects such as chakras, reiki healing, to astrology to channeling spirits. There's something about all those subjects that remind me of fairy tales, so how perfect is it to have a shop in a fairy tale house?

I texted Raven on the way up, telling her that I'm anxious to check out the space, and she shows up while I'm admiring the architecture of the special space. "Lilith," she says. "When I got your text, I was so surprised. When I last talked to you, I was sure that you would want to stay in Los Angeles. I thought there was a special person down there for you."

"There is," I say. "But I think my time in his life has run its course." I sigh.

I met Roman when he needed someone to guide him back to his father, to help mend that broken bridge. Has he completely healed from those old wounds? No. Some scars might always remain. But his father stands beside him now, and with each passing day, their relationship strengthens. This resort they're building together—I see it as more than steel and glass. It's a monument to their reconciliation, even if the final healing takes years.

Roman is becoming someone new before my eyes. Someone steadier, more at peace. And I know that perhaps it was my entire purpose in meeting him - so that I could help them bridge their divide. I'd like to think that my midnight prayers to Brigid, the rose quartz I slipped into his pocket, the hours spent cross-legged on my meditation cushion visualizing father and son embracing—that somehow, in some small way, it all helped push them toward each other.

My mind insists I was just the catalyst for this transformation, nothing more. My heart argues differently—whispering that he's the one person I've been searching for my entire life, my other half. The kind of connection I never truly believed existed.

But I need to silence these feelings. His investors would balk at him dating someone like me with my crystals and tarot cards. They'd question his judgment, his stability. And Serafina would ensure every tabloid splashed our relationship across their pages, humiliating him completely.

Worse, Serafina could whisper the magic words "recovering alcoholic" into the right ears. As a respected hotelier with connections throughout the industry, she wielded enough influence to ensure Michael's resort project would be strangled in its cradle before the first investor's check cleared.

Raven sinks onto a jewel-toned floor pillow, patting the one beside her. I hesitate before joining her, my legs folding reluctantly beneath me.

"Your aura," she whispers, her eyes widening. "It's jet

black, Lilith. Not your usual pink or green. Something's torn you apart."

My throat tightens. Roman's face blazes through my mind like a lightning strike—that smile that cracks open his granite facade, revealing the raw, beating heart beneath. When we're together, my entire body hums with recognition, every cell screaming that I've found the other half of my fractured soul, the missing piece I've been searching for across lifetimes.

God, I want him. Need him. But then I see the Bloomberg headlines: "Kensington Hotels Plummet as CEO Dates Self-Proclaimed Witch." I imagine his brothers' disappointment, his father's concern. Maybe I'm being paranoid. Maybe investors wouldn't care. Maybe I'm just scared of how desperately I love him, how completely he could destroy me. But what if I'm right?

I tell Raven everything—how Roman and his father are staking their entire relationship on this eco-resort, how the project is like some fragile, beating heart between them. "If it fails," I say, my voice cracking, "Michael will shatter. He'll crawl back inside a bottle and never come out. And Roman—God, Roman will never forgive himself. Never forgive his father. Never forgive me."

I grip the edge of the table until my knuckles turn white. "And I'm dying inside, Raven. I found him—my actual soulmate—and now I have to walk away. These billionaire investors Roman needs? They'd take one look at me, at my crystals and tarot cards, and they'd laugh him out of the room. If that doesn't do it, the knowledge of Michael's alcoholism would. His father's dream would collapse. Their relationship would implode. And it would be my fault—all my fault—because I couldn't stay away from a man I had no business loving in the first place."

Raven exhales, her shoulders dropping. We're both spiritual, just in different ways. I read tarot; she does Reiki and sound healing with crystal bowls. Her clients leave with the same peaceful look mine do. She's booked solid for months. "We should work together," I've suggested more than once. "My readings followed by your healing—it'd be perfect." I'd find what's broken, and she'd fix it.

She cocks her head to one side, her waist-length auburn hair cascading over her shoulder like a waterfall of fire. Those sea-green eyes narrow slightly as they study me. "Well, one thing's for sure," she says, her voice melodic but firm. "Your chakras are completely out of alignment. Your root chakra is practically screaming." She taps a slender finger against her lips, adorned with a simple moonstone ring. "See me tomorrow morning, first thing, and I'll do something about that mess of energy you're carrying around."

I force a smile, my lips stretching like an elastic band about to snap. God, when was the last time I actually meant that smile? Before Sera, definitely. Maybe some stones on my back would help.

I've seen clients emerge from chakra sessions looking reborn—eyes bright, shoulders relaxed, as if someone had finally unscrewed a valve letting all that toxic pressure escape. But who am I kidding? My heart feels like it's wrapped in razor wire. No amount of sandalwood smoke or crystal vibrations will fix what's breaking inside me. I've lost him. Period. All my new-age remedies are just expensive Band-Aids on a wound that won't stop bleeding.

Chapter Forty-Three

ROMAN

The hairs on the back of my neck stand up. My phone screen shows seventeen unanswered texts to Lilith since morning, and every call goes straight to voicemail after the fourth ring. When I cornered Miranda at the front desk about it, her perfectly penciled eyebrows arched high. "I'm sorry, Roman, but Lilith gave notice that she'd be gone at least until the 15th, so she's not on the schedule right now."

I know I've been out of pocket. Between my usual resort duties, Dad's investor meetings, and poring over his plans until my eyes cross, I've barely had time to breathe. If someone had told me two months ago I'd willingly sacrifice my scarce free hours to help the man who abandoned us launch his own resort, I'd have called them delusional.

Yet here I am, knee-deep in sustainability reports and blueprint revisions, determined to see this through. The strangest part? Somewhere between location scouting and budget meetings, the stranger who shares my DNA has become... Dad again.

My walls came down when I realized something simple but profound: if he ever tried to vanish like before, I wouldn't let him—none of us would. What I thought was anger was really just fear in disguise—terror that letting him back meant risking another abandonment that would break me beyond repair. Now I can breathe easier knowing my brothers and I hold the power. He's not leaving again unless we say so.

Dad and I even surfed last Saturday. Just us—my brothers all magically had other things to do, even Max, who'd normally cut off his right arm before missing Saturday waves. The morning fog had burned off, leaving the water so damn perfect it almost hurt to look at it. Between sets, we just floated there, faces up to the sun, and talked. Actually talked. Twenty-two years of silence, and suddenly I'm telling him everything like some emotional dam broke inside me.

Told him about Lilith's eyes—amber, like whiskey in sunlight—and how the lavender smell of her skin somehow calms the constant chaos in my head. He told me about Patricia's laugh, how it starts small then takes over her whole body, and how she dragged him back to life after Mom.

The old man actually has a sense of humor—cracking jokes about Uncle Thomas's ridiculous three-legged goat and some crazy Vietnam vet who drinks Jack for breakfast at his local dive in that English village where he spent two decades.

Four hours later, arms feeling like jelly and skin burned to hell, we walked up the beach together, laughing like those missing years were nothing but a bad dream.

After surfing, I invited him to The Bone and Brass for dinner—my flagship restaurant where I knew the staff would treat him like royalty. When he walked in, I stepped forward first and wrapped my arms around him.

"The menu's yours," I said, that old feeling washing over me—ten years old again, desperate for his approval. "Chef Marcelo outdoes himself on everything."

He gave me that hesitant smile before ordering oysters to start and the herb-roasted chicken. Nothing flashy, nothing expensive. Classic Dad—frugal to the bone. I'd somehow forgotten that about him.

He sipped his water. "So, Lilith. She okay with all this father-son time?"

"That's what makes her special," I said. "Unlike anyone I've dated before. She's just... genuine. Sees the bigger picture when everyone else gets caught in the details."

His eyes creased at the corners. "And training for this Ironman with Max next fall? When exactly will you sleep?"

"Not starting that until wc finalize your resort plans," I said. "We're in the critical phase now—financing, blueprints. Once we break ground, I'll ease back. Won't push myself too hard, like you always warned."

"You remember those conversations." He nodded slowly. "Me worrying your intensity would burn you out someday. Still worries me."

"It's who I am, Dad. Lilith says it's my Aries nature—always charging forward. That won't change. But I promise not to run myself into the ground."

Dad and I talked long into the night, our voices growing hoarse as the soda water in our glasses dwindled - I don't drink around him, of course. He insists that I can, that he can handle it, but why tempt fate? The restaurant's balcony overlooks the Pacific with waves crashing against the Palos Verdes cliffs below us.

When his eyelids started drooping, I insisted he take one

of our open oceanfront suites—the Malibu, with its king-sized bed and rainfall shower. As I handed him the keycard, our fingers brushed, and I felt something shift between us, like tectonic plates finally settling after decades of tension.

So, yeah, Dad and I are finally becoming something I never dreamed we'd be—friends.

Now, for some odd reason, Lilith isn't answering her phone. Three calls straight to voicemail. So unlike her. I drive my Aston Martin down to Venice Beach and go right to her store. The crystal dreamcatcher that usually catches the last rays of sunlight in the display window hangs motionless in darkness. The CLOSED sign dangles crookedly against the glass door. Of course—it's 8:17 now. She always locks up around 6, right after the beach crowd thins out.

I speed across town to her pale blue townhome and rap my knuckles against the door, my pulse quickening with each second of silence. When Jack finally opens the door, his usual sparkly eye makeup is smudged at the corners. "Roman, hello," he says stiffly, his shoulders squared beneath his silk kimono robe. My stomach drops. Jack isn't winking, isn't calling me "gorgeous," isn't playfully adjusting my collar. Something is definitely wrong.

"Hey, Jack," I say. "Where's Lilith?"

Jack heaves a heavy sigh. "She's not here."

My heart drops like an elevator with cut cables. The hairs on my forearms stand at attention. Lilith once told me about how the subconscious mind processes millions of data points that never reach our conscious awareness—something like 11 million bits of information per second versus a measly 40 bits that we actually notice. It's why sometimes everything looks fine on the surface, but your gut churns with warning. "That's your third eye," she'd said, touching the center of my forehead with her fingertip, her voice soft and certain. "Trust it when it speaks." Right now, mine isn't just speaking—it's screaming.

"Where is she?"

He shrugs and I want to rip his throat out. "She's..." His voice cracks. "She's gone, Roman. And I can't tell you where she is." He's trembling like a goddamn leaf, but still has the audacity to gesture me into the townhouse. "Cocktail?"

"Fuck no," I snarl, shoving past him. "Jack, what the FUCK is happening?"

He flinches, backing against the wall. "I begged her to face you, but she refused." His eyes dart away from mine. "Said she felt she'd end up destroying you and your father. That she'd rather disappear than watch you both crash and burn. So she ran—vanished without a trace."

Oh, hell no. This is NOT happening. I swear on my mother's grave, if I have to kick down every goddamn door on this planet with my bare fucking feet, I WILL find her. My hands are already shaking, jaw clenched so tight my teeth might crack. But first—Jack. Jack has answers, and I don't care what it takes to get them.

"Okay. Let's have that cocktail."

I enter the apartment, and Jack's already mixing tequila with lime in a salt-rimmed glass. Sweet drinks, ugh, hate sugar, but take it anyhow to be social. Taking the margarita, I settle into the chair opposite his at the dining room table and study his face. Jack's an open book with dog-eared pages—I can practically see the secrets bubbling behind those eyes. Five minutes of my questioning, and he'll spill everything.

"Now," I say. "Let's start over. Why is Lilith gone?"

"Oh, I can't lie to you. But I won't tell you where she is, but I can tell you why she left. How would that be?"

I drag in a ragged breath, my fists clenching so hard my knuckles crack as I fight the crimson fury blazing behind my eyes. Everything was finally falling into place—reconciling with my father after twenty-two fucking years, getting his project off the ground, crushing those investor meetings for him. Demolishing my opponent in that MMA cage until my hands were slick with blood and victory.

And Lilith—Christ—she's been the only light guiding me through this darkness. Now it's all crumbling to ash in my hands, and I swear to God I'll burn the world down before I let that happen. She isn't just my North Star—she's the oxygen in my lungs, the blood in my veins. That.Will.Never.Fucking.Change.

"Why did she leave?"

Jack leaned in, lowering his voice. "It's that Shady Barbie again." He shakes his head. "Don't give me that look—Lilith might absolutely murder me for spilling the tea, but honey, someone's gotta put Miss Thing in check. She's been skating by her whole life on those baby blues and daddy's platinum AmEx. I mean, please. You ask little ol' me? She's been getting away with nonsense since the cradle, which is why she continues to be a hot mess. Somebody has to hold her fabulous ass accountable."

My stomach knotted. "Sera. What happened?"

"Paid our girl a little visit. Threatened to blast you all over Instagram, maybe even get some hit piece in *Forbes* about how the great Roman Kensington is dating—" he made air quotes, "—a 'witch.'" Jack rolled his eyes. "She knows damn well Lil don't cast spells or whatever. Lil reads cards and sells crystals. There's a difference." He sighs. "And she threatened to tell the investors about your father's drunkenness. Guess they don't know about that right now, huh?"

My jaw tightens. I know the distinction between Lilith's spiritual practice and actual witchcraft, but to Sera and her crowd, it was all the same ammunition. And I wouldn't try to explain to my investors the difference, either. They wouldn't understand, the closed-minded pricks.

And Dad's alcoholism? Those investors would bolt faster than paparazzi chasing a scandal. They have no clue—how could they? We've buried that secret deeper than the Mariana Trench. Every glossy magazine profile on the Kensington brothers strategically omitted the chapter where our father vanished into a bottle. One word about that in the article, and that magazine would face a complete Kensington media blackout. Not even worth it when Connor's collecting Oscars like souvenirs and Kalen has stadiums of screaming fans worldwide. We've guarded that boundary like a fortress. So, yeah, those investors are blissfully ignorant about Dad's demons, and that's exactly how the project survives. If Sera starts talking... Dad's dream dies before it takes its first breath.

I wouldn't touch Sera—never raised a hand to a woman in my life—but picturing her Maserati taking a wrong turn at Mulholland gives me a moment of dark satisfaction.

I clench my jaw, feeling the muscle twitch beneath my skin. "Let me guess. Sera threatened to poison my investors against me if Lilith didn't back off." My voice drops lower, harsher. "She was going to paint my father as a unrepentant drunk while convincing them Lilith's some kind of black magic practitioner." I slam my palm against the desk, sending papers fluttering. "I can just see her whispering in their ears about evil spells and hexes, making those superstitious old bastards think their stock portfolios would suddenly combust."

"Oh my God, you hit that on the head! Yes, that's exactly how it went."

I slam my fist against the wall. Damn it. Lilith is gone because she wants to save my father's project. No matter. I'll find her if I have to burn this whole coast down. Jack will crack—I'll make sure of it. But I already know where she is. Carmel. The way her eyes lit up when we drove through those cypress trees, how she gasped at the waves crashing against those jagged cliffs. She practically vibrated with energy there, said the place "called to her soul." She disappeared to Big Sur for that retreat a few months ago too. Those fairy-tale cottages, the misty mornings—it screams Lilith. She's there. I can feel it in my bones. And if she's not? I'll tear apart every town on the goddamn map until I find her.

But Sera—that manipulative bitch is my first problem. My investors are old-school, superstitious as hell. One whisper from Sera about Lilith's crystals or meditation circles, and those cowards will run. She'll twist everything, paint Lilith as some kind of dark sorceress corrupting their precious investment. And if that doesn't do it, Dad's alcoholism will.

I need to shut Sera down. Permanently.

Caspian will help me. Blood or not, he knows his sister is poison. He's seen what Lilith does to me—how she's the only fucking thing that makes sense in my world. Once I tell him what Sera pulled, he'll help me find her weakness. Everyone has one. And I'll exploit it until she backs the hell away from my investors, my father's project, and my life.

"Thanks, Jack," I say. "Listen, I have to go. I have to talk to Caspian."

“Caspian. Sera’s brother, no?”

“Right.”

I storm out and call Caspian from the car, my knuckles white against the steering wheel. "Coming over," I growl, not asking permission. Caspian would walk through fire for me—has before, metaphorically speaking—and I'd burn down the world for him. That's our blood oath.

And right now, I'm drowning.

My chest is a vise, crushing inward with every heartbeat. If anyone can pull me back from this edge, it's him.

Chapter Forty-Four

ROMAN

Caspian opens the door before I can knock. "Hey, Rome." I step into his penthouse on Sunset, a wall of windows framing the glittering LA skyline. Polished marble floors reflect the chandelier's light, leading past a floating staircase to the sunken living room where a white leather sectional faces a fireplace big enough to roast a cow. A Basquiat hangs casually above it. The place is almost as nice as mine.

I nod. "I need your help."

"What's going on?" He looks extremely worried, and I don't blame him. He could tell by the edge in my voice when I called him that there's something very wrong. And he's known me for long enough to know that I don't hit him up like this unless I'm at my wits end. Which I am. The absolute end of my rope.

"Your sister. You have to help me."

"What did she do now?"

I slam my fist against the wall. "She threatened Lilith." My voice comes out like gravel. I tell him how Sera cornered Lilith, how she promised to destroy everything I've built if Lilith didn't vanish from my life.

Caspian's eyes widen. "Jesus Christ. That psycho's been obsessed with you since day one. After you dumped her, my phone would light up at three in the morning—her sobbing, screaming about how you belong to her. I should've warned you she'd snap eventually."

"I don't give a damn about the past." I grab his shoulder. "I need your help. Now."

He jerks back. "What exactly am I supposed to do?"

"Give me something on her. Anything." My voice drops to a dangerous whisper. "I need leverage that'll make her back the hell off before she poisons my investors. You know how she operates—twisting everything, making people believe whatever sick version of reality she's selling." I lean in closer. "Listen to me. Losing Lilith isn't an option. I would burn everything to the ground before I let that happen."

I'm trapped between a rock and a hard place. If Sera isn't dealt with, I'll be forced to choose: my father or Lilith. Choosing Lilith could send this entire resort project tumbling down. These investors are crucial, and even if Dad borrowed from Granddad as a last resort, Sera would still find ways to sabotage everything. She'd stop at nothing to ruin him. Right now, the investors have no clue about Dad's battle with the bottle. Sera would make damn sure they found out he's barely twenty months sober.

Sure, I could also write the check myself if the investors bail. But that's not the real problem. One whiff of scandal—whether it's about Lilith or my father's demons—and the resort's reputation is tarnished before we even open the doors. And Sera? She'd be all too happy to strike the match and watch it burn.

“I’ll see what I can do,” he says. “I won’t let her do this to you.”

I nod, feeling the tension in my jaw. "Thanks. But I want to brainstorm with you tonight." The thought of returning to my empty penthouse makes my skin crawl—pacing across Italian marble floors until dawn, watching the city lights flicker below. Sleep would be impossible. My mind is a hurricane with her at the center. I need to contain this situation before it spins further out of control.

The hatred I feel for Sera burns cold in my chest. Her years-long obsession has finally crossed a line I didn't think even she would dare to cross.

I follow him into his living room and he hands me some scotch, which burns pleasantly down my throat as I study his face, searching for any hint of what he might be thinking about his sister.

"Now what kind of information do you think we need about my sister so that she'll back off you?" His voice breaks the heavy silence between us.

I shrug, rolling the cool glass between my palms. "What do you think? What's her Achilles heel? It has to be something damning enough to keep her quiet."

He laughs, a sharp sound that doesn't reach his eyes. "So it has to be something better than holding over her head the night she snuck out of the house to meet Tanner Pennington, the tattooed bad-boy who rode a motorcycle and made my parents clutch their pearls."

Despite everything, I feel my lips curve into a genuine smile. "Yeah, I don't think teenage rebellion quite covers it. But nice try."

He runs a hand through his hair. "Shit. She'll have my head for this. But I can't stand by while she ruins you." His eyes meet mine. "Twenty-eight years of friendship means something to me. And look, there was always this small part of me hoping you'd end up with my sister, make it official, you'd be my brother-in-law. But that ship's sailed. But you're still family to me, Roman. Always will be."

I lean in, desperate for whatever he's about to reveal.

He exhales heavily. "My sister committed insider trading. Drunk one night, she bragged about making a fortune on Orion Pharmaceuticals right before their miracle weight loss drug hit the market. Remember that pill everyone's taking now? Five years ago, Orion was nothing. After that drug, their stock exploded—twenty times what she paid. Sera had an executive wrapped around her finger." Caspian's jaw tightens. "That's her specialty—batting those eyes and getting men to spill their secrets. This poor bastard never stood a chance."

"Name, please."

Caspian shrugs. "Don't have a name. She didn't tell me that much."

My fingers tap a staccato rhythm against the glass tabletop. I need leverage. Something concrete that would hold up in court—federal court—or she'll dismiss this entire situation with that infuriating laugh of hers.

"This information is promising, but insufficient. I need to establish a timeline for the insider trading. Dates, specifics. Then I'll have Sven breach her email server, search for correspondence with this contact. If we find evidence of a tip-off, she'll have no choice but to back down."

But even as I say it, I know we're grasping at straws. What are the odds she'd leave such an obvious digital trail?

Caspian's jaw tightens. "I have the dates," he says, pulling a crumpled paper from his pocket. "Been carrying this around like a fucking grenade with the pin half-pulled.

Every day I wake up thinking today's the day I call the feds. But she's my blood. My goddamn sister."

I slam my fist on the table, making the glasses jump. "I don't need her in handcuffs. Yet. I need a sword hanging over her neck." I lean in, voice dropping to a razor's edge. "Because if she gets these investors whispering about my father's drinking, or breathes one syllable about Lilith being a witch, I will personally escort her through the gates of hell. Twenty years in federal prison will feel like a spa retreat compared to what I'll do. I'll take everything—her money, her reputation, her future—until she's begging for those prison bars to protect her from me. So I get those dates, and that beautiful mouth of hers stays permanently shut."

He gives me the dates and I text Sven.

Got a job. Meet me at the resort tomorrow at 10.

Got it.

I smile. It's a long-shot, but if it works…Lilith will be mine, with no threat hanging over her head. Or my head, for that matter. My father's secrets will be safe.

God, I hope there's some kind of trail…

Chapter Forty-Five

LILITH

I have to admit, I'm falling for Carmel-by-the-Sea, with its cypress-lined streets and cottages that look plucked from storybooks. This morning, I spread my turquoise mat on sand that felt like crushed velvet between my toes, the misty air clinging to my skin as I flowed through my Vinyasas.

Just four miles south is a dense forest where I go to clear my head. The Japanese call it shinrin-yoku—forest bathing. I sit on pine needles and just listen: wind in the trees, birds, the smell of moss and earth. It's where I can finally breathe.

Further south stretches Big Sur, where ancient redwoods at Pfeiffer State Park thrust upward like nature's skyscrapers, their cinnamon-colored trunks wider than my arms could ever encircle.

Venice Beach has its charms—the people-watching, the energy—but here, nature takes over. Last night, I drove the coastal highway to Big Sur, turned off my headlights, and looked up at more stars than I'd ever seen. The Milky Way was clearly visible, something impossible through LA's light pollution. My new shop is in a little Tudor cottage with leaded windows and a curved roof.

Can this paradise replace Roman? No. My heart still aches for him like a phantom limb—for his stormy dark eyes that soften only for me, for the sandalwood scent of his skin. But I can't risk Sera poisoning what Roman and Michael have painstakingly rebuilt. Their relationship is like a bonsai tree—meticulously tended, beautiful in its fragility. The resort they're creating together is the soil in which their reconciliation grows stronger each day. So I'll stay here instead, letting the waves and trees calm me down when I start to ache for him again.

And I'll be going soon for my chakra balancing with Raven. That'll help me so much, along with meditating, crystal healing and the forest bathing.

This morning, after my sunrise Vinyasas on the beach—sand still clinging to my ankles, hair smelling of salt—I step into Raven's incense-hazed shop. She presses her cool palms against my shoulders, her bangles jingling softly as her amber eyes narrow in concentration.

"Oh, Lilith," she whispers, her voice honeyed with concern, "every one of your chakras are blocked tight as seashells. But your heart chakra is practically pulsing with dark energy. We'll start there, unravel that knot first, then work through the others in the coming days."

So, for three hours this morning, we work on opening my heart chakra. Raven burns sage and palo santo, the smoke curling around us as we sit cross-legged on embroidered floor pillows. She places a rose quartz crystal between my breasts, its cool weight centering me, while smaller pieces of green aventurine form a circle around us.

"Visualize emerald light," she whispers, her voice barely

audible above the singing bowl she occasionally strikes. "See it pulsing outward from your chest, dissolving any walls you've built." I try, I really do, breathing in lavender oil and breathing out the name of everyone who'd ever hurt me.

By the time the heart chakra ritual is over, I feel lighter, as if someone has lifted a granite slab from my chest. The emerald-green candles are burned down to nubs, their melted wax forming tiny crystalline pools on the meditation mat.

Tomorrow, we will work with my root chakra, grounding me to the earth again, and then the day after, the solar plexus chakra, which Raven says is a sickly yellow instead of the vibrant gold it should be. All of these energy centers clogged with the debris of memories—Roman's calloused fingertips brushing my cheek, the scent of his sandalwood cologne, the way his voice would drop to a whisper when he told me he loved me.

I text Jack.

> Loving it up here! I can't wait for you to join me.

I also text him pictures: of the forest with its towering redwoods dappled in golden afternoon light, the beach where foam-tipped waves crash against pristine sand, and the weathered cedar cottage with its peeling blue trim and charming bay windows—the place where Mystic Tides will soon find its new home.

Three gray dots appear on my screen, pulsing hypnotically. They linger there, second after excruciating second, like the pendulum of some invisible clock counting down to an unknown revelation. My stomach tightens. Jack never writes novels unless something's seriously wrong.

I finally get it.

> LILITH SYDNEY! Honey-bunny-sugar-plum! Fab to hear you're thriving in your little hideaway, but RED ALERT Roman knows you've flown the coop and WHY. Oopsie-daisy! But like, don't give me those judgy eyes through the phone—you KNOW my mouth is like a broken piñata around him. Secrets just fall out! He hasn't pinpointed your exact coordinates yet, but that man's brain is like a sexy GPS system. Tick-tock! Spilled ALL the tea about Shady Barbie and her diabolical shenanigans. Sooooo... don't be shocked when Mr. Tall-Dark-and-Temperamental comes storming up your driveway like a romance novel cover come to life. XOXO with sprinkles on top!
> ~Jack

Despite the anxiety coursing through me, I can't help but smile. Classic Jack. But Roman has no idea where I am. Even if he narrows it down to Carmel, what then? My shop isn't open, and I've been crashing at Raven's place—someone he's never even heard of. Carmel has thousands of residents. I'm practically invisible.

I catch myself. Shouldn't I want him to find me? But the truth is, I don't. If Roman tracks me down, Sera will make good on her threats. She always does. Women like her—blessed with beauty, bankrolled by daddy, and willing to fight dirty when necessary—they've been getting their way since the beginning of time. The rich crush the rest of us simply because they can. Serafina's just following the same old script, and I'm the nobody standing in her way. What chance do I have?

Still, I can't help myself. Raven doesn't do tarot, but Raven's friend, Marigold, does. So, I go to her shop, tucked between a vintage bakery and a handmade jewelry store in that quaint town area where every building looks plucked from a Brothers Grimm illustration—all gingerbread trim and storybook shutters.

The moment I push open the door, I smell jasmine, my absolute favorite scent since childhood. Polished oak floors are so pristine that I can almost see my reflection as I walk. Marigold floats toward me, her honey-blonde hair cascading in waves beneath a teal silk scarf, her flowy tunic the color of sunset. Before I can even introduce myself, she enfolds me in a hug that feels like coming home, her arms surprisingly strong for someone so ethereal, and in that instant—her cheek pressed against mine, her heartbeat somehow in sync with my own—I know with bone-deep certainty that she's one of my soul sisters.

"Raven tells me you're suffering from a broken heart," she says. "So let's see what the cards tell us." I follow her back to her reading room, and she shuffles some cards and throws them out - she doesn't put them into two stacks and have me choose a stack. To each their own.

She tilts her head, silver bangles tinkling as she studies the Celtic Cross formation. The final card catches my eye immediately—The Sun, its golden rays bursting from the edges of the worn card, promising happiness on my horizon. Happy with Roman? The thought sends a flutter through my stomach, though I can't imagine how that's possible right now. Still, the card promises joy will find me, one way or another.

My fingers hover over the spread, tracing the air above each revelation. Roman dominates the layout—The

Emperor sits upright in his stone throne, stern and commanding in the position of influence. The King of Wands blazes with fiery Aries energy in the hopes position, his lion-headed staff aglow with the same intensity I've seen in Roman's eyes when he's focused on a goal. And there, in the position of what's coming, the Knight of Cups offers his chalice with a dreamy expression, revealing a tender heart beneath Roman's hard exterior. Together they paint him in vivid strokes—powerful yet passionate, visionary yet vulnerable. And remarkably, each card sits in a position of promise rather than warning.

She studies the cards, her eyes widening. "This man you're mourning—he's still very much in your future. I see something quite promising here." Her gaze flicks up to mine. "What happened between you?" Before I can answer, she waves her hand. "No, no—I see it now." Her finger taps the reversed Queen of Swords. "This woman—cold, calculating—she inserted herself between you. She wields words like knives, thinks only of herself." A soft click of her tongue. “Nasty piece of work, that one. But look here—" she traces the surrounding cards, "—her influence is temporary. These cards suggest she'll fade from your story soon."

She gathers the deck, shuffling with practiced hands. "Let's see what becomes of her, shall we?" Her eyes close briefly as she lays out a new pattern. A small, satisfied smile curves her lips. "Ah. Her own schemes will be her undoing. See the Seven of Swords? Deception. And here—Justice. The scales will balance. I wonder what secrets she's hiding."

I trace my finger over the cards, lingering on the Justice card that sits opposite the reversed Queen of Swords—Serafina, no doubt. The cards whisper of deceit, of secrets kept in shadow. My pulse quickens as I imagine Roman uncovering whatever Sera's hiding. The Tower and the Lovers sit side by side in the outcome position, promising destruction followed by union.

My chest tightens with a feeling I haven't allowed myself since Serafina's threats.

Could the universe actually be conspiring in our favor?

Chapter Forty-Six

ROMAN

I spend the night fighting my sheets, sweating through the damn silk until it clings to me like I'd been caught in a riptide. Every time I close my eyes, there's Serafina, that shark in Louboutins with those blood-red nails and a smile that never touches her eyes.

When my phone buzzes at 5 AM, I nearly knock over the whiskey I'd left on the nightstand. It's Sven.

"Tell me you found something," I say, already sitting up.

"Nothing concrete on Orion," he says, his accent thicker than usual. "But I dug deeper. Six separate trades, Roman. All before major announcements. The SEC would have a field day with this."

"Send it all to me," I say, already calculating how to use this. "I want to see her face when she realizes I've got her."

He rattles off the damning list: the Orion trade from five years back when she'd spilled her secrets to Caspian over three bottles of vintage Bordeaux; Cohen and Friesz law firm stocks purchased days before a merger that sent shares soaring like eagles; dumped shares in Swedish toy company Flicka and Pojke, mere hours before their wooden train set was found to be a death trap for toddlers; Boeing stocks sold just before their planes started falling from the sky like wounded birds; and finally, a massive buy-in to Chinese EV company Red Star Motors, right before they unveiled a revolutionary battery that had Elon Musk grinding his teeth with envy.

I rub my hands together, a surge of adrenaline shooting through my veins. Checkmate, bitch. Two birds, one stone - I'll crush her until she backs off my father and Lilith, and I'll make damn sure she knows I've got Sven watching her every financial move like a hawk circling wounded prey.

If she even thinks about pulling this insider trading shit again, she'll rot in prison for 20 years minimum. My conscience flickers - shouldn't I already be dialing the feds? But hell no - I'd have to reveal how I got this intel, expose Sven, and that's a powder keg I'm not lighting unless I have to. Serafina won't know my hesitation though. I'll stare straight into those snake eyes of hers and make her believe I'm one heartbeat away from destroying her entire life if she so much as whispers about Lilith or Dad to a single living soul.

I call her. "Sera," I say. "Bone and Brass. Tonight. 7." Then I hang up.

My phone buzzes non-stop for the next several hours. I ignore it until curiosity gets the better of me. I scroll through her messages with mounting disbelief.

Are we finally going to talk about us? 💕

Ten minutes after this message…

I knew you'd come around! I'll wear that black dress you couldn't take your eyes off last time. Can't wait to see you tonight. I love you, Roman.

Twenty minutes later…

Spring wedding at Lake Como would be perfect. The wisteria will be blooming against those mountains. We could have the whole resort to ourselves before tourist season!

One hour later…

Should we invite Spielberg? Get Max to reach out to him? I'm starting on the guest list now.

I toss my phone onto my desk. Christ. One dinner invitation and she's planning our wedding and Hollywood guest list. My phone buzzes again. Does this woman ever actually work?

My phone buzzes again and again and again throughout the day. Thirty-fucking-plus messages from Sera about "our special day." I grimace through the barrage of messages that are filled with her wedding wish list.

Annie Leibovitz for photos. Gordon Ramsay himself handling the menu. Jamie Oliver for appetizers. Vera Wang designing her gown. Christ. She drops these celebrity names like they're waiting by the phone for her call. As if Annie Leibovitz gives a shit about wedding photography. As if Gordon Ramsay isn't busy running about 50 different restaurant chains and appearing on approximately a gajillion television shows. The only one who might actually do it is Jamie Oliver—didn't he offer something for Prince Harry's wedding? That's what Sera thinks we are. Royalty. Delusional bitch. I'll give her Vera Wang though—she did design something for Celeste when she married my brother. But still.

Each message makes my jaw clench tighter until I taste blood from biting the inside of my cheek.

I should feel guilty about what I'm about to do to her, but all I feel is rage burning through my veins when I think about her threatening Lilith. The bitch crossed a line. I've always been ruthless in business—crushing competitors, finding weaknesses, exploiting opportunities—but I've never stooped to blackmail. Never needed to. Serafina, though? She's a snake. And I'm about to cut off her fucking head. The five insider trading deals I have documented will destroy her. Not just her career. Her entire life. And I won't lose a second of sleep over it.

I arrive at Bone and Brass at 7 and freeze mid-step. Serafina. Jesus Christ. She's wearing black—not just any black—a dress that clings to every dangerous curve like it was painted on her skin by the devil himself. Her blonde hair cascades down her back, catching the golden hour light like a halo mocking her intentions. Those blood-red lips I used to devour are curved into a smile that's both invitation and weapon. The hemline barely exists, revealing miles of toned legs that once wrapped around my waist, and the neckline plunges so deep I can practically see her heartbeat. Yep. She thinks we're getting back together.

"Roman!" she says, her eyes sparkling with excitement. "I can't wait to show you a picture of the church where I want the ceremony. I'm thinking the Church of San Giovanni Battista in Varenna—that enchanting fishing village on the eastern shore of Lake Como, just a short drive from your resort. The church's weathered stone facade has stood since 1010, watching over generations of lovers. And that town! The Way of Lovers pathway hugs the crystalline water, while Villa Monastero's gardens burst with Mediterranean flowers and centuries-old cypress trees. Those narrow cobblestone streets wind between homes painted in warm terracottas and sunny yellows...I couldn't imagine anything more magical than saying our vows there as spring blossoms perfume the air."

My blood boils. "Sera, we're not getting married. Not today. Not ever."

"Oh, but we are. We are!" Her bottom lip juts out, trembling. "I texted you all the wedding plans today and you never got back. If we weren't getting married, if you didn't want to get married, you would've texted me back to tell me that."

Jesus Christ. The twisted logic hits me like a sucker punch. I don't respond, so that means full steam ahead? My jaw clenches so tight I can hear my molars grinding. How the hell did I miss the Cat 5 hurricane of crazy all those years we dated?

I look Serafina straight in the eye. "Sera. I need you to understand something. What we had—it wasn't love. Not for me." My jaw tightens as I think about the countless nights in hotel suites across three continents. Great sex, nothing more. "It's Lilith. She's..." The words catch, then break free. "She's everything. And I'm in love with her." There, I said it to somebody not named Lilith. Something shifts inside me—like I've just signed my name to a declaration. Even with Sera's mascara starting to run, I can already imagine saying those three words at the resort, at family dinner, anywhere Lilith stands beside me.

Her eyes flash. "Lilith." She spits the name like venom.

"She bewitched you. She admitted it to my face." She leans forward, voice dropping to a hiss. "Black magic. The darkest kind. She's invaded your mind, Roman. Violated you." Her fist slams the table. "How can you not see it? She's cast a goddamn spell on you! She doesn't love you—she's after the Kensington fortune!" Her voice cracks with desperation. "She'll drain every account, every asset. If you marry her, she'll hex you into your grave, and before your body's even cold, she'll be sprawled on some Mediterranean yacht, champagne dripping down her throat while boy toys worship at her feet—all paid for with your money."

I can't help but laugh at the absurdity. Hexes? Black magic? Lilith confessing to some elaborate supernatural trap? Christ. If anyone should be writing fiction, it's Serafina. She'd give my sister-in-law Celeste a run for her money, and Celeste's no amateur—Netflix limited series, Paramount features, even those saccharine Hallmark romances she cranks out like clockwork. "Damn good," as Max always says. Maybe I should connect them; Serafina's delusions could fuel a decade of screenplays. The woman runs hotels, but clearly she's wasting her talents. Hollywood's missing its star fantasist.

I sigh. A village is missing its idiot.

I lock eyes with Serafina, her perfectly plucked eyebrows arching in challenge. "Tell you what," I say, my voice dropping to that dangerous octave my brothers recognize as the calm before the storm. "I'll take my chances with Lilith." My jaw clenches so tight I can feel a muscle twitch beneath my five o'clock shadow. "And you might think in your twisted head that she's an actual witch, stirring cauldrons and casting hexes. I think you actually believe that, which makes you as narrow-minded as anyone I've ever met."

My hands curl into fists at my sides, knuckles whitening.

The familiar heat of anger floods my chest, but it's different this time—protective, possessive. I shouldn't care what this woman thinks, but goddamn it, I do. The thought of anyone slandering Lilith—*my* Lilith —makes something primal rear up inside me.

Now, Serafina's perfectly plucked eyebrows draw together, her crimson lips thinning to a dangerous line. Her manicured fingers grip her champagne flute so tightly I'm surprised the crystal doesn't shatter.

"I still don't believe you're falling for her games," she hisses through clenched teeth. "Wake up, Roman! The woman graduated from City College. City College!" She spits the words like they taste foul on her tongue. "I heard her telling somebody at your gala that she sewed her own dress—with actual thread and needle, like some kind of peasant from the Middle Ages. She probably thinks Chanel is a TV station. Thinks Balenciaga is a kind of cheese. I bet she stares at the row of forks at Eleven Madison Park like they're ancient hieroglyphics. She might know service protocol—left to serve, right to clear in America, ladies first in Europe—but only because she's been a fucking cater waiter, not because she has a single refined bone in her bohemian body. What could you possibly have in common with her?"

Ha. Good question. Truth is, Lilith and I have very little in common. Her tiny Venice Beach townhouse could fit in my master bathroom. Her idea of breakfast is some kind of green smoothie with ingredients I can't pronounce, while I have a personal chef at the resort who prepares eggs Benedict with caviar. She wears flowing skirts with jangling ankle bracelets; I wear Tom Ford suits that cost more than her monthly store rent.

But none of that matters when I'm with her—when her

eyes crinkle at the corners as she laughs, when her wild chestnut curls tickle my chest as she sleeps. She makes the constant buzzing in my head quiet down for the first time since I was ten years old. No, she didn't attend Harvard-Westlake prep school, or Harvard undergrad, or Stanford MBA, or Cornell PhD like I did. I don't understand how her tarot cards work or why she thinks holding a piece of rose quartz can heal a broken heart. But when I'm with her, I'm not Roman Kensington, hotel magnate with the weight of a $50 billion-dollar empire on his shoulders. I'm just Roman. And that feels like finally being able to breathe after drowning for twenty-nine years - since my mother died.

And the fact is, she's everything to me. Light. Heat. Oxygen. Everything.

I lean in close enough to smell the Chanel No. 5 on Sera's neck, my voice dropping to a dangerous whisper that only she can hear in the crowded restaurant. "It's over, Sera. Not just over—fossilized. Ancient history." The crystal tumbler in my hand catches the amber light from the chandelier as I take a slow sip of eighteen-year Macallan. "And I know exactly what you did, threatening Lilith at her bookstore."

Her perfectly glossed lips part slightly, the first crack in her porcelain façade. I slide my phone across the white tablecloth, its screen displaying a series of damning financial records. "Five separate insider trading violations, all meticulously documented. The Cohen and Friesz merger you somehow predicted; Flicka and Pojke, whose stocks you dumped right before it came out that their wooden train set would be recalled; Boeing's nosedive—both literal and financial—that you escaped unscathed." I tap each transaction with my index finger, the platinum Patek Philippe on my wrist catching the light. "The Chinese battery breakthrough. And my personal favorite—Orion's miracle weight-loss drug that's currently financing your new Aspen chalet."

The blood drains from Sera's face, leaving her MAC foundation a shade too dark against her suddenly pallid skin. Her French-manicured nails dig into the leather banquette. "How did you possibly—"

"Not important," I cut her off, enjoying the way her sapphire earrings tremble as she swallows hard. "What matters is that I can picture the whole scene now—federal agents in bulletproof vests storming through your hotel, boxes of evidence stacked in the elevator, your Louboutins clicking desperately as they escort you past all those employees you've terrorized." I smile, not the practiced one I use for investors, but the predatory one my brothers know means someone's about to bleed. "So here's the deal, simple enough even for your Harvard Business School brain: you stay completely silent about my father's past and Lilith's spiritual practices, or I make one phone call and your next outfit comes in prison orange. Understood?"

She nods, finally knowing she's lost. For good.

Sera's eyes glisten with tears. "Roman," she chokes out, clutching at my sleeve. "Please don't do this. Please. We loved each other, I know we did."

I wrench my arm away. "Sera, here's the thing." My voice turns to ice. "What we had wasn't love. It was convenience. Lust. A goddamn business arrangement with orgasms." I lean closer. "Real love? It's a fucking inferno. It's choosing to burn alive, screaming in agony, rather than watch her shed a single tear. It's lying awake at night memorizing the rhythm of her breathing." My fists clench as Lilith floods my mind—rushing that dress to her at the gala; rebuilding her shop after that flood, her smile worth every penny of the six figures I spent. The blood I would spill for her. The bullet I would take for her. "I would tear this world apart with my bare hands for her. And I wouldn't think twice."

She sighs. “Roman.”

I point at her. “Not a word about Lilith to anyone. Not a word about my dad to anyone. Got that? You breathe a word and the fed will get an anonymous tip. And you can do what can, hire a forensic fucking genius to erase all evidence of your trades from your hard-drives, but it’ll be no use. Those trades are out there. They can’t be erased. The feds will find them. And you’ll be fucking toast.” I raise an eyebrow. “Fair warning.”

At that, I drink the rest of my whiskey, throw down my napkin and storm out.

Tomorrow, I’ll do one thing, the first thing in the morning.

Head to Carmel.

But first, I call Jack. "Jack," I say. "Sera won't be a problem anymore. Where's Lilith?"

"Oh my god, what did you do? I need details!"

Jack's practically salivating for gossip, but I can't risk it. My arrangement with Sera hinges on discretion—her financial indiscretions stay buried as long as she backs off. If Jack finds out, the whole city will know by happy hour.

"Not important. Just tell me where to find her."

He sighs with the drama of a soap opera diva. "In CarMEL, silly. I'm sure you knew that. Some cosmic priestess named Raven something is letting her crash in her yurt. Our girl’s scouting storefronts for Mystic Tides: The Sequel. Probably communing with redwood spirits and collecting moon-charged pebbles as we speak."

I nod. Tomorrow at dawn, I'll be in my helicopter

heading north. The five-hour drive isn't an option—every minute away from her feels like torture.

I touch the small velvet box in my pocket. For weeks, I've been working with Silas, who's been in touch with jewelers across three continents to find it: a blue diamond so rare that fewer than twenty comparable stones exist on earth. When I look at its impossible azure depths, I see everything I want to promise her—forever, only her, always. The kind of certainty I've never felt about anything else in my life.

Chapter Forty-Seven

LILITH

Raven and I are sharing tea in her shop, legs folded beneath us on embroidered floor pillows, when the bell above the door jingles. A man stumbles in—unwashed hair, clothes that hang on him like they belong to someone else. His eyes find us, red-veined and vacant. The air around him seems to darken, as if light itself retreats from his presence. My skin prickles, tiny hairs standing at attention. Warning signals flash through my mind faster than I can name them, but the message is clear: danger.

He sways slightly, gaze drifting between us without focus. The sour reek of bottom-shelf whiskey reaches me even from across the room. But beneath that—something worse. Something wrong. His aura pulses like an oil spill—thick, iridescent black that seems to absorb all the light around him, leaving only the sharp edges of his silhouette visible against the California sunshine.

The warmth from my tea cup vanishes as cold seeps into the space. Beside me, Raven's fingers tighten around her mug. Her shoulders stiffen.

"Can I help you?" Her voice cuts through the silence.

He just shakes his head. His gaze drifts to Raven's display of rare crystals. The lavender-pink Taafeite catches the light, its $5,000-per-carat brilliance matched only by its mystical power to transform bad luck into good fortune and bestow divine wisdom upon its keeper.

Next to it sits Musgravite, deceptive in its greyish-green exterior that conceals spectacular rainbow depths within—much like its spiritual properties of fostering new beginnings, restoring balance, and inviting joy into one's life.

His eyes linger on the Painite, similar to the black-and-red stone Roman gifted me for the gala, its dramatic natural beauty renowned for drawing abundance to whoever possesses it. Collectors covet these stones as much for their mystical properties as for their scarcity—each one a tangible promise that happiness and prosperity might be held in the palm of your hand.

His eyes fix on the display case. "That Taafeite. Want it." Before I can respond, his hand disappears into his overcoat and emerges with a gun. The morning light catches on the barrel. My stomach drops. Just moments ago, I'd barely registered his coat—November in Carmel, sixty degrees, the shop just opening. Nothing unusual. Now I see what I missed: the slight bulge at his side, the way the fabric hangs too loose around his frame, the nervous darting of his eyes. My brain had collected all these warning signs and filed them away, useless, but it helps explain my earlier intuition that something was very wrong.

I look at the man, who's staring at the case with pupils blown so wide his irises have disappeared into black holes. His fingers twitch against his thigh—counting, measuring, calculating their worth with manic precision. The muscles in his jaw work beneath his skin like something alive trying to escape. Sweat cascades at his temples despite the arctic blast of air conditioning.

"Lock the fucking door and put the closed sign out NOW!" He screams, waving the gun around wildly. Raven dashes to the door and does as he says.

The man's breathing has gone shallow and ragged, and I can feel the fever-heat scorching off him in violent waves. My throat constricts like it's being crushed. Every hair on my body electrifies. My instincts don't just scream danger—they shriek in primal terror. This man isn't just unstable—he's a detonation with a timer counting down to zero.

Raven's hands tremble violently as she fumbles with the case, nearly dropping it before placing the crystal on the counter with a dull thud. The man's tongue darts out, wetting his lips as his gaze locks onto the stone. A muscle in his cheek spasms, his pupils dilating until they nearly swallow the irises. "Cornelia," he hisses, his eyes boring into mine like twin drills. "You fucking whore. You're already dead. This crystal is going to rip your soul apart and scatter it across dimensions for what you did."

My blood freezes in my veins. This is a predator who's found his prey. Headlines flash through my mind: "Woman Decapitated in Bookstore," "Shop Owner's Throat Slashed by Customer." The subway pusher in New York. The Portland stabber. The Boston Strangler.

He's looking at me but seeing someone else, and that someone else is already dead in his mind.

Chapter Forty-Eight

ROMAN

My turboprop slices through the morning air toward Carmel. By 9 AM, I'm touching down at Monterey Regional. Damn air traffic control—wouldn't clear me for takeoff until 7. Jack's intel on Raven is pathetically thin: no last name, no shop name, just "some kind of psychic." Useless bastard.

I've narrowed my search to ten possibilities—a bookstore, a handful of healers, tarot readers, and astrology joints. Google turned up nothing under Raven's first name. So now I get to play detective, hitting every psychic shop in town until I find her. At least Carmel's small. If she were in LA, I'd be screwed—that city's crawling with hundreds of crystal-waving, card-reading New Age types.

I arrive in town and head straight for the first listing in my search results—a tarot reader tucked somewhere in Carmel's downtown. The streets are lined with faux-Tudor facades, wrought iron signs swinging above doorways, and storybook cottages with thatched roofs.

They call Carmel a "fairy tale city," and walking

through it, I half expect to see dwarves whistling their way home from a diamond mine. The irony is that none of this English whimsy belongs here historically—the Spanish missionaries were the ones who settled this stretch of California coastline in the 1700s. Unlike places that grew organically from their immigrant roots—Holland, Michigan with its authentic Dutch windmills and tulip festivals, or New Glarus, Wisconsin where Swiss chalets and fondue make cultural sense—Carmel's Olde English charm is entirely manufactured to make this place a tourist trap.

But the quaint façade doesn't fool anyone with real money. Behind those storybook cottages and cobblestone streets lurks a playground where Taylor Swift once held hands with Travis Kelce over dinner with Bradley Cooper and Gigi Hadid, where Clint Eastwood once governed from a mayoral office, and where CEOs pretend they're just regular folks enjoying ice cream cones while their security details hover nearby.

I approach a tarot reader's storefront, where purple velvet curtains frame a window display of crystal balls and ornate decks. A handwritten sign on parchment paper announces the next reading at 11 AM.

Undeterred, I next try a reiki healer's bamboo-framed doorway next door, then a chakra balancer with its rainbow-colored wind chimes, followed by a sound healer's studio where Tibetan singing bowls gleam in the window, and finally a place with "pranic healing" painted in flowing gold script above a doorway draped with beaded curtains. Each place is the same story—hushed voices behind closed doors, the faint scent of incense, and not an employee in sight.

I run my hand through my hair, frustrated. I just need one conversation with one person wearing flowing clothes and too many rings. Surely this Raven character is part of their little crystal-clutching community—in a town this size, all these mystical types must gather at the same full moon ceremonies.

Frustrated, I finally duck into a bookstore with a wrought-iron sign hanging above the door. The place smells like incense, and some new age music plays softly from speakers I can't see. Behind the counter sits a blonde woman in a blue dress, her hair catching the light from several salt lamps around the shop. She has a small silver nose ring and eyes that remind me of sea glass. When she looks up at me, she nods like she was expecting me. "You must be looking for Raven," she says, and something in me lifts.

I don't even pause to ask her how she knows I'm looking for Raven. The woman is psychic, after all. I'm starting to grudgingly accept that some people actually do have a gift, and this woman is evidently one of them.

"I am. Where is her shop?"

She writes down an address on lavender stationery with a peacock feather pen, and I thank this mysterious lady before heading straight there.

I pull up to the address in my rented Maserati, tires crunching over the cobblestone streets. The storefront window of Raven's store, called White Light, displays a hand-painted "CLOSED" sign, the letters swirling in purple and gold against weathered driftwood. I shake my head, jam my hands into the pockets of my tailored slacks, and take three steps back toward my car before something freezes me mid-stride.

A prickling sensation crawls up my spine—that inexplicable awareness Lilith always describes as the "third eye opening." My breath catches. The late morning sun glints off the crystal wind chimes hanging in the window, casting rainbow prisms across the sidewalk at my feet. Despite myself, I pivot back toward the darkened shop.

I peer through the smudged glass window, my breath fogging the pane, but see only darkness beyond. The lights are off, and I shake my head, running my fingers through my hair in frustration. Why are the lights off? The antique brass clock on the building across the street reads 10:17 AM, but Raven's shop sits abandoned in shadow.

The heavy velvet curtains, deep purple with silver moons embroidered along the hem, block any hint of California sunshine from penetrating the gloom. My stomach tightens. The shop's ornate wooden sign swings slightly in the breeze, the hours "9AM-7PM" mocking me as I glance down at my steel-toed boots, the leather still new enough to creak when I flex my foot. Something told me to wear them this morning instead of my usual loafers—some primal instinct I couldn't name—and now I understand why as I position myself to kick the wooden door in.

I get into the shop and freeze. A man has a gun trained on Lilith and a woman with auburn hair—must be Raven. Just like that, the gunman swings around to face me. Perfect. My gaze drops to my steel-toed boots—the ones I'd inexplicably decided to wear this morning. Funny how intuition works. The voice in my head that said "wear the boots" apparently didn't think to add "and maybe grab a weapon while you're at it."

Something primal takes over. All those years with Caspian in the ring crystallize into this one moment—this is what we trained for. I pivot toward the gunman, my leg already arcing through the air. The weapon skitters across the floor. My body moves on autopilot: feint, jab, roundhouse. He crumples like wet cardboard. Only then does the burning in my shoulder register. Blood soaks my shirt—the bastard got a shot off. The pain hits me like a freight train, delayed by adrenaline's mercy. Christ, it feels like someone drove a hot poker through my flesh.

No matter. I grind my boot heel into his spine, pinning him to the floor while he thrashes like a dying fish, still clutching that pathetic crystal. My eyes snap to Lilith and the redhead huddled behind the counter, trembling violently.

Fuck. My chest caves in at the sight of Lilith—her face drained of color, eyes wild with terror. This woman who walks barefoot through Venice at midnight, who laughs in the face of my rage—now reduced to this quivering shadow. The radiance that's always pulled me toward her like a goddamn magnet has been snuffed out. It hits me like a sledgehammer—I've been basking in her light without even knowing it, and now that it's gone, I'm drowning in darkness. I'd kill this bastard with my bare hands to bring that light back.

I call the police while grinding my Italian leather boot into this bastard's spine, feeling each vertebra crunch beneath my heel.

Lilith's jade eyes are wide with terror, her olive skin paler than usual, and somehow that sight drowns out the searing, white-hot pain radiating from my shoulder. Warm blood soaks through my custom Tom Ford shirt, the crimson stain spreading like spilled wine across the Egyptian cotton. A metallic scent fills my nostrils. I know that significant blood loss leads to unconsciousness, but I force my vision to stay clear, my muscles taut as steel cables. The police better hurry—if I pass out, this piece of garbage will lunge for Lilith again. Mind over fucking matter.

I hear the sirens wailing closer, then the heavy thud of

tactical boots as cops storm into the shop. My vision blurs at the edges. I close my eyes, picturing Lilith's face—those amber eyes, that gentle smile. The cops are here, so she's safe. That's all that matters now. The world tilts sideways, colors swirling into darkness as my consciousness slips away like water through open fingers.

Chapter Forty-Nine

ROMAN

I wake up in a sterile hospital room, the antiseptic smell burning my nostrils as fluorescent lights stab at my eyes. Two faces swim into focus when I come to - Lilith's and my father's. Lilith is perched on the edge of the vinyl chair beside the bed, her slender fingers clutching mine so tightly her knuckles have gone white, her usually radiant face now drawn and pale with dark circles shadowing her topaz-jade eyes.

My father hunches on the other side of the bed, his salt and pepper head dipped low, weathered hands wrapped around a dented cardboard coffee cup that's been squeezed nearly flat. When I blink my eyes open, Lilith's face transforms instantly, color flooding her cheeks as relief washes over her features like a sunrise. "Oh, thank God!" she whispers, voice cracking. My father's head jerks up, coffee sloshing over his trembling fingers, crow's feet deepening around his bloodshot eyes as all the years we've been apart seem to dissolve in a single moment of naked vulnerability.

"Roman," Lilith says. "Thank God you're awake."

I grip her hand tighter, my fingers crushing hers like I'm dangling off a cliff. My head feels like it's been stuffed with cotton balls soaked in novocaine—thoughts trying to wade through quicksand. I've obviously been given painkillers. My usual mental state is a Category 5 hurricane of rage, blood-red memories whipping around like shrapnel, slicing at me from the inside out for twenty fucking years. And being with Lilith usually feels like the first perfect wave of the morning—clean, bright, electric. But this? This is like being underwater with earplugs in, wrapped in a strait-jacket, my emotions mummified. Artificial. Chemical. Wrong.

I fucking hate it.

I blink against the harsh hospital lights. "Yeah, I'm awake. Sort of." The painkillers make everything float six inches above reality. I should feel something stronger seeing Lilith again—relief, joy, something—but the meds have muffled everything to a dull hum. Just days ago, I was telling Jack I might never see her again. If Serafina had her way, that would've been it. Game over. No more Lilith in my life. Even if I'd managed to win Lilith back, my father would've been collateral damage, and that would've poisoned whatever Lilith and I rebuilt.

Funny how much I care about the old man's happiness now. When he was sober, he was the kind of dad who'd spend hours teaching me to throw a curveball. He's got that same gentleness Cameron has—the brother who never raises his voice even when he should. And here's Dad, sitting beside my hospital bed after driving six hours from Carmel, while none of my brothers made the trip. Not that I blame them. They've got their own fires to put out.

Dad shifts his weight from one foot to the other, his weathered hands fidgeting with his phone. "Your brothers are here," he says, glancing toward the door where the fluorescent hallway light spills in. "I'll go find them." His eyes dart to the nurse's station visible through the half-open blinds. "We're not supposed to crowd around the hospital room. The protocols are people can only come in two by two—like Noah's ark." He attempts a smile that doesn't quite reach his tired eyes.

A smile tugs at my lips. I stand corrected. All seven of my brothers drove the full six hours to be here. My chest should swell with gratitude, but the morphine has wrapped everything in cotton. Still, beneath the haze, a cold realization forms: they wouldn't have come unless something was seriously wrong. Did the doctors tell them something they didn't tell me? Were they racing against time to say goodbye?

Cameron's the first one through the door, flashing that million-dollar smile. "Rome," he says, voice thick with relief. "We almost lost you."

Lost me? From a shoulder wound? Give me a break.

"What happened?" My throat feels like sandpaper.

"Two hours in surgery. Touch and go the whole time." Cameron's smile fades. "Bullet nicked an artery. You nearly bled out right there in the shop before the ambulance even arrived. Then surgery and you've been out ever since." He shakes his head. "Man, you've got to stop with this hero complex."

My jaw tightens despite the pain meds. "Listen, jackass," I growl, "if I hadn't stepped in, Lilith would be in the morgue instead of me in this bed." I turn away, wincing. Even drugged to the gills, Cameron still manages to piss me off. Hero complex. What was I supposed to do? Let the woman I love die? Not a chance. I'd walk barefoot over broken glass for her. A bullet? Small price to pay.

Cameron holds his palms up. "Easy, easy now. I'm just trying to tell you to take it easy for awhile. You're going to have to dial it back for a few months while your shoulder heals."

Fuck that. I'm supposed to be training with Max for the Ironman next year. My shoulder will heal up in no time. No matter how much rehab I'll have to do to get it there.

Chapter Fifty

LILITH

Oh my god. My hands won't stop trembling, even hours later. Every time I blink, I see that wild-eyed man, his knuckles white around the matte black pistol, the barrel wavering between Roman and me like a cobra deciding where to strike. The hospital's antiseptic smell burns my nostrils, mixing with the lingering copper scent of blood that seems to have soaked into my skin. My soul sisters have been texting non-stop—Jade sending healing crystals via DoorDash, Hazel promising to cleanse my aura once I'm home.

Roman's back in my life somehow, his tall frame now crumpled in starched white sheets, monitors beeping a rhythm that had been terrifyingly erratic just hours ago. His eyelids fluttered open hours after his emergency surgery, revealing those stormy eyes I thought I'd never see again. The relief flooded through me like warm honey, but the doctor's grim expression tells me we're only at the beginning of this winding, treacherous path.

A part of me melts at the sight of him, my heart fluttering like the pages of a book caught in a summer breeze. I love him with an intensity that makes my chest ache. He saved my life—not metaphorically, but literally.

The police report confirmed what I already knew: the wild-eyed man who stormed into my shop that day, knocking over crystal displays and sending tarot cards scattering across the hardwood floor, was deep in the grip of a meth-induced psychosis. I still see those dilated pupils when I close my eyes, the hand gun glinting under the amethyst glow of Raven's shop lights. If Roman hadn't burst through the door, ready for a fight, I'd be nothing but a crime scene photo.

Another part of me twists with anxiety. My fingers fidget with the moonstone pendant at my throat as I wonder how Sera could possibly keep quiet about me and my beliefs and the darker truths about Roman's father that could shatter everything Roman and Michael has built.

I step into Roman's room, my heart lifting when his face brightens at the sight of me. His smile—God, that smile could power all of California during a blackout. "Lilith," he murmurs, extending his hand across the starched hospital sheets. I take it as I sink into the chair beside him, my knees suddenly weak. "You holding up okay?"

I can only shake my head. The irony nearly makes me laugh—or cry. He's the one with tubes snaking from his arm, monitors beeping out his vital signs, bandages covering where a bullet tore through him and nearly drained his life away before the ambulance even arrived. Yet here he is, concerned about me.

"I should be asking you that," I say, giving his fingers a gentle squeeze while brushing back a lock of hair from his forehead.

"Jack told me why you left," Roman says, his voice low. "It's handled, Lilith. All of it."

My brow furrows. "Sera—"

"Isn't going to bother us anymore." His eyes hold mine, steady and certain. "Trust me."

"But how—"

"That's all I can say right now." A flash of discomfort crosses his face, tightening the skin around his eyes. "Tomorrow, we're out of here. I've had enough of this place. I'll have my pilot fly the chopper back to LA since I sure as hell can't right now."

I nod, but anxiety still gnaws at my insides. What if he's underestimating her?

As if reading the doubt written across my face, he squeezes my hand again. "Sera is not a problem anymore. I promise."

I tilt my head, studying him. Not mind-reading—just Roman knowing exactly what I'm thinking, as always. Our connection runs that deep.

I swallow hard. "I believe you."

His eyes hold mine. "Lilith," he says, the rough edge in his voice sending a shiver through me. "Remember when I said nothing would hurt you while I breathe?" He gestures to his bandaged shoulder. "I meant it."

The weight of what he's done settles in my chest.

If our positions were reversed, I wouldn't hesitate. That's how I know this is real.

Epilogue

LILITH

One year later

I sigh with happiness as I trail my fingers along the bamboo trim of my new space—a sun-drenched sanctuary nestled within Michael's new eco-resort. The polished stone floors catch the light streaming through floor-to-ceiling windows that frame the Pacific like a living painting. Roman and Michael had unveiled blueprints for this dream one starlit evening after the groundbreaking ceremony, their Kensington eyes alight with excitement.

"The heart of the eco-resort will be a verdant courtyard surrounded by alternative healing spaces," Michael had explained, his weathered hands gesturing enthusiastically. "Each practitioner will have their own custom-designed sanctuary. I've scoured the country for the most gifted healers—Reiki masters, Chakra Balancers and Sound therapists." His voice had grown reverent. "And I need your intuitive gift with the cards to anchor our tarot services." He'd then draped his arm around Roman's broad shoulders, and

Roman—my brooding, temperamental Roman—had actually beamed at his father, the decades of hurt now invisible. "Roman is entrusting your talents to my project, which means everything to me."

So, here I am at Tides of Renewal, Michael's eco-resort in Laguna Beach that wouldn't exist without Roman's influence. When Michael started to realize his dream of an environmentally conscious luxury getaway, Roman didn't just nod—he mobilized. Within weeks, he'd assembled a team of investors over dinner at his penthouse. I watched him pore over blueprints until dawn, his fingers tracing the lines of what would become living walls and solar arrays. He called in favors from the most innovative sustainability architects in California, the ones with two-year waiting lists. When permit issues threatened to derail everything, Roman simply made a few calls, and suddenly bureaucratic roadblocks vanished. The property itself—a boutique beachfront that Roman had acquired years ago but rarely visited—he transferred to Michael at below market value. "It deserves someone who'll transform it," he told me with a shrug. Though much smaller than Roman's Palos Verdes flagship, Michael's 100-suite sanctuary offers an intimacy that marries luxury with environmental consciousness in a way I've never experienced.

When it opened last week, Roman stood at the entrance of Michael's singular high-rise masterpiece. Unlike Roman's sprawling properties elsewhere, this tower represented his and Michael's environmental vision. He ran his hand along the sustainable, reclaimed wood flooring, remembering how he'd selected each plank himself. The handwoven natural-fiber rugs beneath his feet had been commissioned from artisans who shared his ethos.

"The walls," he explained to the resort's new manager,

"are finished with zero VOC paint—water-based, latex-free. No toxic compounds." He demonstrated the low-flow toilets: "Reclaimed water, but powerful enough to avoid complaints."

In the showroom suite, he pulled back covers made of 100% natural fibers with organic cashmere filling. "The mattresses are wrapped in 100% organic cotton." He pointed toward the ceiling. "Solar panels and geothermal pumps handle all heating and cooling and the heating and air are pumped through the rooms with reverse ionic technology. Every drop from the taps is purified through reverse osmosis."

I nodded appreciatively, examining the bathroom products. "Are the toiletries also organic?"

"Especially those. The soaps, lotions, shampoos, anti-aging serums—all organic." Pride crept into his voice. "The paint throughout the resort is Zero VOC—no volatile compounds—water-based, latex-free."

And then Roman swept his hand across the gleaming hardwood floor, the scent of lemongrass and eucalyptus lingering in the air. "All cleaning products are 100% organic. The floors shimmer from beeswax and coconut oil polish, not chemicals. The sheets guests will sleep on were laundered in lavender-infused, biodegradable soap. Even the glass sparkles from vinegar and essential oils, not ammonia. You won't find a single toxic substance in any bathroom—just cedar and sage." He nods. "The hot tub is powered by the sun, as is the salt-water pool. The hot tub and the pool are maintained and cleaned by a combination of ozonators, mineral purifiers, and baking soda and vinegar."

Later, in the flagship restaurant, Roman introduced the chef to the new organic menu. "I've met every rancher personally," he said. "The grass-fed beef, pasture-raised chickens and eggs, wild-caught sustainable fish—I've visited the ranchers and verified the humane treatment myself. Same with the organic vegetables. Nothing enters this kitchen I haven't personally vetted."

Every detail in this resort whispers luxury and a commitment to sustainability and non-toxicity, and, because it's such an innovative concept, the only issue was getting the word out. The Malibu elite noticed first, then Silicon Valley tech moguls, then European royalty. *Vogue* did a twelve-page spread. *Architectural Digest* featured the penthouse suites on their cover. Reservations became impossible to secure—even for celebrities—with Michael's creation now booked solid for the next two years.

Michael's new resort was all due to Roman, who had transformed from his father's harshest critic to his most trusted confidant.

And Roman has his own project that he's proud of - the underwater suite idea. His face lit up when he spread the blueprints across the table. "Got the permits yesterday," he said, tapping the paper where an underwater glass dome stretched beneath the resort. "Your idea's becoming reality." I traced my finger along the curved walls of what would be America's first underwater suite. The thought of lying there, watching silver fish dart through azure waters above the bed, made my heart race. "We'll christen it," he promised, his eyes meeting mine. "Just us, champagne on ice." I couldn't help but smile, already feeling the cool glass against my palm as the ocean moved overhead.

Before Michael's resort opened, the Kensington brothers gathered at sunset on the unfinished cliffside terrace overlooking the Pacific to honor their mother. Catherine's memorial had been postponed for months—the garden in Los Angeles with its manicured hedges and imported roses never felt right. This place, with the salt spray catching the golden light and the waves crashing below, had been her favorite spot to bring the boys as children. Asher, ever the perfectionist, had arranged white orchids in crystal vases along the stone balustrade and placed framed photographs of their mother—her smile radiant, her eyes the same stormy dark as Roman's—on easels where the ocean breeze couldn't disturb them.

Right after the memorial service, the resort's grand ballroom transformed for Michael's wedding to Patricia Jenkins, Max's mother-in-law. White orchids and champagne-colored silk draped every surface, the Pacific Ocean glittering beyond floor-to-ceiling windows. During the intimate reception, Cameron raised his crystal flute with a mischievous grin, declaring Max and Celeste "step-siblings by marriage," which sent ripples of laughter across the room. Even I couldn't help smirking. But watching Michael's weathered hand tenderly cover Patricia's as they swayed to their first dance, their eyes locked in that private language only true lovers speak—that wasn't funny at all. That was two souls finding their missing halves after decades of searching.

Now it's my wedding day to Roman. At Roman's suggestion, Michael will walk me down the aisle. After the ceremony, I'll move in Roman at his penthouse, of course, although we have plans to move to Malibu on a cliffside estate overlooking the ocean. And the best part? Jack will live in the guest house! Roman knows how important it is that Jack and I don't lose touch, and this gesture from him means more to me than almost anything else. It shows just how committed he is to my happiness, as I am just as committed to his.

We're keeping the ceremony small and intimate – just

his brothers, Caspian, Jack, and five of my soul sisters gathered around us. No bridesmaids or groomsmen standing awkwardly in matching outfits. When Roman slipped that light blue diamond ring onto my finger – platinum-set and catching the light like nothing I'd ever seen – his eyes told me he understood why I'd never want some massive production filled with strangers.

"This blue diamond symbolizes commitment," he whispered, "I researched it and that's what I came up with." It does symbolize commitment and fidelity, but I know he chose it for more.

That rare blue stone – known for bringing peace, calming turbulent emotions, releasing negativity, healing wounds – mirrors his transformation. Roman's inner tempest has calmed to gentle swells since he and his father buried the hatchet. Now, he channels his remaining intensity into grueling training sessions with Max, their shared suffering through the Oceanside Ironman last spring forging a brotherhood stronger than blood as they prepare for Kona's legendary World Championship next week.

The grueling preparation for the two Iron Mans - Roman and Max had to complete the Oceanside Iron Man to qualify for Kona, which apparently was on Max's bucket list - forged a bond with his youngest brother he never imagined possible. "The noise in my head," he told me last night, fingers tracing the diamond's facets, "it's finally gone." This blue gem isn't just my engagement ring – it's the symbol of his journey to peace.

The ceremony takes place at sunset on the resort's private beach. I slip away from my new Mystic Tides boutique, leaving behind the lingering scent of sage and sandalwood. Michael offers his arm with a smile that reminds me so much of Roman. As we walk toward the shore, my bare feet sink into warm sand. When I finally see Roman waiting by the altar, his normally stern face softens. The ocean breeze ruffles his dark hair, and something inside me settles into place. The cards were right all along. This man—this complicated, passionate man—is my destiny. The universe aligned to bring us here.

After we exchange vows, Michael raises his glass, his hand trembling slightly. "To Roman and Lilith," he begins, his voice catching. He clears his throat. "My son and I... we've walked a rocky road. Twenty-two years away from him—from all my boys—and not a single day passed when I didn't wonder how they were. When Roman first saw me again, he couldn't even look at me. I understood why." He pauses, meeting Roman's gaze across the reception hall. "This past year changed everything. And Lilith—" Michael smiles at me, his eyes crinkling at the corners. "—you've given my son something I never could. Peace. When he's with you, that famous Kensington temper just... melts away. You two fit together like you were made for each other."

Roman rises to his feet and wraps his arms around his father, holding on like he's afraid Michael might vanish again. My vision blurs, and I brush away the wetness on my cheek. Decades of absence dissolve in seconds as Roman's voice, usually so commanding, breaks just slightly when he whispers, "I love you, Dad." The impossible has happened right before my eyes—the stubborn, explosive Roman Kensington has opened his heart again. As I watch them, something settles in my chest, warm and certain.

Whatever comes next, I'll treasure being part of this moment.

Next in The Kensington Brothers Series

vinci-books.com/TheMalibuSecret

Some hearts aren't ready to risk breaking... but some collisions can't be avoided.

Tattoo artist Tally Steele avoids love—until a near-fatal accident puts her in the care of Dr. Cameron Kensington. Their undeniable attraction threatens to shatter their walls, but passion can't heal all scars.

Turn the page for a free preview…

The Malibu Secret: Chapter One

TALLY

I slam my needle down on the tray. "For the love of—would you stop squirming?"

The redhead in my chair—who calls herself "Shallow" like that's a normal human name—flinches again as I try to finish the cursive "M" of "Mortimer" on her lower back. March isn't even over, and this is already boyfriend tattoo number five for the year.

"I thought redheads were supposed to have, like, superhuman pain tolerance," I mutter, dabbing away a tiny bead of blood.

"Sorry," she whispers, then immediately jerks again.

I shake my head, wondering what drives someone to permanently ink every temporary man onto their body. Part of me wants to lecture her about how these guys never stick around—trust me, I know—but another part of me almost respects her stubborn optimism. While I'm over here refusing to get even one romantic tattoo until I meet a unicorn who won't bail, she's collecting an entire gallery of failed relationships like they're souvenirs.

I cap my needle gun and step back. "Well, Mortimer has officially joined the skin parade," I tell the lovely Shallow, who's been my most loyal—and most idiotic—customer. "Right above the VIP entrance, as requested."

She's got a goddamn boyfriend museum all over her body. Slade occupies her left forearm (lasted three weeks), Nash rides her right shoulder blade (cheated with her cousin), Lincoln decorates her ankle (stole her cat), and Wilde (ironically the most boring) circles her belly button. The douchier the guy, the cooler the name. So, assuming that relationship between douchetude and cool names, that'll mean that good ol' Mortimer will be a wonderful guy who'll treat her like royalty. I mean, nobody names their kid Mortimer unless they're planning for him to grow up honest and dependable, right? Maybe the universe is finally cutting her a break. Or maybe she'll be back next month for a "Bartholomew" tramp stamp. Jesus.

She rubs her lower back—newly minted Mortimer territory—and wrinkles her nose. "I know, I know. Terrible name. But you ever see *Arsenic and Old Lace*?"

"The one where sweet little grannies poison lonely dudes with elderberry wine laced with arsenic, strychnine, and just a pinch of cyanide for a kick? Yep. Why?"

"Cary Grant's character was Mortimer," she says, jazz-handing like she just pulled a rabbit from a hat. And fair play—Cary Grant was basically the Ryan Gosling of his day, if Ryan Gosling had the voice of a British butler and eyebrows that could seduce you from across a football field. So maybe Mortimer has a fighting chance after all. Even if the name peaked sometime around 1943, when people thought Mortimer, Mildred and Hubert were names you'd actually inflict on a child.

Shallow slaps her card on the counter, wincing as she

rubs the fresh ink on her back. I ring her up, watching her go with a head shake. Ten bucks says she's back before Valentine's Day wanting "Poindexter" or "Eggbert" etched somewhere else. Girl better pray she doesn't fall for some dude with a name like Bartholomew Christopherson—she's running out of virgin skin at this rate.

Eight hours later, I'm finally clocking out. My fingers are cramping from the nonstop tattoo gun action today. Maya —my business partner and supposed "other half" of Manic Muse, my tattoo studio—texted at 6 AM with some bullshit about food poisoning. Yeah, right. More like she's nursing a hangover the size of Texas after that warehouse rave she "wasn't planning to attend" last night.

I need a drink the size of Jupiter right now. Thank god I'm hitting up our Malibu spot with Celeste and Liv tonight. Yeah, Malibu—land of the douche canoes—but what can I do? My bestie Celeste went and married Max Kensington, billionaire extraordinaire who practically has his name stamped on every grain of sand there. Their whole setup started like some medieval arranged-marriage bullshit that I thought died with corsets and the plague, and I thought she was batshit cray for doing it, but damn if those two didn't pull a romance novel twist. From "I can't stand his face" to "I can't keep my hands off his face" in record time. Love's weird like that.

I spot Celeste and Liv at our usual table on the Bluetide Grill deck, the ocean breeze tousling their hair. Despite marrying a billionaire, landing that screenwriting gig, and having little Violet at home, Celeste hasn't changed. There she sits in worn Levi's, a faded t-shirt, and those ridiculous rainbow Docs she loves so much. That knockoff Vuitton she haggled for in Cabo is perched beside her, red hair twisted into her signature messy bun. Max filled her closet with designer everything, but whenever she's with us, it's like the fancy shit stays home. Sometimes I wonder if she's just more comfortable this way, or if she's afraid we'll call her Princess Moneybags if she shows up in Prada. Maybe a little of both.

I slide into the booth, drumming my fingers on the table. "All right, ladies. Spill the tea. What's been happening?"

Celeste shrugs, tucking a strand of perfect hair behind her ear. "Nothing much, really. Just the usual."

"Right," I snort. "Just the usual mind-blowing sex with your movie-star-looking husband while you're raking in screenplay money. God, how do you survive the boredom?" I catch Liv's eye and she smirks. We both know the drill. In an hour, Celeste will check her watch and make her excuses—Max and little Violet waiting at home, the perfect little family in their perfect 20,000 square foot house. Meanwhile, Liv and I will order another round, maybe hit another bar after, stumble home whenever the hell we want. No texts to answer, no one to check in with. Just sweet, uncomplicated freedom. And honestly? I wouldn't trade it for all the Max-clones in the world. One-night stands don't come with custody arrangements.

Celeste sips her drink with that cat-who-got-the-cream smile. Must be nice getting laid on the regular—definitely one perk of the whole marriage package I hadn't considered.

"How's life treating you?" she asks.

"Jesus Christ." I blow my bangs off my forehead. "Today was a three-energy-drink nightmare." I dive into my highlight reel of the day's clients—the frat boy who fainted during his tribal armband and the middle-aged woman who wanted her ex-husband's name covered with a particularly anatomical mushroom. I roll my eyes. "So, yeah, when Maya decides to be 'sick,'" I say, making little bunny ears with my fingers, "my entire existence turns into a dumpster fire. Like, congratulations on your self-inflicted misery, now I get to suffer too."

Celeste's eyebrows shoot up. "So there's this guy at Max's studio who's been asking about you—"

"Hard pass," I cut her off. "I'm not about to make awkward small talk with some trust fund bro who keeps flashing his fancy-ass Philippe Patek watch at me like it's supposed to make my panties drop."

"It's Patek Philippe," Celeste says primly. "They're actually quite—"

"Jesus, who names their kid Patek?" I snort. "Though I guess it beats Mortimer. At least Patek sounds like he might know how to have fun without his mommy's permission."

Celeste laughs. "It's actually named after two guys who started it—Antoni Patek and Adrien Philippe. They created this super high-end watch company in Switzerland back in the 1800s. The Swiss don't mess around when it comes to timepieces."

"How do you know this random watch trivia?" I ask, shaking my head. "I thought Patek Philippe was some new luxury brand all the rappers started flexing in their Instagram posts like five years ago." Then I shake my head. Of course Little Miss Married-to-Money knows all about fancy-ass timepieces. I bet her husband could buy the whole damn factory with his pocket change. I take a deep breath, trying not to roll my eyes. Maybe she has changed after all.

"No, no," Celeste says, swirling her wine. "But it is weird how everyone suddenly cares about them. I always thought Rolex was the ultimate status symbol, but now it's all about Patek Philippe."

"Holy shit, is this what girls' night has devolved to? Drooling over fancy-ass watches worn by trust fund babies?" As soon as the words leave my mouth, I wince. *Nice one, Tally.* Celeste's husband Max probably has a whole damn collection of those Patek whatever-the-fucks stashed in some climate-controlled safe. And he's actually decent, despite the silver spoon. His brother Roman isn't half bad either—managed to fall for some crystal-waving tarot card reader, which still blows my mind. Maybe I've been too quick to write off the entire Kensington clan.

Celeste's eyes meet mine for a second before she loses it, cackling so hard her mascara starts to run. I'm right there with her, snorting like an idiot. Jesus, we're ridiculous—usually debating the merits of dick pics while normal people worry about climate change or whatever. But fuck it. Some people march with cardboard signs; we judge tattoo designs and talk shit. Not exactly solving world hunger over here, but at least we're honest about it—unlike that customer today who wanted "Deep" tattooed on her wrist while talking about her spiritual awakening at Coachella.

Later on, I'm driving home stone-cold sober. Five years ago, a cop pulled me over after girls' night. I got lucky—he let me go with a warning that still makes my hands shake on the wheel sometimes. Now I nurse one drink all night, tops.

The streetlights flash across my face as I grip the wheel, thinking about Celeste. It's not the hot-as-hell husband who looks photoshopped in real life. It's not his bank account that could fund a small country. It's that look in her eyes now.

A few years back, we were the same—not happy, but not unhappy. Both of us just existing, her with her screenplay rejections and her mom's cancer battle, me with my own shit. Now? That bitch radiates. She's crossed over from that gray zone of not-happy-but-not-unhappy into just plain happy. Meanwhile, I'm still stuck in that same twilight of not-happy-but-not-unhappy, watching the clock tick.

But I've made my choices. Damn right I have. The whole white-picket-fence-and-hubby routine? Hard pass. Same goes for popping out kids. While other little girls were playing house, I was mixing watercolors until they bled through the paper. Liv was the one obsessed with her Easy Bake Oven—no surprise she's slinging gourmet appetizers now. Me? Give me a Lite Brite or that impossible silver-screen Etch-A-Sketch any day. God, that thing was a nightmare at first, but once I cracked the code? Magic. One of my favorite foster families nearly lost their minds when I twisted those little knobs into the perfect Beatles Revolver album cover at age eight. Their faces when they recognized those four floating heads and that wild lettering? Priceless.

Love is garbage. It's not like my childhood prepared me for happily-ever-after. Mom chose prescription painkillers over stability, which meant I got the grand tour of the foster care system. Every few months, some government lackey in sensible shoes would interrupt my Etch-A-Sketch masterpiece to stuff my belongings into trash bags. And I never wanted to leave my mother. Never. I mean, sure, Mom was orbiting Saturn half the time, and I became a Hot Pocket connoisseur by third grade, but she was mine. Those substitute rando mothers with their fake smiles and forced hugs? Couldn't hold a candle.

And then—HOLY CHRIST—a deer materializes out of nowhere, eyes blazing like hellfire in my headlights. I wrench the wheel hard, tires screaming against asphalt as my Jeep launches sideways, the world spinning violently as metal crunches and glass explodes around me. Three, four rolls—each one hammering my body against the restraints until I'm hanging upside down, blood rushing to my skull. Those movie scenes where people walk away from wrecks? Complete horseshit. Every breath feels like knives between my ribs, and something warm trickles down my temple that I'm desperately hoping isn't brain matter.

It takes everything in me to dial 911, my trembling finger missing the buttons twice before finally connecting. The room spins like a carnival ride as I press the phone to my ear, darkness creeping in from the edges of my vision until I mercifully slip into unconsciousness.

The Malibu Secret: Chapter Two

CAMERON

I'm working the ER when they wheel her in—dark hair with rainbow streaks spilling across the white gurney sheets, cheekbones that could cut glass even beneath the angry purple bruising spreading across her right side. My heart stutters when I realize it's Tally, Celeste's friend from both weddings. The fluorescent lights catch on the blood seeping through her torn blouse, revealing lacerations across her abdomen. Her eyelids flutter, consciousness slipping in and out like a tide, and her normally full lips are pale and cracked. My fingers tremble slightly against the cold metal rail as I guide the gurney toward Bay 3, remembering how she'd laughed at Max's reception, champagne glass dangling between slender fingers, completely unaware of my staring at her from across the room. Now those same fingers lie limp against sterile sheets, and I've still never spoken a single word to her.

The trauma team descends in a choreographed rush—one nurse cuts away her bloodied clothes while another starts an IV line, a third attaches cardiac monitors that immediately fill the room with urgent beeping. I call out orders as I check her pupils with my penlight: "Get a trauma panel, type and cross for four units, and push 1 of morphine." Her oxygen levels dip and I motion for intubation equipment. "Let's get her to CT stat—I need to rule out internal bleeding and head trauma before she crashes completely."

My fingers dig into her abdomen, probing for internal bleeding or swelling, the heat of her skin burning through my latex gloves. Her eyelids flutter—delicate as moth wings—revealing irises the precise blue of Mediterranean waters at noon. "Fucking perfect," she hisses through clenched teeth. "A Yalie doctor. Just my goddamn luck." Her gaze drops to my wrist, zeroing in on my watch gleaming under the merciless hospital lights - the antique Patek Philippe, given to me by my granddad on my 16th birthday. "Bet you've got a whole fucking vault of those at home, don't you, Scrooge McDuck?" A savage smile cuts across her bloodless face, that single dimple appearing like a battle scar before her eyes roll back, lashes slashing shadows across skin pale as death.

I shake my head. "Didn't go to Yale. Johns Hopkins." I tap the face of my watch—the only Patek Philippe I own, unlike my brothers who collect them like trading cards. Something in Tally's eyes tells me she knows me and thinks that I'm a trust fund baby playing at being doctor. Had she been watching me at those weddings too? My family is incredibly wealthy and she assumes I'm the same, which I admittedly am, thanks to a half-billion trust fund set up by granddad for all of us Kensington boys. Still, she probably doesn't know me as the black sheep of a dynasty, the one who chose a year in Kenya's dust with Doctors Without Borders over boardroom battles and trust funds. The one whose annual salary wouldn't cover what Roman makes in a day.

I can still see her at Max and Celeste's wedding—that burgundy halter dress that framed her shoulders like artwork, the slit that revealed legs strong enough to kick down doors. Her short dark hair shot through with defiant rainbow streaks. She stood there like someone who'd parked a Harley outside the church, and I couldn't look away if I'd wanted to.

Of course, being mesmerized by her meant I froze like a statue. My brothers would've strolled right up—Roman with that cocky grin, Silas with his smooth one-liners, Max already making her laugh. Ansel would've had her feeling like his oldest friend within minutes. Kalen would've channeled that rock star confidence, while Connor—despite those childhood years when he could barely order pizza without stammering—would've drawn on that Oscar-winner charisma. Even Asher, who treats romance like an abstract theorem, would've managed better than me. My palms went clammy just watching her from across the room. I've always been this way around beautiful women—admiring from a distance, tongue-tied and hesitant. The irony is I probably respect women more than any of my brothers, yet I'm the one who can never seem to approach them.

Which is why I'm still stunned—thunderstruck—that I convinced a woman like Alecia to marry me. My Alecia, with those freckles scattered like constellations across her nose, hair blazing like summer wheat under a merciless sun, and eyes that cut through me—green as absinthe and twice as intoxicating. Her laugh that first day slammed into my chest like a fist. How could a goddess like her even acknowledge my existence? But I knew—Christ, I KNEW—the instant I saw her that I would drown in her. And I did. And she did too. One weekend in her Arts District loft was all it took. I would have slit my own throat before letting her slip away.

Three years ago, her laugh was silenced forever when a drunk driver obliterated her car with my baby girl Stephanie inside. All because I couldn't handle a goddamn cold. We ran out of NyQuil, to my chagrin. I never run out of anything because I make sure to replace everything once it gets low. I never, ever just run out of toilet paper, paper towels, toothpaste, cold medicine, aspirin, anything that's necessary. Yet we did run out of NyQuil, a fact that haunts me to this day. Why, why, why didn't I get a bottle of NyQuil when I happened to be at the store instead of running out completely? But I didn't, so, that early morning when I was so sick, we needed to get some in the house ASAP.

The coughing fits had been ripping my lungs apart for hours when Alecia kissed my burning forehead at 1 AM and whispered she'd be right back. She took Stephanie because I was too pathetic to move. Three blocks away, that bastard plowed through a green light at 80 mph without touching his brakes. I heard the sirens screaming through our neighborhood and knew—KNEW—before my phone rang. My soul recognized the sound of my world ending.

I'd resigned myself to a life of solitude. Then I spotted Tally across the crowded room at Max and Celeste's wedding. My heart stuttered. The champagne flute nearly slipped from my fingers. I kept stealing glances at her while pretending to listen to some cousin's medical woes. Three times I started toward Celeste to ask about her friend, and three times I retreated. What would someone with galaxy-blue hair streaks and sleeve tattoos peaking beneath her cocktail dress want with a guy who spent his days in scrubs and his nights hunched over medical journals?

Now, here she is, and I'm attending her after her accident. The fluorescent lights cast a harsh glow on her bruised skin.

Her voice comes out like sandpaper. "Hit me with it, doc." She narrows her eyes at my badge, then recoils. "Dr. Kensington? Christ. You're Max's brother." She clutches the paper-thin sheet to her chest, fingers digging into the fabric. "Brilliant. Absolutely brilliant. Next dinner party at Max's, you'll have this little tableau burned into your memory, won't you? Me, splayed out like a science experiment." Her jaw tightens. "I'm guessing the hospital gown came after you got quite the anatomy lesson."

She didn't recognize me until she read my name tag. This realization hits like a sucker punch—while I'd been stealing glances at her all night at Max's two receptions, memorizing the curve of her smile, the way she cocked her head, and the way she threw her head back when she laughed, she hadn't even noticed me in the crowd. When she called me Scrooge McDuck, it wasn't because she knew who I was. She just took one look and decided. And hell, maybe she's right. I've held dying children in refugee camps and stitched wounds by flashlight, but at the end of the day, I'm still a Kensington. Maybe wealth clings to me no matter how far I run from it—like some designer aftershave I can't wash off.

I clear my throat. "Your CT scan and MRI results aren't back yet, but I need to ask you a few questions."

"Shoot," she says, wincing as she shifts position.

"Can you tell me how the accident happened?"

"Damn deer." She sighs. "Not that I should blame her—poor thing was just being a deer. But she darted across the road and next thing I knew, my Jeep was rolling."

I run through the standard checklist. Seatbelt? Yes. Airbag deployment? None to deploy—her '97 Jeep predates mandatory airbags. Windshield impact? No. Alcohol consumption? The lab work confirms what she tells me—BAC of .02, nowhere near the legal limit.

I glance at my watch. "What day is it today?"

She arches an eyebrow. "Depends. Has the clock struck midnight yet? Because if it has, we've crossed into Friday territory. If not, we're still clinging to Thursday by our fingertips."

Good enough. She seems to have a sharp memory, so I don't suspect a concussion. But I go through the rest of the protocol anyway. I check her pupils with my phone flashlight, ask her to follow my finger with her eyes, test her balance by having her stand on one foot, and quiz her about who the president is. She passes everything, rolling her eyes at my ministrations.

She finally grips the edge of the bed, her knuckles paling. "Listen, doc. I need to get out of here." Her jaw tightens slightly. "My tattoo studio on Mateo is in trouble if I don't show up. Maya—she's not the most reliable—called in sick yesterday, or maybe it was today? Is it past midnight or not?" She leans forward, concern in her eyes. "She might not come in again today, and if I'm not there, that's twelve appointments canceled. Twelve. That's rent money I can't afford to lose while I'm stuck here." She gestures toward the clipboard. "Please. Sign the papers."

I grip the side of her hospital bed. "Ms. Steele."

"Oh please." Her eyes flash, her voice dropping to a husky whisper. "You've seen me naked. Tally is just fine."

Yes, I've seen her naked and it is a sight to behold. Heat floods my face. "Tally," I say, my voice rougher than intended. I lean closer, close enough to catch the faint scent of her perfume beneath the antiseptic. "You cannot leave. Not right now, anyhow. Not when every minute counts after trauma like this. The protocols don't catch everything—I've seen patients walk and talk perfectly, then collapse hours later from a brain bleed no one detected. I won't risk that. Not with you. Celeste would kill me if you died on my watch."

She rolls her eyes and crosses her arms so tightly it's like she's physically holding herself together. "Goddamn it," she hisses through clenched teeth. "But yeah, I've heard of that talk and die thing. Liam Neeson's wife? Hit her head skiing, said she was fine, then—dead. And Jesus—Celeste's father." Her voice cracks. "Laughing with the EMTs one minute after that skier crashed into him. Next day we were picking out his casket because his brain just—" She makes an explosive gesture with her fingers near her temple. "Fuck. You win. Not risking that." Then she shakes her head. "But if Maya wants to call off again for another fucking hangover, I'm firing her ass and getting somebody I can rely on."

"You do that," I say with a smile. "Anyhow, need to do my rounds. I'll be back when I get the results back from your scans."

She salutes me like she's in the military and I leave her there, my pulse hammering so violently I can feel it in my fingertips. During ER rounds, her scent haunts me—Tom Ford Black Orchid invading my senses, making it impossible to focus. The black truffle, black orchid and black plum notes mixed with that intoxicating patchouli and chocolate—it's not just a perfume, it's her essence distilled. Dark. Dangerous. Utterly consuming. Like her. I want to drown in it.

A few hours later, I return with results that bring visible relief to her face. "The scans came back clean—no internal injuries," I tell her, watching her shoulders relax. "You'll probably need to stay tonight for observation, but you should be free to go home tomorrow morning."

And then I go about the rest of my rounds, the scent of Tom Ford's Black Orchid following me around like a ghost.

The Malibu Secret: Chapter Three

TALLY

I swear, every time Cameron Kensington walks into a room, the temperature rises ten degrees. The man didn't just win the genetic lottery—his entire family bought out all the tickets. Put any Kensington brother in a suit and watch the photographers at *GQ* start a bidding war, but Cameron? At 38, he's aged like fine whiskey. When he runs his fingers through those dark waves or flashes those dimples—which he knows damn well what they do to women—I have to remind myself to breathe. Those sapphire eyes could make a nun question her vows.

But now I'm back at my apartment, and unless I wreck another vehicle, I've seen the last of Cameron. My poor Jeep—Jaspress, I called her, because I always loved the name Jasper but it felt too masculine for a car—is completely destroyed. Damn deer came out of nowhere. No work today either. The accident's still got me rattled, even though they discharged me from Cedars around 3 AM, plus, my left hand - the dominant hand, alas - is fucking stiff as hell. Cameron said it's strained. I can't grip a tattoo gun right now.

Cameron pushed for them to keep me overnight, but with no beds available except maybe a gurney in some hallway, they sent me home. If my brain had hemorrhaged while I slept, Mom would've hit the lawsuit jackpot—her opioid days finally paying off. But here I am at two in the afternoon, channel-surfing with a perfectly clear head. Guess I survived.

I am having a slight problem getting around, though, as my body is stiff from whiplash. Guess it's whiplash, because my scans showed nothing broken and whiplash is more of a muscle thing. Shit, I'll probably have to get some kind of neck brace. That'll be lovely at work. My regulars won't stop giving me shit about something like that.

A thunderous knock rattles my door. I lurch forward to answer it, but white-hot pain sears through my lower back, dropping me back onto the couch with a gasp. My muscles seize into concrete, each spasm a lightning strike up my spine. "COME IN!" I scream, desperation clawing at my throat. God, I don't even care who's there anymore—the devil himself could be on the other side of that door, but if he can drag me to the bathroom before my bladder explodes, I'll gladly follow him to hell.

Cameron steps through the door and my breath catches. Last night's green scrubs were one thing, but now—blue t-shirt stretched across shoulders that could carry the weight of the world, jeans hugging thighs that have clearly seen their share of training miles. His dark waves fall just past where they should, begging for fingers to brush them back. When he shoves his hands in his pockets, the motion pulls the fabric tighter across his chest and I have to bite my lip to keep from making a sound. That jawline could slice through diamond. Damn.

"Just checking on you," Cameron says gently.

I nod. "Hello there, Yalie boy," I say, my voice suddenly husky. "Sorry. Meant Johns Hopkins boy. Still playing doctor, I see. Anyhow, I really gotta use the little girls' room and—" My back spasms again and I cry out, the pain searing through me like a hot knife. He's at my side in an instant, his cologne hitting me before his hands do.

"I'd really like some help," I whisper, hating how vulnerable I sound.

When his fingers grip my waist, it's like being branded. Every nerve ending screams to life. Sure, I'd seen him at both of Max and Celeste's weddings—the first one that was as real as a Prada purse being sold from back of a Cabo van and the real tear-jerker one in England —but I'd dismissed him as just another perfect-faced Kensington with their obscene wealth and country club smiles. So he saves lives in Africa and has dimples that could make a nun question her vows. Big deal.

But holy hell, I wasn't prepared for this—this molten heat flooding my body as he practically carries me toward the bathroom. His breath fans against my neck, and I swear I can feel each individual exhale like a promise against my skin. My heart hammers so hard I'm certain he can hear it. God help me, I can barely remember my own name.

After finishing in the bathroom, I hobble into the living room where Cameron waits, armed with a warm towel and cold compress.

"Lie down," he says, gesturing to the couch. I stretch out on my stomach as he places the icy compress against my lower back. I flinch but bite my lip. The dragon tattoo that curls across that same spot took four hours and I barely winced—I can handle this.

"That's quite a bruise," he observes. "Black now, but it'll cycle through green, yellow, and finally a yellowish-brown before it's gone. Usually takes two weeks, though this one might need longer."

I manage a nod as he removes the compress. His fingertips begin working the tissue around the injury, sending little sparks racing up my spine. My breath catches. My muscles clench involuntarily beneath his touch. I close my eyes, suddenly aware of how long it's been since anyone has touched me like this—clinical as it may be. His hands are here to heal, not to explore, though my body doesn't seem to understand the difference. Wasn't there some study about endorphins from orgasms being natural painkillers? Maybe I'm just self-medicating in my mind.

His fingers work the skin around my bruise with practiced precision. "Increasing circulation," he explains. "Helps the blood flow, speeds healing. I promise I'm not being fresh."

My body begs to differ. I bite my lip to keep from saying so, amused by his quaint phrasing - "fresh." Cameron with his old-timey expressions, probably the kind of guy who says "swell" unironically. I never thought I'd be attracted to someone like him—this doctor who supposedly, according to Celeste, makes five-star meals on weekends and keeps a song-writing journal. Something about that combination makes my pulse quicken under his touch. Last boyfriend couldn't even microwave without setting off the smoke alarm because the dumb shit put a metal bowl into that microwave and set the damn thing on fire. I mean, who doesn't know by now that you can't put metal in a microwave? Kent Rogers, my idiot ex, that's who.

I've heard Cameron plays piano too, just like his brothers—especially Kalen and Ansel. A doctor with artist's hands. No wonder I can barely breathe when he's this close.

His voice drops to a rasp. "I need you to unzip your jeans. Just enough for me to see the bruising."

My fingers tremble at the zipper. The metal teeth part with a sound that echoes in my ears like thunder. I ease the denim down, revealing the thin strip of my thong and the curve of flesh beneath. The cool air kisses my exposed skin.

"It's spread lower," he murmurs, his breath warm against my back. Ice touches my skin—a shock that melts instantly into heat as his fingertips trace the edges of the bruises. His touch is clinical, but my body doesn't know the difference. Every nerve ending ignites.

Two decades of dawn runs and punishing squats have sculpted me here. I know what I am. And I know what his quickening breath means as his hands work over me.

He applies heated towels, but they're nothing compared to the inferno building between my legs. I bite my lip to keep from arching back against him, from begging his fingers to slip beneath the thin fabric, to feel his mouth replace the ice. I want to burn. I want to shatter.

Dammit. I'm burning alive. Every nerve ending screams, my skin electric under his touch, my core clenching with a need so fierce I can barely breathe. I have to do something before I combust.

I flip onto my back, the sudden movement making him jerk backward. His eyes—those impossible eyes that shift between oceanic blue and forest green depending on how the light catches them—lock with mine, pupils dilating instantly. He swallows hard, that perfect throat working as he tries to drag his gaze away from my exposed skin. I grab the hem of my shirt and yank it up, revealing the purple-blue stain across my abdomen. "This needs your attention too," I whisper, my voice husky, unrecognizable.

His hands hover, trembling slightly, before pressing the ice against my skin. I gasp at the shock of cold against heat. His fingers work the tender flesh, and I arch involuntarily into his touch. He's looking everywhere but at my face, while I'm desperate to capture those kaleidoscope eyes, to make him see exactly what he's doing to me.

He clears his throat. "I should probably get going."

"Already?" I sit up, catching the way his gaze drops to my collarbone before darting away. His pupils are dilated, his breathing shallow. "You sure about that?"

He hesitates. "Not really. But I should. Being here with you like this—it crosses every professional boundary."

"Since when is a follow-up visit crossing boundaries?" I tilt my head, widening my eyes in mock innocence while my heart hammers against my ribs. The flush creeping up his neck betrays everything his words won't admit. "I mean, isn't checking on discharged patients just good medicine?"

I slip open the first button of my blouse, then the next. The bruises from the Jeep accident map across my skin in purple-green constellations. Cameron's eyes widen as I reach behind to unhook my bra. This is reckless. This is stupid. This will haunt me forever if anyone finds out.

But who would he tell? Breaking doctor-patient boundaries would torpedo his medical career faster than I could say "malpractice."

Celeste would never forgive me. Her golden rule: friends don't hook up with friends' relatives. Especially not her husband's brother. The Kensington family gatherings would become unbearable—and I've already missed their famous annual gala last year with the living art installation. Art is my weakness; I never miss the *Pageant of the Masters* in

Laguna if I can help it, and from what I hear, Asher did something similar as that Laguna festival at last year's Kensington gala. I want to attend this year's gala where Asher's planning something spectacular again, and it'll be…uncomfortable…if Cameron and I hook up and I have to run into him there.

If Cameron and I crash and burn like all my relationships... but God, the heat spreading through me demands satisfaction in a way logic can't touch.

He's shy. I've watched him shrink into corners at both weddings, his eyes darting away whenever a woman approaches. Even with that jawline—the kind that could cut glass—and those broad shoulders straining against his tailored suit, he'd rather study the pattern in the carpet than meet a woman's gaze. I've seen them circle him like sharks, touching his arm, laughing too loudly at his mumbled jokes. Each time, he'd flush crimson and find an excuse to escape. If I want him, I'll need to be the predator here.

"Cameron," I say, arching my back until my breasts nearly graze his chest, "does this bruising look serious to you? Feel how tender it is." I'm pointing at the bruise across my now-bare breasts.

"I—Christ—I can't—" His pupils dilate until his eyes are almost black, fixed on my skin like he's drowning in it.

I shove him onto the other end of the couch. "You can and you will." I devour his mouth, and Christ, the taste of him—dark chocolate and sin. My body ignites. Bruises? What bruises? Back pain? Gone. There's only him, his hands gripping my hips hard enough to leave marks, his tongue claiming mine. He kisses me with a violence that matches my own, and I know with absolute certainty he'll obliterate every sensation except pleasure. I need him to burn through me like wildfire, scorching away everything but this moment. This isn't about connection—it's about consumption. He's a feast laid out before a starving woman, and I will take, take, take until there's nothing left of either of us. Right. Fucking. Now.

Grab your copy…

vinci-books.com/TheMalibuSecret

About the Author

Bella Christina lives with her hubby and two fur-babies in Southern California. When she's not binge-watching *Grace and Frankie*, *Succession* and *Downton Abbey*, she's reading historical and women's fiction and scouring the beach for sea glass and sand dollars.

www.ingramcontent.com/pod-product-compliance
Lightning Source LLC
La Vergne TN
LVHW030914080826
845145LV00013B/2896

* 9 7 8 1 0 3 6 7 3 3 9 1 9 *